Windrush: Cry Havelock

Windrush: Cry Havelock

Jack Windrush Series – Book IV

Malcolm Archibald

For Cathy

Time upon time, the sepoys struck their blows,
Digging in about them, the white warriors fought well.
On their feet they wore boots, on their bodies' kilts.
Tassels of silk on their hats and trembling aigrettes
The white warriors went into battle like elephants on heat
With no fear of death, they set their faces to the front.

Indian song about Sir Colin Campbell's relief of Lucknow, 1857

Prelude

'Jack Baird Windrush.' The words whispered through the night. 'Do your duty, Jack Baird Windrush.'

When the words faded, a bearded face leered at him with hate in its eyes.

Jack started up with tight beads of sweat already formed on his forehead and streaming in rivulets down his back. Looking into the darkness, he struggled to control his breathing. Jack had never liked confined spaces. Living in the open air was best for him, and here he was in claustrophobic darkness surrounded by nightmares. He took a deep breath. Where was he? Under the ground; he was under the ground somewhere, and there was great danger of a kind he had never encountered before, together with some new and terrible sorrow.

Jack closed his eyes, opened them again; nothing had changed. There was darkness and confinement and danger. He reached out, feeling the earth under his fingers. He was underground. Why was he underground? He struggled backwards, trying to escape back to the open air. Where was he?

The call of a jackal awakened him, and he lay sweat-sodden and scared. Oppressive heat pressed down on him and the high-pitched hum of insects reminded him where he was.

India. He was back in the land of his birth after an absence of twenty-two years. That voice echoed in his head as he swung his legs over the side of the bed and stood up. 'Jack Baird Windrush.'

Nobody had called him that for many years; he had never informed anybody of his full name. Opening the door of his bungalow, he peered outside. The configuration of the stars was familiar, although he had not seen it since his early childhood.

'I'm home again,' Jack said and shivered. India was in his blood; something of him belonged here. Even the distant howl of a jackal was strangely reassuring; it was part of the land, as natural as the nocturnal croak of frogs and the smell of spices that permeated every native village and town. He was in India, timeless, friendly, familiar and home.

'Jack Baird Windrush.' He reached for a memory that lived in the shadows of his mind. He couldn't grasp it; the voice was female and elusive, yet comforting. Wondering from which part of his childhood it had come, he reached for a cheroot, lit it and inhaled calming smoke deep into his lungs. Something momentous was about to occur; there had been good and bad in that dream. Well, let it happen. He was Captain Jack Windrush of the 113th Foot, a veteran of Burma and the Crimea and he was alone in the world, rejected by his family and with nobody outside the regiment to care a damn for him. Well then, in that case, why should he care for anybody outside the 113th?

Damn them.

Damn them all.

Chapter One

'Don't you ever feel the heat, Jack?' Elliot dragged the back of his hand across his forehead, leaving a temporary dry track that perspiration soon refilled. 'This is unbearable.'

Jack took a breath of the perfumed air. 'It will get a lot worse before it gets better. It's only April; wait until June, and we'll really know about it.'

'I forgot.' Elliot threw him a glance that combined jealousy with admiration. 'You were born in this country, weren't you?'

'So I've been told.' Jack straightened his uniform. The details of his early life were so confused and contradictory he had never worked them out. 'I don't remember much about it; I was young at the time.'

'That explains it then.' Elliot adjusted the crimson cord on his shoulder. 'God, I miss the old uniform. This one is so dull in comparison.'

Brushing an inquisitive insect from his single-breasted scarlet tunic, Jack gave Elliot a final glance over and nodded. 'This new uniform is a bit more practical than the old; easier to keep clean.' He forced a smile. 'You'll do, Arthur. You're fit to fight the French.'

'Or the Russians.' Elliot pulled back his shoulders. 'You'll pass fit to muster too, Jack.' He took a drink from a small silver flask and replaced it inside his tunic. 'Scotch courage. Right then, let's go; God knows what this will be like and Jeffreys has invited some guests along too.' He sighed. 'I miss the old days; things were never this formal when old Colonel Maxwell was in charge.'

'Life has changed,' Jack agreed, 'and not for the better.'

The officer's mess stood on its own within a rectangle of impeccably cropped grass, kept free of leaves or other litter by an industrious native gardener. With so many new men in the regiment to replace the losses of the Crimea, Jack was not surprised he didn't know either of the sentries at the door. He acknowledged their salutes by lifting a hand to his shako.

'Here we go, then,' Elliot murmured and stepped aside. 'After you, sir.'

'Quite right too,' Jack said. 'I am the senior officer here.'

'Rank before beauty,' Elliot responded.

Stout and red-faced, Major Snodgrass greeted them formally, looked them up and down, made unnecessary adjustments to Jack's jacket, frowned irritably at Elliot's nervous grin and ushered them in. 'Don't forget,' he said quietly, 'Colonel Jeffreys likes things done properly. He will allow none of the lax ways of his predecessor.'

'Yes, sir,' Jack said.

'And there are East India Company guests,' Snodgrass said. 'Don't let the regiment down.'

'We won't, sir.' Jack noted the Victoria Cross prominent on Snodgrass's chest. He had been awarded the medal after supposedly killing a prominent Cossack officer at Inkerman. Jack knew that Charlotte Riley, wife of Sergeant Riley, had shot the Cossack – but Snodgrass had accepted the credit.

'Deep breath, Jack,' Elliot murmured as an immaculate Pathan servant opened the door into the dining hall.

They walked into a wall of noise and conversation with the officers of the 113th Foot standing in small groups, nursing glasses and puffing on cheroots or cigars. The uniforms of the guests shone among them; the two native infantry regiments and the native cavalry regiment who shared the Gondabad cantonment with two companies of the 113th. Snatches of conversation drifted to Jack as the officers spoke to each other or issued sharp orders to the soft-footed servants. As was to be expected the John Company – East India Company – officers were far more fluent in the native languages.

'Hey, brandy and water and quick about it.'

'*Mero lagi pani!*'

'Not quite like England is it? This heat is insufferable!'

'Queen's officers eh? They know nothing about India and like to parade their ignorance at every opportunity.'

'I thought we had a punkah-wallah to keep the place bearable. The old duffer must have fallen asleep. I'll give him toco and wake him up.'

'Blasted John Company wallahs; they think they know everything about this damnable country.'

Amidst the casual conversation, Jack heard snatches of what they called shop-talk as men discussed their respective regiments.

'Your Queen's soldiers fought well in the Crimea, I heard,' a tall, bronzed lieutenant in the uniform of the Bengal Native Infantry said. 'You'll find things different here. Our men would have given the Ruskies the right-about turn, I can tell you.'

An ensign of the 113th with the peeling red face of a griffin gave a snort. 'Your sepoys? They'd hardly be a match for white troops.'

'Oh, I wouldn't agree,' the Company lieutenant said. 'Given the opportunity, my boys are second to none in the deadly charge, the skirmish and the escalade. Military ardour is bright in my sepoys.'

'Don't they run when they meet European troops?' the ensign sneered. 'Just a rabble of blacks, aren't they?'

The lieutenant's face closed into a frown. 'There is no army in the whole of Europe in which military discipline is better maintained; there are no soldiers more faithful, braver or more strongly attached to their Colours and their officers than those of the Bengal Army.'

The ensign laughed. 'I heard that blacky is as deceitful as his colour is black and as selfish as he is double-faced.' He saw Jack listening. 'Don't you agree, sir? These sepoys have all the faults of Irishmen and none of the courage.'

Jack grunted. 'They fought well enough in Burma,' he said, 'and the Sikhs gave us hard knocks a-plenty. I suggest you read your regimental history Mr.... What's your name?'

'Shearer, sir. John Sebastian Shearer of the Hertfordshire Shearers.'

'Indeed, Mr. John Sebastian Shearer of the Hertfordshire Shearers,' Jack said. 'Well, you'll learn, no doubt – or cholera or the Sikhs will teach you.' He dismissed Shearer with a sharp inclination of his head.

Down the centre of the room, the table dominated. A splendid array of bone china, silver cutlery and sparkling crystal almost hid the white linen table cloth and proclaimed the 113th was now fit to take its place alongside any regiment in the British Army.

'Colonel Jeffreys shelled out for most of this.' As always, Elliot had all the gossip and most of the knowledge.

Jack remembered the canvas tent they'd used as the officer's mess during much of the Crimea campaign. 'We are living like lords of Gondabad,' he said.

'Lords of Gondabad,' Elliot repeated with a small laugh. 'I may enjoy this cantonment after all.'

Standing proudly in the centre of the table were two huge brass mortar cases, inscribed with the regimental number and the slogan: *Captured at Sebastopol 1855*. Now they did duty as bottle holders and served to remind new officers of the recent history of the regiment.

'You lack battle honours,' a splendidly whiskered captain of the Bengal Native Infantry pointed out. 'My men have been winning battles since Plassey.'

'Oh?' Elliot raised his eyebrows. 'In the 113th we don't rely on history. We make our own. Inkerman and Sebastopol, don't you know?'

The memory of the letter that pressed against his breast tempered Jack's small smile of satisfaction.

Helen!

He heard loud laughter from Major Snodgrass as somebody admired his medal and saw Shearer in light conversation with a young cornet of Bengal Native Cavalry.

The atmosphere altered as Lieutenant-Colonel James Jeffreys entered the room and the officers of all regiments stiffened to attention. The servants, efficient and impassive, seemed to vanish into the background.

'Good evening, sir.' As the senior major, it was the duty of Snodgrass to greet the colonel and ensure everybody present behaved correctly.

'Good evening, Major Snodgrass.' Jeffreys returned the formal salute and gazed around the room. Tall and slender, he stood as erect as a Guardsman and noted the name, rank and bearing of every man present. 'Take your places, gentlemen.' Jeffreys stepped to the head of the table and stood beside his seat until all the officers were ready. He sat down slowly.

'We cannot sit until his Majesty is comfortable on his throne.' Elliot intended his whisper only for Jack's ears, but in the hush, it was audible to at least half the officers present. Snodgrass glared at him.

'Did you have something to say, Lieutenant Elliot?' Jeffreys' voice was acidic.

'No, sir,' Elliot said.

'Then kindly keep quiet until a senior officer speaks to you. Junior officers should learn there is a time and place for conversation.'

Behind each diner, an Indian servant waited. Dressed in white and adorned with a scarlet cummerbund, they could have been carved from marble.

The officers ate in strained silence except for the music of the regimental band outside the building. Jack tried to recognise each tune and hoped to avoid the colonel's eye. He wondered which was worse: advancing against Russian artillery or enduring a full mess dinner under the gaze of Colonel Jeffreys and Major Snodgrass. Each required a different form of courage, active and passive, yet each was draining.

Thankfully, the evening wore on and after an eternity of courses while sweat soaked the back of Jack's tunic the servants replaced the water glasses with wine glasses. Decanters of whisky, Madeira, port and sherry appeared, to circulate clockwise around the table and empty at an astonishing speed. Jack knew he was no drinking man and pressed the side of his foot against Elliot's, to warn him not to imbibe too deeply.

'Careful, Arthur.'

Elliot shifted away, filled his glass with whisky, drained it in a succession of quick swallows and filled it again before passing the decanter on to the next man. Only when each officer's glass was fully charged did the colonel lift a small brass bell and ring it softly. The sound seemed to echo around the quiet room.

Colonel Jeffreys rose to his feet and lifted his glass. 'Gentlemen,' he said crisply. 'The Queen.'

The assembled officers stood up as one and lifted their glasses in salute. 'The Queen.'

On cue, the music outside halted and after a few tense seconds, the strains of *God Save the Queen* crashed out. Jack stood in silence, glass in hand as he pretended to have noble and patriotic thoughts. Instead, he felt the letter in his breast pocket and remembered the contents which he had read a score of times and still refused to accept.

The tune stopped abruptly and Colonel Jeffreys sat down. He lifted his glass again.

'Gentlemen of the 113th! We drink to the regiments whose officers have graced us with their presence. The native regiments of the Bengal Army of the Honourable East India Company!'

The officers of the 113th stood up and lifted their glasses to their guests. Once again Jack barely sipped at his and frowned at Elliot, who drained his glass in a single swallow.

The Company officers responded in kind, with toast following toast so within an hour, Jack felt light-headed and wondered if drinking to excess might not be a bad idea after all.

'Now gentlemen,' Jeffreys' tone had altered from crisply officious to benignly paternal. 'You may relax. Light up, smoke and talk for this is your home.'

Jack looked around as a buzz of conversation began. On the wall behind the colonel, a portrait of Queen Victoria hung below the cased Colours of the 113th. He remembered these Colours standing above the remnants of his shattered company at Inkerman, when the Russian dead lay piled before them in the drifting mist and his men robbed corpses for ammunition. Now, they presided in mute splendour, a memory of past suffering and glory. Every morning and every night the youngest ensign in the regiment had the duty of dusting the Queen's portrait and ensuring the Colours were safe.

'Gentlemen.' The colonel spoke again, his voice cutting through the conversation as smoothly as a bayonet through a straw-stuffed target. 'This regiment, our regiment, has been given a bad name in the past. We have suffered from poor morale and low-quality men.'

There was silence as the officers of the113th Foot – the Baby Butchers, –waited to hear what their new colonel had to say. Becoming aware of a slight drumming, Jack looked down to see his fingers beating a rapid tattoo on the table-top. He withdrew them hurriedly, hoping the Colonel had not noticed. The officers of John Company listened in respectful silence, smugly aware that their regiments were blessed with excellent reputations.

'We partially redeemed ourselves in the Crimea.' Colonel Jeffreys didn't mention that he had joined the regiment since then. He clearly preferred to have his officers imagine he already considered himself as one of them. 'However, there is much work to be done. A regiment takes its motivation from the top, from the officers, so you gentlemen must show an example to the men. They must look up at you with respect and devotion.'

Jack nearly smiled. He tried to imagine Donnie Logan or Thorpe or Coleman or any of his Crimea veterans looking up at any officer with respect and devotion.

'To gain their loyalty and trust, we must form ourselves into a tight bond; we must be as close as a family and know each other as intimately as you know the boys in your form at school.'

Jack kept his face immobile. His family had disowned him when they found out he was illegitimate and he had endured his school years with a passive hatred which still surfaced from time to time.

'To that end, the junior officers will sing songs.' The Colonel eased his gaze over the assembled men. 'Lieutenant Elliot, I hear you have a musical ear. Sing for us.'

'Yes, sir.' Elliot surprised Jack by immediately standing to sing.

Once more the trumpet clangs to war! That blast is widely heard!
And from its brief repose in peace is the martial spirit stirred
The British soldier hears the sound and rises in his might;
The sepoy feels the thrill of joy and girds him for the fight!'

Officers of both Queen's and Company regiments cheered, and a Company officer jumped up with a song of his own. Jack listened to the words.

The valour of our Sepoy sires lives in us o'er again
The British banner in our keep has never met with stain!'

There were other songs, some familiar, others locally composed but all dealt with a similar theme, the valour of British soldiers and sepoys fighting side by side. After half an hour or so Colonel Jeffreys ordered:

'There is a tradition in many regiments for officers to play games; as of this moment it is also the tradition in the 113th.' He looked down the length of the table. 'Young gentlemen of the Company regiments are of course welcome to participate. Officers of more seniority are invited to repair to the ante-room with me.'

'It has never been a tradition in the 113th' Snodgrass murmured and raised his voice. 'I think it is a first-class idea, sir. 'We will start with High Cockalorum, gentlemen, and then try some wall racing. Servants! Clear the table; *jildi!*'

As the servants moved smoothly to obey, Elliot winked at Jack. 'You will enjoy yourselves, by order,' he whispered.

'What the devil's High Cockalorum?' Jack asked.

'We'll soon find out.'

High Cockalorum proved to be a military variation of a children's game where the officers climbed on each other's backs to create the largest possible human pyramid.

'Come on Jack, don't be shy!' Elliot threw himself into the game with such enthusiasm that Jack had to join in.

As the drink flowed, the men grew more daring, until at one point Jack was at the apex of a pyramid that pressed him against the underside of the ceiling. At another, he was struggling under the weight of a dozen men with a lieutenant's boot in his ear and Ensign Shearer's knee heavy on his shoulder.

When the pyramids collapsed with shouts and laughter, the officers began wall-racing.

'What's the deuce is wall racing?'

'Watch and learn, young man,' Elliot slurred his words. 'Watch and learn.'

For a moment Jack watched as young officers launching themselves at the wall at great speed and ran as far as possible in a nearly horizontal position. A few minutes later he was balancing along the wall and whooping with the best of them. When he landed heavily on the floor, he came to his senses and regarded his antics with a mixture of disgust and embarrassment.

'These are the antics of school-boys,' he said and withdrew to the more tranquil atmosphere of the ante-room.

'It was a bad move, taking over Oudh,' Irvine, a Company captain in his late thirties was saying as he nursed a brandy glass. 'Nevertheless, we have now the opportunity to extend the blessings of British rule, tranquillity and security to the people, but the sepoys resent it.'

'I can see nothing wrong in taking over Oudh,' Snodgrass said.

'Many natives can,' Irvine explained. 'They believe we are appropriating all of India. In the last ten years we – the Company – have followed the Doctrine of Lapse, so if the ruler of a state dies without leaving a direct male heir, the Company has the right to take it. In local custom, you see, an adopted heir can rule.'

'Damned good thing if you ask me,' Snodgrass said, glancing at Jeffreys to ensure he agreed. 'We're far better than the perverted and dissipated creatures that rule these blessed places.'

'That may well be so,' Irvine sipped carefully at his brandy, 'but they were native states governed by the indigenous peoples according to their local customs and practises.' He twirled the brandy around his glass. 'In the last decade, we have taken over by one method or another Jhansi, the Punjab, Satara, Nagpur and Sambalpur, and now Oudh. The Indian princes must be uneasy; they are our allies and our friends and must feel we threaten their security.'

'There's not much they can do about it.' Snodgrass was drinking whisky at a rate that would put Elliot to shame. 'If these damned black princes start trouble the Company will just smash them.'

Irvine raised bushy eyebrows. 'As I said, Major Snodgrass, they are our friends. We have neither desire nor intention to smash them, as you put it. Anyway, it's not only the rulers who suffer. When we took over Oudh – or Awadh, to use its real name, we put thousands of men out of work. There were two hundred thousand men in the army alone and Lord alone knows how many in the royal household, plus thousands of armourers.' He shrugged.

'Two hundred thousand men!' Snodgrass marvelled. 'That is a large army to have on our border.'

'Yes, I realise the numbers may sound threatening, but Awadh was friendly and our biggest recruitment area. Now, thanks to the Doctrine of Lapse, we have tens of thousands of disaffected men there, *within* our borders.'

'Are they so disaffected?' Jack felt himself rapidly sober.

'There is a new feeling of unease in the land,' Irvine said. 'Things are happening that I for one don't understand and I have been in the Company's service for over twenty years.'

'What sort of things?' Jeffreys asked.

Irvine put his glass on a table and shook his head when the imperturbable Pathan servant offered a refill. 'There are silly, inconsequential things that individually make no sense at all, but when put together indicate an unhappy country. For example, down in Baroda some men are taking a pariah dog around the villages and feeding all the local dogs.'

'Why?' Jack asked.

'Only they know.' Irvine shrugged. 'The Maratha god of the sword is a dog, so it could mean there is violence imminent. Or it could mean the natives fear the Company will end all forms of caste; everyone sharing the same food, don't you know?'

'I don't know at all,' Snodgrass said.

'Nor do I, frankly,' Irvine admitted. 'Then there are the chapattis.'

'What the devil?'

'Small cakes...' Irvine began.

'I know what a chapatti is, for God's sake,' Snodgrass said. 'I want to know how they are suddenly famous.'

'I don't *know* why,' Irvine said. 'It's something I have never come across before. A stranger will appear in a village with four chapattis. He gives them to the *chowkidar*, the watchman, and asks him to bake another four and take them to the next village along.'

'Why?' Jack asked.

'Nobody knows,' Irvine said. 'I doubt even the villagers understand, yet it is undoubtedly a message.' He grinned. 'India is a strange place, full of intrigue, mystery and danger, which is why I love it so much. I intend to settle here when my time is up.'

'Don't you wish to go home?' Snodgrass ran a hand through his luxuriant whiskers.

'This is my home,' Irvine said. 'I am what is known as a 'serious' officer. I think it my Christian duty to teach these misguided souls about our Lord. We have to use kindness and slow the process of taking over their lands and decreasing their pay as we do. The more of India we annexe, the more my sepoys lose their *batta* – the money we pay them for serving beyond the Company's borders.'He smiled. 'No soldier likes to lose part of his wages.'

The tall servant moved slightly, spilling a single drop of wine onto Irvine's shoulder.

'Be careful, blast it!' Irvine shouted as the man salaamed in apology.

'I am no expert,' Jack waited until the servant withdrew a pace. 'But interfering with people's religion is pretty fundamental, is it not?'

'We must spread the truth,' Irvine said. 'We must hasten the time when the people throw off the dark cloud of idolatry and superstition which has hung for ages over this land – *our* land and our responsibility.'

Jack shifted uneasily. 'You know them better than I do,' he said, 'so I must bow to your experience. I do know England has failed to persuade most of Ireland to convert from Catholicism to the Church of England despite centuries of attempts.'

'These are both branches of Christianity,' Irvine pointed out.

'Opposing branches,' Jack said. 'And when King Charles the First tried to impose Episcopalianism on Scotland, he ended up on the losing side in a bloody war.'

Irvine laughed. 'There will be no bloody war in Bengal,' he said. 'Our sepoys are the match for any native army – no, they are the match for any *ten* native armies combined. And as we now possess the Punjab, we will have the magnificent Khalsa as well. That's the Sikh army, don't you know?'

'But the sepoys themselves?' Jeffreys asked. 'Are they to be trusted? There have been cases when they have disobeyed, even mutinied.'

Irvine shook his head. 'These were isolated misunderstandings, sir. The sepoys are the most loyal men and the best soldiers in the world,' he said. 'I would stake my life on their fidelity.'

Jeffreys lifted his glass. 'I'm glad to hear it,' he said. 'If ever we have another set-to with the Russians, we may need your sepoys. There was hard fighting at Sebastopol, God knows, and we needed more men than we had.'

'My sepoys would have shone,' Irvine said stoutly.

'Now you, Windrush; go back and join your colleagues,' Jeffrey's ordered. You are a young man still, far too junior in years to be jawing shop with us oldsters. Go and enjoy yourself.'

'Yes, sir.' Jack had no alternative but to obey orders, although he wished to learn more about the current situation in India.

The evening ended in raucous laughter and singing as one by one the officers decided to return home. The older married men were first, and then the older single men as the younger became rowdier without their elders' moderating influence.

'Come on, Arthur.' Jack took the glass from Elliot's hand. 'It's time you were getting to bed.'

'I'm not ready yet,' Elliot tried to snatch his drink back. 'I'm not leaving until I'm ready.'

'Come on.' Handing the glass to an expressionless servant, Jack took Elliot's arm. 'Time to go.'

'You're not my father!' Elliot's words slurred as he shouted. 'You can't order me around as he does!'

'No, but I can.' Colonel Jeffreys must have drunk equal to any man in the room yet he was as precise of speech and stance as if he had not touched a drop. 'Get back to your quarters, Elliot! You're a disgrace.'

'He had a bad time in the Crimea, sir,' Jack defended Elliot.

'We all had a bad time in the Crimea. If he cannot handle his drink, then there is no place for him in a regiment of British infantry.'

'He'll be all right, sir. I'll take care of him.' Sliding an arm around Elliot's back, Jack supported him. 'Come along, Arthur.'

Jack supported Elliot outside the mess and along the path with wan moonlight as a lantern. Jeffreys watched for a moment, turned around, slammed his boot on the ground like a sentry and marched away.

'It's not fair,' Elliot slurred. 'It's not fair.'

'No, it's not,' Jack knew there was no point trying to get any sense from Elliot when he was drunk. 'Come on, Arthur. We're nearly home.' A jackal howled beyond the cantonment; the sound of India.

'I've to be a general.' Elliot staggered sideways, nearly pushing Jack into the prickly hedge that bordered the path. 'My father expects me to be a general and I'm only a lieutenant.'

'You're only twenty-two,' Jack said. 'Nobody can be a general at twenty-two.' He tightened his hold as Elliot's feet slipped from under him. 'Not even the Duke of Wellington was a general when he was twenty-two.'

'I'm only a lieutenant. You're a captain, and I'm as good an officer as you are.'

'Better, probably,' Jack murmured. He heard something moving outside the cactus and wondered if it was one of the servants or if there was some wild animal on the prowl. 'Come along, Arthur.' He adjusted his grip on Elliot and inhaled deeply of the hot night air, momentarily wishing he had brought his revolver.

'Here we are.' Jack stopped where the mohur tree marked the driveway to Elliot's bungalow. Half-seen by starlight, the lawn was close-cropped, and the sound of insects and frogs filled the air. 'Come along home.'

As an unmarried Lieutenant, Elliot occupied one of the smaller bungalows, but it was palatial by the standards he could have expected back in Britain. Hardly seen in the dark, brilliant purple bougainvillaea coiled around the colonnaded porch which protected the front door from the scorching sun of the day.

With the alcohol still coursing through his system, Jack was uncaring of the neighbours. He raised his voice. 'Awake inside there!'

The response was immediate as lights flared behind the windows and Indian voices came in reply. The watchman stormed out first with his iron-tipped staff ready to repel any threat to his master's house.

'Rambir!' Jack shouted. 'Help me with the sahib here!'

More servants scurried out, some stopping to salaam with both hands to their forehead as they recognised that a British officer was making all the fuss, others concentrating on Elliot, who was now breaking into song:

> *In Nottingham, there lives a jolly tanner*
> *With a hey down, down, a down, down.*
> *His name is Arthur-a-Bland,*
> *There is never a squire in Nottinghamshire*
> *Dare bid bold Arthur stand.*

Jack grinned. Despite their years of campaigning together, he had never heard Elliot sing that particular song before. 'You're out of tune, Arthur. Come on, and these nice people will help you to bed.'

Elliot turned aside and grinned vacantly. 'Bed? I know a song about beds,' he said and began to sing.

> *There was a monk of great renown*
> *There was a monk of great renown*
> *There was a monk of great renown*
> *He fu—'*

'Enough,' Jack slipped a hand over Elliot's mouth. 'There are women and children around. I don't know what your mother would say.'

Rambir and the butler took hold of Elliot, faces impassive. They had seen drunken British soldiers before.

'We'll take care of the sahib,' Ramdass the butler salaamed to Jack.

'All right, Ramdass.' Jack had found it surprisingly easy to pick up some Urdu phrases. He watched as the servants gently and expertly eased Elliot up the stairs and through the large front door of the bungalow. Trying to imagine how British servants would have coped, Jack shook his head and turned away. Elliot was in good hands. He would wake up washed and shaved in his bed, without knowing a thing about it.

As Jack followed the path around the cantonment, a pale moon gleamed above the surrounding palms, and small bats flitted around, feasting on the plentiful insect life. He knew if he returned to his bungalow he wouldn't sleep. There was too much in his mind for rest and the night's mixture of formality, conversation and stupidity had only acted as a reprieve from his thoughts.

Extracting a cheroot from his inside pocket, Jack lit up and inhaled the sweet smoke. He looked around; he was in India, in effect ruled by the Honourable East India Company and the spiritual and actual second home of the British Army. India was the jewel of the Empire and the landmass from which Britain drew much of her wealth, power and prestige. And for the next ten years or so, this would again be his home.

He began a slow walk around the British cantonment, listening to the regular fall of his feet on the ground and the sounds of the Eastern night all around. Tall palms thrust upward among the dark foliage outside the camp, where sentries patrolled in bored routine, swearing under their breath as British soldiers always did and always would do. The world would be a strange place if British soldiers ever stopped grousing, swearing and complaining.

Jack stopped at the edge of the broad road that separated the officers' bungalows from the barracks of the other ranks. His men were over there: Riley, Thorpe, Logan, Coleman, Whitelam and the rest. These were the men he had fought and suffered beside throughout the Burmese War and the horrors of the Crimea. Men who had stood at his side at Inkerman and the Redan, who had crouched under the parapet of the Sebastopol trenches; companions, comrades and, he liked to think, friends.

Under the old commander, Colonel Maxwell, such bonds of friendship were cherished and valued. He could have slipped over the road to pass an hour with the sentries, shared a pipe of tobacco and a joke and spoken of old times along the Woronzoff Road or how the new Enfield rifle compared to the Minié that had done such sterling work in the Crimea. However, Colonel Jeffreys had stopped such friendly intercourse.

'Officers and men live different lives,' Jeffreys had announced on his first day on taking over command. 'It is your duty to lead and theirs to obey.'

'My men saved my life more than once,' Jack began, only for Jeffreys to cut him short.

'They were doing their duty for an officer's life is worth more than theirs,' Jeffreys said. 'There will be no more mixing with the other ranks unless duty compels it. We must maintain a proper and respectful distance and speak to the men only through the agencies of the sergeants. That is what sergeants are for; to relay and translate our orders into language the troops can understand.'

Drawing on his cheroot, Jack peered across the road, wondering how his men were coping with this new regime. After the ordeal of the Crimea, to be shipped to India must have come as something of a shock to them.

For a moment Jack contemplated breaking the Colonel's rules, crossing the road and talking to his men. Then he shook his head; they were soldiers. They knew rules and regulations governed the lives of the officers every bit as much as they did other ranks. Instead, he watched as the sentries marched on their pre-ordained routes and tossed away his half-finished cheroot, so the glowing end arced into the dark. Sighing, he followed the road to where the flagpole soared upright toward the sky. At the base of the pole was a granite slab, inscribed with the names of all the British regiments that had garrisoned Gondabad in the previous thirty years. Jack stopped and waited until a cloud eased away from the moon, so the light returned.

A bat fluttered past, its shadow a strange reminder of his nightmare. Jack fought his shudder. His gaze passed over the famous regimental names and numbers on the slab. He recalled the legends attached to the men who had garrisoned Tangiers, the bloodied battalions at Quatre Bras, the stubborn soldiers who faced the Sikhs and the unfortunate 44th cut down to the last man at Gandamack. And there, near the bottom of the list, was the Royal Malverns. Jack felt his hand shaking as he produced another cheroot and scratched a light.

The Royal Malverns, his family regiment, had been here from 1830 until 1835; he was now twenty-four years old, so he had been born here, in this cantonment at Gondabad. Jack looked around; fate played strange tricks sometimes.

There was the murmur of voices, and he saw that the sentry opposite him was Riley, the gentleman thief with whom he had shared so much in the Crimea. About to call a greeting, Jack realised Riley was not alone.

'What are you up to, Riley?' he said softly and peered into the darkness.

Jack saw that Riley was with Charlotte, his wife. He smiled, knowing how close the two were and opened his mouth to interrupt them. Instead he turned away. Riley was one of the few men he genuinely trusted and even with Charlotte at his side he would be a better sentry than most men. Besides, this was peaceful Gondabad, in the heart of British India and with two companies of the 113th as well as two native infantry regiments, and three troops of native cavalry within call. Nothing could happen here.

'Good luck Riley,' Jack said quietly. 'And you Mrs. Riley.' He stepped back toward his bungalow, pulled on his cheroot until the tip glowed brightly and he thought of Helen.

A picket of sepoys marched smartly past on some mission of their own. The naik in charge threw Jack a perfect salute. He responded, watched them disappear into the barracks and allowed his mind to return to Helen.

'Sahib!'

The voice came from the darkness beyond the cactus. Jack frowned; he hadn't recognised the voice. It came again in a husky whisper.

'Sahib; sir!'

'Show yourself, whoever you are.' Jack felt at his belt and grunted when he remembered he had neither sword nor pistol with him. 'Come out!' He lifted his fists, ready to face whoever emerged from the dark be it badmash, dacoit or a servant seeking a favour.

Dressed in a mixture of European and Indian clothing, the man had a ragged blue turban on his head and a long, old-fashioned pistol at the waist of his baggy red trousers.

'Don't come any closer.' Jack glanced around, hoping a sentry was within earshot. 'How did you get past the pickets?'

'They did not see me, sahib.' The man stopped about ten yards away. Slightly built, he leant heavily on a stick. Jack guessed his age at somewhere between fifty and seventy. 'I am here to warn you.'

'Are you indeed?' Jack wished he had at least his sword with him. 'Warn me about what?'

'There is a scarlet storm coming to India.' The man's voice was husky, his words hoarse.

Jack frowned, wondering if he was speaking to some madman, or perhaps a fakir. 'I am not here to listen to your nonsense,' he said.

The man leant closer. 'You are a British officer, a captain of the 113th Foot,' he croaked.

'I am.' Jack tried to retain his patience while wondering if he should summon Riley and have this madman removed. 'And who might you be?' He stepped back as the man suddenly slammed to attention.

'Fraser, sir, Private, 78th Foot.'

'You're a British soldier?' Jack heard his voice rise.

'I was, sir. I was invalided out in 1820.' He limped forward, face wrinkled with curiosity. 'Beg pardon, sir, but what year is it now?'

'It is May 1857,' Jack said. 'Have you been in India all this time?'

'Yes, sir. I was wounded you see,' he tapped his left thigh. 'I lost some use of my leg, so the army had no further use for me. There was nothing for me back home; the landowner emptied my glen for sheep.' As he spoke, Fraser's voice strengthened. 'India is my home now, sir.'

'I see,' Jack said. 'There seems to be a few British soldiers deciding to stay here.'

'Yes, sir. It's a fine country except bad times are coming.' Years of service compelled Fraser to stand to attention.

'What sort of bad times, Fraser? Oh, stand easy, man! You're not on parade now!'

'I move around with the natives, sir, and I hear them talking about a scarlet storm. I don't think they know themselves, but there's talk of kicking the British out of India. There's a prophesy our rule will end a hundred years after the Battle of Plassey, sir, and that was in 1757.'

Jack nodded. 'So I believe, Fraser.'

'The sepoys are unhappy sir. I've heard them talking in the markets about the new cartridges having a covering of pig and cow fat. The Moslems think pigs are unclean, sir and will hurt their religion and cows are sacred to Hindus, so if they bite or touch cow fat, it damages their caste.'

Jack frowned, remembering his recent conversation with Irvine about unrest in some of the East India Company's native regiments. 'Is this discontent widespread?'

'I wander about quite a lot, and I've heard the same sort of stories from the borders of the Punjab right across to Calcutta.' Fraser's voice strengthened the more he spoke.

'I'm sure his Excellency the Governor- General knows about them,' Jack said.

'There is more, sir,' Fraser glanced around him.

'Carry on.'

'Some of the people believe we intend to convert them all to Christianity and others are saying the Company is grabbing all their land.'

Jack remembered Irvine's conversation. 'They seem to have reasons for discontent.' He thought of the bravery and sacrifice of the sepoys during the Burmese War. It was wrong to ill-treat such soldiers.

'I thought I should warn you,' Fraser said. 'And I have. What you do next is up to you.' He stepped back just as another cloud concealed the moon.

'Wait!' Jack strode forward, but Fraser had gone. He lit another cheroot, turned around and walked to his bungalow. He had much to ponder.

Chapter Two

Lying on his bed with the mosquito net loose above him and the night sounds muted by the walls of his bungalow, Jack lit the lamp. Soft light diffused around the room. Whatever Elliot believed, the humidity affected him, so he stripped off his clothing and lay naked, staring at the lizard that crawled along the ceiling on its never-ending hunt for insects.

Fraser's words reverberated through his head. Unhappy sepoys, soldiers grumbling about new cartridges and British land grabs. Were such things his concern? He was a British officer, a man in command of a company of soldiers in the heart of India. Of course it was his concern. He would pass on the information to Colonel Jeffreys first thing in the morning. It may well only be bazaar gossip, the sort of grumbles soldiers always had. Yet there had been unsettling incidents with native regiments refusing the new cartridges and a sepoy named Mangal Pandey attacking British officers.

Jack sighed. Fraser hadn't given him any new information, so there was no need to interrupt the colonel's sleep. Irvine's earlier conversation proved the authorities knew what was happening and had plans to remove the grievances. After all, John Company, the Honourable East India Company, had been in India for centuries and knew the people well.

Stretching out, Jack dragged over his tunic and pulled out the letter from his inside pocket. It was crumpled and well-thumbed from constant use, and he knew the contents by heart, yet he opened it with care and scanned the words. It had been his nightly ritual ever since the letter had arrived and every time he read, he felt sick and hoped he had misunderstood the meaning.

'*My dear Jack*' it began.

Jack ran his fingers over those words as if by touch he could bring the writer closer to him. Her writing was large and bold, slightly untidy. Jack could picture her so clearly; he could see the crinkle of her eyes and the set of her mouth.

'*I hope you are in good health and the remainder of the campaign in the Crimea was successful.*'

He re-read the words. He had spent so much time with Helen over there; they had shared experiences, danger and dreams of a mutual future.

'*I often think of our times together and smile at the memories. My father always spoke highly of you, and he took an interest in your career, as did I.*'

Her father was Colonel Maxwell, who had commanded the 113th Foot through much of the campaign in the Crimea. Now he had left, promoted to brigadier and sent on to England, taking his family with him.

'*As you know, I became very friendly with your brother William before the Russians captured him. He was repatriated in a prisoner exchange and was on the same ship as we were when we sailed home.*'

Home. Helen had never been to England until that point and still thought of it as home. The eternal nostalgia of the exile, as Jack knew well.

'*Father and Mother both approved of our friendship so when William asked their permission for my hand in marriage, they gave it and I, naturally, had no hesitation in accepting.*'

Jack read the passage three times, mouthing the words silently as moths fluttered around his lantern and the lizard crept slowly across the ceiling. 'Oh, naturally,' he said. 'So brother William not only has my house and land, but he has also stolen my girl.'

He put the letter down, closed his eyes and swore. Damn him; damn William to hell, and damn Helen too; the lovely, vivacious, unpredictable Helen. Damn them both. Damning them didn't help, so Jack continued to read.

'*I was not happy to learn how you had abandoned William and allowed him to be taken deep into Russia, and now I have learned certain things about your history that are frankly quite disturbing.*'

'I did not abandon William,' Jack said to himself. 'He chose to remain a prisoner with his drinking and womanising!'

'*Indeed, Jack, I find I am quite disappointed in you. I had thought you to be a gentleman and now I know you are not. William and I will be happy if we no longer have anything to do with you. I do not wish you to reply to this, the last message I will ever send you.*'

The letter ended with three curt words:

Helen Windrush (Mrs).

Jack re-read the entire letter, slowly, knowing it would hurt him, knowing he could do nothing to assuage the pain yet still reading. He leant back as the sweat from his hands soaked into the paper, smudging the ink and blurring some of the words. It didn't matter; he knew them off by heart and could repeat the sentences blindfold if he needed to.

His Helen was gone, married to his half-brother. For over two years he had imagined taking her to Wychwood Manor and showing her his favourite places, introducing her to the Malvern Hills and the villages, fields and woods where he grew up. Now Helen would see all these places with his brother, William, who had turned his back on him as soon as he learned he was illegitimate.

Illegitimate. The word echoed through Jack's head. He was the bastard son of General Windrush and some servant girl; who she was he did not know and never would. It had been some casual sexual encounter that mattered nothing to his father but infuriated his stepmother, so she denied him all access to his father's home. Rather than having him commissioned into the prestigious Royal Malverns, Jack's mother had sent him to the 113th, the last refuge for ne'er-do-wells, blackguards, criminals on the run, and men discarded by other regiments.

Jack looked at the bottles on the sideboard, pondered for a moment and discarded the idea. Drinking would not alter anything. He lifted the letter again and read it, savouring Helen's signature as he relived the times they had spent together. Sighing, he put the letter down and lifted a Hindustani dictionary. He was determined to learn the language, although the words blurred and the image of Helen intruded every time he turned a page.

'Sahib!' The voice was soft, but urgent. 'Sahib!'

'Hazura.' Jack struggled to open his eyes. His Dogra butler stood at the side of the bed. 'Have I overslept?'

'No, Sahib.' Hazura was immaculate as always. Tall and slim, he sported a fine curling moustache and a turban that seemed over-large for his head. 'There is a soldier-sahib to see you.'

Jack lifted his silver Hunter from the sideboard. 'It's five in the morning, Hazura. I've only been in bed for two hours, for God's sake.'

'Yes, Sahib.'

'Send him away, Hazura. Tell him to report to me at a respectable hour.'

Hazura salaamed. 'It is a sergeant, Sahib. He said it was urgent and he must see you.'

About to blast the man to obedience, Jack killed his bad temper. Hazura had grown old in the service of John Company; he was not a man to wake an officer unless there was a good reason for it. 'All right, then, Hazura. Give me a minute to get some clothes on, and I'll see this fellow.'

Unshaved and not-yet-awake, Jack stumbled to the front door to see a sergeant standing at attention.

'O'Neill!' Jack's momentary pleasure at the sight of a familiar face altered to concern. 'What's the trouble, Sergeant?'

'We have two men missing, sir.' O'Neill threw a smart salute.

'Have you reported to the duty officer?'

'Yes, sir.' O'Neill remained at attention. 'Mr. Hargreaves said I should tell you, sir.'

Jack nodded. Lieutenant Hargreaves was one of the new young officers who had joined the regiment to replace the casualties of the Crimea. 'He was probably wise. Who is missing – let me guess, Thorpe and Coleman?'

'No, sir. Thorpe and Hutton.'

Jack frowned. 'I don't know much about Hutton.'

'He's a new man, sir; a wild young lad from Manchester with a taste for women and drink.'

'Stand at ease for God's sake, O'Neill.' Jack tried to get his sleep-fuddled thoughts together. 'All right; any ideas?'

'They'll be in a brothel in Gondabad, sir, depend on it.'

'Bloody fools,' Jack said. 'Thorpe should know better.' He pondered for a moment. 'Ever since he won that blasted medal outside Sebastopol, he's thought he's something special! All right Sergeant. My compliments to Mr. Hargreaves and ask him to inform the colonel then meet me outside the barracks in ten minutes. Bring a picket of a dozen steady men, Riley, Logan, Coleman… You know best.'

'Yes, sir.' O'Neill saluted again and loped off into the dark. Somewhere in the night, a leopard gave its sawing cough. Jack grunted. Thorpe and Hutton were prize fools to risk the pox and God-knows-what- else consorting with prostitutes, but at least they had taken his mind off his problems.

Pulling on his uniform, he allowed Hazura help him with his sword and pistol, checked his revolver to ensure it was loaded and stalked off to meet O'Neill.

The bugler was busy, calling out the guard and the official words ran through Jack's head as he crossed over to the barracks side of the road.

Come and do your guard, my boys, come and do your guard
You've had fourteen nights in bed, so it won't be hard.

Naturally, the 113th had refined the words:

> *Come and do a picket boys, come and do a guard*
> *You think it's bloody easy, but you'll find it's bloody hard.*

The picket was waiting for him, mostly Crimea veterans, grumbling as they fastened their tunics and made final adjustments to belts and buckles. Jack frowned at one familiar face.

'Armstrong! You were with us in Burma. Where have you been since?'

Armstrong was a saturnine Borderer with a mouth like a man-trap. 'In Scotland, sir.'

'Why were you not with the regiment?'

'I had to go and sort something out, sir,' Armstrong said and relapsed into silence.

'You deserted,' Jack said.

'Yes, sir. I had to sort something out at home and then I was in Greenlaw.'

Greenlaw was the military prison at Penicuik, south of Edinburgh. 'I see.' Jack knew he would never hear the full details. 'Glad to have to back, Armstrong. If you try to desert again, I will shoot you myself.' He raised his voice. 'Right, men, you know that Thorpe and Hutton are absent and you'll know where. How many of you know the brothel area of Gondabad?'

There was an uneasy silence.

'You know, Coleman, and so do you, Logan.' Jack ignored the expected protestations of innocence. 'You take point along with me. Sergeant O'Neill, take the rear. These two idiots could be dragged away and murdered in the native town. I want them safely back in barracks so I can kill them myself.' Jack hid his smile as he looked at the familiar faces. Since his promotion to captain and their posting to Gondabad, he'd had much less time with his men. 'March.'

Gondabad was a sprawling town of some thirty thousand souls, with a tangled spider's web of narrow, stinking streets and alleyways around the crumbling Moghul fort in the centre. There was also a suburb where the local merchants lived secret lives behind high-walled gardens.

The watchman at the gate in the decaying mud-and-stone town walls stepped out to challenge them, saw they were British soldiers and retired to his habitual semi-doze.

'It's a bit like home.' Logan's Glasgow accent cut through the dense humidity of the night.

Jack ignored him. 'Coleman; you know Thorpe best. Where will he be?'

Coleman hesitated for only a minute. 'I don't know, sir.'

'Well you'd better damned well start to know, Coleman!' Jack snapped. 'Anything could happen in this sort of place. Unless you want Thorpe murdered or worse.'

'He might be in a place I've heard of, sir,' Coleman muttered softly.

'Take us there,' Jack pushed Coleman ahead into the first of the alleyways. Even at night, there was an all-pervading smell of fruits and spices, together with a hint of incense and the urine of cattle, goats and humans. A waft of high-pitched music came from deep in the interior.

The alleys were narrow and dark, with windows shuttered to keep out the daytime sun and night-time thieves, stinking puddles on the ground and the rustle of rats and unseen horrors. Even with a dozen fully armed and stalwart British soldiers around him, Jack felt vulnerable in this place. This town of Gondabad was raw India, far removed from the glamour of John Company's offices and the counting of cash through trade.

The native music continued, punctuated by a sudden outbreak of barking from pi-dogs and the harsh voice of a man. A woman screamed, a child began to cry and then silence, brittle with menace. The music started again, sinister in the dark.

'This way, sir'. Coleman sounded as calm as if he was walking through a market town in England. Stopping where the alley narrowed even further, he glanced ahead. 'There's a place down here I think Thorpey might be, sir. We call it Madame Dora's but the locals have another name for it.' He touched a hand to his bayonet. 'It could be a little rough, sir.'

'Thank you for the warning, Coleman.' Jack felt the comforting weight of the revolver in its holster. He raised his voice slightly. 'Be prepared for anything, men.'

The resulting growls were reassuring. Roused from their sleep and sent on a march to the native town in the small hours of the morning, his men would not be in the best of tempers. He stifled his involuntary grin. God help the *badmash* who got in their way.

Moving in single file up the alley, Jack was very aware how vulnerable his picket was with shuttered windows overlooking them and hidden doorways leading to only-God-knew-what on either side. Although the men carried rifles and bayonets, this was a civilian area, and they were under the rule of law. Whatever happened, he would be responsible for any damage to property or injuries to people, military or civilian. With Fraser's warning of the previous night raw in his head, he could sense a new tension in the air. It was as if the town was watching him, waiting to strike at these men from the far north who had occupied so much of this ancient land.

There was a sudden bang of wood on hardened mud as a shutter opened behind them, the querulous sound of a female voice and the staccato barking of a dog.

'Here we go,' somebody muttered.

For a few moments frantic barking and the shouts of angry dog-owners filled the air.

'Bloody dogs,' Logan commented. 'We should shoot the buggers.'

'We should shoot you, Logan.' O'Neill gave the inevitable response. 'And I might if you don't keep your mouth shut, you bloody Scotch dwarf.'

'Aye, right, Sergeant. It would take more than you.' Logan probably meant his words to be a whisper, but they carried further than he intended in the confinement of the alley.

Jack said nothing. It was better for the men to work these things out themselves without the interference of an officer.

'Up here, sir.' Coleman opened an ornate metal gate by turning his back on it and kicking with his heel. The gate creaked backwards to slam against a mud wall. The sound set off another dog.

'You pick your places, don't you?' Jack said. 'How on earth did you find this?'

'Oh, Madame Dora's is well known, sir,' Coleman said. 'It's one of the best whore houses in Gondabad.'

'If this is one of the best...' Jack left the rest unsaid. He remembered the French army in the Crimea supplying women for the benefit of the men. They were clean and safe, which was a much more sensible arrangement than anything the British Army did. Perhaps the powers that be in Horse Guards believed British soldiers were hymn-singing angels who spent their evenings reading improving books rather than the flesh-and-blood men they were.

The metal gate led to a short passageway that stunk of every offensive smell Jack could imagine, and others he had no desire even to consider. At the far end was an arched Moorish door, heavily studded with iron and with a small grilled window in the centre.

'Here we are, sir.' Coleman stood aside, duty done.

Jack stared at the door, momentarily unsure what to do next.

'With your permission, sir?' O'Neill stepped forward, as Jack had hoped he would.

'Carry on, Sergeant.'

'Logan, Riley, Murphy, Whitelam – you follow me when I enter and don't stop for anything. Coleman, Parker, and Regan – stay out here and don't let anybody in. The rest of you wait inside and don't let anybody out.'

Without waiting for confirmation, O'Neill lifted his boot and kicked massively at the wooden door.

'113th Foot!' he roared. 'Open up in there!'

O'Neill's voice had carried across the battlefields of the Crimea and Burma. Now it shattered the fragile peace of the restless town and yet again awakened a score of dogs.

Lights appeared behind the upper windows of the building.

'Open up!' O'Neill emphasised his roar with another thunderous kick that rattled the door on its hinges. There was the scrape of bolts, and the door creaked slightly.

'Follow me!' Without waiting for the door to fully open, O'Neill barged inside with his four chosen men at his heels. Either he was already familiar with the interior layout of Madame Dora's, or he had some sergeant's skill at navigation for he raced up a flight of internal stairs without hesitation.

'Thorpe! Hutton! We're here for you, you idle bastards! Come out now, or I'll have you both hanged for desertion. 113th! 113th!'

The men at his heels shouted the same so the cacophony of noise increased, doors opened and patrons and their girls peered out.

In the meantime, Jack took a more leisurely approach as he watched a surge of people descend to the front door, where the 113th halted them with loaded rifles and loud voices. Jack looked over the assembly of scared men and angry women. It was a pretty typical cross-section of Indian society, he decided, with clerks and lawyers as well as farmers and merchants of all ages from sixteen to sixty. One middle aged, dignified woman stared at him, bold-eyed.

'Sir,' Riley said. 'That's Dora. She will know if Thorpey's here.'

Jack stepped into the press of bodies. 'Miss Dora?' he enquired politely. 'I am Captain Jack Windrush of the 113th Foot.'

He expected the tirade of abuse but not the large man who stepped forward and lifted an iron-shod staff.

'The Wrath of Shiva will come upon you!'

'That could be true.' Jack tried to sound calm. He knew any overreaction would only encourage this man to violence, and then his 113th would retaliate, with goodness knew what ultimate consequences. 'But before Shiva begs angry we are searching for two wayward private soldiers. Once we retrieve them, we will be gone and leave you in peace.'

'There is a scarlet storm coming to India,' Madame Dora said. She was about forty, Jack guessed, with a caste mark low on her forehead and intense brown eyes.

'So I've heard.' Jack noted that Dora used the same phrase as Fraser had.

'It will blow you back to England,' Dora shouted.

'Bloody cheek!' Williams lifted his hand as if to slap her.

'Restrain yourself, Williams.' Jack glanced upstairs as there was a sudden outburst of noise and then O'Neill's voice bellowed out.

'Stand still, Hutton, or I'll shoot you where you stand!'

'That's Hutty told,' Riley said casually. 'Stupid Mancunian bastard.'

There was the sound of heavy feet clattering on the stairs, and Logan appeared with his rifle at the high port. 'Got them, sir. The locals don't like us much.' He shifted aside as something heavy sailed through the air to bounce on the ground at his feet.

'Form a square, men,' Jack ordered. 'We're not popular here.'

Thorpe looked bemused as O'Neill pushed him down the final few steps, reached behind him and dragged Hutton to join him.

'Sorry I took so long, sir,' O'Neill said. 'These two were out of uniform.'

That was as neat a euphemism as Jack had heard for some time. 'I take it they were not alone.'

'No sir; they had company.' O'Neill shoved them both into the middle of the square.

'Let's get out of here before we start a war.' Jack wondered if he was better to lead from the front or take the rearguard. As an officer, he should take the position of most danger.

'Yes, sir.' O'Neill hesitated for only a second. 'Beg pardon sir, but do you remember the way back?'

'Not well,' Jack admitted.

'Shall I take point then, sir?'

'Yes, please, Sergeant.' Thank God for O'Neill.

The first stone rattled from the gate as they reached it. The second stone passed high over Jack's head, hit the wall of a building and bounced back.

'113th!' Jack watched his men pass. Hutton ducked as the volley of stones and crockery increased, with men and women in other buildings joining the denizens of Madame Dora's in pelting the British. '113th; hold your ranks!'

If the men remained in formation, they would be safer. Any individual soldier who strayed could be snatched away and murdered in the tangle of dark alleyways. These native towns were as dangerous to strangers as the rookeries of London or the closes and wynds of Glasgow. The noise of shouting men and women and the crash of stones on walls and ground increased.

Logan cursed as a rock thumped onto his shoulder. He lifted his rifle as if to fire, glanced at Jack and lowered it again.

'Keep moving,' Jack ordered. 'Hold your fire. These are civilians.'

'There's a scarlet storm coming!' That was Dora's voice, high-pitched and piercing. 'It'll chase you back to England!'

'You'll lose half your custom then, you poxed-up bitch!' Thorpe retaliated quickly.

'Keep quiet and listen for orders!' O'Neill shouted over his shoulder.

Jack looked forward. Dawn was breaking above the town, easing tendrils of light through the gaps between the houses and shining on the shakos of the white-clad 113th as they pushed through the lanes. Above them, shutters opened, rubbish was tipped out, stones thrown, and shutters closed again. Faces appeared and reappeared, brown and dark-brown, male or female, shouting insults, screaming hate or worried and fearful. The roar of abuse increased. The barking of dogs became frantic.

More stones battered down, bouncing from shoulders, knocking off shakos, cutting heads and faces.

'Scarlet storm!' The English phrase was heard above the background noise, either partial or in its entirety. 'Scarlet storm!'

The gunshot came as a surprise, echoing through the narrow lanes. Jack didn't see where the ball landed but smelled the burned powder and saw the slow drift of smoke across the face of a building to the left.

'Anybody hurt?'

There was a pause. 'No, sir!' O'Neill replied. 'All present.'

'Pick up the pace,' Jack said. 'The sooner we're out of here the better.'

Williams yelled as a stone struck his mouth. He swore, spat out blood and carried on.

'Permission to fire, sir?' Coleman asked.

'Denied; keep moving.' Jack ducked as a brass pot hurtled toward him. It hit the wall at his side and clattered to the ground.

'Sir!' O'Neill shouted. 'Ahead of us.'

Another lane crossed theirs at right angles. A crowd waited at the intersection, brandishing metal-tipped staffs, swords and long muskets and shouting as the British approached.

'Halt.' Jack lifted his hand. His men obeyed, eyeing the shifting mass ahead, the long robes of the men and the array of weapons they carried. Jack raised his voice above the hubbub. 'Bayonets, fix!'

The sinister hiss of British soldiers drawing bayonets from their scabbards would quieten any crowd. The sharp snick of the picket fitting them under the barrels of the Enfield rifles penetrated even the rising roar.

Stepping to the front of his men, Jack formed them into a solid block, taking his time to make it appear he was unafraid of the screaming mob. The veterans of Sebastopol and Inkerman stared forward without expression, with the newer members of the unit shaking, either with excitement or fear, Jack neither knew nor cared. They would do their duty, and in time they would be skilled veterans, or they would die. In the British Army, there was no alternative.

'Sergeant O'Neill,' he said. 'Take the rear.'

'Sir!' O'Neill slammed to attention and threw a salute. There was a trickle of blood on his face where some missile had nicked him.

With the lane behind them also beginning to fill up with yelling men, Jack knew he had little room to manoeuvre and no time to hesitate.

'O'Neill, Logan, Riley; face the rear. The rest of you, load!'

The men took cartridges from their ammunition pouches, ripped them open with their teeth and tipped the gunpowder down the barrel of the rifle.

'Caps!'

The cap was a cone which contained a chemical compound known as fulminate of mercury. Each man lifted a cap from the cap-box on their belt and fitted the cap onto the lock of the rifle. Despite the noise, they remained disciplined, with the younger men copying the veterans and trying to ignore the stones and other missiles that bounced all around them.

'Aim high!' Jack shouted, 'above their heads!' He made sure each man hoisted his rifle with the muzzle pointing to the sky. He had no desire to have a civilian death on his conscience. So far this was just a local disturbance; if he shot some unarmed man, the local population might rise en-masse with who-knew-what consequences.

One young soldier's hands were shaking.

'Thorpe; remove that man's rifle and take his place.'

The Enfield weighed nine pounds and together with the long triangular bayonet was a heavy weight for a man to point skyward for any length of time.

Coleman nudged Thorpe's elbow. 'Can you remember how to fire it, Thorpey? Or are you too important now you've got a Victoria Cross?'

'Bugger you, Coley! You never got nothing, you!'

'Fire!' Jack ordered.

In the confined space, the report of the rifles was shockingly loud. Grey-white smoke choked the alleys as the mob in front withdrew a pace.

'Reload,' Jack ordered when the echoes faded away. The sound of men preparing their rifles filled the new hush. 'Now lower your bayonets and follow me.'

Drawing his sword, Jack rested it against his right shoulder and marched boldly toward the crowd. A stone hurled through the air from somewhere in the rear. He ignored it and strode on, aware the mob was facing the gleaming bayonet points of his men, and knowing his 113th would not hesitate to stab and thrust. These were not parade-ground soldiers but veterans who had seen all the horrors of war.

Two natives stood their ground; one was tall with the arrogance of a Pathan and a scarf shielding the lower half of his face, the other older, with a bushy grey beard and venomous eyes. Unrelenting, Jack strode on, meeting the bearded man's gaze, seeing the smouldering hatred and knowing he would not break away. He had faced Burmese dacoits and Russian Cossacks, so a fat Indian civilian could not intimidate him. The Pathan stepped aside and watched from the shadows of a deep doorway. The bearded man began to shout, gesticulating angrily with his finger as Jack stepped toward him.

'Shall I shoot him, sir?' Coleman sounded eager to help.

'No, Coleman.' Jack nearly added, *but thank you for the offer.* Some of the crowd were backing off; the sound altered from defiance to anxiety, yet the bearded man shook his fist and stood directly in front of Jack.

'Leave him to me, sir,' Coleman sounded angry. 'It's not right he should do that.'

Jack pressed on, with the pressure of the 113th behind him. The bearded man was forced back, first one step, then two. He continued to shout with his breath hot, foul and spiked with betel in Jack's face. Jack slipped on something foul, recovered and continued, stepping over the man as he stumbled and fell. The soldiers of the 113th had no such sympathy; their iron-studded boots crunched down, deliberately stomping the bearded man as they marched onward.

In front, the mob dissipated. There were one or two stones and then nothing. Jack glanced over his shoulder; only the masked Pathan remained, watching from the shelter of an arched doorway. His gaze locked with Jack's and he nodded once and drew a finger across his throat in silent menace before gliding back into the darkness. Jack ignored him and led his men clear of Gondabad and on to the British cantonment.

Chapter Three

'He just refused to move,' Jack said. 'You know there is often trouble in the poorer quarters of Gondabad, as there is in any town. Good God, man, there are riots in Worcester and London and Birmingham every other weekend when the drink is in them. It's normal.'

'So I've heard.' Elliot rested his feet on a stool as he sipped at a glass of sherry.

'I'm not concerned about the stone throwing and shouting,' Jack said, 'but this fellow simply refused to move. I had my sword out, we had fired a warning volley, and we were advancing with a dozen bayonets – and he stood there haranguing us as if he had every right to do so.'

'Blasted cheek of the man,' Elliot agreed.

'More nerve than cheek,' Jack said. 'I've never seen the like. There was a Pathan as well. He stepped aside and drew a finger across his throat.' Jack demonstrated for Elliot's education.

'To a Pathan that's probably a sign of affection,' Elliot said. 'They're ugly brutes at the best of times.'

'His face was half-hidden,' Jack said. 'And he kept in the shadows, yet I'm sure I've seen him before.'

'Never met one in my life,' Elliot said. 'Don't want to either, because they're ugly brutes.'

'I admire your logic,' Jack told him, shaking his head. 'Damnit, the more I think about it, the more I'm sure I've seen him before, but for the life of me I can't say where.'

Elliot waved his glass in the air for a servant to refill. 'Never mind; it will come to you. What did the old man say about your two black-guards?'

Jack frowned. 'He was less angry than I thought. I wondered if he would get the triangle out, but instead, I have to take the entire company for a five-day route march to teach us discipline.'

'Your men were lucky,' Elliot said. 'The Colonel was light-handed because Thorpe won the Victoria Cross at Sebastopol.'

Jack nodded. 'It wouldn't look good if the regiment flogged a hero.'

Elliot grinned. 'Some hero! Did you tell Jeff about the bearded fellow?'

'I did. And about Fraser's warning about the sepoys. He didn't seem particularly interested. He called it bazaar gossip and people trying to stir up trouble.' Jack shook his head as a servant offered him sherry. 'No, thank you.'

'If the company men don't seem concerned,' Elliot said, 'I don't think there is anything to worry about.' He grinned. 'After the Crimea, this is a cushy number anyway. True it's hot. Yes, it's humid, but you can't compare this to the trenches outside Sebastopol, can you?'

Jack shook his head as his mind darkened with memories. 'No,' he said shortly. The Crimea had been hell on earth, yet Helen had been there. Here, stranded in Gondabad in the north of India, he had nothing but the regiment. Jack sighed and stretched. 'Best get back to my bungalow,' he said. 'I've an early start tomorrow with this route march.'

'What a bore,' Elliot agreed. 'Serves you right for not looking after your men properly.' He waved his glass for a refill. 'I'd see you out if I could be bothered.'

'You should jump to attention and call me sir.' Jack stood up and handed his glass to the willing servant. 'Never mind, as soon as Queen Vic promotes you to general you can have me saluting you all day long.'

'All day and every day,' Elliot grinned. 'By God, I'll make you suffer.'

As always, Jack took a deep breath as soon as he stepped outside. He wished he had been gentler with the sherry. Still, it was too late now; he had to get back to his bungalow and get some sleep before taking his men on the route march.

'Be on guard, Captain.' The words came in a husky whisper from beyond the cactus.

'Is that you, Fraser?' Jack asked.

'Be on guard. The Scarlet Storm is coming.'

'Show yourself!' Jack's shout set a dog barking, with others joining in. 'If you want to play childish games, find somebody else,' Jack said. Turning around, he marched steadily to his bungalow.

His watchman was waiting outside, sitting on the steps of the veranda and carelessly tapping his staff on the ground.

'Make yourself useful,' Jack snapped. 'There's a fool out there in the dark talking about a scarlet storm. Go and chase him away. Don't hurt him, just chase him away.'

Pleased to have something to do, the watchman loped into the dark. Jack heard him shouting a challenge, and then he walked into his house. 'Wake me at two,' he said to the butler before undressing and collapsing on the bed. Immediately he did so, images of Helen came to his mind.

'Go away!' Pressing a pillow over his face, Jack tried to block out the pain. He imagined her laughing with William; he imagined her strolling up the serene heights of the Malvern Hills; he imagined her taking William's hand and pressing against him as they climbed the sweeping staircase to the front door of Wychwood Manor. He imagined William lifting her over the threshold and carrying her inside and up to their marriage bed. 'No; go away!' Screwing tight his eyes, he tried to sleep, and the dark tunnel returned, with all the horrors it contained. There was fear and hatred and those words – 'Jack Baird Windrush'.

There were names from his distant and near-forgotten past.

'Two o'clock, sahib.' The butler stood beside his rumpled and sweat-soaked bed.

'What?' Jack looked up, dazed from a night of disturbed sleep. 'Oh, thank you.' He staggered to his feet to find servants waiting to dress him. Somebody handed him his sword belt while capable hands buckled on his holstered revolver. Within half an hour Jack had breakfasted and was out of his bungalow in the early morning air.

He walked past the nearby servant's cottages and into the barracks where bored sentries slammed to attention on his approach.

Jack's Number Two Company was waiting for him to arrive. He stood thirty yards away, quietly proud of his position as commander of these men. They stood in a solid block in their white drill, traditional summer dress in India, black shakos polished and the Enfield rifles held in right hands. He scanned them, recognising the veterans from the Crimea and the few who he had known in Burma five years before.

'Right then, men. Fifteen miles out and we make camp. Tomorrow we'll cover twenty miles, and so on. It's a round trip, so we'll see a bit of the countryside.'

There was no response. Men who had endured the trenches outside Sebastopol and the hell of Inkerman would shrug off a peacetime Indian route-march while the new members of the regiment hoped to look and act as hard-bitten as the veterans.

'Stand to your front!' Jack ordered. 'Number Two Company; form fours!' He waited until they had completed the manoeuvre. 'Left! Right wheel!'

It felt good to be giving parade ground orders to a regiment in peace rather than ducking within a Crimean trench. 'Quick march!' The rhythmic crunch of iron-shot boots echoed from the single-storey bungalows and the tall, airy barracks where the men slept, ate and lived. Jack saw a group of wives watching, some holding small children despite the early hour. Charlotte Riley was in front, waving to Riley, who disregarded discipline for a second to lift his left hand in farewell.

'By the left... left wheel.' Jack glanced over his men; they were behaving impeccably, *his* company of the 113th Foot showing what a

Queen's regiment could do, displaying the flag to the natives of British India. 'Forward march!'

The first few miles were along a pucka road, a metalled road laid by the British to improve communications. The boots rang on the hard surface as the men swung along, disposing of their tiredness in the rhythm of the march. After an hour Jack gave permission for them to march easy and the company relaxed and began to talk, with some lighting pipes, so the sweet smell of tobacco drifted behind them. One or two smoked cigarettes, a habit they had acquired in the Crimea.

'Is such laxness allowed, sir?' Ensign Shearer asked. 'We were taught to keep other ranks under discipline at all times.'

Jack nodded. 'You're just out of the Royal Military College, aren't you?'

'Yes, sir!' Shearer looked about eighteen with sweat already running down his sunburned face.

'You'll learn that what the college teaches and what happens in real life are two different things, Shearer. The men are not a different breed from us; we are all part of a whole, the regiment needs us all.' Jack remembered the attitudes he had as a young officer. Serving with the 113th had taught him humility as much as anything else.

'But, sir,' Shearer glanced behind him, where Coleman and Thorpe were joking together; the latter with a clay pipe hanging from his lower lip and his collar undone. Already the heat was increasing; within half an hour officers and men would be walking amidst a haze of dust that would stick to the sweat on their faces.

'Get back to your men, Shearer. They need to know their officer cares for them.' Jack listened to the murmur of conversation and the crunch of booted feet on the ground. He nodded in satisfaction; his men were all right.

They moved from the pucka road onto a *cutcha* road, new, unmade but still broad. Tree-lined and unmetalled, deep ruts on the surface made marching more difficult. The sun had risen now and struck a harsh glare from the surface into the slitted eyes of the men.

A bullock-cart jolted in front of them with a family perched on top of its load and a pencil-thin native walking alongside, tapping a long staff on the ground.

'Something's ahead, sir,' Shearer reported, self-importantly.

'Keep marching,' Jack ordered. 'They will move aside for us.'

Others were using the road, men herding goats, a gaggle of sari-clad women swaying under the burden of the water-jugs balanced on their heads, more bullock carts, a holy man with a long white beard and wise eyes, a plump merchant in a gharry. Some of the 113th called out raucous greetings, others waved or whistled. The natives stepped aside for this company of *lalkurti* - British soldiers. The griffins pointed excitedly when a small herd of cheetal - the common spotted deer - scampered across the road in front of them. Everything was as it should be, peaceful under the benign rule of the Company, idyllic except for the punishing sun.

By seven o'clock the men were feeling the heat and Jack had to run a hand around his collar to ease the friction. He savoured the fact he was in India, the land of his birth and his second home. It was strange, colourful, mysterious and often strikingly familiar.

When the heat became intolerable, Jack called a halt. 'This will do!'

Pleased to stop, the men slumped to the ground until Jack ordered them to set up camp. The sergeants translated Jack's orders into hectoring commands to create order out of chaos.

'The sergeants are our Godsend,' Jack said quietly to Shearer. 'Without them, this army would fall apart. They understand the men, and they know us. A good sergeant is worth his weight in rupees. A very good sergeant is worth ten griffs like you.' He smiled at Shearer's expression. 'It's all about experience, Shearer. I have no doubt you are as brave as a hundred lions, as patriotic as the Union flag, yet when the bugles call and the bayonets bloody, sergeants are the backbone of any army.'

With the muggy heat increasing, Number Two Company settled down to endure the day. Rather than allow the men all afternoon in idleness, Jack had them drill and set out pickets to scour the countryside.

'Never let the men get too idle,' Jack advised. 'Idle soldiers sulk and plot mischief.'

'I thought there would be battles,' Shearer said. 'Peacetime soldiering is a bore; nothing but parades and mess-meetings and dinners.'

'If you are ever unfortunate enough to be involved in wartime soldiering,' Jack said soberly, 'you will long for the boredom of peace.' He looked away, remembering the sounds and smells and horror of Inkerman.

'We had a toast at the college,' Shearer said. 'Here's to a bloody war!' He looked quite proud of his desires. 'After all, fighting is our job.'

'It is,' Jack agreed. 'And sometimes it is a job I hate.'

Shearer stiffened. 'It is our duty to defend and expand the borders of Empire. As soldiers of the queen, we must fight her enemies, seek glory and honour the flag.'

Jack smiled. 'Just why did you choose the 113th, Shearer? If you are seeking glory and honour, there are regiments with a much longer and more illustrious history.' In the British Army, the rule-of-thumb was the lower the number, the more senior the regiment, so the First of Foot, the Royal Scots, was known as Pontius Pilate's Bodyguard because of its age. The 113th was one of the newest infantry regiment and the least considered. Its nickname of the Baby Butchers showed the near-contempt in which other units regarded it.

Shearer was silent for a moment. 'I heard the regiment fought well in the Crimea,' he said at length.

Jack nodded. 'I am glad we have done something to enhance our renown.' *But was improving the reputation of a regiment worth the sacrifice of so many men?*

Jack looked away. He had grown up knowing he would follow the family's military tradition. Ever since he'd joined the 113th, he had tried to claw his way back into respectability by acts of bravery and by forcing the often-reluctant soldiers to become as professional as any regiment in the army.

'I don't know about glory,' Jack said slowly, 'but recently we've had more than our share of fighting.' He looked around. 'It will be good to have some peaceful days in cantonments to consolidate and allow the new men to settle in.' Was he saying too much to a griffin? Probably, but if Shearer was to be an efficient officer of the 113th Jack should include him in everything.

'The Crimean War ended last year,' Shearer said. 'Surely enough time to recover.'

In an instant, Jack was reliving the horror of Inkerman when his 113th built a wall of dead bodies as a barricade against the attacking Russians. He could see the frozen slush in the trenches outside Sebastopol. He could hear the roar of the Russian artillery and hear the screaming wounded outside the Redan.

'Too many men will never come back,' Jack spoke as if to himself. 'And the rest of us, those who survived whole in body, will carry the Crimea inside our heads forever.'

Shearer was too young to know when to withdraw. 'You did your duty,' he said.

'Now you do yours,' Jack said. 'Go and attend to your men.'

'Isn't that the sergeants' job?'

Jack felt the anger surge through him. 'They're your men and your responsibility! Look after them, damn it! Move!' He pushed Shearer away.

He wanted to be alone with his memories and the residual guilt of the survivor. He thought of Helen and of the men he had lost and recalled the fear and horror. He wished the politicians who had caused these insane, bloody wars could campaign with the 113th for just one week before they made their fatal decisions. His men may be foul-mouthed, they may haunt brothels and be prone to brawl, they may prefer to drink themselves into a stupor rather than listening to opera or reading the classics, but when the call came, they were ready to put their lives on the line. Jack looked over the camp with some pride; the Duke of Wellington had called them the scum of the earth, but they never let down their comrades when it mattered. In Jack's opinion, they were better men than the vast majority of frock-coated politicians and lords who made the decisions that sent them to die.

He shook away the thoughts. This dreaming would never do. He had a company to command, men to feed and ensure they had a bed for the night and water to drink. If soldiering were only about fighting, his job would be so much easier.

They heard the drums as they marched along the broad road with their boots crashing in unison and their rifles slung at fifty different angles. Jack remembered books he had read as a child where soldiers sang as they marched. Whoever had written those books had never marched in India when dry weather brought throat-clogging clouds of dust.

'Sir!' Sergeant O'Neill marched at his side. 'Drums, sir.'

'I hear them, O'Neill.'

'Yes, sir. They've been sounding this last hour or so.'

'They're *dhaks*,' Jack said; the word sprang from nowhere into his mind. 'Traditional Bengali drums. I wonder what message they are sending.'

'It could just be some festival, sir,' O'Neill sounded doubtful.

'It could be,' Jack said. 'All the same, keep an eye out, O'Neill. There may be a rogue tiger or a group of dacoits or some *badmash* on the road.'

'I'll pass the word on, sir, although the boys are a bit wary already.'

They passed through an area of jungle, with long-tailed grey langur monkeys screeching at them from the trees and an explosion of brightly-coloured minivets far above. The drums continued, to stop abruptly with no warning leaving an unnerving silence.

'What's happened?' Thorpe asked.

'I dunno, Thorpey.' Coleman looked around. 'I think I prefer the drums.'

They marched onward past fields with isolated copses of trees until they arrived at a village, empty save for a single brass *lota* bowl that lay abandoned beside the well.

'Where are all the people?' Jack held up his hand, ordered a halt and looked around. He had been in a hundred native villages, and always there was bustle and confusion with men sitting under the shade trees and women with bundles on their heads and children around their feet. This village was eerily empty. There was only a single pi-dog sniffing hopefully around.

'Dacoits,' O'Neill said shortly. 'That's what the drums were saying. Remember we heard the like in Burma, sir?'

'I remember,' Jack agreed. 'Burma was a wild territory with a rogue king. India should be more settled; John Company is in command here, with the rule of Law and military garrisons to ensure order and stability. If the villagers are scared of dacoits, they should come to us. God knows we tax them high enough.'

'Maybe they're scared of us, sir?'

Jack raised his voice as he saw the 113th scatter all around the village. 'Keep together! We don't know what's happened here. O'Neill, send pickets to search the area. I want relays at the well to refill the water-bottles.'

There was no sign of disaster, no scatter of bodies, no blood; only houses that showed evidence of rapid evacuation with household goods lying on the floor, a small heap of clothes here, a bowl of un-eaten food there.

Jack called over his lieutenants. 'Prentice, Fairgreave, Kent – ten minutes to fill the water-bottles at the well and then we're leaving. Something is very wrong here.' He looked over to a peepul tree. There should be a gathering of old men around the tree-trunk, passing the day in conversation as they watched village life. Instead, the branches were laden with watchful birds.

'This is sinister,' he said to O'Neill.

'Yes, sir. Our boys are ready.' O'Neill didn't have to elaborate. They both knew O'Neill referred to the men who had been with him since Burma and those he had fought beside in the Crimea. Jack's promotion had done nothing to weaken the bonds formed in war.

'Keep them alert, O'Neill.'

'Sir!'

'Prentice, send a picket forward to check the road ahead; Kent, arrange for a ten-man rearguard.'

'Are you expecting trouble, sir?' Prentice spoke with an assumed drawl.

'Always,' Jack said.

'This is India, sir, not the Crimea. I've been out here since '54, and there hasn't been anything the Company's armies could not handle.'

'You recently transferred to the 113th didn't you, Prentice?' Jack didn't like junior officers questioning his orders.

'Yes, sir.'

'From where? No, never mind. In this regiment, we obey orders without question. Get it done!'

'Yes, sir.' Shrugging, Prentice casually moved away.

'On the double!' Jack roared. He could feel O'Neill watching.

They left the village more warily than they entered, with the men watching the fields and copses of trees on either side.

'Shearer!' Jack called the ensign over. 'Take three men and liaise between the advance guard and rear guard. Inform me of any development. Got it?'

'Yes, sir.' Shearer nodded, eager to be involved. 'What is happening, sir?'

''Damned if I know, Shearer but something is not right.'

They marched on, boots crunching on the ground and the men edgy, watching their surroundings. Birds circled above, their calls somehow sinister in the punishing heat.

'We'll be in Gondabad soon,' Jack said quietly.

'Yes, sir,' Shearer agreed. 'The advance party reports all quiet ahead.'

'Good,' Jack had contemplated sending O'Neill up front with his veterans, but such a move may have undermined the authority of his officers. 'And the rear guard?'

'I'm going there now, sir.'

'Off you go then.' Jack lit a cheroot, more to show a lack of concern than out of any desire to smoke. Fine dust raised from the marching men descended in a cloud to cover them in a white film. Already the sun was reflecting off the road, increasing the heat, drawing sweat from officers and men.

The drums started again, sombre, insistent, disturbing.

'I'll be glad to get back to the cantonment.' The furrows on Lieutenant Kent's face made him look old.

'We'll be fine, Kent. Make sure your men are alert.'

'Yes, sir.' Kent was keeping to the centre of the road. 'What do you think is happening?'

'I don't know. How long have you been in India, Kent?'

'Fifteen years, sir. I came out in '42.' Kent flinched at the call of a monkey.

'You know the country better than I do, then. Have you seen much action? Afghanistan? The Punjab, Burma?'

'No, sir. I've been on garrison duty in the south all the time.'

Jack frowned. For a man to spend fifteen years in India yet avoid all the wars argued for the damnedest of bad luck; or no thrust at all. Kent seemed to be the sort of officer the 113th used to have but had gradually removed either by natural wastage or carefully considered postings. 'This might be something or nothing, Kent. I'm not sure yet.'

'Sir!' O'Neill hurried up. 'Thorpe thinks he can smell smoke, sir.'

'Send Thorpe to me.' Jack knew O'Neill would not approach him with a triviality.

'Smoke sir.' Rivulets of sweat ran down Thorpe's tanned face.

'Could it be a cooking fire?'

'No, sir,' Thorpe shook his head emphatically. 'I know how smoke smells, sir.'

'If I recall, Thorpe, a magistrate found you guilty of arson and gave you a choice between jail and joining the army.'

'Yes, sir. I can smell buildings burning, sir, and cooking meat. It smells sweet, not like animals. I think it's people, sir. Dead bodies.' Thorpe shook his head slightly to dislodge the bead of sweat that hung on the end of his nose.

'Thank you, Thorpe.' Jack dismissed him and strode forward to join the advance guard. He tried to look less worried than he felt.

'Come on, lads. We might have work ahead of us.' He had made it his business to know the men's names and faces, yet many were still strangers. Most had the thin, suspicious faces of urban slum dwellers, sharp-eyed and underfed, with bodies small in stature and quick in movement. 'Stay with me.' Lengthening his stride, Jack paced ahead with the picket hurrying at his heels.

'Sir! Listen!' The leading man, a Liverpudlian named Parker, pointed ahead. 'That's gunfire, or I'm damned.'

Jack stopped, feeling the sweat soaking through his tunic and the sudden jangling of his nerves. He recognised the feeling as a warning of danger.

'I don't think you're damned, Parker.' He heard the high-pitched crack of a pistol, followed by the deeper bang of an Enfield. Only officers carried revolvers while the men used rifles. Another shot sounded, followed by a fusillade. Dear God in heaven; what was happening? Had some group of badmashes been foolish enough to attack a British cantonment?

'Spread out. Watch your flanks. You, corporal,' Jack pointed to a man and searched for his name. 'Corporal Evans; give my compliments to Lieutenant Prentice and tell him there is smoke ahead and possible gunfire. Tell him we are hurrying ahead and ask if he would kindly increase the pace of the men. Have you got that?'

'Yes, sir,' Evans said.

'Off you go then.' Jack turned away. 'The rest of you follow me. Load, but I want no firing unless I give a direct order.' He did not want some poor civilian killed if the man was only celebrating some local god or hunting a tiger.

The next shot was distinct, followed by another, and then a ragged volley. 'What in God's name are they firing it?' Jack spoke without expecting a reply. 'Dacoits would never come near a British cantonment!'

'Dunno, sir,' Parker said. 'Will I run ahead and find out? I'm a bit of a scud.'

'No,' Jack said at once. 'If there's trouble I want us arriving all together, not in penny packets.' He raised his voice. 'With me, men!'

They advanced at the double with rifles at the high port and boots pounding on the pucka road. The firing increased, and Jack heard a high-pitched scream.

'That sounded like a woman,' Thorpe said.

'You should know if anybody does,' Parker muttered. 'What's happening?'

The trio of native horsemen emerged from a copse fifty yards in front of them but reined up when Jack and his picket pulled up short.

'Who are you?' Jack asked sharply. He had to shout so the horsemen could hear him.

'Musgrave's Horse.' The man was heavily bearded with a twisted turban and what might have been a uniform tunic, dark blue and ornate.

'Oh, thank God,' Jack said softly and then louder. 'Are you Company cavalry?'

The man's teeth showed white behind the beard. 'Yes, sahib. We are Company cavalry.' More riders formed behind him, bearded, wild-looking men in all sorts of uniforms who ranged across the road and merged into the trees on either side. They sat their horses like experts and some fingered the tulwars or sabres they wore.

'What's happening ahead?' Jack asked as the firing continued, now with more screaming. 'Have you sent a patrol to find out?'

'No sahib,' the bearded man called. 'We already know. The Scarlet Storm has arrived.'

'What?' Jack frowned. 'Don't talk in riddles man! Stand aside. I'm Captain Windrush of the 113th Foot, and we're coming through.'

'No, sahib,' the bearded men said. 'You are not.' He snapped an order, and his men drew their swords and formed up behind him, some bearded faces grim, others grinning but all with their swords held against their right shoulders.

'The devil we're not!' Jack wasn't sure what was happening. He knew the sowars, the native cavalry, were as loyal as the sepoys. 'Stand aside when I order you, sowar!'

There was a further outburst of shooting from the direction of the cantonment and more shouting. Somebody screamed, the sound distinct.

'That was another woman.' There was concern in Parker's voice.

There was no reason for a woman to scream in a British cantonment. 'Stand aside sowar, damn you!' Flicking open the button that secured his revolver in its holster, Jack felt his men tense behind him. The situation was getting ugly, and these capable-looking cavalrymen outnumbered his small picket. Musgrave's Horse? He had never heard of them. 'Who's your commander? Where are your officers, sowar?'

The sowar spokesman shouted an order and the cavalry began to move forward. Another order and they presented their swords for the charge. More appeared from the trees, so the horsemen outflanked and heavily outnumbered Jack's small advance party.

'Form square!' Jack gave the only order he could. 'Bayonets… fix!' He heard the snick as experienced hands fitted the triangular blades. Each of his men now held a weapon sufficiently long to repel a cavalryman provided discipline held and their courage didn't crack. These were British soldiers: they would stand and die rather than run.

'Unless you withdraw I will treat you as hostile!' Jack shouted to the mounted men. *What the devil is happening here?* These were Company sowars who had taken the salt of the East India Company, men who had proved their loyalty on a hundred battlefields across India over the past century. He could not think of them as the enemy; they were friends.

The cavalry began to move faster, still with their swords extended. Jack didn't see who gave the order as a bugle sounded, thrilling in its purity.

'Sir,' Parker said. 'The black bastards are attacking us!'

There was no doubt of it. This situation was no exercise organised by Jeffreys, no drunken game created by an over-exuberant cavalry commander. These sowars, these British-trained men were advancing on his small party of the 113th.

Jack grunted – the sowars had made a mistake. Cavalry needed room in which to manoeuvre and on which to build momentum for a charge. These men were too close – at most they would manage to gain a trot before they hit the 113th, which may work against broken troops but not against disciplined British soldiers. Feeling sick at heart, he gave orders that would set his Queen's infantrymen fighting Company cavalry.

'Present!' The Enfield rifles slammed down, ten muzzles pointing, ten perspiring British soldiers wondering what was happening as they aimed at allies and friends, ten soldiers obeying orders, ten fingers poised on ten triggers.

Jack swore, hoping the sowars would withdraw. He couldn't fire on these men. There must be some mistake. Yet if he didn't fire, the sowars could sweep right over his small detachment and wipe them out.

The horsemen were closing; he could see every detail of their faces, see the flaring nostrils of the horses, and see sunlight glittering on the points of the swords. Oh *God; I may start a war here. Or perhaps one has already begun? My duty is to my men first and foremost.*

'Fire a volley at thirty yards!'

'Sir?' Parker looked around. 'They're John Company, sir.'

'I know what they are; obey orders, damn it!'

The cavalry was picking up speed, the hooves causing the ground to tremble. The sowars let out a great yell, and some leant forward, in their saddles, thrusting out their swords, so the viciously-sharp points were three feet closer to the British.

The rifles pointed, men altering aim as the enemy advanced through shimmering heat that distorted their bodies and shapes.

Oh God, let this be the correct decision. 'Fire!'

The shots rang out; powder smoke jetted in the old familiar way, acrid, white and ugly. Three sowars fell. The rest roared out their battle-cry and increased their pace.

'Load!' It was mechanical now. Fate had case its dice and training took over. Jack mouthed the orders, knowing his men would obey. 'Home! Return! Cap! Volley at twenty yards.'

The men obeyed, biting the cartridges, pouring down the charge, ramming like automated demons, bringing back the Enfields, putting on the percussion caps.

'Ready... present!' The rifles extended again. The sowars were closing fast, and Jack knew he had hesitated too long.

'Fire!'

Four more sowars staggered in their saddles or fell; one horse screamed. The remaining riders powered closer to Jack's tiny group – they were Company cavalry, as brave and skilled as any fighting men in the world.

Jack aimed his revolver. *I should have fired sooner; my hesitation has cost these soldiers their lives in some skirmish for which I don't even know the reason.* 'Present bayonets!'

The foot-long triangular blades thrust forward in a sharp-pointed hedge. They looked puny in comparison to the long swords of the pounding cavalry.

'Number Two Company of the 113th will advance!' Lieutenant Prentice's voice was welcome. 'Halt! Prepare! Load, fire!' The orders came in quick succession at the exact time the sowars reached Jack's men. Intent on the situation in front, Jack could not spare even a glance for what was happening at his back until the rifles volleyed out. At least ten sowars fell, and the cavalry wavered.

'Load! Fire!' Jack ordered. He heard the crunch of boots and Prentice was beside him, smiling.

'I thought it best to come up, sir.'

'You thought correctly,' Jack said. 'Glad to see you, Prentice.'

The sowars withdrew in good order, vanishing into the trees without fuss or noise. Only the dead and wounded were left.

'These seem to be Company Irregulars, sir! I thought it was a band of dacoits.' Prentice sounded curious.

'I don't know what's happening, Prentice.' Jack ordered his men to form up. 'We're marching into the cantonment. Keep alert.' He raised his voice. 'Load!' There was a rattle of cartridge boxes and the ripping of paper and then silence. A long-tailed green parrot squawked high up and then more silence, broken only by the whinnying of injured horses and soft moaning of the wounded sowars.

Jack looked around. 'O'Neill; take ten men and act as the advance guard. If anybody tries to stop you...'

'We'll kill the bastards,' Logan said with an evil grin.

'Quite,' Jack said. Logan was always morose unless he was drunk or in action. He raised his voice. 'Quarter column and watch the flanks. If anybody attacks, shoot them flat.' About to tell his men not to wait for orders, Jack considered for a moment and decided it was best to leave it. He did not want a Johnny Raw from some industrial hell's kitchen firing on an innocent villager just because he looked out of place.

They moved forward quickly, stopping for nothing and with firing breaking out ahead and then becoming desultory. The smell of smoke increased.

'Sir!' Coleman threw a hurried salute. 'The Sarge... Sergeant O'Neill says to tell you there's trouble sir. The cantonment is alight, and there's sepoys killing us everywhere.'

'That makes no sense, Coleman.' Jack glared at him. 'I'll come myself. Prentice; take charge – bring the men and take care.' He ran forward.

The smoke was denser now, acrid in the back of his throat while intermittent gunfire sounded. Somebody was shouting; a child's voice screamed 'mother' again and again and then ended abruptly, a man laughed high pitched, and there was a renewed spatter of gunfire.

'Jesus, sir,' Thorpe said. 'Something's happening in the cantonment.'

'Sir!' Coleman pointed to the side of the road.

The woman lay face-down with her dress pulled to her waist and a gaping wound in her left shoulder. Bare legs gleamed, and her blonde hair was a tangle across her back.

'Dear God in Heaven!' Jack stopped only for a moment to crouch beside the body. Pulling down her dress to make her decent, he felt for a pulse. There was none. Turning her over he saw her eyes were wide open. Both her hands were closed into fists, with her nails broken and fingers smeared with fresh blood.

'That's Mrs. Alcorn, sir,' Coleman said helpfully. 'Sergeant Alcorn of Number One Company's missus.'

'Thank you, Coleman,' Jack said. He stood up, pulled out his revolver and moved on. He felt sick.

'Sir!' O'Neill called to him from behind a cactus. 'Careful sir; there are sepoys ahead.'

'There are meant to be, O'Neill. They're on our side.'

'Not today they're not, sir,' O'Neill said. 'Look ahead.'

The cantonment was a shambles, with the 113th barracks ablaze and half the officer's bungalows surrounded by mobs of red-coated sepoys. The noise increased with every step, high-pitched laughter and yelling, the occasional eruption of gunfire mingled with the crackle of flames, the pounding of feet on the ground and the constant rumble of voices.

There is a scarlet storm coming to India. Jack remembered Fraser's warning. *Well, here it is. The sepoys have revolted.* He looked around the cantonment. Number One Company of the 113th should be here, together with headquarters staff and a few dozen servants as well as two regiments of native infantry and three troops of Company cavalry. All he could see was mobs of native infantry running around with no order or discipline, and a scattering of bodies on the ground.

'Oh, Jesus, there are women there,' Parker said. 'What's happened?'

I don't know.

Parker was correct. Women in light-coloured night-clothes lay bloody and dead among the bodies of British officers and the occasional servant or sepoy.

There was no training to help him in a situation such as this. The native troops, the utterly loyal sepoys and sowars, had mutinied. Despite the warnings, the sight was shockingly unexpected. The loyalty of the sepoys was the bedrock on which British India stood. Sepoys were men of solid character, whose conditions of service was superior to those of the Queen's infantry. For a moment Jack could only stare in total disbelief.

'Where are our men, sir?' Prentice was remarkably calm. 'Where is Number One Company?'

'I wish I knew, Prentice.' There was an outburst of firing even as Jack spoke. 'That was volley fire so it could be them now.'

'Yes, sir,' Prentice said, and reminded: 'The sepoys also fire in volleys, sir.'

'Advance in echelon by platoon,' Jack ordered. He had witnessed Colin Campbell's Highlanders marching and firing in echelon at the battle of the Alma and had trained his company until they were proficient. It was an ugly irony that his first chance to see how it worked was against a rabble of soldiers who until very recently had been friendly.

Jack had never thought to see a British cantonment in flames, or British-trained sepoys acting like a rampaging mob. He saw a large group around his bungalow, yelling and shouting as they threw all his possessions outside and destroyed them. He saw a tall naik pulling on his dress uniform and parading around to the cheers and laughter of his fellows, and a grey-haired Havildar lifting his dress sword and holding it up to examine the quality.

'Permission to fire, sir?' Prentice asked.

'Denied,' Jack said immediately. 'There are a hundred of us,' he said. 'If all the sepoys have mutinied there are over two thousand in the cantonment, plus the sowars.'

'What is your plan, sir?'

'Gather as many survivors as we can and get out,' Jack said. Everywhere he looked there were burning buildings, and among the drift of smoke, scattered British bodies lay in a score of positions.

A group of sepoys looked up as they passed and some pointed, yelling and waving their rifles. Others joined in, shouting challenges or cursing. When they realised these British were capable of retaliation, they didn't attack.

'Look!' Prentice nodded to the nearest bungalow where a group of sepoys clustered around something that struggled on the ground. 'What's happening there?'

'It's a woman!' Riley was looking around in something like horror. 'Sir! They've got a British woman!'

Jack nodded; he felt the anger rise hot within him as he realised what was happening. The sepoys had surrounded a British woman and were watching while three men kicked her back and forward.

'It's Mrs. Pringle,' Prentice said suddenly. 'Lieutenant Pringle's wife. He's in Number One Company.'

I was speaking to her last week, Jack thought. *She's from Northumberland, a lovely lady.* 'Kill the bastards,' Jack said softly. What happened was more of a massacre than a battle as the men of the 113th, confused by this mutiny of the sepoys and angered beyond reason at the sights and sounds, charged forward. Intent on their fun, the sepoys hardly had time to look up before the privates of the 113th began work with bayonet and rifle butt.

'Mrs. Pringle!' Prentice was first to the crumpled form of the woman. He looked up. 'She's dead, sir.'

'So I see.' Jack had seen death take many forms in his five years as a soldier, but nothing he had seen shocked him as much as he was at that moment. To have sepoys turn on British women and burn a British cantonment in India, a place the British felt was a second home, was beyond comprehension. He wanted time to withdraw and think about events, to put things in perspective and consider the reasons for this nightmare. However, he knew he had to deal with the situation as it arose and worry about the whys and wherefores later.

'Sir!' O'Neill gave a formal salute. 'Riley and the rest are worried about their wives and families, sir. They ask if they can go to search for them.'

Jack glanced toward the British barracks, from which smoke and flames spiralled to the sky. 'No,' he said softly, hating himself. He felt

O'Neill stiffen. 'We stick together, sergeant. There are thousands of these sepoys here; if we break into small formations, we're inviting them to destroy us piecemeal.'

'Yes, sir. But the women, sir.'

'The barracks are aflame, O'Neill. The women won't be there now.' Jack didn't say that they may all be dead, like Mrs. Pringle. 'We'll move toward the firing.' He set off again with his company in formation, stamping their boots and looking for blood. Jack had never known such anger in British soldiers. He remembered the men after Inkerman when they had been incensed at the Russians' bayonetting British wounded. This situation created a deeper hurt; the men felt shocked, betrayed and outraged by the murder of their women.

'Sir!' Ensign Shearer had been physically sick. Now he pointed a shaking finger at the bungalow of Lieutenant Harris. 'Sir; oh my God.'

The sepoys crowded outside, laughing as they tossed something back and forward outside the burning building. Jack only watched for a moment before he realised they were throwing a baby boy in the air and laughing as they caught him. The child's cries of fear rose high.

'Oh, dear God!' Jack said. 'Prentice; keep the men in check. O'Neill, accompany me with a picket.' He was moving before he had finished speaking, running toward Harris's home with his revolver in his hand.

Sepoys crowded around the bungalow, mixed with a sprinkling of servants and a few men Jack did not know. However, he recognised the tall man who caught the baby boy.

'You!' It was the Pathan servant who had spilt a drink on Irvine at the guest night. 'Sarvur Khan!'

The Pathan lifted the baby by his left leg and casually tossed it upwards and backwards into the bungalow. For a second the child's screaming body was lit by the orange flames, and then it vanished into the fire. The screams increased and ended with a whimper. Jack squeezed the trigger of his revolver as a surge of sepoys rushed toward him. He shot two, swearing, and then O'Neill and his men fired a volley. The sepoys parted and ran, leaving bodies on the ground. Sarvur Khan was not among them.

'Where is the bastard?' Jack looked around as the private soldiers bayonetted the sepoy wounded. 'Reload.' He felt his anger rise. 'What kind of people murder children? Who does that sort of thing?'

'Sir.' O'Neill was at his elbow. 'Over there.'

There was a bank of white powder-smoke ahead, with either the same mob of red-coated men or another group attacking another of the bungalows. 'Elliot!' Jack said softly. 'That's Elliot's house.' He allowed himself a humourless smile. If anybody organised resistance, it would be Elliot.

'Form a square,' Jack ordered. 'Move forward and if anybody tries to stop us, shoot them flat.'

The men gave a grim cheer – not the full-blooded roar of British soldiers going into battle but something more subdued, more savage. He had given the correct order in the circumstances. If he had said 'no quarter', he knew it would be both welcomed and obeyed.

They moved forward step by step until the sepoys realised what was happening and turned toward them.

'Fire,' Jack said. 'Don't wait for orders. Fire at will and be careful; our men are in the bungalow.'

Faced with this new advance by an unknown number of disciplined soldiers, the mob of sepoys scattered. 'Keep in formation!' Jack ordered when some of his younger men surged forward in pursuit. He raised his voice. 'You in the bungalow! I am Captain Jack Windrush of Number Two Company, 113th Foot!'

'Lieutenant Elliot, sir.' The welcome answer came through the crackle of flames and the incoherent roar of the crowd. 'With half a dozen men and a few civilians!'

'Bring them out, Elliot. The sepoys have gone for the minute.' Jack kept his finger on the trigger of his revolver, hoping the sepoys would return so he could kill. He watched as Elliot emerged with six men, two of them wounded, and a gaggle of servants, with two British civilians.

'Sir.' Riley spoke from the ranks behind him. 'My wife...'

'The men's wives and children, Elliot? Any news of them?'

Elliot was tired and smoke stained, with the front of his uniform jacket torn. He held a revolver in his right hand. 'Yes, sir. Colonel Jeffreys' packed them off to Cawnpore three days ago when we heard there was trouble brewing.'

Jack felt the relief pass through his men. 'Mrs. Pringle was left behind, and others.'

'Yes, sir. Mrs. Pringle said her son was too sick to travel, and most of the officers' wives refused to go with the rankers.'

Jack swore. The officers' women had put class differences before their safety. Class was the curse of British society. He didn't ask what happened to Harry Pringle. 'Tell me more.'

'The sepoys just rose sir. It was quiet yesterday, tense but quiet and then very early this morning they just erupted and attacked everybody.'

'Both native regiments?'

'Yes, sir and the sowars as well. They must have arranged it in advance.' He hesitated as loud shouting came from the darkness around. 'I've seen one man running between the groups of sepoys, sir, as if he was organising them.'

'Who?' Jack guessed the answer even before Elliot spoke.

'Sarvur Khan, sir, the colonel's servant.'

Jack nodded. 'We'll deal with him later, I promise you. Have you heard from the colonel, Elliot? Or Major Snodgrass?' Jack heard somebody shouting close by, the words indistinct but Urdu.

'The Major went with the rankers' families, sir. He took an escort of twenty-five men from Number One Company.'Elliot started as a rifle cracked. 'Sorry sir, my nerves are a bit on edge.'

'That's not surprising,' Jack said. 'If Snodgrass took twenty-five men, and I had Number Two Company, there would be about eighty men of the 113th here.'

'Yes, sir.' Elliot agreed.

'Where are they?' Jack looked around. He saw Captain Irvine of the Bengal Native Infantry spread-eagled on his back with a score of ugly gashes to his body and face. Only a few days ago he had praised the loyalty of his men.

'They were in the barracks when the sepoys mutinied, sir,' Elliot sounded near-hysterical. 'As far as I know, the sepoys barricaded the doors and set the buildings on fire.'

'Dear God,' Jack said again. 'They were burned alive? Our men?'

'Yes, sir. I got some of the pickets to my bungalow.' Elliot was striving to control his emotions.

'You did well, Arthur.' Jack looked up as a rifle fired nearby, then another.

'The sepoys are recovering, sir,' Prentice said. 'They're collecting again.'

There were groups of sepoys gathering in the shelter of the bungalows with white trousers and cross-belts gleaming in the sun. The tall figure of Sarvur Khan moved from group to group, talking to the Naiks and Havildars.

'Time to move,' Jack decided. 'We'll take a quick tour of the cantonment, show the flag and get out.'

With the servants and civilians in the centre of the square, Number Two Company moved slowly around the cantonment. The scenes were shocking, with bungalows on fire, pet dogs hacked to death and a litter of British and servants' bodies across the lawns or sprawled over the cactus plants. The smell of burning bodies from the barracks was nauseating.

'Unless they are surrendering,' Jack ordered, 'if any sepoys come close, shoot them.'

He marched the square around the officers' bungalows, hoping some survivors might creep from cover, hoping the sepoys would attack so he could have them destroyed.

'There's the colonel, sir,' Prentice said. 'What's left of him.'

Colonel Jeffreys lay on his side, faintly ludicrous in his embroidered nightshirt and with his sword in hand. A dozen wounds seared his body, and somebody had crushed his head. Insects were already busy on his corpse.

'Murdered by those he thought were friends,' Jack said.

'Yes, sir.' Prentice didn't say more. They moved on, across the pucka road and onto the area occupied by the other ranks. Two sentries of the 113th lay on their backs, one with an expression of surprise on his face and a bullet hole in his chest, the other with his bayonet bent and a score of wounds in his body. A single sepoy lay at his side, moaning softly until Logan kicked him to death. Coleman and Thorpe watched without expression.

Riley pulled Logan away. 'Come on Logie; Charlotte may still be here.'

'She's not here, Riley,' Jack said quietly. 'All the rankers' wives and children were sent away.'

There were more bodies inside the compound, a confusion of butchered corpses where men had run from the burning barracks and into the rifles and bayonets of the waiting sepoys. None were fully dressed; some had jackets and no trousers; some were in their under-clothes, and two or three were fully naked. There was an ugly growl from the men as they saw how their comrades had been cut down and hacked to pieces as they lay helpless on the ground.

'Poor buggers had no chance,' Elliot said.

'The sepoys murdered them,' Kent spoke in little more than a whisper.

'That's what it was; pure bloody murder,' Elliot agreed.

'We'll get the bastards,' Logan said. 'Just you wait, you filthy black murderers, we'll get you.'

'Sir,' O'Neill said softly. 'Somebody's moving over there.' He nodded to the left.

'A sepoy?'

'I dunno, sir. I saw movement behind the store hut. I don't know who it was.'

'Right, sergeant.' Jack knew he should send a sergeant or a junior officer with a picket to investigate. 'I'll go.' It was the wrong decision; it was a bad decision, but Jack wanted to kill; he wanted to rend and destroy more than he had ever wished to do so in his life. This terrible betrayal of trust, this mutiny by men on whom the British had relied, this appalling breach of loyalty, had shaken him, so he wished to strike back.

'Logan, Coleman, Thorpe; come with me.' Deliberately choosing Crimea veterans, Jack left the security of the square and ran toward the store hut. The door hung on one hinge, the windows were smashed, the roof smouldered and sparked, yet it was in better condition than most of the buildings in the cantonment.

'I'll go ahead, sir,' Coleman said. 'It's not right for an officer to go first.'

'Stay behind me, Coleman,' Jack hauled out his revolver, booted the sagging door open and thrust inside. 'Halloa!'

Although the interior was dense with smoke, sufficient light seeped from the smouldering thatch to reveal that the hut had been looted. The remaining contents were strewn over the floor in a confusion of uniforms, shakos and belts, ammunition pouches, neck-stocks and a hundred other items the military mind thought was indispensable to the art of legal slaughter.

'Sir!'

The elderly corporal whose duty had been to look after the store hut had died at his post. He lay spread-eagled with a bullet hole in the centre of his forehead and a look of astonishment on his face.

'Rest easy, Corporal Greener.' Jack stepped over the body and peered into the hut. About forty feet long, temporary walls and doors divided it into compartments. 'Is there anybody in here? Show yourself!'

There was a faint rustling, and Logan was immediately down on one knee with his rifle pointing.

'Only a rat,' Thorpe said. He looked around. 'These sepoy lads have a lot to learn about starting a fire,' he said. 'My Aunt Alice could have done a better job than this.'

'You can teach them next time,' Coleman muttered.

Revolver in hand, Jack took three short steps. 'Come out! Come out you sepoy bastard so I can shoot you!'

Kicking down each door as he came to it, he glared into each compartment in turn before moving on to the next. 'There you are!' He saw movement in the second last. Stepping forward, Jack saw a mass of dark hair, extended a hand and hoisted the owner upright. 'Right you bastard! Oh, sorry miss!'

The woman grabbed his arm. 'You're British,' she said. 'Oh, please God, say you're British.'

'Captain Jack Windrush, Ma'am, 113th Foot.' Jack stared for a second.

'Who did you say?' The woman was about forty, with the light olive complexion of a Eurasian. Her eyes were brown and nervous.

'Captain Windrush of the 113th.'

'Oh, thank God!' The woman's shoulders sagged although her eyes never strayed from Jack's face. '*Captain* Jack Windrush. I thought... the sepoys... they've been killing us.'

'You're safe for the minute,' Jack didn't want to give false hope. 'We are number Two Company of the 113th. The sepoys control most of the cantonment, so we're leaving soon. What is your name?'

'Jane,' the woman hesitated slightly. 'Jane Niven. And before you ask, yes, I am Eurasian.'

'How do you do, Miss – Mrs.?'

'Mrs.,' Jane said, 'I'm widowed.'

'Well, Mrs. Niven, we'll soon have you out of here.'

'Wait!' The woman put a hand on Jack's shoulder. 'There are two of us here. Mary!' she called sharply. 'Mary! It's all right – they're British.'

There was movement from a corner, and another woman appeared. She was younger, perhaps in her late teens or early twenties and trembling. Tears moistened her eyes and coursed down her cheeks.

'It's all right, Missus,' Logan said awkwardly. He touched a hand to the brim of his shako as if in salute. 'We're the 113th. We're not sepoys.'

The woman stood close to Jane, looking at the soldiers as if they were monsters from a gothic horror story. She held her ripped clothes together to cover herself.

'Mary had a rough time with the sepoys,' Jane explained. 'She's a bit wary of soldiers now.'

'Not surprising, Miss,' Coleman tried to help with rough humour. 'Anybody would be a bit wary of Thorpey.'

'You're safe with us, Miss,' Logan said. 'We'll rip any bastard who tries to hurt you.'

'Watch your language, Logan,' Jack said. 'Thorpe, check outside; Logan, take the rear, Coleman, look after the ladies.' He followed Thorpe outside, where the heat smashed them like a hammer, and Number Two Company fought their impatience as they waited for him to emerge.

'What is happening now, sir?' Elliot straightened his tunic as he spoke.

'We're leaving before the mutineers get themselves properly organised,' Jack said. 'We don't have sufficient men to retake and hold the cantonment against their numbers.'

They left the cantonment by the pucka road, marching slowly to allow the civilians to recover and keep up and after an hour, Jack ordered them onto a track that led west and south.

'Where are we going?' Jane asked.

'Honestly, I am not sure,' Jack said. 'I want somewhere secure to consolidate and discuss what's happened.'

'There is an old temple about two miles away,' Jane said. 'Not many people know it's there and there is no reason for the mutineers to visit.'

Jack nodded. 'Do you know the way?'

'I would not have mentioned it otherwise!'

'Take us there, then.' Jack ignored her outburst. Anybody who had been through what she had could be excused frayed nerves.

Without speaking, Jane led them on to another, even smaller track where they had to walk in single file and watch their feet for snakes. Jack sent Elliot to the front and counted his men past before he took a position in the rear, the place of most danger. If anything happened, he wanted to be in the centre of it, not two hundred yards away.

He shook his head. His world had turned upside down, but he was still a soldier, and he had his duty to perform. That was something secure to hold onto.

Chapter Four

Much overgrown and colonised by monkeys, the temple was in ruins, with massive buildings decorated with ornate carvings while a very welcome spring bubbled in the centre of what had once been a beautiful courtyard. Strange gods and goddesses peered down at these northern intruders through a tangle of invasive trees and creepers.

'Elliot; set up a defensive perimeter,' Jack ordered. 'I want three men at each corner and a picket of five men to patrol the area.'

'Yes, sir,' Elliot said.

'Once you've done that, report to me. You too, Prentice, Kent and Fairbairn. Leave the ensigns and NCOs in charge of the defences.' Jack gave a little bow to Jane and Mary. 'If you two ladies could join us, you would be very welcome.'

'Why them?' Fairbairn asked. 'They're women and civilians.'

'They were also in the cantonment when the sepoys mutinied,' Jack said. 'Their information could be valuable.'

'They're Eurasian,' Fairbairn said. 'Why are they still alive when we saw the white women killed? They might have sided with the mutineers.'

'They didn't,' Jack said softly, 'and I'll thank you not to question my orders again, Mr. Fairburn. Not if you know what's good for you.' He held Fairburn's gaze until the lieutenant looked away.

With the men busy digging trenches, making rifle-pits and clearing fields of fire in case of attack, Jack brought the officers and women into the courtyard and under the blank gaze of a prominent, many-armed Hindu deity, invited each to tell his story.

'The day after you left,' Elliot said, 'Colonel Jeffreys got notice of impending trouble. There was a mutiny at Meerut on the 10th you see.'

'The devil, you say!' Jack said. 'Meerut's a major cantonment!'

'Yes, sir. It's worse at Delhi. Three native regiments, the 38th, 54th and 74th Bengal Native Infantry, mutinied and grabbed the city. They proclaimed the old Moghul Emperor, Bahadur Shah Zafar, as Emperor again and all sorts of rebels are flocking to the Peacock Throne.'

'Dear God.' Jack tried to digest this ugly piece of information.

'There's more, sir. The sepoys at Mean Meer were also grumbling and threatening mutiny. Their commanders had them disarmed and sent home.'

'Dear God in heaven. The whole Company army is revolting!' Jack took a deep breath. British power in India rested on the three Company's armies: Bengal, Madras and Bombay. The overwhelming majority of Company soldiers were Indian, with only a handful of European units supplemented by a few Royal or Queen's regiments. If the native regiments rebelled, then Company control in India was in serious jeopardy.

'Yes, sir. That is the fear.' Elliot stopped for a second to gather his thoughts. 'The reports were confused, and Colonel Jeffreys was concerned in case the Gondabad sepoys may emulate their cousins elsewhere.'

'He was right to be concerned,' Jack said.

'Yes, sir.' Elliot hesitated again. 'The mutineers are called pandies now, sir, after a sepoy of the 34th Native Infantry called Mangal Pandey. He attacked his adjutant on the parade ground in March, and was executed a few days later.'

'Pandies? A soft name for a mutineer,' Prentice said grimly.

'The men adopted it quickly,' Elliot said.

'I know about Pandey; the name doesn't matter. Tell me more of what happened at Gondabad,' Jack said.

'The senior officers had a meeting, sir, and the colonels of the native infantry swore from Monday to Christmas that their men were loyal. They refused to have them disarmed. As there was only a single company of the 113th here, Colonel Jeffreys offered to send for another Queen's regiment to enforce any disarmament, but the Company colonels rejected any suggestion their men would mutiny.'

'Where are they now?' Jack asked. 'I saw Captain Irvine among the dead.'

Elliot shook his head. 'I don't know, sir. I presume they're all dead. The pandies killed Colonel Jeffreys.'

'I saw his body,' Jack said.

'With most of our regiment in Malta or penny-pocket sized garrisons up and down the country, sir, and Major Snodgrass away, you are now in command of the largest contingent of the 113th,' Prentice pointed out.

Jack blinked. While acutely aware he commanded Number Two Company, he had never considered his relative position. 'So be it,' he said quietly. At that moment, with the ordered world of British India turned upside down, it didn't matter if he commanded a picket of the 113th or if he was Governor- General. He would do his duty and get his men to safety, and the devil help any murdering mutineer who got in his way.

'Carry on, Elliot.'

'When the Colonel sent the women and children away the sepoys must have guessed our suspicions.' Elliot reached inside his tunic for his silver hip-flask. 'They were restless, nothing more; there was no sign of mutiny. And then they seemed to go mad. They attacked everything and anybody to do with us or John Company.'

Jack remembered the warnings he had heard and passed on. 'It's hardly a coincidence that all these outbreaks occurred at the same time. This is more than just a local mutiny,' he said. 'We passed a deserted village yesterday.' *Was that only yesterday? It feels like weeks ago.*

'Do you think the whole country is in rebellion, sir?' Kent asked. 'Is this the end of Company rule in India?'

'No,' Jack said flatly. 'This is a few disgruntled sepoys.'

'There are hundreds involved,' Prentice reminded. 'Maybe thousands.'

'Most are followers,' Jack tried to find a silver lining. 'As in any riot or any mutiny, there will be a few malcontents stirring up trouble and a majority of followers too stupid or too lazy to think for themselves.' He thought back to the chaos in Gondabad. 'Did you notice any particular man among the mutineers, Elliot?'

'Nobody springs to mind. Some of the native officers tried to stop their men. The sepoys killed them.'

'How about the servants?' Jack asked.

'I didn't see many,' Elliot frowned. 'Only the colonel's pet Pathan.'

'Sarvur Khan.' Jack couldn't stop himself blurting the name.

'That's the fellow,' Elliot said. 'Sarvur Khan. He was involved in the attack on the Colonel, I think; he was certainly in the mob that came from the colonel's bungalow.'

'I want him,' Jack said. For a moment the entire perplexing situation coalesced into the face of one man. Sarvur Khan personified the mutiny and all the murders, the brutality and the shocking breach of faith. 'I want him dead.' He remembered the face in his recurring nightmare. *Sarvur Khan.*

'That's not like you, Jack.' Elliot reverted from an officer of the 113th to becoming a friend.

Jack felt Jane's gaze fixed on him. He didn't care; they could all think whatever they liked. He had seen Sarvur Khan working as a trusted servant in the Mess, and now the Pathan was heavily involved in the mutiny of children, women and men of the 113th. He had seen Khan personally throw a baby into a fire. 'I want him dead,' he repeated. 'We have to eradicate this poison from India before it infects us all.'

'It seems to have already affected you,' Elliot said.

'I'll thank you to keep your opinions to yourself, Lieutenant Elliot!' Jack snapped.

'Yes, sir.' Elliot stiffened to attention as the men looked around, interested in raised voices from their officers.

'Murdering black bastards.' Fairbairn glowered at Jane and Mary as if they were in some way responsible for all the ills of India. 'We should kill every single one of them. Show them all what happens when they oppose England.'

'Control yourself, Lieutenant!' Jack understood Fairbairn's anger and humiliation, yet he knew that indiscriminate slaughter was not the answer. 'And watch your language when there are ladies present.'

'They're not ladies, they're—' Fairbairn started, until Jack glowered at him and ordered him to tour the sentries.

'Ensure every man has his bayonet loose in his scabbard; make sure their picket route overlaps their neighbours,' Jack said. 'My apologies ladies; feelings are running a little high at present.'

Jane nodded graciously. 'It's understandable, Captain Windrush.'

'Mrs. Niven,' Jack tried to keep his voice gentle. 'Could you tell us what happened to you? Start at the beginning, please.'

'I am Jane Niven,' Jane spoke quietly yet with some authority. 'I act as a tutor to the children of the officers and sometimes the men.'

'Why did you not go to Cawnpore with the other women and children?' Lieutenant Kent sounded nervous.

'Colonel Jeffreys decided I am not British enough.' Jane faced him squarely. 'He said the British women might feel uncomfortable with Eurasians – half-breeds, he called us – along with them.'

Jack stifled his desire to swear. He remembered Myat, the Burmese girl he'd been so attracted to as a griffin ensign, only to learn she was married to a British sergeant. 'You are very welcome with us.' He injected iron into his tone, in case Fairbairn or any other of his officers objected. 'And if anybody, officer or other rank, treats either of you as anything other than a lady, you let me know.'

He was not sure what expression crossed Jane's face. He only knew he had said the right thing. Even the quiet Mary, palpably shocked by her experiences, gave him a small smile and a long look from under her eyelashes.

A parrot screeched nearby. Mary started and Jane took her arm. 'It's all right, Mary.'

'We've got pickets out,' Jack said. 'My men know their job. You're safe.'

The women nodded, with Mary looking at Jack as if he was her saviour. He frowned and continued. 'Now, Mrs. Niven, could you tell me what happened this morning?'

'It was last night. We were at home, and the sepoys came.' Although she was sitting on a squared off block with her back straight, and her head held proudly, the tremble in Jane's voice gave away the emotions within her. She looked away.

'They grabbed Mary, and one was going to stab her with his bayonet. She escaped, and we ran.'

There was so much left unsaid that Jack nearly asked for details. He tried to picture the scene; two women alone in a bungalow, not thought sufficiently British to save, not thought Indian enough by the sepoys to leave alone. Two unprotected women and a horde of soldiers bursting in, intent on murder and maybe rape – how had they escaped?

'We did not know where to go,' Jane continued. 'We heard firing from the officers' bungalows, and the soldiers' barracks were on fire, so we hid in the forest.'

Jack imagined them sheltering under the trees, watching as the sepoys killed and plundered.

'Then the sowars came, searching for British soldiers. They found two privates near us and killed them both. The first private fought hard and strangled a sowar. The second soldier made a lot of noise as they hacked him to pieces. We saw the sowars looting the store hut, and then we thought they would not be back there, so we hid until you came.'

'Was your daughter badly hurt?' Jack indicated Mary who now sat with her back to a carved pillar, mouth slightly open, staring into nothing. She had somehow managed to cobble her torn dress together.

'My daughter?' Jane frowned. 'Mary Lambert's not my daughter; she's my assistant!'

'I'm sorry.' Jack apologised immediately. 'I thought…'

'You thought that because we are both Eurasian, we must be re-lated?' Jane's voice was as cold as anything Jack had ever heard.

'I thought you were a mother looking after her daughter.' Jack felt the colour rise to his cheeks.

'I never knew my mother.' Mary's voice was soft and rendered more attractive by her faint Indian accent.

'I never knew mine, either,' Jack told her and immediately pressed shut his mouth. Why on earth had he made that admission? Fortu-nately, none of the officers appeared to have heard or understood the implications, although Elliot was watching him through narrowed eyes. Jane lifted a hand as if in sympathy and dropped it just as quickly. A pi-dog howled outside, setting off chattering from the monkeys.

'What do we do now, sir?' Elliot brought Jack back to the matter in hand.

'We go to the nearest British garrison town,' Jack had made his de-cision. 'Cawnpore.'

'That's where the Colonel sent the rankers' families,' Kent said.

'How far is Cawnpore?' Prentice asked.

'Look.' Jack unsheathed his sword and drew a quick sketch map of northern India in the dust. 'Here is the River Ganges, flowing across the country. Over here is Delhi, the old capital.' He stabbed downward. 'And here, about 270 miles to the south-east of Delhi, is Cawnpore, or Kanpur to give it the correct name.'

Prentice nodded. 'Yes, sir. Where are we?'

Jack traced a faint line to the south. 'Here is Gondabad, and there, 140 miles or so north-west, is Cawnpore.'

'A bit of a march then,' Elliot said. 'Is it safer for the women in Cawnpore?'

'I hope so,' Jack said. 'As far as I recall the 1st, 53rd and 56th Native Infantry are there, with the 2nd Native Light Cavalry, and some British artillery. It is, as you know, the divisional headquarters with Sir Hugh Wheeler in command. He's a man of tremendous experience with over fifty years in India, so if anybody knows how to handle native troops, he does.'

'When do we leave?' Prentice asked.

'We consolidate for a day or so, gather what supplies we can and scout the countryside,' Jack said at once. 'We have wounded, sick and bewildered men to care for.' He glanced at Mary. 'And ladies.'

'Don't you worry about us,' Mary said quickly. 'Jane and I will take care of ourselves.' She lifted her chin and looked Jack directly in the eye. 'You have your duty to do, Captain Windrush.'

Jack nodded slowly. There was always his duty to do. He held Mary's gaze for a fraction longer than he'd intended. She had the loveliest brown eyes.

The temple was alive with monkeys, snakes and a million insects, all of which seemed either to bite or sting. Sitting on a pedestal, a huge statue of a four-armed goddess stared out benevolently as she held a long-necked musical instrument and a rolled-up scroll.

'That is Saraswati,' Mary explained quietly. 'She is the goddess of knowledge, music and the arts, hence the veena – the musical instrument – and the scroll.

'I see,' Jack said. 'Is she important?'

'Very,' Mary said.

'Then why is the temple in ruins?' Jack ran his hand over the foot of the figurine. 'I don't believe in Hindu gods, but this was once a beautiful place, and the workmanship of the stonework is extremely impressive.'

'The Mogul Empire was Moslem,' Mary said. 'They persecuted the indigenous Hindu population. There were massacres; the Hindus abandoned scores of temples, the Moslems destroyed others and built mosques on top; they killed or enslaved unknown numbers of people, tens, maybe hundreds of thousands.' She stopped. 'It was not a good time to be a Hindu or a Sikh.'

Jack looked around at the slowly-crumbling temple where once holy men preached peace and a love of music and knowledge. 'There is an amazing potential for peace, and so much history in this country. Why do people ruin it with violence?'

Mary touched his uniform, smiled, and said nothing.

Jack kept them three days in the temple, giving the men time to rest and recover before they began their march to Cawnpore. He checked their ammunition, distributed it out as fairly as he could, and sent out small pickets to inspect any local villages and see what food they could find. 'No firing,' he ordered. 'We don't know how many mutineers there are, or if they are in this part of the country.'

The men sat quietly, some still in shock, others visibly angry at the massacre at Gondabad.

'Do we have any poachers among us?'

A long-faced, saturnine man touched a hand to his forelock rather than saluting. 'Matthew Whitelam, sir.'

Jack nodded. 'I should have known you'd be a poacher, Whitelam. You're a Lincolnshire man, aren't you? Yellowbellies are famed for their poaching skills.'

'Yes, sir.' Whitelam seemed pleased at Jack recognising his home county. 'Are you from Lincolnshire, sir?'

Jack shook his head. 'Herefordshire, Whitelam.'

'Yes, sir. Imagine a Hereford man knowing about a Yellowbelly.'

Jack forced a smile. 'You're one of my men, Whitelam. It is my duty to know about you. I want you to do some poaching; you'll know the likeliest lads in the company. Pick a few and see what you can snare. No shooting, but we need food.'

Whitelam's grin was probably bad for discipline although undoubtedly good for morale. 'There's Hutton, sir, and Armstrong. He's a nowter from the north, but frit of nobody even when he gets wrong.'

'I'll take your word for it, Whitelam.' Jack didn't pretend to understand broad Lincolnshire. 'No firing, mind.'

'No firing sir.' Whitelam's grin was infectious. 'Imagine being ordered to do what the magistrates jailed me for.' He waved to Mary. 'Don't you worry my duck; we'll get you safe from the niggers.'

Mary waved back. 'I won't worry when there are men like you around, Mr.... What's your name?'

'Whitelam. I'm Matthew Whitelam.'

'Off you go,' Jack said, warming to Mary. Many women would whisk aside their skirts when close to private soldiers. He was strangely glad Mary was not of that kind.

'I've been watching you, Captain Windrush.' Jane had been gathering some early mangoes. 'So, you are little Jack Windrush.' Stepping back, she ran her gaze up and down him. 'You turned out all right.' She fingered his uniform. 'But why join the 113th, and not the Royal Malverns?'

Jack shook his head. 'It's a long story,' he said. 'How do you know about the Royal Malverns?'

'That is also a long story.' Jane patted his chest. 'How is your father?'

'Did you know my father?'

'I knew him well,' Jane said. 'And I knew you as a baby.' She smiled and held out her hand, palm downward, close to her knee. 'Last time I saw you, you were this height and just learning to walk.' The light faded from her eyes. 'And then you were sent home, and I never saw you or heard anything more about you.'

'Were you my *ayah* – my nanny, Mrs. Niven?'

'In a manner of speaking,' Jane sat down on a vegetation-smothered square of carved stone and invited Jack to join her. Above them, birds circled, and the goddess stared out from blank stone eyes across the tangled wilderness. 'What do you remember about your early childhood, Captain Windrush?'

Jack shrugged. 'Very little. I know I was born in India and sent home to be educated.'

Jane nodded; her eyes were bright and very intent. 'Do you remember anything at all about your time here?'

Jack pondered. 'Sometimes at night, strange images come through my head. A smiling face, the touch of a hand, a voice calling, but nothing I can make sense of.'

Jane sighed. 'You don't remember me, then?'

'No. I'm sorry.'

'I would be surprised if you could. You were very young. Too young.' Jane looked away for a second. Jack could see she was tense, nearly trembling. 'Do you remember your mother?'

'My mother?' Jack was surprised by the question yet answered it frankly. There was something about this woman that inspired respect, and he knew instinctively he could trust her. 'Until I was eighteen years old, I believed my stepmother was my real mother. I did not know otherwise until the day of my father's funeral.'

'Your father is dead?' Jane said the words quickly. 'I am sorry.'

'Don't be,' Jack said. 'I hardly knew him. He was always in India or somewhere. I doubt I saw him half-a-dozen times in my life. I'm sorry, I forgot you knew him as well.'

'We used to meet here,' Jane said slowly, holding his gaze. 'In this very temple.'

'Oh, I see,' Jack said. 'You mean…'

'I mean that for a while we were close. In the absence of a wife, men sometimes need the comfort of a woman. It is as natural as breathing, so I don't want you to think ill of him.'

'No, no of course not,' Jack said. He knew many soldiers out East took native or Eurasian women as mistresses, but had never imagined his father doing such a thing. Strangely it made him more human.

Reaching out, Jane touched his arm. 'You must have a girl somewhere?'

Jack shook his head in instant denial. 'No.'

'Oh.' Jane looked disappointed. Her voice was soft as she continued. 'Why not, Jack? I presume you would go to a public school in England. I hope you did not indulge in the practices that I hear are so prevalent in such places?'

For a moment Jack was confused and then shook his head violently. 'Oh, God no! No! I am not that way inclined.'

'I am glad to hear it,' Jane said. 'You must think me very forward to broach such a subject.'

Jack felt himself blush. 'I have never spoken of such a thing to a woman before,' he admitted.

'And never should again, I hope,' Jane said. 'You will wonder at my interest in you.'

'Yes, a little,' Jack said. The questions made him uncomfortable, yet he did not want to leave Jane's company.

'Your father and I spent a lot of time here,' Jane was smiling again. She stood up and walked around the courtyard, touching the Hindu goddess with her open hand. 'He always vowed... well, never mind what he vowed. You are like him in many ways.'

'What was he like?' Jack asked.

'He was more assertive than you,' Jane said. 'He was tall and proud and confident. His men would have followed him anywhere; that is something you share.'

'He commanded the cream of the British infantry,' Jack said. 'I have only the lowly 113th.'

Jane frowned. 'Your men depend on you. They deserve better than to be insulted.'

'It wasn't an insult,' Jack said. 'The 113th are not considered among the army's best regiments, although the men performed well in the Crimea.'

'That's a bit better.' Jane's frown dissipated. 'When people are loyal to you, Jack Windrush, you should respect their loyalty and repay it double.'

Jack opened his mouth to protest and quickly closed it again. There was nothing he could say.

'Now, tell me about your girl. The one you denied a few moments ago.' Jane was smiling again.

'I had a girl,' Jack said and suddenly found himself telling the whole story, from his friendship with Helen in the Crimea to the growing romance and then how he lost her to William, his half-brother who got his house and lands as well as his commission in the Royal Malverns.

Jane listened without a word. Only when Jack had finished did she speak. 'Do you still have the letter she sent?'

'Yes.' Jack produced it from inside his jacket. Crumpled and sweat-stained as it was, he handed it over.

'May I?' Jane asked.

'Yes, of course.'

She opened it and read the contents. 'I see. Do you understand you are a very fortunate young man?'

'Fortunate?' Jack stared at her. 'How am I fortunate?'

'You have friends who care for you, men who respect you and you have escaped a woman who obviously cares more about material things than she does for you.' Jane folded the letter and handed it back. 'Why are you keeping this?'

Jack opened it again, running his gaze across Helen's handwriting. 'I don't know. It's a reminder.'

'Yes. It's a reminder of a girl who betrayed you. It must hurt every time you read her words. Do you like revisiting hurts?'

Jack looked at Helen's letter again, unsure how to react.

'The best thing you can do, Jack Baird Windrush, is to destroy this nonsense and find a decent girl who will return your loyalty.' Abruptly standing up, Jane walked away, speaking over her shoulder. 'And that's my last word on the subject of Helen Maxwell!'

Jack sat for a long time, holding Helen's letter in his hand. He didn't notice Mary coming out of the temple ruins until she was at his side. 'Jane can be very direct sometimes,' she said. 'She means well.'

'I take it you have you been listening?'

'Yes, I have,' Mary admitted freely. She sat near him. 'I have not thanked you for saving our lives.'

Jack shrugged. 'Don't be silly,' he said. 'There is no reason for thanks.'

'I won't forget.' Mary watched Jack fold the letter and put it in his breast pocket. She sat beside him as he stared at nothing, and when he stood up, she watched him walk away.

Chapter Five

Jack looked around at the circle of officers. After three days in the temple, they still looked worse for wear, with wary eyes and mouths compressed into tight lines.

'Well, Sergeant? What did you find?'

'Pandies, sir,' O'Neill reported. 'I took out a patrol like you said and scouted the area. It's thick with pandies.'

'How many? What type?'

O'Neill took out a small notebook. 'There was so many I had to get it written down, sir. That fellow, Parker, he's a scholar and he did the writing for me.' He scanned the page. 'We headed west first, sir and saw a troop of sowars in the open ground. They were laughing and carrying on, sir as if they hadn't got a care in the world. Certainly, they were not looking as if they expected us to return and sort them out.'

'Their time will come,' Jack said. 'Depend on it, O'Neill, Britain won't allow a few mutineers take our India from us.'

'No, sir. So with the sowars all over the open ground, we headed north, sir. There were a load of sepoys, sir, camped in the forest. They've taken over a couple of the villages and are all spread out between them and over the paths and road as well.'

'How many and what regiments, O'Neill?'

'About three hundred, sir and I saw at least three different units there. They were all Bengal Native Infantry, sir; 44th and 17th, and some of the 37th.'

'So they are to the west and the north of us.'

'Yes, sir, and south as well, sir.'

'How many did you see in the south?' Jack was taking mental notes. O'Neill screwed up his face. 'Not sure, sir. We stayed within the forest and looked out on them. I would not like to guess at the numbers.'

Jack grunted. 'Ten? Fifty? A thousand?'

'More than fifty, sir. Maybe a hundred or so.' O'Neill sounded apologetic. 'Then we looked east, and the lads from Gondabad are still around, or some of them anyway.'

'Thank you, O'Neill.' Jack dismissed him. 'So there we are, gentlemen. The mutineers surround us. I will welcome any suggestions and then decide what is best to do.'

'We were going to Cawnpore, sir,' Elliot said. 'I still think we should continue. We did plenty of night movement in the Crimea; march in the dark, rest in the day and destroy any pandies that get in our way.'

'Thank you, Elliot. Anybody else?'

'I think we sit tight, sir,' Kent said. 'We are safe here; the mutineers don't seem to want to come to this temple. Maybe it's sacred to them. We can wait until they've gone and then we can move away.'

'We're British soldiers, damn it!' Prentice said. 'Form the men up and march through the blasted pandies. Shoot any we meet and get through to Cawnpore, join the army there and come back to show what happens to mutineers.'

'Bravo!' Fairgreave said. 'Hang every mutineer we come across, and every black bastard we meet. If they are not for us, then they're the enemy. I would not trust a single one of them. Hang them all.'

Elliot raised his eyebrows. 'That's some hanging spree,' he said. 'Even Judge Jeffreys left some people alive after the Bloody Assizes.'

'It's what they deserve,' Fairgreave said, shrugging.

'There will be no reprisals against the innocent,' Jack said. 'Not by any man under my command.'

'That sort of weakness created this mess,' Fairgreave said. 'We won this land by the sword, and we should rule it by the sword. Teach the pandies they can't rebel against Englishmen, by God.'

'Enough!' Jack felt his anger rising. 'I said there would be no reprisals against the innocent. Do you have anything constructive to say?'

'I think we do as Lieutenant Prentice suggests. March for Cawnpore and destroy any mutineer we come across. And any who sympathise with them.' Fairgreave glanced at Jack. 'Leaving the innocent well alone, sir.'

Jack took a deep breath. He could understand the desire for revenge and the anger that caused his men to wish vengeance on anybody who was involved with or who could sympathise with the rebellion. There was also the fearful consciousness that in India the British were vastly outnumbered by the indigenous peoples, who may have hidden secret knowledge of the attack. Jack thought of the urbane, hidden face of Sarvur Khan and felt an immediate desire to kill and destroy. Oh yes, he could understand the desire for revenge; he shared it in the fullest possible measure.

'Get some sleep if you can.' Jack decided. 'We are heading for Cawnpore.'

They left in the stifling heat of the night, one hundred and ten men of the 113th, with Jane and Mary walking in the middle of the column and Jack at the head. The men had their tunics undone and had blackened any part of their equipment capable of reflecting the light and dyed their white summer uniforms with mud to make them less conspicuous. All wore handkerchiefs or some other square of cloth tucked into the back of their shakos to protect their necks from the sun.

'They look a mess,' Prentice disapproved. 'They don't look like British soldiers at all.'

'They certainly don't look like Hyde Park soldiers,' Jack agreed. 'However, they look very like the men who fought at Inkerman.'

'We must assert our moral superiority over the natives,' Fairbairn advised, with all the assurance of his twenty years. 'And the best way is always to always smart.'

'Elliot; take the rearguard. Prentice, take the left flank; Kent the right, Fairbairn, you liaise between us all.' Jack watched his men march. They looked tired as they stumbled past him in the dark, but they also looked determined.

The forest waited, crisscrossed with paths, dark with menace and mystery. Few British soldiers felt at home in these close confines, and only those with long experience of India or Burma were not apprehensive of the strange sounds and sensations.

'I should be a corporal now,' Thorpe said, 'since I won the Victorious Cross.'

'It's not the Victorious Cross,' Coleman sounded patient. 'It's Victoria's Cross, named after the queen, see? It's to show everyone that Queen Victoria's cross with you and you aren't to be trusted.'

'What the Queen cross with me for?' Thorpe asked. 'I haven't done nothing.'

'Exactly,' Coleman said. 'You haven't done nothing except visit half the whore houses in India and spread the pox around.'

'I haven't got the pox!' Thorpe sounded indignant. 'I checked! Anyway, how would the Queen know what I've been doing?'

Coleman nudged Parker. 'The Queen knows everything. That's why she's the Queen.'

Jack raised his voice slightly. 'Keep the noise down, lads; the enemy could be listening. 'And don't heed Coleman, Thorpe. Your Victoria Cross is to prove you're a brave soldier.'

Taking the lead, Jack moved slowly, very aware the enemy could be watching him from only a yard away, secure in the cover of the trees. He remembered this jungle-creeping from his time in Burma and thanked God there were veterans such as O'Neill and Coleman with him. They may be troublesome in times of peace but when the trumpets called such men proved themselves a hundred times over.

Moving from cover to cover, Number Two Company tried to avoid the villages scattered across the land. They moved in silence and refrained from smoking near villages in case the whiff of tobacco gave them away. They watched for any sign of mutineers, moved by night and camped in daylight. 'Triple sentries,' Jack ordered, 'and every man keep his rifle to hand and have it loaded.'

'Is that wise, sir?' Kent asked. 'Some of the men may be a little irresponsible.'

'It may save their lives, and ours,' Jack said. 'You ladies,' he pointed to Jane and Mary. 'Keep well within our lines and never stray beyond.'

'We have to leave sometimes,' Jane said.

'In God's name; don't you understand a simple order?' Jack realised the expedition was straining his nerves. 'I am sorry. Mrs. Niven. For what reason would you wish to leave the safety of my men?'

'Nature may demand it,' Jane said, 'and women like some privacy in such matters.'

'Oh, of course!' Jack said. 'I will give you a steady married man to act as permanent escort,' he said. 'He'll look the other way.'

'Thank you,' Jane rewarded Jack with a sweet smile.

'Blasted women.' Jack gave the necessary order. 'And make sure to look after them as if they were your mother and sister.'

'Yes, sir,' Riley said. 'They'll be safe as the Bank of England, sir.'

Jack grunted. 'With you around, Riley, the Bank of England would be in great jeopardy.'

It was Whitelam who heard them first. With his senses tuned to listening for gamekeepers in the Lincolnshire Wolds, he knew something was different even before the veterans of Burma and Crimea.

'Somebody's coming, sir,' he said.

'I can't hear anything.' Jack lifted his head. 'Are you sure?'

'I'm sure sir. I can feel it on the ground.'

'Right, Whitelam.' Jack lifted a hand to halt the company. 'O'Neill; take Coleman, Thorpe, Whitelam and Logan, see what's happening. The rest of us, keep still and keep down.' They slid into a copse as O'Neill led his picket along one of the narrow paths which formed a network across the entire Indian sub-continent.

'Are you all right, ladies?' Jack kept his voice low.

'We're all right,' Jane spoke for both of them. 'Mr. Riley is looking after us.'

'Keep still unless I order otherwise.' Jack loosened the revolver in his holster.

'Sir.' O'Neill returned quicker than Jack had expected. 'Pandies sir. They're right around us.'

Jack swore softly. 'How many?'

'Hundreds, sir, maybe thousands.'

'Jesus,' Jack said quietly. 'Show me, O'Neill.'

They moved forward slowly, step by step through the night with the sound of the river in the distance and the growing murmur of the mutineers. Now even he could feel the ground trembling with the tramp of marching feet and smell the unmistakable aroma of sepoys en-masse. The sudden blare of music settled any remaining doubts.

'They're in regimental formation,' O'Neill said. 'Look, sir; they are marching by unit, with the bands and even the Colours.' He stared at Jack. 'They may have mutinied, but they are still soldiers.'

'You're right, O'Neill. They've kept their cohesion, which makes them even more dangerous.' Jack watched them march past, British-trained and equipped soldiers, the most effective native fighting force in Asia, and all seemingly intent on destroying British rule in India.

'Where are they headed?' Jack pondered.

'Possibly Delhi.' The voice came from the gloom to his left and Fraser, still in native clothes, limped out from behind a tree. 'Or maybe Cawnpore.'

'What? Where did you spring from?' Jack put out a hand to prevent O'Neill shooting Fraser. 'It's all right, Sergeant. He's a friend.'

Fraser squatted in the shelter of a thorn bush. 'Have you heard the latest happenings?'

'We try to keep away from native villages,' Jack said. 'They don't know we're here.'

'Yes, they do,' Fraser told him. 'Everybody knows there is a company of Queen's infantry wandering through the country.' His smile was grim. 'The natives here know all and say little.'

Jack grunted. 'As long as the mutineers don't find out. We're on our way to Cawnpore to join the garrison there.'

'You haven't heard then,' Fraser said. 'The sepoys mutinied there as well. Wheeler is under siege.'

Jack felt O'Neill stiffen at his side. 'Our wives and children are there.' Despite his slide of dismay, he tried to keep his voice neutral.

'If they are,' Fraser said, 'they'll be inside Wheeler's entrenchment. Listen.' He lowered his voice as another company of sepoys marched past, their white trousers gleaming through the dark, white cross-belts immaculately maintained and every man holding his firearm in the approved manner.

'I'm listening,' Jack said.

'This is not isolated. The mutiny has spread up and down the Ganges. Delhi has fallen, and there was a bloody massacre at Meerut. The mutineers' control both.'

Jack nodded. He already knew some of this, but confirmation was always valuable. 'Continue please, Fraser.'

Watching the mutineers march past, Fraser leant against the bole of a tree and chewed a betel nut. 'There is a small British force marching to try and retake Delhi from the rebels; I don't know how many. There were more outbreaks – the 25th Bengal Native Infantry rioted in Calcutta; the 55th mutinied at Murdan; the 9th mutinied at Allygurh, the 15th and 30th at Nuseerabad.' Fraser shrugged. 'Things are bleak for John Company.'

'Holy Mary,' O'Neill blasphemed and crossed himself. 'The whole Company army is up in arms.'

'Not only them,' Fraser said. 'Some of the native princes are looking unstable as well. The Oude Irregulars have mutinied too, and the Rani of Jhansi is rumoured to be on the rebels' side.'

Jack tried to focus on what immediately concerned him. 'You say Cawnpore is under siege?'

'Yes, sir,' Fraser said.

'We were heading to Cawnpore,' Jack said. 'No point now. Where is the nearest British force?'

'General Wilson is gathering men to retake Delhi, somewhere, and Colonel Neil and General Havelock are meeting at Allahabad, 120 miles from Cawnpore along the Ganges. I'm not sure, but I think Neil hopes to relieve Wheeler in Cawnpore.'

Jack nodded. 'Thank you, Fraser.'

'The rebels are trying to restore the Moghul Empire with Bahadur Shah Zafar as their leader,' Fraser said. 'He's an ancient, white-bearded old creature, so he hardly inspires confidence. More importantly, a man called Nana Sahib leads the rebels at Cawnpore and another fellow who seems to be connecting the different rebel groups.'

'Who is that?' Jack already guessed the answer.

'I don't know much about him, except he's called Sarvur Khan.'

Jack felt the chill creep through him. 'We know the name.'

'He's a bad one,' Fraser said. 'Try to keep out of his way.'

'No.' Jack shook his head very slowly. 'I will not. If I don't find Sarvur Khan in the course of my duty, then I will scour India for him once this war is over.'

'Jack.' Jane had been listening. 'What would you do if you find him?'

'Kill him,' Jack said. He didn't mention his nightmare.

'Please, Jack.' Jane put a hand on his arm. 'Don't let these terrible events turn you into a killer.'

'I'm a soldier,' Jack said. 'It's my duty to kill.'

'It's not your duty to hunt down men simply to kill them.' Jane patted him gently.

'There is evilness in that man.' Jack couldn't explain more. He only knew that some skein of fate bound him to Sarvur Khan.

'Captain Windrush.' Fraser's cracked voice interrupted the conversation. 'Remember that Colonel Neill and General Havelock are meeting at Allahabad.' He withdrew into the trees, leaving Jack with even more concerns.

'We'll tell the men the news,' Jack said. He knew it was customary only to inform the officers. The other ranks were expected to obey without question or information. After two campaigns he was also aware that his men responded better when they knew what was happening and why they were marching or fighting.

'Wheeler's a good officer.' Jack addressed the assembled ranks of Number Two Company. 'He'll look after our people until we arrive.'

Riley looked concerned. 'Did you hear if all the women and children got safely into Cawnpore?'

'Sorry, Riley, I did not learn much. I know General Wheeler is holding out in the city and there is a force gathering at Allahabad to relieve him.'

'Charlotte will be all right.' Logan lifted his chin. 'If anybody can survive, Charlotte can, Riley. Don't you fret.' He faced Jack squarely. 'Isn't that right, sir?'

'I know your wife well, Riley and I'm sure Logan is correct.' Jack held Riley's worried gaze. 'I don't think there is a pandie born who is a match for Charlotte.' He raised his voice again. 'Now gather round and listen, everybody.'

Jack related all that Fraser had told him. He was surprised at the silence from men who were usually only too ready to give their opinions on everything under the sun.

'Are we marching to Allahabad now, sir?' Prentice asked.

'That's the idea,' Jack said. 'Our single company is not powerful enough to make a dent in the mutineer positions. We have to join a larger force.' While part of him regretted losing his independent command, he was also glad to be joining an army sufficiently powerful to challenge the mutineers.

'The whole country is against us,' Kent said. 'Maybe we'd better leave India completely.'

Jack felt a shudder run through him. When he first joined the 113th such defeatist talk would have been commonplace. Now, after five years and hard-fought campaigns against Burmese and Russians, the temper of the regiment had altered, and the officers were more confident than they had been. 'So far as I can judge, Lieutenant Kent, the rebellion has not spread from the Ganges valley. It seems to be confined only to disaffected sepoy regiments and some native states.'

'Other native states could mean half of India,' Kent said. 'We'll be kicked out of the country.'

Jack felt the ripple of unease pass through the men. They had seen their cantonments destroyed, their colonel killed, and their families sent into the unknown. Now one of their officers, a man they would rely on to lead them in battle, was telling them they faced defeat.

'Lieutenant Kent,' Jack controlled his voice. 'We are not going to lose India. The mutineers have taken us by surprise. I know you have recently posted to this regiment from another unit, so you are maybe not fully aware who we are.' He waited for a moment to allow his words to sink in, knowing the men were listening intently.

Jack raised his voice slightly more. 'We are the 113th Foot. Once we were the Baby Butchers; after the Crimea, we became the Defenders of Inkerman. The 113th are at their best when things look bad, as they do now. The rebels appear to be hunting us in a country we think of as our second home.'

Jack realised every man was watching him; every face was concentrating on him. 'Well, Lieutenant Kent, and all the other men of the 113th here, this *is* our second home. I was born in this country, and I'm damned if I'll let it slide back into the anarchy it was in before we arrived.' Jack wondered why he suddenly felt so passionate about India – he only knew that he did.

'Sir!' Riley sounded sick at heart. 'How about Charlotte and the rest of our families? They're in Cawnpore.'

'I know,' Jack was aware of Jane and Mary watching him. He couldn't read their faces. 'We'll join the army at Allahabad, lift the siege of Cawnpore, kick the pandies so hard they won't know what hit them and return India to British rule.' The men stared at him, some blank of expression, others concerned. He had hoped for more enthusiasm. Somebody whispered: 'Holy Havelock; bring your Bibles, boys.'

Holy Havelock? What did that mean?

'We're the 113th,' Jack spoke quietly again. 'Not some stuck-up, dandified regiment whose officers never venture further from London than Tunbridge Wells.'

He saw the men's expressions alter. Many British regiments had two different sets of officers, the Hyde Park Strollers who squired the ladies while their regiment was in a British barracks, and the practical, less wealthy officers who took over when Horse Guards posted the regiment abroad. The former looked down on the latter as socially inferior. As one of the least desirable units in the Army, the 113th did not possess Hyde Part Strollers; their officers remained with the men wherever they travelled.

'We're the 113th.' Jack spoke slightly louder. 'We do the jobs other regiments don't do.' He saw some of the men nod at that, paused and continued. 'Or rather, we do the jobs other regiments *can't* do!'

He saw backs straighten, shoulders pulled back, heads coming up – there were even a few smiles.

'Don't forget what we have done, at Inkerman, at the Redan and in the trenches outside Sebastopol. We held the Russians, we met the best they had and,' he paused, then spoke slowly and loudly, 'we smashed them!'

There were a few cheers and men looked at him, nodding.

'So if we defeated the best the Czar produced, what do you think we'll do to a few mutinous, back-stabbing pandies?' He waited for a response. The low growl was heartening. He helped them along. 'We'll destroy them!' He shouted the words. 'What will we do?'

'We'll destroy them!' the men responded.

'What will we do?'

This time the reply was a full-blooded roar. 'We'll destroy them!'

'That's right.' Jack held up his hands for silence. 'Until now, we've been creeping around avoiding the pandies. Well, not any longer. It's not the 113th way to avoid trouble. We are marching to Allahabad to join Havelock, and then we are relieving Cawnpore and setting our families free.'

The men were standing up, some stamping their feet. Jack wondered if the mutineers could hear them, hoped the sentries were alert and continued. 'We're marching tomorrow morning early, so make sure your rifles are clean, bright and slightly oiled, keep them loaded and ensure everybody has sufficient ammunition. Keep your bayonets loose in their scabbards, keep alert...' He waited for a second, 'and if any blasted pandies get in our way, we'll treat them like we treated the Cossacks.'

The men cheered and Jack allowed them to do so. One part of him hoped the noise alerted the mutineers, even although he knew the enemy would vastly outnumber them.

'Take command, Prentice,' Jack said. 'I need a few moments to think.' There was no need to explain anything to his junior officers.

'Yes, sir.'

As always, they had camped within a copse of trees to shield them from travellers or hostile rebels. Ensuring his revolver was secure in its holster; Jack stepped to the edge of the trees, produced and lit a cheroot. He looked over the flat plain, with the fading light punctured by the flickering lights of village fires and smoke hazing the sky. There was a peaceful beauty here, as well as a new sense of uneasiness Jack had never experienced before. He tried to recall vague memories from his early childhood, remembering laughter, bright eyes and a feeling of security.

'You did that well.' Mary's voice interrupted his reverie. 'The soldiers were unsure what was happening.'

Jack had heard her coming. 'It's better that they should know.'

'You're deep in thought. What are you thinking?'

'I hate to watch this country tearing itself apart.' Jack inhaled deeply and allowed the smoke to trickle from the corner of his mouth.

'Why do you care?' Mary asked. 'You're a soldier. You're British. You'll go home to your northern island when your time here is finished.'

Jack leant against the tree and allowed his eyes to roam across the vastness of India. 'I was born here,' he said slowly. 'Part of me will always belong here. All of me hates to see these people, the hard-working, innocent, honest people of the land, trapped between these mutineers and us.'

'Do you hate them?' Mary's voice was low.

'Do I hate who?'

'The mutineers.' Mary said. 'Do you hate the mutineers?'

Jack thought for a long moment. 'Yes,' he said softly, 'yes, I do.'

Mary moved closer to him. 'Don't.' She said. 'Please don't.'

'They murdered scores of my men,' Jack said. 'Burned them in barracks or shot them when they emerged. They butchered the colonel and women and children.'

'I know,' Mary said. 'Your men talk about the murder of the women. They also hate. They are filled with hatred. They frighten me sometimes when they look at me as if I was a murderer too.'

Jack nodded. 'They won't touch you.'

'They won't touch us when you are there,' Mary corrected softly. 'If you were not here, they might. To them, I am another potential rebel, a black.' She looked downward, avoiding his gaze. 'Do I look black to you?'

Jack took the cheroot from his mouth. Although they had been together since Gondabad, he had never properly looked at her before; she had only been a female civilian to be cared for, a shadow of Jane. 'I have never thought about it.'

'Well; do I?' Mary stepped out from the shadow of the trees and into the last slanting light of the sun.

For a moment Jack was back in Burma with Myat sliding past, smiling mysteriously. Except this woman was more vulnerable than Myat had ever been, and her question asked so quietly, hid far deeper concerns. In a way Mary was like India herself, unsure quite what she was. Mary was half British and half Indian, not quite belonging to and never entirely accepted by either people.

'It's like walking a tightrope.' She must have read his thoughts. 'Balancing between one culture and the next, never being sure what people are thinking about you, knowing nobody trusts you.'

Jack thought of his own life as the illegitimate son of a general and some unknown servant girl. Before he learned he was a bastard, Jack had been confident and assured of his place in society. Ever since his stepmother told him he was no longer part of the family, Jack had been a man out of place, neither a proper gentleman nor a man from the ranks. How much worse would it be for this woman?

'Black, white, brown or green.' He shook his head, understanding something, yet only a fraction, he suspected, of the life that fate had given her. 'I don't know, and I don't care. You look beautiful.'

Mary stiffened and looked at him. 'I was not fishing for a compliment.'

'And I was not giving you one,' Jack said. 'I was only speaking the truth.' He watched her slide back into the trees and pulled again at his cheroot. Tomorrow they would begin the march to Allahabad. Tomorrow was the beginning of a new phase. He heard Mary stop and he glanced over his shoulder. She was watching him.

Chapter Six

'Heads up, men,' Jack surveyed them. After months in India, most were sun-browned to the same hue as any Indian, with only the red-heads retaining the pale complexion that peeled and reddened under the heat. Their uniforms were similar to those worn by many of the mutineers, and their weapons and training were not much different.

'As I said, we are no longer creeping by night and hiding by day,' he said. 'As from now, we are marching like soldiers. From a distance, we are no different to a company of mutinous sepoys. We march in the open.'

'Sir,' Kent said. 'What if we meet any real mutineers?'

'We are the 113th,' Jack said. He gave no more instructions; his men knew what he meant.

'Keep your rifles loaded and ready,' Jack ordered, 'and your bayonets loose in the scabbards. You griffins – I want you to watch the veterans and learn from them. The old hands, I want you to have patience with the Johnny Raws; you were like them once and probably even greener. We are all the 113th, all part of the regiment.'

Marching under the summer heat with the dust filming them and their boots crunching on the road, the 113th was in no mood to stop for anybody. Twice they saw bodies of red-coated mutineers marching northward and once a group of irregular horsemen demanded their destination.

'Allahabad,' Jack said and marched on.

'The *Gora-log* are there,' the horsemen said.

'*Achcha*' Jack shouted back. 'Good.'

The 113th continued to march. A dozen horsemen pursued them and rode alongside. Savage looking men with an assortment of arms and steel breastplates below spiked helmets, they could almost have come from the pages of the *Arabian Nights*, save for the muskets some carried. Galloping past the stubbornly marching column, they reined up fifty yards ahead and held up their hands as if demanding the infantry should stop.

Jack felt his anger rise. *How dare these insolent rebels attempt to halt my men?* He spoke over his shoulder. 'Front rank!'

'Sir!' As O'Neill spoke, Jack thanked God for his Crimea veterans.

'Do you remember when we trained to march and fire in the Crimea?'

'Of course, sir.' There was satisfaction in O'Neill's face.

'Carry on, sergeant.' Jack stepped aside. There was no need to give further orders – his men knew what to do.

The column marched on, boots raising fine dust that rose high to settle on the rear ranks and the road behind them. Jack saw a stick-legged Indian peasant look up briefly and then return to his labour. The warfare of armed men, sahibs or whatever, was no concern of his. He would be happy only to be left alone.

'Right lads,' Jack heard O'Neill's voice, rich with Donegal. 'On my word.'

There was the snick of soldiers fitting caps on their rifles. Two more steps.

'Present.'

Without looking back, Jack knew the front two ranks were aiming their rifles as they marched. The horsemen were only thirty yards in front, unsure what was happening. Some unslung their muskets; others drew tulwars and headed toward the advancing column.

'Aim.' There was no urgency in O'Neill's voice.

'Come on you bastards.' Logan's harsh, unforgiving Glaswegian voice sounded.

Two more steps, the boots crashing down remorselessly.

'Fire,' O'Neill said without emotion.

Eight rifles fired in unison, the noise deafening. The horsemen in front staggered, with three men falling from their saddles.

'Front two ranks, take the flank,' O'Neill said and the front two ranks separated from the main body to march beside the road. 'Present!'

The next two ranks readied their rifles. The horsemen saw death pointing at them, and while some turned to flee, others charged forward, decreasing the space between infantry and cavalry at a frightening rate.

'Fire!'

There was immediate chaos in the advancing horsemen with tumbling riders and horses. The charge ended in kicking carnage.

'Bayonets… fix!' Jack ordered as his column continued its remorseless march. 'Finish them.'

There was no mercy as the 113th plunged forward. Memories of the massacre of Gondabad combined with the frustration of hiding for the last few days as the men charged in with bayonets. The British butchered the cavalrymen in an ugly, sordid affair that left no survivors and gasping, sweating infantrymen of the 113th looked in something like satisfaction at the bloodied dead.

'Form up,' Jack ordered. 'March.'

'The pandies will have heard the commotion,' Elliot said.

'Let them.' Jack glanced back over his men. The minor victory had heartened them. They marched slightly straighter, with heads up and their shoulders back despite the crippling heat. India may be in danger of falling, but this company of the 113th were still soldiers, still fighting, still men. There was hope for this unhappy country.

Another day, another night of pickets and slow conversation, of nervous sentries with their fingers on warm triggers, of men twitching in disturbed sleep, of heat and humidity and questing flies, and of Jane's voice singing old lullabies. Jack watched as teenage soldiers crawled closer to listen and some dashed homesick tears from eyes that had seen far more than boys of their age should. He saw Jane holding a weeping boy's hand as his colleagues watched in nostalgic memory or envious regret for the childhood they never experienced.

'She's a kindly woman,' Jack said.

Mary lay with her back to a tree, watching him as he slumped beside her after completing his rounds of the pickets. She smiled and handed over a mango. 'She's adopted your young soldiers.'

'They're a wild bunch, but some have a good heart.'

Mary lifted her chin slightly. 'Riley and a shy soldier with steady eyes are taking care of us as if we were family.'

'Whitelam.' Jack identified Riley's companion at once.

Whitelam had found a soul-mate in Riley, and next day they discovered an abandoned *tonga*, a local pony trap, next to a burned-out village. While men with practical skills restored the cart to something like working order, others had found an ancient horse. As they marched on, day after day, Mary and Jane sat in discomfort on the jolting, spring-less cart in the midst of the column, with a tattered hood keeping off the worst of the sun.

'Enjoying the ride, ladies?' Jack asked.

'Your men are doing their best to help us,' Jane replied.

Jack nodded. The presence of two women helped focus the attention of the men. They had something for which to fight.

The cavalrymen had been watching them for some time, riding on both flanks at a distance of some three hundred yards.

Flapping his hand in a vain attempt to clear away some of the dust, Jack looked left and right. 'If they are mutineers, then they're having a good look at us. The longer they delay attacking, the closer we are to Allahabad. Let them wait.'

'If they come on both flanks at once,' Prentice said doubtfully, 'we'll be in trouble.'

'Then we form a square and blast them,' Jack told him. 'Keep marching.' He looked down the column. 'How are the women faring?'

'They're bearing up.'

After days of jolting and creaking in the tonga, Jane and Mary were increasingly tired, but both refused to complain. Jack nodded; they were made of the right stuff. He stepped aside to allow the men to march past and slid between the ranks to speak to the women.

'Don't be concerned about the horsemen,' he marched alongside them. 'They can't hurt us from there.'

'I'm not concerned,' Jane lifted a hand. 'We are surrounded by a hundred stalwart British soldiers led by the redoubtable Captain Windrush.'

'Maybe not so redoubtable,' Jack said.

'Your men think otherwise,' Mary called over. 'They have been telling us all sorts of things about you.'

Jack smiled. 'Barrack-room gossip,' he said. 'Half will be lies and the other half simply not true.'

Jane smiled. 'Perhaps,' she said.

'We are nearing Allahabad,' Jack said. 'You should be safe there and get some rest.'

'Your men will be leg-weary,' Mary said. 'They've marched for days and days, and nobody has fallen out.'

'If they fall out the mutineers will murder them,' Jack said. 'I have a good sergeant to shout them back into formation and save their lives. Leg-weary or not.'

Jane eased herself up slightly from the cart. 'My legs are not weary,' she rubbed at her backside. 'Quite another part of me is suffering.'

Mary looked momentarily scandalised but gave a small smile and slid her hand behind her. 'Me too,' she said.

'Not long now.' Jack hid his smile. 'Then you can ease that part as well.'

'Sir,' Ensign Shearer was obviously anxious. 'The cavalry is closing, sir.'

'Thank you, Mr. Shearer.' Jack tried to sound calm. He raised his voice. 'Form a square; Prentice, take the left side, Elliot, the right, Kent the rear and I will command the front. Riley and Logan look after the ladies. You two, get underneath the waggon until I say it's safe.'

'We'll be all right, Captain Windrush,' Jane said.

'You'll do as I say!' Jack ordered sharply.

Expecting the order, the men moved with the skill of long practice. Formed into two ranks with the front man kneeling and his rear-marker standing, they obeyed Jack's order to fix bayonets and faced outwards, waiting. The dust settled slowly. Somebody swore softly.

The cavalry merged into a single thirty-strong body and advanced at a trot with the sun glinting from breast-plates and steel helmets and reflecting from the blades of drawn swords.

'Here they come!' Jack felt the gravel in his throat. He took a quick sip of his water bottle to lubricate his voice. 'Load!' he shouted above the drumming of horse's hooves. 'Home!'

He stepped to the face of the square. The cavalry was approaching behind a screen of dust. Wellington must have had a similar view at Waterloo. 'Return! Cap!'

The men were ready – bayonets fixed, rifles loaded.

'Aim! Volley at fifty yards!'

Seventy yards, sixty, the cavalry closed, partly concealed behind a curtain of dust, and then one man spurred ahead of the rest on the right flank of the square.

'He's a white man, sir!' Elliot said. 'A blasted renegade!'

Jack felt, rather than heard, the growl from the men.

'It's bad enough when the blacks rebel,' Thorpe said, 'but when your own people join them, it's worse.'

'Hold your fire!' Jack shouted.

The rider approached the square. 'Who the devil are you?'

'Number two Company, 113th Foot, British Army,' Jack shouted back. 'Who the devil are *you*?'

'Captain Potts of the Allahabad Rangers. Where have you sprung from?' The man wore European civilian clothes with an oversized white turban around his head. He carried a Sikh tulwar and had a revolver thrust through his cummerbund.

'Gondabad,' Jack said.

'Good show!' Potts shouted. 'We thought you were all dead up there.' He rode closer to Jack. 'You'd better follow me into Allahabad then. General Havelock will wish to speak to you.'

'We've made it, men!' Elliot shouted. 'They're British!'

Too tired to cheer, the 113th could only raise a croak. Jack felt Mary's hand on his sleeve.

'Thank you, Captain Jack,' she said. 'And I forgive you for shouting at me just now.' She squeezed lightly and returned to the *tonga*.

Chapter Seven

Jack had never met a soldier with such a penetrating gaze. Havelock's eyes were bright and hard and perceptive. Jack knew that General Henry Havelock was in his early sixties and this was his first independent command in a career which spanned Burma, Gwalior, Afghanistan, Persia and the Punjab.

A fighting man, then, Jack thought.

Havelock's North-East accent was hidden behind his curt military sentences while his lack of inches compared to Jack's nearly six feet tall was immaterial. One look at this man and Jack knew he was as capable as any officer he'd ever met.

'Gondabad fell some weeks ago,' Havelock said as he faced Jack across the desk in Allahabad Fort. 'Where have you been since?' He listened as Jack recounted his movements, nodded from time to time.

'Tell me which Company regiments you saw in rebellion, their numbers and in which direction they were heading.'

Jack had been prepared for the question and listed the regiments they had encountered. 'Lieutenant Prentice was most helpful in identifying these units, sir.'

Havelock nodded. 'I will bear his name in mind. How many men did you lose on your march?'

'Three sir; I lost two from heat exhaustion and one from fever,' Jack said.

'Another three men gone to meet their Maker.' Havelock touched the Bible that sat on the desk in front of him. 'I presume you have thanked the Lord for your preservation and for that of your men?'

'I have not, sir,' Jack said truthfully.

'Then I expect you will do so at the first opportunity, Windrush.'

'Yes, sir.' Jack was glad Havelock didn't ask him to sink to his knees there and then.

'We are in the midst of a dangerous situation, Windrush.' Havelock spoke with utter sincerity, 'And only with divine help and the strength and loyalty of our men will we succeed in bringing peace to this land. God bless us all.'

'Indeed, sir,' Jack agreed.

'Are you by chance related to the late General Windrush?' Havelock continued before Jack could reply. 'No, his son is Captain William Windrush of the Royal Malverns. He won renown at the Redan. Well, Windrush, perhaps you will add further lustre to the Windrush name here in India.'

'I'll do my best, sir.'

'With God's guidance, that is all we can do.' Havelock nodded Jack's dismissal. 'Your men will stay in the fort for the present, Windrush. 'When I am ready, we'll march to Cawnpore, relieve General Wheeler and rescue the women from their peril.'

'Yes, sir.' Jack withdrew gratefully. Havelock was undoubtedly the most unsettling senior officer he had met.

Strategically placed, Allahabad was an iron gate controlling the route from Calcutta to the North West, the road along which British reinforcements must travel to relieve Cawnpore. Previous rulers had recognised the city's importance, and in 1575 Abu'l-Fath Jalal-ud-din Muhammad, better known as Akbar had built a fort on a prime defensive position where the Ganges merged with the Jamuna. Now Allahabad Fort was the headquarters of the small British force that hoped to turn the tide in the rebellion they had inadvertently provoked.

'This is some building,' Elliot murmured. 'These Mughal emperors knew their stuff.'

Red-walled and massive, Allahabad Fort frowned over the huddled houses in princely pride. The footsteps of Jack and Elliot echoed from solid stone, while a native woman followed them at a few yard's distance, her blue sari nearly brushing the ground.

'It's said to be the most haunted building in India,' Elliot said.

'Trust you to know such things.' Jack followed as Elliot led the way to a great stone pillar, thirty feet high, with a carved lion on top. He touched the smooth stone as Jack admired the view north.

'This is one of the Ashok Pillars.' There was something like awe in Elliot's voice. 'It was built hundreds of years before Christ.' He caressed the stone nearly reverently. 'What amazing things this place has seen, what tremendous people have been here before us.'

'And now Captain Windrush and Lieutenants Elliot and Prentice of the infamous 113th Foot are gracing it with their presence,' Jack said.

Jack looked at the view. A faint mist only enhanced the beauty of the land, with trees draped in soft grey and the slow drift of the rivers a background to the murmur of voices.

'We think we are civilising this land,' Prentice said softly. 'Yet one of the greatest emperors the world has ever known built this huge fort more than a century before Great Britain even existed.'

Jack glanced at him. He was not used to such words from junior British officers, whose conversation commonly centred on hunting or women. 'You seem to know a lot about India.'

'I've been in India all my adult life,' Prentice said. 'We are guardians here, not owners. We are only the latest in a line of peoples stretching back further than we yet know.' He touched the pillar and indicated the massive fort. 'Look at the architecture here, sir, and feel the age and the sheer scale of it. How can we feel anything but respect for people who can create such a tremendous place?'

Jack grunted. 'These people have also murdered our men and women.'

'With respect, sir, Boadicea murdered quite a few Romans when she led the Iceni in rebellion against Rome,' Prentice said. 'And we revere her as a heroine. Perhaps these mutineers see themselves in the same light.'

Jack raised his eyebrows. 'We can feel sympathy for their cause after we have defeated them,' he said. 'At present, all I see are sepoys who have broken their oath of fidelity. Men who pretended friendship and loyalty then stabbed us in the back.'

'Yes, sir,' Prentice said. 'I was not suggesting we let them win, sir.'

'I'm glad to hear it.' Jack lit one of his last cheroots and inhaled.

'We are on the southern frontier of Oudh,' Elliot murmured, 'and near to the disaffected districts Juanpure, Azamgarh and Gorakhpur.'

'You've been doing your homework,' Jack said. 'A few days ago, you didn't even know where Cawnpore was.'

'I've been boning up.' Elliot indicated the smiling young woman who stood a few yards away. 'If you want to know the country, ask a native.'

'I thought your father was a religious man.' Jack glanced at the woman and away again. 'Would he approve of such activities?'

'He's not here,' Elliot said. 'And anyway, if he wants me to be another Wellington, I should act like Wellington, and he slept with every woman in sight.'

Jack thought of Myat once more and smiled. 'As long as you can trust her,' he said. 'Be careful she does not slit your throat in the night.'

'I'll be careful.' Elliot touched his revolver. 'I sleep with this under the pillow.' He looked around at the fort and the sprawling town beneath. 'The 6th Native Infantry were here, you know. When they offered to march against Delhi to support the British, their officers praised their loyalty. Officers and men cheered each other on the parade ground, and the same evening the sepoys rose and murdered the officers and eight young lads who had only arrived in India a few days before.'

'So I heard,' Jack said, and nodded to Prentice. 'So you be careful who you befriend, Prentice.'

'I will, sir,' Prentice plainly regretted his earlier words. 'I did not mean I sympathise with the mutineers, sir.'

'If I thought you did,' Jack spoke slowly, 'I would ensure that you were no longer a British officer. Our first duty is to the Queen, and then to the men under our command. Politics of any kind is irrelevant.'

'Yes, sir,' Prentice said.

'Did you hear about Lieutenant Brasyer? He saved the day and the fort.' There was admiration in Elliot's voice. 'He started off in the ranks, you know. It was he who disarmed the remnants of the 6th and held the fort.'

'Men like him deserve to be remembered,' Jack said. 'But he won't be. He'll be forgotten, and some titled ass will gain the plaudits and rewards.'

'And sometimes the women will get the rewards as well,' Elliot said shrewdly.

'What?' Jack didn't understand.

'The fair Helen.' Elliot did not withdraw. 'Who won your brother William, the hero of the Redan.' His sarcasm was evident.

Jack touched the letter in his breast pocket. There was too much hurt for him to continue the conversation. 'Allahabad seems quiet now.'

'Yes,' Elliot agreed. 'It was not quiet when the pandies were in charge. They burst open the doors of the jail, and all the thieves, bad-mashes and blackguards ran riot. They attacked anything European and progressive, ripped down the telegraphic wires, destroyed the railway, robbed the treasury and raped, tortured and then murdered the whites and Eurasians.'

Jack thought of Jane and Mary in the hands of these creatures. 'Inhuman monsters.' The words didn't adequately describe his feelings. He didn't add more. Elliot understood.

'When there was nobody left to kill and nothing to loot, the mutineers decided they had enough of rebelling and scurried home.'

'And so we came in,' Jack said.

'Not quite. The local landowners already disliked us after we tried to impose British land reforms on practices they had followed since

God was a toddler. When the sepoys left, a fellow called the Maulavi rose up to lead the landowners.'

'There's always somebody wanting to be a leader when others have done the dirty work,' Jack said sourly. 'Chaos brings out the opportunist.'

'Yes, sir. Colonel Neill arrived and soon gave this Maulavi fellow the right-about-turn. Neill recaptured Allahabad, sent the women and children to Calcutta and consolidated our position here.' Elliot spoke like a school teacher. 'The Maulavi fled to Cawnpore and, as you know, we are gathering forces here.'

'We have four regiments, or bits of them, in Allahabad,' Jack said, 'with a few guns plus some volunteer cavalry and odds and sods, such as us.' He looked around the massive fort where his men were making themselves at home.

'It is not much to try and retake India,' Elliot said.

'I'm sure there will be more arriving.' Jack said softly. 'The mutineers won't grab India without a fight, I can tell you.' He pulled on his cheroot. 'You'd better go, Arthur – there's a lady there waiting patiently for you. You too, Prentice, you'll have work to do.'

As the 113th rested and recovered after their trek across India, General Havelock and Colonel Neill prepared for the coming campaign. The fort and city of Allahabad buzzed with activity. Neill gathered camels and carts for the Commissariat and Transport Department, while Captain Brown of the Artillery and Captain Russell of the Ordnance worked all the hours they could in the stifling heat.

On the 30th June 1857, Havelock sent Major Renaud with an advance party to test the route to Cawnpore. Renaud commanded four hundred mixed Queen's and Company soldiers, together with three hundred Sikhs and over a hundred horsemen.

'About a third of our manpower,' Elliot calculated. 'I hope this Havelock fellow knows what he's doing.'

Jack remembered those steady eyes. 'I think he does. In fact, I am sure he does.'

Three days later, Havelock ordered Captain Spurgin with a hundred men and two guns to take a river steamer toward Cawnpore, and then he sent for Jack.

'You arrived in time for the advance, Windrush,' Havelock said. 'Your Crimean veterans will come in useful when we meet the mutineers.'

'Yes, sir.' Jack watched Spurgin's steamer chug up the Ganges, her decks full of men and the water churning up creamily in her wake.

'I understand Colonel Jeffreys sent some of your regimental families to Cawnpore for safety.' Havelock's eyes were unwavering, yet full of sympathy.

'Yes, sir. He sent them away a day or two before the outbreak at Gondabad. Major Snodgrass and a small escort accompanied them.'

'You may have heard the rumour that General Wheeler hauled down his flag and the mutineers have taken over.' Havelock said.

The pounding of Jack's heart increased. 'I had heard, sir.'

'I don't yet know if it is true or merely bazaar gossip,' Havelock said. 'Let us hope the Lord sees fit to care for our loved ones as well as the defenders of the city.' He sounded sincere.

'I hope He does, sir,' Jack said. His men had been shocked when they heard the stories, with Riley turning aside in horror and battered little Logan putting an arm around him in awkward companionship. 'When are we leaving to retake the city, sir?'

'When I am ready, Windrush,' Havelock said. 'Rest your men, ensure they have all their equipment and inform them there will be trials and tribulations ahead, but with God's help, British arms and the right will triumph.'

'Yes, sir.'

'May the good Lord give me wisdom and strength to restore tranquillity to the disturbed districts.' Havelock looked directly at Jack with those sharp, shrewd eyes. 'Speed is a priority to save the women. There will be no private carriages for officers, Windrush, and only a minimum of baggage.'

'My men are used to marching with nothing except what they can carry,' Jack said. 'And with some having family in Cawnpore, they would march through Hell to rescue them.'

'There is no need for the blasphemy, Windrush,' Havelock rebuked. 'This will undoubtedly be a hard campaign. The enemy will be stern in their desire to stop us.'

'Yes, sir. I am sure they will,' Jack said. Within him, he knew he wanted the mutineers to fight. He wanted revenge for the men he had lost. He needed to kill Sarvur Khan.

'You look worried.' Mary stood beside the Ashok pillar, gazing at the river and the view beyond. From up here, the land appeared beautiful, fertile and peaceful.

He lit another cheroot. 'I am worried,' he admitted. Images of Sarvur Khan filled his mind, together with a terrible feeling of foreboding.

'Your men are well but unsettled.' Mary folded her skirt beneath her and sat gracefully on a nearby block of stone. 'I have lived in cantonments much of my life; I know when soldiers are unhappy.'

'They are concerned about their families.' Jack drew on his cheroot.

'And you are worried about them,' Mary said.

'They're my men,' Jack said. 'It's my job to worry.'

Mary gave a little smile. 'Not all officers worry about their men.'

Jack thought for a few moments. 'We've been through a lot together. You get close to people when you've stood side by side in battle or waited in trenches for the Plastun Cossacks to come through the night.' He lapsed into silence; his mind clouded with memories. 'And a few were with me in the Burmese war.'

'Even so,' Mary said, 'some officers keep a distance between themselves and the men.'

'Maybe I should do the same,' Jack said. He drew on his cheroot and blew out aromatic smoke.

'Why don't you?' It was a direct question asked in a tone so gentle that Jack knew Mary was genuinely interested in his answer.

He inhaled again, considering how much he could safely tell her. Safely? He could be killed any hour of any day; did it matter if this woman sneered at him for his illegitimate birth? Yes, it did. For some reason, he valued her good opinion. 'I would feel a fraud,' he said slowly, wondering if he was destroying something fragile by saying too much. When he moved, he felt Helen's letter press against his chest. *Damn Helen Maxwell.*

'In what way?' Mary spoke in a quiet voice again, so thoughtful and so different from Helen's youthful impulsiveness.

Should he tell her? Jack shrugged – if he didn't, she might think he was a man of mystery, a dark stranger with a brooding secret like the hero of a Gothic romance. He gave a sudden, bitter smile; nothing could be further from the truth. 'I'm not entirely from the officer and gentleman mould.' He had drawn on his cheroot before he continued, so short spurts of tobacco smoke accompanied each word. 'My father was an officer of the Royal Malverns, scion of many generations of a military family, but my mother was not his wife. She was a kitchen maid or some such, a brief, meaningless affair to ease my father's concupiscence.'

'You make it sound very sordid.' Mary had been listening. 'I wonder if she felt like that, or indeed if *he* felt like that. Perhaps their relationship was significant to both their lives, something unique and precious despite the differences in their social position.'

Jack frowned and said nothing. He was uncomfortable with the turn the conversation had taken.

'After all,' Mary continued. 'Your father did not abandon you. He sent you to England to be educated and had you brought up as his son. It was your step-mother who disowned you, not your father.'

Jack examined the glowing end of his cheroot, stepped forward and tossed it into the void. Far below, the river ran brown, glittering under the sun. 'You are a persuasive woman.'

'And you are a man who worries about things you cannot alter.' Mary met him statement for statement. 'Do you think you are less of an officer or less of a man because of an accident of birth? Your soldiers certainly do not.' A gentle smile lifted the corners of her mouth. 'Do you think less of me because my mother was a Rajput and my father a British officer? Do you think less of me because I am the product of a brief, meaningless affair to ease *my* father's concupiscence?'

Jack turned to face her, again consciously comparing her to Helen. 'No.' He spoke more shortly than he intended.

'Nor do I about you; and nor should anybody else with even a modicum of sense,' Mary said. 'You are no fraud, Captain Jack; you are a soldier of the Queen and a respected – a highly respected – officer of the 113th Foot.'

Jack took out another cheroot, contemplated it for a moment and put it back in his pocket. He studied Mary. 'You are very serene sitting there,' he said. 'You look as if you are waiting for an artist to paint your portrait.'

'Only if you are the artist.' Mary was smiling. 'There is nobody else here. Only us.' Standing up, she extended her hand to him.

'What?' Taken by surprise, Jack stared at her.

'What do you think? I want to hold your hand. Or am I not sufficiently respectable for you?'

Unused to such forward behaviour from a woman, Jack hesitated. 'Tomorrow we march for Cawnpore,' he said. 'Tomorrow we return to the war.'

'I know,' Mary said softly. Her hand was warm and dry in his. 'Come home safely, Jack Windrush.' She lowered her voice so even he couldn't hear. 'Come safely to me, Captain Jack.'

Chapter Eight

'It is one hundred and twenty miles from Allahabad to Cawnpore.' Elliot gave the statistic with some satisfaction. 'And there could be pandies every yard of the way.'

Jack inspected his men. Havelock had split the 113th, leaving half in the fort with Lieutenant Fairbairn and Ensign Shearer in charge. Now Jack's sixty men of the 113th helped make up the 979 British infantry, with contingents from the 64th and 84th Foot as well as the kilted 78th Highlanders and the Company's Madras Fusiliers. Eighteen volunteer British cavalry accompanied them, as well as thirty irregular native horsemen and a hundred and thirty proud Sikhs.

'I don't fully trust those Sikh fellows,' Kent said. 'We were fighting them only a few years ago, and now they pretend to be on our side. Like as not they'll turn traitor the minute the mutineers appear.'

'If you don't trust them,' Jack said, 'I recommend you keep a strict watch on them, Lieutenant Kent.' He had hoped to leave Kent in Allahabad, but Havelock had insisted he accompany the relief column. Jack shrugged; obeying disliked orders was all part of the soldier's bargain.

General Havelock's small army included his son, Lieutenant Havelock as Aide-de-Camp and the experienced Stuart Beatson and Fraser Tytler as Assistant Adjutant-General and Quartermaster-General respectively. Captain Maude, an energetic man of great experience, was in charge of the artillery.

'So Cawnpore has fallen,' Elliot said. 'Wheeler surrendered to Nana Sahib. I never thought I'd see the day a British general surrendered to a native.'

'That's the shave,' Jack spoke quietly. 'If it's true we don't hold much in the north of India now. Please God, Sir Henry Lawrence keeps the flag flying in Lucknow.'

'I heard the sepoys who wanted to remain loyal are turning,' Elliot said. 'They're scared of the mutineers. The Rani of Jhansi is said to have murdered all the British in her country too, after promising safe conduct.'

Jack thought again of Boadicea and wondered if the Romans experienced the same feelings of hurt and betrayal he was experiencing, or if they had only known hatred and a desire for revenge, as seemed to fill Colonel Neill.

'There were uprisings in Gwalior as well,' Elliot said.

'The unrest is spreading.' Jack felt for a cheroot; he only had a few remaining and no way of renewing his stock. This war was showing him many types of hardship.

'Here's the general,' Prentice said.

At five foot five, Havelock should not have been an imposing figure, but there was something about his white-haired, neat figure in his blue frock coat that inspired confidence.

'Men,' Havelock didn't need to shout for his voice to carry to every man in the relief column. 'You will by now have heard the news from Cawnpore.'

There was a deep growl from the soldiers. Jack focussed on his reduced company; Riley was white-faced under his tan, with O'Neill grim at one side and Logan's mouth moving in silent obscenity at the other.

While the 64th and 84th were mainly composed of young Johnny Raws with sun-reddened faces and peeling noses, the 78th Highlanders were veterans of the recent Persian War and looked ready to recapture all of India on their own. They spoke in whispering Gaelic and thrust stubby pipes into whiskered mouths as they waited for Havelock to continue.

'We are going to avenge the fate of British men and women,' Havelock said. 'I know you will all do your duty. Trust in the Lord and all will be well.'

'Not what I would call a rousing speech,' Elliot murmured as they marched out of the great fort and toward Cawnpore. It was four in the afternoon with the air heavy with the oncoming monsoon.

O'Neill eased a hand around the inside of his collar and looked upward. 'I wish the rain would come and end this humidity,' he said. 'At least we won't die of thirst.'

'No.' Parker was smiling. 'We'll drown instead.'

With five Highland pipers wailing in the van, Havelock's small column crunched grimly on. Brayser, the ex-gardener turned officer led his Sikhs while Captain Maude fussed over the artillery. In their wake, the supply waggons creaked onto the hard road, lagging further behind by the minute.

'No straggling,' Havelock ordered his infantry. 'Stay in the column.'

They marched along the Grand Trunk Road with the men toiling in the dull heat until the heavens opened and the first deluge of the rainy season descended upon them.

Thorpe looked upward. 'Maybe once we can have a war in good weather,' he said. 'Burma was just humid heat, Crimea was mud and cold and snow, and now we have some beggar emptying the sea on us.'

'We're not allowed to fight on pleasant days,' Coleman told him easily. 'The generals on both sides get together, you see, and decide they'll only fight in foul weather so they can go hunting and horse-riding when it's fine.'

Thorpe grunted. 'I thought so,' he said, 'I bloody thought so.'

The land on either side, once fertile and well populated, had been devastated by war. Frogs and crickets greeted them with a monotonous grating, villages lay in ruins with vultures and insects competing for obscenely dead bodies while wild pigs ran from the outraged boots of soldiers who interrupted them from feasting on human corpses. Worst of all were the bodies that hung from roadside trees; native men of all ages swung slowly with their accusing eyes following the progress of the marching column.

The opening volley of the monsoon hammered them. For a few moments, men faced upward, trying to catch the falling rain in their mouths as they marched, and then they bowed their heads under the relentless downpour. The dust on the road settled and turned to mud as the column marched on beside the weeping trees that lined the Great Trunk Road.

'The land looked better from the fort,' Elliot said.

Kent glanced fearfully at the hanging men with their twisted necks and limp bodies and water dripping from their pointed toes. 'Bloody pandies! They've hanged everybody!'

'No, they haven't,' Jack said. 'We have. Renaud has been executing rebels, and anybody he thinks might be a rebel.' He shook his head. 'Poor India.'

'Murdering pandy bastards.' The voice came from the ranks of the 113th.

The column swung on, regular as on parade, with officers ignoring the deluge, scant cavalry on the flanks and the level, dreary plains sliding past. Marching behind the 113th, the men of the 64th and 84th staggered on the road and wilted in the humid heat.

'They lads won't last.' Logan jerked a thumb behind him.

He was right. After only three hours, Havelock stopped the column for the night. The men tried to camp on the sodden ground.

'Where are the tents?' Kent asked. 'Where are the commissariat waggons?'

'Still back there.' Prentice nodded toward Allahabad and the unseen supply train. 'You'll have to rough it.'

'This is nothing,' Elliot said. 'You should have been with us on the first night in the Crimea.'

Jack eyed his sodden, grim-faced men. 'That's hardly a comfort, Elliot. Now, who the devil is this?'

The volunteer cavalryman trotted along the 113th, shouting. 'Where is Captain Windrush? I need Captain Windrush!'

'Here!' Jack stepped out.

'General Havelock would like to see you.' The rider was about forty, with a shiny red face beneath a broad-brimmed hat, and with a makeshift lance in his right hand. Three long-barrelled revolvers were shoved ostentatiously through his scarlet cummerbund.

'And you are?' After five years as a commissioned officer, Jack was not inclined to jump to the orders of a sweating civilian.

'Oh! Tom Plankett, I'm an indigo planter—'

'Very good, Mr. Plankett. In future, you will carry your message correctly and address me as sir.'

'I manage an estate of—'

'I don't care a twopenny damn what you do. Pray inform General Havelock that Captain Windrush sends his compliments and he will be with him directly. Go.'

Havelock rode at the head of the column, unsmiling and with a volunteer cavalryman at his side. Fastened to the pommel of his saddle by a long cord, a native walked awkwardly at the side of the volunteer.

'The cavalry caught this man skulking by the road,' Havelock said. 'He claims to know you.'

Jack looked closer at the prisoner. 'Yes, sir. He is Private Fraser; he warned me about trouble many weeks ago.'

'Oh? Did you take heed of his warning?'

'I passed it on to Colonel Jeffreys, sir. Fraser is no Mutineer.'

Havelock nodded. 'Release him,' he ordered casually. 'Now, Fraser, what do you have to say for yourself?'

'The mutineers have captured Fatehpur, sir.' Fraser ran a hand around his neck where the cord had left a red mark. 'They are waiting for Major Renaud there.'

Havelock snorted. 'Why did you not inform him, Fraser?'

'Major Renaud would have hanged me on sight, sir,' Fraser said casually.

Havelock didn't comment as he gestured to the closest volunteer. 'You fellow – Plankett, isn't it? Gallop ahead, find Renaud and tell him, with my compliments, not to progress any further. Inform him the rebels are at Fatehpur. Go, man!'

Nodding, Plankett kicked in his heels and pushed ahead.

'Fraser; you seem to be a useful man. Do you wish to re-enlist?' Havelock asked. 'You are over age, but you'll be doing the Lord's work.'

'Yes, sir,' Fraser's Scottish accent was distinct under the sing-song cadences characteristic to Indian veterans.

'As you already know Captain Windrush, you may join the ranks of the 113th,' Havelock said. 'On a temporary basis.'

'Yes, sir.' Fraser accepted his re-enlistment without visible emotion.

They marched on with the volunteers guarding the flanks until they met and merged with Renaud's force by the side of a copse of trees. Rain hammered down, bouncing off the hard surface of the road, dripping from shakos and forage caps and the manes of bedraggled horses. The men stood in ranks, silent, keeping the muzzles of their rifles pointed downward, inwardly cursing India, the army and life in general.

'Report, Renaud,' Havelock ordered. 'What intelligence have you gathered?'

'Sir,' Renaud said, 'the mutineers at Cawnpore are commanded by Nana Sahib, with a bodyguard under a fellow called Tantia Topi.'

'Very good.'

'Topi is advancing toward us with some 1400 sepoys, about the same number of local rebels and ex-Oudh soldiers, a few hundred cavalry including some ex-Company sowars and a dozen guns.'

'Very good, thank you, Renaud.' A sharp order from Havelock sent Fraser Tytler and a handful of horsemen forward to reconnoitre. 'The rest of us can have breakfast,' Havelock said calmly.

'That's very civil of the general,' Elliot said.

'It may not be a good idea.' Kent looked around warily. 'If the mutineers come across us here, they could slaughter us.'

'They might try,' Jack said. 'Have you seen any action, Kent?'

'I have not had the opportunity, sir,' Kent said.

'You are about to, I think.' Jack nodded forward. 'Just keep calm, let the men know you are there and trust them.'

Elliot sighed. 'Here we go, then.' He looked up. 'Listen! Was that artillery? It's hard to tell in this damned rain!'

'It was thunder!' Kent said, just as a cannonball crashed into the camp, throwing up a column of mud and earth and rolling to a halt a few yards from the position occupied by the 113th.

'Solid looking thunder, don't you know?' Elliot said, as Kent backed away.

Jack said nothing as Tytler rode hard toward them with his horse throwing up a fine spray from the road. He reined up in front of Havelock, flecks of froth covering his horse and his forage cap awry.

'The mutineers are coming, sir!'

'So I gathered, Tytler,' Havelock said. 'How many?'

'There is a whole army, sir; a column of infantry on the road, with two cannons in front and cavalry on both flanks. As soon as they saw me, the cavalry advanced at speed, and I had to ride hard to escape.' Tytler fought to control his horse.

'The pandies are attacking us.' O'Neill's voice was distinct above the diminishing hammer of rain. 'They must think we're unarmed women.'

Logan laughed. 'Come on, you pandy bastards!'

'You know what to do, men,' Jack called. 'Obey orders and trust in your comrades.'

'Aye,' Logan replied. 'We'll lace these buggers.'

There was a growl in reply, with a few muttered prayers and many more curses. Riley was quiet, looking to his front as he slid the bayonet from its scabbard and tested the edge. The rain eased to a halt, leaving only a fine mist drifting upward from the warm ground. The smell of wet earth was pleasant, as was the call of birds.

'That will be the famous Tantia Topi, coming to pay us a morning call.' Havelock gathered the officers. 'He's Nana Sahib's adviser. Captain Maude, take a hundred men and eight of your guns there.'

He pointed to a coppice a few hundred yards away, vague under the mist. 'The Irregulars will take the left flank, the volunteer cavalry the right and the remainder of us will form a line of column. I presume the enemy think they are only opposing Renaud's force.' He looked as lugubrious as ever. 'We will surprise him.' He raised his voice. 'Officers, prepare to deploy on my word.'

'What's that village ahead called?' Kent sounded anxious.

'Fatehpur,' Elliot replied shortly.

From their position to the south, Fatehpur looked a difficult proposition if Tantia Topi chose to defend it. The Grand Trunk Road ran straight through the middle, past solid stone houses surrounded by enclosed gardens, while the plains on either side were deep in monsoon floods.

'Tantia could hold this place for hours; we'd have to take it building by building.' Elliot ran his experienced eye over it.

Jack nodded. 'This could be bloody.' He looked around – an array of small hillocks lay between the flooded fields and the British, with a scattering of tiny hamlets and mango groves.

'Look!' Prentice pointed forward. 'There's movement in that mango grove. No civilian in his right mind would stand between two rival armies. Ten guineas to a brass farthing that Tantia's men are there.'

Jack nodded. 'We'll just have to turf them out, then.' He took a deep breath, touched the letter in his breast pocket and for some reason thought of Mary. He would never see her again, but at least she would be safe in Allahabad.

The British waited, rifles loaded, faces grim until Havelock ordered a general advance toward Fatehpur.

'Stand to your arms, men,' Jack said. 'O'Neill, take ten men as skirmishers – Coleman, Thorpe... the usual suspects.' He glanced at his men. They were silent, determined, shifting slightly to relax muscles. Coleman muttered something to Thorpe, who gave a small, quick smile. Unusually there was none of the black humour with which British soldiers habitually eased the tension before battle. This coming battle was different; they were fighting men they had thought of as friends.

The British advanced slowly, each step accompanied by a splash as their feet sunk into the muddy ground.

'Come on, you murdering black bastards.' Logan glanced at Riley, who stared ahead, his eyes focussed on the copse where Maude's men and the artillery waited.

The mutineers opened rapid fire with their cannon, the sound surprisingly loud as always. Kent started and grabbed at his shako.

'Don't mind the shine, Kent,' Jack said. 'Stand tall; the men are watching.'

The mutineers appeared on the road ahead, infantry marching steadily and cavalry on the flanks. Their artillery fired again, aiming at the main British force advancing in three columns toward them. Smoke coiled along the ground, hazing the ranks of the mutineers as they marched, red coats like flowing blood and white trousers twinkling through the heat haze. Overhead, pregnant clouds threatened a renewal of the deluge.

'There goes Maude,' Prentice said as the British artillery advanced from the copse to within four hundred yards of the advancing enemy. Cannon fired at cannon, with Maude's skirmishers also busy, the range of their Enfield rifles taking the mutineers by surprise.

'Aye, that's what you get for not accepting new rifles,' Logan snarled. 'See what you're missing?'

The mutineers halted in seeming confusion. In the middle of them, a man gave orders from the back of an elephant.

'There's Tantia Topi,' Elliot said. 'Bastard-in-chief to the head murderer.'

'We're after you, elephant man,' Logan shouted.

'Watch your flanks,' Jack warned.

The mutineer cavalry had been riding on both flanks, far outnumbered the small numbers of riders with which the British could oppose them. On the left, the eighteen or so British volunteers rode out bravely and in a frantic skirmish turned back the mutineers.

'Good lads, these volunteers,' Elliot approved.

'Not so good over there,' Prentice pointed to the right where native cavalry under British officers guarded the flank. 'Listen!'

Faint through the continuing duel of the cannon, some of the Mutineer horsemen could be heard shouting to Havelock's native cavalry. The sound carried above the thunder of the guns and crackle of musketry, with isolated words reaching them, high-pitched, sinister in the stifling heat.

'I'd wager my pension and yours they're trying to get our sowars to change sides,' Prentice said.

'Oh, God no! If they succeed, we'll have no cavalry left!' Kent glanced over his shoulder as if preparing to run away all the way back to Allahabad.

'Our sowars don't look too happy at all,' Prentice loosened his revolver in its holster.

'Look! There's Pallister, the sowar commander.' Jack saw the slender figure shouting an order, and the thin, stirring bugle call of the charge came to them, high above the hammer of the guns. 'Jesus! He's charging alone!'

They watched the drama unfold. Pallister had sounded the charge, lifted his sword and spurred forward toward the mutineer ranks. One other British officer immediately accompanied him and then four of his native troopers. The remainder hesitated, unsure what to do. Some looked toward Havelock's small army, others to the mutineer cavalry opposing them.

With the odds in their favour, the mutineer cavalry also sounded the charge and crashed into the much smaller British force. Amid a flurry of activity, with the sun flashing off sword-blades, Pallister was unhorsed and lay on the ground, stunned.

'He's a goner,' Kent said.

'No, look!' Elliot pointed as a few of Pallister's men formed a body around him and carried him off the field while others fled. The mutineer cavalry waited for a few moments, turned and retreated. With the skirmish over, a couple of horses lay kicking on the damp ground, half hidden by mist and rising steam.

'Who can you trust in this damned country?' Kent asked.

'Ourselves,' Jack said quietly. 'And the men.' Again, he fingered Helen's letter. *And nobody else.*

While Jack had been watching the cavalry, Maude had pushed forward his guns to within two hundred yards of the mutineers; in a hectic exchange of fire he had either destroyed the opposing artillery or forced them to run and now concentrated his fire on their infantry. White smoke added to the mist haze as Maud's artillery battered the enemy ranks.

'Advance,' Havelock ordered briskly. 'Take the village.'

'Cry Havelock,' Elliot misquoted Shakespeare, 'and let loose the dogs of war.'

The British moved forward in three columns – elements of the 113th, the 78th Highlanders, the 64th and 84th Foot marching to engage a much larger body of mutineers on the plains of India. After months of massacres and disasters, Havelock's men were drawing Britannia's sword.

With Maude's artillery and accurate musketry flaying them, the mutineers stood to face the oncoming British until a shot crashed into Tantia Topi's elephant. Tantia Topi fell clumsily, unhurt but shaken. Temporarily bereft of their commander, the mutineers lost heart and began a slow withdrawal.

'They're running!' Prentice said.

'Get the bastards!' Quiet Whitelam shouted.

'Keep your ranks!' Jack ordered. 'Stay together!' In the right-hand column, the 113th marched forward steadily as the mutineers' withdrawal turned into a rout.

With the 64th in the centre and the left, the 78th Highlanders as the hinge and the 84th beside the 113th, the British pushed on. Not yet defeated, the mutineers formed up behind the garden enclosures until the British came close and the accurate fire of the Enfields forced them back to the mud wall of Fatehpur itself.

Malcolm Archibald

'Here's where it gets interesting,' Elliot said as he marched three steps in front of his men. 'It's not much of a place, is it? A few houses and a wet road.'

'And there's the irregular cavalry,' Jack said, 'with the mutineers chasing them. Halt.' He waited until the broken remnants of the British right flank guardians fled past, to the jeers of the 113th, and then ordered, 'Prepare! Fire a volley at the enemy cavalry!'

'Fire!'

Other officers took up Jack's shout and volley after volley crashed out. The mutineer horsemen reeled back in disarray, leaving a tangle of dead and injured men and horses on the ground. The advance continued, stolid and disciplined. As the right column had been disposing of the cavalry, the centre and left had pushed past the defending wall at Fatehpur and attacked the fast-retreating enemy rearguard.

'They're broke!' Elliot shouted as the mutineers finally turned and ran, leaving behind all their artillery, bags and baggage. 'We've beaten them! Havelock has beaten the pandies!'

Jack reached for a cheroot to celebrate and swore when he remembered he had none left. 'That must be the easiest battle I've ever fought in,' he said. 'The pandies hardly fired a shot at the 113th.'

'Let's hope for more of the same,' Elliot said.

'Maybe the mutiny's over.' Kent sounded hopeful. 'Maybe now they've been defeated in battle the rebels will surrender?'

'Maybe,' Elliot said. 'Although I doubt it.'

The men cheered at this first success for weeks. They knew the British habit of losing the first few encounters and then grinding out an eventual victory, yet their exhaustion proved stronger than their elation. The cheering didn't last. Unable to advance another step, they halted, collapsing with the heat, and reached for water bottles or crawled into whatever shade they could find.

Havelock looked over the field of battle. 'Thanks be to Almighty God, who gave us victory,' he said. 'Now we will march to retake Cawnpore.'

After their nineteen-mile march and decisive victory, Jack, remembering the slaughter of the Alma and Inkerman, expected scores of casualties, but the British had only lost a dozen men, all by sunstroke. Not a single mutineer shot had taken effect.

'Loot!' Coleman said loudly. 'We have two six-pounders and ammunition, ten other pieces of artillery, tumbrils of all sorts of goods and a victory. I'll march with Havelock any day of the week.'

Ignoring the victory and the bloody corpses of the slain mutineers, Riley stared forward. Jack knew he was thinking of Charlotte, held prisoner by Nana Sahib.

Chapter Nine

'Jack.' The voice was soft and feminine. 'Jack.' It was also persistent. He stirred and looked up. Mary stood in the shade of a palm tree, smiling down at him.

'What the devil!' Jack stared at her. 'What the devil are you doing here? You should be safe in Allahabad!'

'It's not safe in Allahabad.' Mary squatted beside him, her eyes serene. 'Colonel Neill is establishing a reign of terror that Herod would be proud of.'

'For God's sake, woman! We're on campaign. The pandies could attack any minute and destroy us.' Jack felt his temper rising. 'You could be killed, or worse.'

'That is as possible in Allahabad under Colonel Neill as here.' Mary didn't flinch from his tongue. 'In fact, we're probably safer here with the 113th to protect us.'

Jack shook his head, sighing. 'How did you get here?'

'In a commissariat waggon,' Mary admitted at once. 'We asked the driver to give us a lift.'

'We? How many of you are there?' For a moment Jack had a vision of a score of women packed into the waggons and all descending on his 113th for sanctuary.

'Only Jane and I,' Mary said. 'Are you not pleased to see me?'

Contrarily, Jack knew he was. 'You make sure you look after yourself,' he said.

'You too, Captain Jack,' Mary said softly.

'It's good to see you again,' Jack said, reluctantly and cursed inwardly as Lieutenant Kent blundered up with a request for help in something he should have been able to manage by himself. By the time Jack had sorted the matter out Mary had vanished.

After a day of rest in which Havelock disbanded the Irregular cavalry and used them as baggage guards instead, the tiny army resumed its advance on Cawnpore.

'You Sikhs,' Havelock ordered, 'I want you to burn Fatehpur; show the rebels what happens when they oppose us.'

Elliot tipped back his hip-flask as they tramped on through the rain. 'I never trusted these Sikh fellows anyway. You don't know when they'll turn and stab you in the back.'

'The Sikhs are all right.' Jack defended them. 'I had a Sikh orderly in Burma; you could not find a better man.'

With only eighteen horsemen left to both guard the flanks and scout ahead, Havelock was blind and vulnerable, yet pushed on remorselessly.

'I hear Colonel Neill is coming up in support,' Jack said.

'God help the pandies if he gets here,' Elliot said. 'He'll hang everyone in sight.'

Jack nodded. He had a sudden, sickening picture of Jane and Mary hanging from one of the sad trees beside the Great Trunk Road. 'Go and look after your men,' he said curtly. 'Young Parker had a rusty lock on his rifle this morning; the men have to care for their equipment in this damp weather.'

Elliot opened his mouth to say something, closed it quickly and said, 'Yes, sir,' and marched stiffly away.

Jack felt for a cheroot, swore at his empty pocket and chased away the images of Mary and Jane. He had sufficient to think about without introducing any more women into his life. He touched the crumpled letter in his breast pocket. *Damn Helen Maxwell.*

'What if she's dead,' Riley said. 'What if the murdering bastards have killed Charlotte?'

'They won't have.' Logan clamped an empty clay pipe between his teeth. 'Your Charlotte is too intelligent to get herself killed. She'll be fine, you'll see.'

'Do you think so, Logie? Honestly?' Riley looked to Logan for support, for reassurance, for anything to ease the burden of worry from his mind. Five paces in front, Jack could only sympathise, there was nothing he could do to help. Charlotte Riley was from a much lower class than Riley, their gentleman ranker, and had followed him faithfully to the Crimea and now out to India. Indeed, Jack had never seen a married couple so devoted as the Rileys'. A ranker's wife could be widowed by shot, shell or cholera on Monday morning, bury her man in the afternoon and choose another by noon on Tuesday. Many soldiers and their wives took their marriages lightly, and some women had a couple of men in reserve for when their current husband died. That was not the case with Charlotte, or with Riley.

'I heard Nana Sahib had them all shot down like dogs,' Riley said.

'I heard different,' Logan said stoutly. 'I heard the women and children, and some of the men were spared and are held safe.' He chewed on the stem of his pipe. 'Nana Sahib would be a bloody fool to hurt them now we're coming to get him.' Logan removed the pipe from his mouth and jabbed it into Riley's arm. 'Trust me, Riley, son, your Charlotte is in the pink.'

Women again, Jack thought. They were always a worry. Men were better off without them; life would be so much simpler. God, he wished he had kept a cheroot. This constant blasted rain and humidity were wearing him down. He marched on with the thoughts and images chasing each other through his head – Helen, the men hanging by the side of the road, the massacre at Gondabad and always Sarvur Khan. The road stretched before him, jarring his ankles with every step while the sweat irritated the old Burmese wound in his leg. Now he had Mary and Jane to worry about as well as his men, and half the blasted rebels in India gathering to murder him.

Jack swore, thought of the march to Balaclava and then of Helen. He touched the crumpled letter in his breast pocket and sighed. *Damn Helen Maxwell.*

'Pandies!'

Jack's mind leapt back to the present. Borrowing a telescope from a panting Fusilier captain, he peered forward. About half a mile ahead a small town ran parallel to the road, with men moving behind solid earth walls and the sinister muzzles of artillery glowering outward. An earth-and-rock barricade wall blocked their onward passage, with the bobbing heads of defenders visible behind.

'That's Aong,' Elliot said quietly.

As so often in this part of India, there was a scattering of settlements, too small to be termed villages, around the main town, with one between the British and Aong. It looked empty under the rain.

'It seems as though we will have to fight to get past Aong.' Jack examined the ground.

Havelock lifted his binoculars. 'I can see two guns. Captain Barrow, take the volunteers; ride ahead and see what's happening.'

The volunteers cantered forward; there was the sharp crack of artillery, and they returned at speed, with a cannonball bouncing along the road behind them. On sight of the volunteers, a body of seven hundred red-coated mutineers advanced from Aong to occupy the huddle of houses between them.

'Good tactics,' Jack approved.

'Cavalry, sir.' Prentice pointed to the left. 'And there.'

Jack nodded. British trained, the mutineers had sent their cavalry to harass the British flanks while they waited with artillery and infantry in the centre. It was a classic manoeuvre, time-honoured and dangerous.

'Tytler, take the Madras Fusiliers and move around Aong. Captain Maude, bring your battery to the front and fire on the entrenchment.' Havelock gave crisp orders. 'Renaud, take two companies of Fusiliers and the 113th, push the Pandies from the hamlet.'

Renaud nodded to Jack. 'Watch how the professionals fight, Windrush!' He gave a grin. 'You Queen's soldiers have a lot to learn about warfare in India.'

'Bloody arrogant Company wallah.' Logan gave his own professional opinion as he slotted his bayonet in place.

They moved forward in extended order, silent and with bayonets glittering. The mutineers opened up with volley fire, jets of white smoke obscuring the front of the hamlet as the British advanced.

'Right boys!' Jack felt the pent-up anger of the 113th. 'Remember Gondabad!' Drawing his sword, he dashed forward, knowing his men were following. A few yards away, Renaud did the same.

'Cry Havelock!' Elliot used the same slogan as before. 'And let loose the dogs of war!'

'Did Shakespeare not write "cry havoc"?' Prentice asked.

'Only because he had never met our general.' Elliot was grinning again.

'Remember Gondabad!' Jack's men echoed his shout and together with the Madras Fusiliers, they charged. Jack saw Renaud stagger and fall and then they were in the hamlet among the red-coated mutineers. There were a few moments of frenzied fighting, bayonet to bayonet, flashes of bared teeth in brown faces, of moustaches and huge brown eyes, of drifting powder smoke and wild curses.

'Come on lads!' Jack emptied his revolver at the defenders. 'Gondabad!'

'Up the 113th!' Somebody shouted, and then the mutineers were withdrawing, leaving a litter of dead behind them and the mounting roars of the victors.

'We're coming for you!' Coleman shouted. 'You back-stabbing murdering bastards!'

'Charlotte!' Riley screamed. Kneeling at the corner of a house, he loaded and fired at the retreating mutineers. 'Charlotte!' Logan was at his side, small, scarred and ugly, guarding him like a West Highland terrier.

'Look, sir.' Rivulets of sweat had formed light grooves on O'Neill's powder-black face. 'Their cavalry is attacking.'

Jack swore as he saw the mutineer cavalry advance on the British baggage train, half a mile in the rear.

'They're after loot.' Thorpe was cleaning blood from his bayonet.

'Maybe,' Jack reloaded his revolver. 'The baggage train has our food and ammunition, our tents and equipment. Without it we're crippled; it's a good move by the mutineers.'

'There's the 78th!' O'Neill said.

A line of British soldiers, distinctively Highland by their kilts, opened fire on the cavalry. Jack saw the individual jets of smoke merging into a whole, saw men tumble from the mutineer's saddles and then the cavalry withdrew. Distance muted the sound of musketry, so it sounded like the innocent popping of children's toys.

'Well done the Sawnies!' O'Neill said.

'We're advancing again,' Jack said and waved his men onward. The 113th and the Madras Fusiliers marched out of the village toward the town of Aong as the mutineers fired a few scattered shots and withdrew. Maude's artillery battered the enemy rearguard.

'They're fighting better today,' Jack said, as one of the Fusiliers crumpled to the sodden ground.

'We trained them well.' Prentice was five steps to his right and two in the rear, marching erect with his sword in hand.

'Keep the pace up.' Jack broke into a trot, hoping to get his men into the cover of the town before the mutineers could recover and blast them with artillery or volley fire.

Spread out to offer a less tempting target, the 113th moved into Aong, to find it deserted save for the bloodied bodies of dead and wounded mutineers and a litter of baggage and stores.

'They must have plenty of ammunition to leave so much behind.' O'Neill rapped his knuckles on the breach of a cannon. 'And guns.'

Jack checked his watch. 'It's two hours since the action began,' he marvelled. 'It seemed a lot quicker.'

Birds circled above, waiting for the men to pass so they could feast on the corpses and fragments of dead bodies that lay scattered around the village. While the griffins tried to come to terms with what they had just seen and endured, the veterans played cards, sought shade, drank from their water bottles or slept. Jack was constantly amazed at the ability of the British soldier to sleep in any situation.

'Two battles, two victories,' Elliot said. 'Maybe the tide has turned.'

'Maybe,' Jack said. He looked up as one of the volunteer cavalrymen trotted up to Havelock and spoke earnestly.

'Something's up,' Elliot said.

'Go and find out what's happening, Arthur,' Jack ordered. 'You're the best man for gathering information.'

Elliot was back within ten minutes. 'I asked the volunteer,' he said. 'He's an ensign of the something-or-other Native foot, a man without a regiment since they mutinied.'

'Poor bugger.' Jack felt for a cheroot. 'I must get some smokes,' he said. 'What did your ensign say?'

'He said he was scouting ahead and the pandies have reformed up the road at a place called Pandu Nadi. He said there's a stone bridge over a stream and it will be the very devil to take.'

Jack nodded. 'I doubt the general will have us fight two battles in the one day.'

'Maybe Holy Havelock will have us all kneel down and pray instead,' Private Armstrong said. Nobody laughed.

'The mutineers are going to blow up the bridge!' The words spread through the camp, with rumour and speculation adding details and lies.

'They're looking for you, Thorpey,' Coleman said seriously. 'The pandies heard about how Queen Victoria is cross with you and how handy you were with your pig-sticker.'

'Have they heard that, Coley?' Thorpe looked up in alarm. 'How do they know my name?'

'All the women know your name,' Parker joined in. 'When we were in Gondabad all the bints spoke about you and your medal and how big you were.'

'They want a British soldier as a sacrifice,' Coleman continued. 'They're going to smear you in gun-oil and spread you across the bridge to show how much they hate us.'

'Never!' Thorpe scoffed doubtfully. 'They never said they want me at all.'

'True Briton they did.' Coleman nodded to Parker. 'Ask Parky there. Isn't that right, Parky?'

'As true as I'm from Manchester,' Parker said.

'God.' Thorpe unsheathed his bayonet. 'I'd better get this sharpened then. They're not smearing me in gun oil and sacrificing me, I can tell you.'

Coleman shook his head. 'I'm only saying what I heard.'

'If they blow up the bridge,' Elliot said, 'that could delay us for days. After all this rain the river's in spate, and there's no ford nearby. We'll have to find boats.'

'Up!' Havelock shouted back down the column. 'Up and march!'

'We'll soon find out what's happening,' Jack said as they continued the advance with the countryside cowering under the monsoon rains and their boots splashing through surface water on the road.

'How far is this Pandu Nadi?' Jack asked.

'About five miles,' Elliot said.

'Nana Sahib is doing all he can to prevent us relieving Cawnpore,' Jack said.

'He'll fail,' Elliot responded. 'Have you heard the men? They'll march through Hades to avenge the women and children. The mutineers don't know what devil is within British soldiers when roused.' He grunted. 'Look at them.'

Riley was staring ahead, his eyes tormented as he thought of Charlotte. At his side strode Logan, as ugly as any medieval church gargoyle and a hundred times more dangerous. Thorpe was chewing on something with Coleman telling obscene jokes, Parker was hiding an animal he had rescued, and Williams was striding along, humming some Methodist hymn.

They marched on, with some men falling through heat exhaustion to lie on the road until the baggage waggons, trundling far in the rear, collected them. Jack glanced over his shoulder, hoping Jane and Mary were safe.

'They're waiting for us at the bridge.' The news passed along the column as men adjusted the slings of their rifles, searched for pipe tobacco and hitched up their trousers. 'Bloody pandies don't know when they're beaten.'

Despite their recent defeats, the mutineers were confident of victory. They still far outnumbered the British and halted at the far side of a river, a natural defensive position that they soon augmented.

'They'll be hard to shift from there,' Prentice said.

'Maybe they'll run away when they see us,' Kent hoped.

A sender stone bridge leapt across a deep ravine, at the bottom of which a swollen river churned angrily over rounded boulders. On the opposite side, the mutineers had mounted two heavy guns behind earthworks filled with men.

'It's like a miniature Alma,' Jack said. 'A river to cross under fire from artillery.'

'Except there are a lot less of us,' Elliot said, 'and these are not civilised European troops we are fighting. The Russians took prisoners; these brutes butcher anything white.'

'Helloa,' Prentice said. 'They've woken up!'

As soon as the British column appeared, the mutineers' cannon opened fire. The long dirty-white jets of smoke revealed their position as the ugly flat boom echoed across the plain.

'They have a twenty-four pounder, sure as death,' Prentice said. 'Heavy metal. And the other,' he ducked involuntarily as a second gun roared, 'that is a carronade I think, a short-range smasher. They'll be the very devil to advance against.'

Havelock surveyed the bridge and the defences through a long telescope before giving sharp orders.

'Maude, we need your guns again. And I want men down there,' he pointed to the lateral ravines, 'see if the rebels like more of our Enfields.'

'My men are good shots, sir,' Jack volunteered, and on Havelock's nod, he led twenty of the 113th into the ravine. 'I'll have your rifle, Riordan.'

'But sir, I'll need it.'

Jack ignored Riordan's protests. 'Elliot, you and Prentice look after the others.'

'Yes, sir.' Elliot gave the only possible reply.

The sides of the ravine were steep and defended by thorn bushes and rocks, but they were also screened from the mutineer's fire. With O'Neill, Thorpe, Parker and Coleman at his back, Jack knew he was in good hands. He would have brought Logan and Riley, but he needed to leave some experienced men with Elliot in case the mutineers decided to attack the British positions.

'We've already beaten them once today,' Coleman said, 'can we not have one battle a day in future?'

'I'll be sure and tell Tantia Topi,' Parker said. 'He'll listen to me.'

'Will he Parky?' Thorpe asked.

'Oh, we're old friends,' Parker said. 'We used to go drinking along Scotty Road.'

'You never did!' Thorpe said.

'Every Friday,' Parker said and ducked as a mutineer's bullet whizzed past.

'Watch your flanks!' Jack warned. 'The pandies might have skirmishers out.'

Fortunately, the angle of the ravine allowed the British to outflank some of the mutineers' positions. Ignoring the roar of the torrent below, Jack nestled behind a rock and aimed his borrowed rifle, blinking away the sweat and peering through the heat-haze. 'Fire when you're ready,' he said.

The sharp bark of the Enfields followed on his last word and Coleman's evil chuckle. 'There's one pandy who won't rape a white woman again.'

Although the mutineers returned fire, they were outranged by the Enfield rifles and their casualties soon mounted.

The booms of the mutineers' artillery continued until Maude manhandled his guns forward and brought them into action. After only a single British volley, the opposing artillery ceased. Maude subjected their positions to a heavy bombardment.

'Help the guns, boys,' Jack ordered. 'Target the mutineer officers.'

'The Fusiliers are attacking, sir,' O'Neill reported as the Madras Fusiliers and the 78th Highlanders swarmed toward the bridge, losing men to enemy fire. As they neared the far side, there was a massive explosion and a huge plume of smoke. Pieces of masonry rose high in the air and began to descend through the smoke, some landing in the ravine among the men of the 113th.

'Oh Jesus, they've blown the bridge!' O'Neill stared at the mess.

'Watch your heads, men!' Jack watched with a heavy heart. If the mutineers had destroyed the bridge, they could delay the British advance for days, giving the enemy time to gather more men and leaving Havelock's tiny army very vulnerable.

The smoke flattened and eventually cleared. Jack saw that although there were ragged holes in the parapet and some British casualties, the bridge itself remained intact. The mutineers' explosives hadn't succeeded.

The Fusiliers and Highlanders were cheering as they charged across the remains, faces contorted with fury. They reached the mutineers' guns in moments and began work with the bayonets. After a few seconds of frantic slashing and stabbing, the enemy was running again.

'That was a smart piece of work,' Jack said. He watched Maude limber up and haul his artillery across the bridge, unlimber in minutes and fire after the mutineers. 'General Havelock knows how to defeat the enemy. What a pity we didn't have him in the Crimea.'

'Thank the Lord we have him here,' Prentice said.

'I'm sure Holy Havelock would agree.' Elliot uncorked his hip flask and took a deep draught. 'We should thank the Lord.'

Chapter Ten

It took all day for the baggage train to cross the damaged bridge with Mary and Jane cheerfully waving as they passed the 113th.

'Wave back, then, Jack,' Elliot urged. 'She's your girl after all.'

'She's not my girl,' Jack said and ignored Elliot's amused grin.

'She's a better girl than Helen Maxwell ever was,' Elliot said softly.

Once they reached the far side, Havelock called for an overnight halt. After two battles in one day, the men lay in exhaustion.

'We're getting there, Riles.' Logan looked without appetite at the hunk of raw beef that was their food for the day. 'Every day brings us closer to your wife.'

Riley leant against the trunk of a peepul tree, staring northward. 'She'd better be alive,' he said. 'These pandy bastards had better not have hurt her.'

'You'd better eat,' Logan said.

'I'm not bloody hungry.' Riley bit into his army-issue biscuit and took a sip of beer to wash away the taste.

'You'll need your strength.' Without another word, Logan began to gather wood for a fire. With the ground sodden it was not an easy task, yet for a veteran of the Sebastopol siege it was not impossible. Jack watched for a few moments and then extracted a few spare tent poles from a commissariat waggon.

'Here, Logan. Firewood.'

'Thank you, sir.' Logan's scowl may have been one of gratitude; it was hard to tell.

'How's he bearing up?'

'Riley?' Logan was immediately defensive. 'He'll be all right, sir. He's worried about his missus.'

'I know.' Jack felt for his non-existent cheroots. 'You take care of him, Logan and hopefully we'll be in Cawnpore soon.'

'Yes, sir.'

The heat and humidity of the night combined to make sleep impossible. Jack lay fully dressed on his cot with his arms folded behind his head and his mind full of possibilities and worries. Twice he unfolded Helen's letter and read the contents, and twice he refolded it and tucked it away.

He thought of Riley, suffering at the thought of Charlotte either dead or in the hands of the mutineers. He thought of the rapid successes over the enemy of the last few days and compared them to the long-drawn-out agony of the Crimea. He thought of the massacre at Gondabad and the dead men hanging beside the Great Trunk Road out of Allahabad. He thought about Sarvur Khan.

This confused campaign was his third within five years and the worst. In Burma and the Crimea, he had been facing a known enemy of his country – this was a civil war, fighting people who had been friends and colleagues only weeks before. It felt wrong, yet he knew his men hated these mutineers even more than they had hated the Russians.

And then there was Mary and Jane. Jack knew he would probably never see either of them after this campaign, yet both remained in his head for entirely different reasons. Jane had been open about her friendship with his father, and for that reason alone he wanted to ask her a thousand questions, yet he didn't know how. With Mary... Jack smiled. He felt extremely comfortable with Mary, yet there was also an edge of excitement he enjoyed. He had never been sure how Helen would react to anything he said or did; she had been impulsive, a devil-may-care youth who sought adventure. Mary was more considered, she was far more mature. Jack knew that even thinking about her brought a smile to his face. Elliot had been wrong though – she wasn't his sweetheart and never would be. He fell asleep with that certainty.

'We have twenty-three miles to march before we reach Cawnpore.' Havelock addressed his assembled officers. 'Nana Sahib is leading seven thousand men to try and stop us.'

He waited for comments. There were none.

'I have also heard there are two hundred women and children still held in Cawnpore.'

Jack looked up, thinking of Riley. 'That's good news, sir.'

'I agree, Windrush. The Lord has given us hope and with God's help we shall save them, or every man of us will die in the attempt.'

There was no cheering from the officers; Havelock was not a man to inspire cheers. Instead, there was a low fighting growl and the nodding of heads. Jack looked around the tiny band of warriors who were intent on defeating a much larger army, storming a city with a garrison of unknown numbers and freeing the captives inside. They didn't look like heroes, only like ordinary British soldiers on campaign, yet they had already defeated larger armies of trained enemy soldiers and thrown them out of defensive positions.

'We are short of rum for the men,' Havelock continued, 'and more importantly, we are short of Enfield ammunition. I have requested both, plus another two hundred European troops from Colonel – now Brigadier General – Neill.' He looked directly at Jack with his sharp gaze. 'We will need more men, gentlemen; for once we have relieved Cawnpore, I intend to relieve Lucknow.'

Jack knew the sepoys had mutinied in that graceful city of palaces, where Sir Henry Lawrence commanded a garrison of British men, women and children in the Residency building. Lawrence was repelling massed rebel attacks and hoped for relief by somebody.

'Fight, march, fight.' Elliot had managed to requisition one of the scarce bottles of rum for himself. 'That's all we do.'

'It's what we're paid for,' Jack said. 'It's part of the soldier's bargain.'

The day brought a sixteen-mile march to Maharajpur with an unrelenting sun drawing sweat from the men until they were dehydrated and staggered with heatstroke and exhaustion. Somewhere in front was Nana Sahib's army, and beyond that was Cawnpore itself, and the suffering women and children.

'Captain Barrow,' Havelock ordered. 'Ride ahead and see what's happening.'

Sweltering in the heat, Barrow of the Madras Fusiliers touched a hand to his hat and spurred on, northward. Within half an hour he reported to Havelock with two loyal sepoys of the Bengal Army. Their nervous reserve did nothing to disguise their courage.

'Did you hear the shave?' Elliot asked.

'Tell me,' Jack said.

'Nana Sahib is in position ahead, waiting for us.'

'Does that man never give up? Thank goodness Havelock has his measure.' Jack's fingers fluttered toward his empty top pocket. God, he missed his cheroots. 'Where is he?'

'The road splits ahead,' Elliot said. 'The Grand Trunk goes straight on, and a smaller road leads to Cawnpore. Nana Sahib is about half a mile along the branch road with five thousand men and eight pieces of artillery.'

'Five thousand men!' Jack sighed. 'About four times our number. How strong is his position?'

'I don't know, yet,' Elliot said. 'Give me time, but these Indian lads know all about terrain. He'll have found a good spot to defend, depend on it.'

'We'll see,' Jack said. 'Make sure the men have ammunition, and they have all eaten. I don't like them fighting on an empty stomach.'

Nana Sahib had chosen his position with care, with an area of marshy ground, watered by monsoon rains, acting as a defensive barrier for his centre.

'The marsh will slow down any advance,' Jack said, sweeping the area with his borrowed telescope. 'Nobody could charge across that, and if they tried, the mutineers have artillery.' He pointed to a baked-mud earthwork where a twenty-four-pounder howitzer and a long nine-pounder poked their long snouts forward. 'Death in a brass casing. We can't try a frontal attack, then.'

He focussed on Nana Sahib's left, where a walled village crowned a wooded hillock a mile from the mighty Ganges River. The gaping muzzles of three twenty-four pounder cannon grinned evilly forward.

'We'll be outranged and outgunned as well as outnumbered by trained men,' Jack said. 'Perhaps Nana's right flank is weaker.'

The telescope revealed a mango grove, dripping with water, with another walled village inside, from where two more cannons angled across the front of the lines. The mutineers' position was about a quarter of a mile in length, a great crescent of armed men, waiting.

'He's aimed his guns toward the road junction,' Jack said. 'If we try to advance that way, he'll be able to dice us with concentrated fire. He's a sound soldier, this Nana Sahib.'

Well aware of the strength of the mutineers' position and the numerical weakness of his force, Havelock didn't waste lives with a frontal attack.

'Some of you men,' he addressed his officers, 'may be students of military history. Do you remember Frederick the Great at Leuthen?'

'He made a flanking attack,' Elliot said at once.

'Which is exactly what we will do,' Havelock said. 'We've beaten the mutineers three times so far on this march. With God's grace we will inflict another defeat, and then it's onto Cawnpore and the rescue of our women.'

The men ate first, sitting by the side of the road, knowing they were going into the largest battle of the campaign so far, knowing Nana Sahib had mustered his entire army to stop them, but determined to win.

'One more battle,' Riley said. 'One more and I'll see Charlotte again.'

'That's the way, Riley.' Logan sat at his side, sharpening his already viciously sharp bayonet. 'We'll give these pandies a towelling and it's full speed to Cawnpore and rescue your wife, eh?'

Something like a smile twisted across Riley's mouth. 'Yes. I don't trust these pandies with women and children.'

'They'll be all right. Charlotte's too canny to be hurt by any bad-mash.' Logan patted Riley's shoulder. 'Cheer up, Riley – we've been through too much to stop now, and Charlotte will be waiting for you, eh?'

Jack walked away. He couldn't help and felt he was eavesdropping on a very personal conversation. They marched forward, toward the mutineers' positions, toward Nana Sahib's main army, and with Cawn-pore the prize in the distance. The rain began again, hissing onto the paddy-fields, pattering onto trees and bouncing off the road.

'Cry Havelock,' Elliot shouted,' and let loose the dogs of war!'

'Havelock,' Prentice repeated the name without enthusiasm.

With his few mounted volunteers riding around his force, Havelock advanced the column along the Grand Trunk Road until about half a mile from the fork where a line of trees gave some cover.

'We'll halt here,' Havelock said, 'and engage the enemy. Barrow, take a company of the Madras Fusiliers ahead, on either side of the road. Make lots of noise and act like the whole army.'

'Yes, sir.' Barrow was a grey-headed Captain with a cheerful smile. 'Did you hear the general, Fusiliers? You are to pretend you're the whole army!'

'We are the whole army, sir!' a Fusilier sergeant shouted. 'These Queen's men are just here to make up the numbers.'

'Cheeky bugger!' Logan reacted predictably. 'Go on, John Company; give them hell!'

Jack watched as the cavalry and Fusiliers extended into skirmishing order and spread out on both sides of the road. Within a few minutes, the mutineers' artillery opened fire, lambasting the road junction they believed Havelock's men would have to take.

'Bloody fools; they should have held their fire until they saw the main body,' Prentice said. 'They're wasting ammunition and firing at nothing.'

With the mutineers blasting away, Havelock led his main force through the screen of trees that sheltered them from the left flank of Nana Sahib's position.

'We've left the baggage behind,' Kent said, 'the pandies could take it and cut us off from Allahabad.' He looked over his shoulder. 'Havelock has forgotten the basic rules of war.'

'He knows what he's doing,' Prentice said.

'But we're trapped between the mutineers and the Ganges,' Kent said. 'If they attack us, we've nowhere to retreat.'

'We won't be withdrawing,' Jack said quietly. 'There's no retreat in this war. We fight and we win, or we die, and British rule ends.'

'Havelock outsmarted you again, pandy-boy,' Elliot said as the mutineers hastily tried to drag their guns to meet the new threat on their flank.

The British marched on, ignoring the mutineers' shot that soon battered down on them. Men fell to lie still or thrash in agony under the pelting rain.

'When do we fire back?' Kent ducked as a roundshot screamed overhead.

'Don't bob!' Jack said. 'The men don't like to see officers bobbing. We're advancing to Nana Sahib's flank.' He checked on the men; they marched steadily, rifles slung over their shoulders, heads down. The 113th had faced worse in the Crimea; they were dogged and determined but some of the younger soldiers in the 84th and 64th winced as the mutineer's heavy artillery thundered around them.

In front and on the left flank, the kilted 78th fixed bayonets.

Jack nodded. 'Havelock is going to do a Gough,' he said and raised his voice. 'Bayonets... fix!'

'Get the buggers!' Logan's voice was distinct. 'Take the bayonet to them!'

The British marched on, with three of the mutineers' guns able to bear on them and the iron balls crashing out, killing and maiming the advancing men.

'Give the order!' Jack heard Riley's voice behind him. 'Give the order!'

'The 78th will charge,' Havelock ordered.

'Why not us?' Riley asked.

Although Jack had seen the advance of Campbell's Highlanders at the Alma, and the stand of the 93rd at Balaclava, it was the first time he had witnessed a full Highland charge. He watched with professional interest.

Colonel Hamilton was in the van, and the pipers played the high pibroch of the glens to encourage men who needed no encouragement. There was no other sound, no cheering and not a shot was fired as the 78th swarmed forward with kilts swaying and bayonets probing. The twenty-four-pounder fired grape-shot as they crossed flooded fields, felling men and causing the waters to foam and fizz. As the Highlanders closed with pointing bayonets, the gunners panicked and left the cannon. Now there was a cheer as the 78th leapt over the defending wall of the village and down into the mutineers' positions.

'Shabash the 78th!' O'Neill shouted.

For a few moments, there was a frantic melee as the Highlanders raised and plunged home their bayonets, and when the triangular blades bent, they finished the job with rifle-butt and then pushed on, rolling up the mutineers' flank.

'It's us now!' As the Highlanders dealt with the rebels in the village, the whole British line advanced against the enemy's positions. The mutineers hadn't been idle, and their twenty-four-pounder opened fire.

'We're pushing them back!' Elliot said. The mutineers were slowly abandoning their positions in the face of the British bayonets, but they were not going easily. A British soldier looked in horror as a tulwar sliced his arm clean off; another fell sideways, his left leg severed. The mutineers were not giving in easily.

'The twenty-four-pounder will cause damage,' Jack said. He saw Havelock gallop across to the 78th and point urgently sideways.

The gesture was sufficient. With hardly a pause, the Highlanders flowed over to the gun in a welter of tartan, bare knees and gleaming bayonets. Some of the mutineers attempted to fight back; others turned at the sight of the charging 78th. The result was never in doubt as the Highlanders thrust forward with bayonet, boot and rifle-butt.

'The pandies are running.' Beads of sweat balanced on Elliot's eyebrows.

'Not very fast,' Jack said. 'They're still organised.'

The bulk of the mutineers withdrew to another village around a mile down the road, where they waited for the pursuing British.

'Stay in your formation, 113th!' Jack restrained the more eager of his men and glanced over the advance. The 64th were on the left, the 113th and the 78th in the centre and the Madras Fusiliers on the right. In front, still vastly outnumbering Havelock's column, the mutineers shouted challenges.

Exhaustion and heat forced the British to stop, with men collapsing on the road and others draining their water-bottles as they faced this new threat. The rebels waited, peering down the sights of muskets and rifles, brandishing the terrible tulwars, preparing the artillery. Jack focussed his telescope and swore. Sarvur Khan was in the centre of the enemy lines, smart and suave as ever, with a long Khyber knife thrust through his belt and a *jezail,* the Afghan musket, balanced over his shoulder.

'You bastard,' Jack said softly. 'You murdering, oath-breaking bastard.'

Havelock rode in front of the British, small and dapper, with his eyes darting around, seeing everything. He knew his men. Rather than appeal to glory or valour, he used the old British method of inter-regimental rivalry.

'Come, who is to take that village, the Highlanders or the 64th?'

'How about the 113th?' Coleman asked indignantly.

'Who cares about the baby butchers?' an Irish voice jeered. 'Watch the 64th and learn how it's done!'

Jack couldn't understand the Gaelic response of the Highlanders, but there was no mistaking their resolve. They quickly formed a line, pushed the light company to the flank to provide covering fire and advanced, shoulder-to-shoulder with the younger men of the 64th Foot.

Jack and the 113th could only watch as the mutineers' skirmishers held their ground for only a few moments until the 78th and 64th scattered them and plunged on to the village.

'Should we join in, sir?' Coleman stamped his boots on the ground.

'We should stay put and wait for orders,' Jack said.

As the 78th and 64th cleared the village, the Madras Fusiliers advanced into the flanking plantation and drove out the defenders at the point of the bayonet.

'Now's our time,' Jack said as the 113th and the remainder of the British followed on, joined up with the 78th and 64th and formed up as Havelock gave his usual brisk orders.

'Consolidate,' Havelock said briefly, 'fill your water bottles and march on. Follow the enemy.'

'We don't know what's ahead,' Jack said. 'The mutineers may have fled right back to Cawnpore, or they may try another stand.'

Elliot nodded, wiping the sweat from his face. 'We'll soon find out.'

Filling their water-bottles from the village well, the British moved on, regiment after regiment with their equipment rattling and boots chunking on the ground, men sweating, swearing and wilting under the sun as the Indian plain slid past. Ahead, the road rose to a small ridge, apparently shimmering in the heat.

'Cawnpore's not far away now,' Logan said. 'Your Charlotte will be pleased to see you, eh?'

'I hope so,' Riley said. 'I've gone to a lot of trouble getting together all these men and guns, just to rescue her.'

'Aye, Queen Vicky done you proud,' Logan said.

The instant Havelock's men breasted the rise the mutineers' artillery opened up. Orange flames jetted through a haze of smoke, and busy artillerymen could be seen darting around the breeches of their guns.

'Oh, good God.' Jack stopped. 'Nana Sahib has gathered all the mutineers and rebels in Hindustan.'

The rebel army stood before them, once more blocking their route to Cawnpore, with a twenty-four-pounder in the centre, flanked by a pair of smaller pieces. Rank upon rank of mutineers waited for the British to attack.

'And there's Nana Sahib himself.'

The rebel chief was sitting on an elephant, walking up and down the ranks of his men while a band played the wailing Indian music that Jack found strangely appealing. He stared at Nana Sahib, wondering what was in his mind as he led his army against the people who had occupied India for so long they thought of it as home. A stray shaft of sunlight flashed on a ring on Nana Sahib's left hand.

'Lie down.' Havelock's order came. 'Lie on the ground.'

Rather than stand to offer an easy target, the British lay down in their ranks, as they had done at Waterloo.

'Keep your locks dry,' Jack shouted. 'Keep the rain from the muzzles! Anyone with a rusty rifle will have me to answer to – if he lives!'

'It's nearly impossible to keep away the rust in these conditions,' Elliot responded.

'They can try,' Jack replied. 'It may save their lives.' He glanced over his men. 'Nana against Havelock in a straight fight! We've marched twenty miles today and fought a quite stiff action. Our artillery is still trundling up the road, while our horses are exhausted, and the few cavalrymen we have are utterly knocked up.'

'All the odds are in Nana Sahib's favour,' Prentice agreed.

Jack looked forward. 'How many men does Nana Sahib have?' Nana Sahib had arranged his army in three units, with the twenty-four-pounder already hammering at the British ranks. 'Eight thousand? Ten thousand? And by the look of it, many of them are fresh against our haggard few hundred.'

Elliot sipped at the contents of his silver hip-flask and offered it to Jack. 'He must have emptied every man from Cawnpore.'

Shaking his head to the flask, Jack checked his revolver. 'This won't be an easy victory.'

'No victory is easy for the men who fall.' Elliot drank again.

With his previous horse shot from under him, Havelock now rode a small pony, which was hardly an inspiring sight compared to the huge elephant of Nana Sahib. Ignoring the plunging shot from the muti-neers' twenty-four-pounder, Havelock turned his back on the enemy to address his men. Jack thought his voice was more higher-pitched than usual, either through tiredness or nervous strain.

'The longer you look at it, men, the less you will like it. Rise up. The Brigade will advance, left battalion leading.'

'Never us,' Elliot muttered. 'Does that man not know I need to be a hero, so I can advance in rank and be a field marshal and please my father?'

'Obviously not,' Jack said. 'You'll have to remind him. Here we go again.'

'Cry Havelock!' Elliot shouted.

'And let loose the dogs of war!' Prentice finished for him.

They moved forward slowly, with solid shot from the twenty-four-pounder hammering them, pulping men into scarcely recognisable jel-lies of blood and brain, meat and crushed bone. Behind the regular deep boom of the gun, Indian music drifted toward them as Nana in-spired his men to fight.

At three hundred yards, with the mutineers' forces becoming ever clearer, the cannon changed to grapeshot that scythed through the British ranks. Men fell, screaming, with legs and arms missing and intestines spilt over the sodden earth.

'Good shooting,' Elliot approved. His nerves had calmed as soon as the battle began, as they always did. 'We trained them well.'

'Too well,' Prentice said.

With Major Sterling and Lieutenant Henry Havelock well in front, the 64th led the assault. Men were dropping, the dead to lie still, the wounded to writhe and kick and groan but the remainder advanced in a silence whose grimness must have chilled the defenders. Only when they were close did the 64th let out a cheer, lower their bayonets and plunge forward toward the massive cannon.

'*Shabash* the 64th!' O'Neill shouted as the British advanced.

There was a sudden roar of musketry from the mutineers, accom-panied by orange jets of flame through thick powder-smoke. Men fell, knocked back by the force of musket-balls, to lie still or twist in pain. After the first volley, the mutineers' fire altered to a long-drawn clatter and then as the British wall advanced, they turned and retreated, still in some formation.

'Stand and fight, you cowards!' Logan shouted. 'I want to kill you!'

'Look,' Elliot touched Jack's arm. 'The guns.'

For hours the British artillery had been bogged down a mile in the rear with their bullocks too exhausted to move. Now four cannon had arrived in the midst of the brigade. They hurriedly unlimbered and busy gunners loaded, aimed and fired with more speed than Jack had ever witnessed before.

'The pandies don't like that much,' Elliot said, as Havelock waved them on.

The 113th crossed the earthwork barrier with its dead and dying mutineers, knowing they had defeated a more numerous enemy, knowing they had won once more and not caring about anything except the result. They pushed on with the artillery punishing the retreating mutineers and the miles to Cawnpore diminishing with every hour.

'Look! Away in the distance; there are our artillery barracks!' Prentice pointed forward. 'There's Cawnpore!'

The fast semi-tropical night was rushing in on them as the mutineer army finally disintegrated and fled, leaving nothing between Havelock's men and Cawnpore except a couple of miles of open territory.

'We've done it.' Prentice sounded amazed. 'Holy Havelock's battered our way through to Cawnpore.'

'We've beaten them in five battles,' Elliot said, 'and today they outnumbered us by five to one and in a good defensive position.'

Jack nodded. 'We lost some good men, though. I'd guess about a hundred casualties there.'

'Stuart Beatson's gone, I hear,' Elliot added quietly. 'Cholera.'

'The Adjutant-General? We'll miss his hard work.' Jack ran his gaze down the length of the column. There seemed very few men to retake a city. He heard a snatch of conversation from the ranks.

'This time tomorrow, Riley, you'll be with Charlotte,' Logan was saying. 'You can cheer up then and stop being such a sour-faced bugger.'

'The men sound happy,' Elliot said. 'Normally after a battle, they are quiet and thoughtful.'

'They know we're saving the women,' Jack said. 'They're hungry and tired, with no shelter or food, but they've won their self-respect.'

Dapper and unruffled, Havelock rode his pony around the men, told them he was "satisfied and more than satisfied with them", nodded and withdrew to his tent.

'High praise from Holy Havelock,' Jack said. 'Tomorrow the men get their real reward.' He saw Riley stare toward Cawnpore, touched Helen's letter and shook his head.

Bloody woman.

And then he looked down the road, wondered where the baggage train was and hoped Mary was all right.

Chapter Eleven

There was an explosion from Cawnpore during the night as the men lay muttering and shaking with reaction on the damp ground. Some looked up from fitful sleep; others turned over and heard nothing.

'What the devil?' Jack jerked upright.

'I've no idea,' Elliot said.

The reflected glare faded slowly while a whiff of powder-smoke reached them from the city, some two miles away. 'Nana Sahib is saying goodbye,' Jack guessed. He lay down again, decided he couldn't sleep and rose to inspect his men. Most were asleep, with the pickets on watch leaning on their rifles and staring at Cawnpore or into the darkness around the camp. One of the 113th had died of dysentery during the night.

'There's pandy cavalry out there,' Coleman said. 'I can hear their hooves hammering.'

'If they get too close, Coleman, you have my permission to shoot them.'

'Oh, aye, sir, I'll do that all right.' Coleman sucked on an empty pipe. 'Did you hear the shave, sir?'

'Which one, Coleman?'

Coleman dropped his voice to a whisper. 'They say Nana Sahib murdered all the women and children, sir.'

Despite the humidity of the night, Jack felt a chill run down his spine. 'Oh God, I hope not. Best not let Riley hear that, Coleman. He is anxious about his wife.'

'I know, sir.' Coleman lifted his head. 'I hope it's only a lie.'

'So do I, Coleman, so do I.' Taking a deep breath, Jack continued his circuit of the British lines. The darkness of India seemed to become more intense, the heat more oppressive.

When rumour crystallised into fact, the mood of the British hardened.

'Not Charlotte,' Riley said, again and again. 'They can't have killed Charlotte.' He sat on the ground, head in his hands, with Logan at his side.

'It may not be true,' Logan said. 'Charlotte might have got away.' He looked up, face twisted in grief for his friend. 'Tell him, sir. Tell Riley that Charlotte could still be alive.'

'I wish I could, Logan,' Jack said truthfully. Riley was a friend as well as one of his men. They had gone through a lot together in the Crimea, and he was as close to him as to a brother; closer, Jack thought, remembering how his half-brother William had treated him.

'We'll be in Cawnpore today, Riley.' He tried to help. 'We don't know anything for sure until then.'

'We'll kill them all, Riley,' Logan responded in the only way he knew, the law of an eye for an eye he had learned in the horrendous slums of Glasgow. 'We'll kill every murdering black pandy bastard in India. Don't you worry, mate. We'll get them for you.'

Jack put a hand on Riley's shoulder and turned away. Nothing he said could help. He expected the tears in Riley's eyes; he was surprised at the raw emotion that Logan didn't bother to hide. Iron-hard men such as Donnie Logan were not expected to show sympathy and grief.

This campaign was changing them all.

Jack had never experienced the atmosphere with which Havelock's column entered Cawnpore. The determination and anger on the march from Allahabad was compounded many times by the ugly rumours.

British soldiers were not naturally bloodthirsty; they were professionals who fought when they had to, but these men wanted to kill.

'It's as well that Nana Sahib has not stood again.' Elliot said. 'He blew up the magazine and fled; we all heard the explosion. The lads would have killed every single one of the mutineers after hearing of the murder of the women.'

Thinking of Riley, Jack nodded. 'We'll get the bastard,' he said. 'We'll hang draw and quarter him.'

Elliot glanced at Jack, opened his mouth to speak, thought better of it and closed it again.

Some of the inhabitants of Cawnpore gathered to watch the British arrive. Most cowered away or ran when they saw the set faces of the British soldiers. These were not the rough, friendly raucous *lalkurti* they had come to know, but another breed entirely. The city waited in apprehension close to fear to see how the British would react.

'Did you hear what happened here?' The 113th clustered outside the house known as the Bibighur, where Nana Sahib imprisoned the women and children. Elliot spoke quietly, with his knuckles white as he gripped the hilt of his sword.

Jack nodded. 'I heard.'

Elliot continued; he had to talk to release the images of horror from his mind. 'Old General Wheeler trusted in Nana's loyalty, but Nana turned traitor and assumed the leadership of the mutineers and rebels.'

'We know that.' Jack wished Elliot would keep quiet so he could be alone with his thoughts.

'So Wheeler got the few defenders and all the woman and children into a shallow entrenchment, surrounded by thousands and thousands of the rebels. He held out for three weeks, repulsing every rebel attack and the women and even the children playing their part.'

Jack thought of an open entrenchment under the Indian summer sun, with women and children lacking food or medical supplies and having no sanitation. He thought of the rebels firing at them day and night and the wounded piling up, and the women exposed to hideous sights and sounds. 'I see.' He didn't hear the harshness in his voice.

Elliot continued, speaking slowly and with a vacant expression on his face. 'Seeing the condition of the women, Wheeler agreed to surrender as long as the women and children were given safe passage out of Cawnpore. The men, you see, would take their chances.'

'He was thinking of the women and trusting to the word of Nana Sahib.' Jack touched the butt of his revolver.

'Nana Sahib agreed and brought boats to Sati Chaura Ghat on the Ganges. He promised the British safe passage to Allahabad. When Wheeler brought the garrison out of the entrenchment and onto the ghat, the mutineers attacked with swords, rifles and bayonets.'

Jack pictured the scene, the heat and the flies, the hope of the women, the crying children and the sudden swoop by the mutineers. He thought of the swish of the river, the fear and the shouts, the women screaming, the men trying to fight back, the blood swirling greasy on the water. He said nothing.

'They had no chance,' Elliot said. 'The pandies burned the boats and murdered nearly all the men, old General Wheeler among them. They dragged the woman and children who survived from the river. They robbed the survivors of everything they had, all jewels and personal possessions and rebels took them to a building known as Savada Kothee and then here, to the Bibighar.'

Jack nodded. The Bibighar stood within the compound of the cantonment magistrate. It was respectably sized, large but not huge and had a courtyard with a central well.

'The house of the ladies,' he translated without effort or expression.

'If you say so,' Elliot said. 'About two hundred women and children crammed in here, some wounded, all in fear, many recently widowed. Cholera came, and dysentery.'

Jack thought of the sounds and smells and feelings of these women, imprisoned so far from home, hoping the British relief column could save them. He said nothing.

'Nana Sahib did not bother about the women,' Elliot said. 'He put some prostitute called Houssaini in charge, and she made them work, grinding corn for food. Nana wanted to keep the women as insurance, hostages, but when he heard our column was advancing and smashing everything they put in our path, he ordered them all murdered.'

'Yes.' Jack said only one word. If he said more, he would un-man himself by breaking into tears, and English gentlemen did not cry. He looked toward the well, imagining the women and children here waiting for relief with their hopes rising as they learned about Havelock's victories.

'I heard two versions of the story,' Elliot spoke in a steady monotone. 'The first said Nana Sahib himself ordered the sepoys to put their muskets through the windows and shoot the women, and the second said it was the prostitute, Houssaini, who gave the order.'

'It matters little who gave the word,' Jack said.

'I heard that the sepoys fired one volley and then couldn't continue; they were sickened by the screams of the children and women and refused to fire more. Nana or Houssaini called them cowards and all sorts of things. Either Nana or Houssaini called up a bunch of butchers, with a Pathan in charge.'

'Sarvur Khan.' Jack knew the name without being told.

'Yes, sir. He was said to be Hossaini's lover. He and the butchers entered the building and chopped the women up with meat cleavers.'

'Oh, sweet Jesus in heaven,' Jack said. 'Oh, dear God.' He looked toward the well, knowing there was worse to come.

'They stripped the bodies, men, women and children – defenceless, innocent children and women, and threw them down the well. This well in this compound.'

Jack nodded again. The men of the 113th were around the building, together with the 78th Highlanders and the 64th and 84th Foot. 'I'm going inside,' he said.

'Best not,' Elliot said.

'I have to,' Jack said. He entered the Bibighar. Riley and Logan were already there; Riley was fighting to keep back his tears, while Logan's arm was tight around his shoulders. Logan's face twisted with grief for his friend, and he was intoning the same word again and again.

'Bastards; bastards; bastards.'

A fur of flies feasted on the blood that in places was an inch deep on the floor, with the walls marked and scored with the scars of cleavers. Women's and children's clothing was piled in the corners and scattered through the echoing rooms and in the courtyard itself. Jack saw a baby's bonnet floating in a puddle of blood, while a pink ribbon tangled around a tuft of fair, downy hair.

'Oh, dear God in heaven.'

He saw a great-bearded Highland sergeant pick up a blood-soaked child's jacket and press it to his lips while tears rolled unheeded down his cheeks. He saw some of the men secreting small pieces of women's clothing inside their tunics and swearing revenge on the pandies.

God have mercy on the mutineers now, because I won't, and these British soldiers won't. Not after this.

'I must find Charlotte,' Riley said. 'I must find Charlotte.' Sinking to his knees, he paddled about in the blood, lifting pieces of clothing, inspecting them and putting them away. 'That's not hers. That's not hers.'

'What's that madman doing?' A broad- faced corporal of the 84th asked and jerked back as Logan grabbed him by the throat.

'None of your business! You mind your own affairs!'

'Logan.' Jack pulled him clear. 'Ignore them. You look after Riley.'

'Yes, sir,' Logan said, glowering hatred at the startled corporal. 'Come on Riley, I'll help.' Without hesitation, Logan joined Riley on his knees in the blood and searched through the debris for anything that may have belonged to Charlotte.

Blinking the tears from his eyes, Jack walked to the well. He had been dreading this moment ever since he heard what it contained. Taking a deep breath as the crowd parted for him, he looked in.

The reality was worse than anything he could have imagined. Bloodied heads and bare arms, naked legs and gashed torsos of women and children filled the well to within a few feet of the brim.

'We have to get them out.' Riley sounded nearly calm as he stared down at the scene of sickening slaughter, buzzing with questing flies. 'Charlotte's in there somewhere. We have to get them out.'

'Come on Riley.' Jack eased him away. 'Come on.'

'Sir.' Riley pulled against him. 'Sir, Charlotte's in there! I must get her out.'

'Somebody will retrieve her, Riley,' Jack said. 'She'll get a Christian burial. I promise you.'

'Charlotte!' Riley raised his voice to a shout, 'Charlotte!'

'Come on Riley,' Logan said urgently. 'Come away with me.'

Coleman and Thorpe appeared with Parker, who had a small dog in his arms. 'Come on Riley, son,' Coleman said. 'Charlotte is safe now.' He looked up at Jack. 'We'll take care of him, sir.'

'He's one of my men,' Jack said.

'If he gets into trouble,' Coleman explained rationally, 'you'll have to put him on a charge, while me and the boys will just cover it up.'

'Off you go then, Coleman.' Jack understood the logic.

'The boys are going mad,' Elliot reported later. 'They've found a warehouse full of wine and spirits, and they're drinking themselves to insanity and attacking any native they come across.'

Jack thought of the butchery of the women and children. 'That's not surprising,' he said.

'It's like Badajoz all over again,' Elliot said.

'I didn't think British soldiers would act in such a manner.' Kent had been in the town. 'It's disgusting; drinking, looting and rioting.' He lowered his voice and spoke in hushed tones. 'I even believe they were cavorting with the women of the town. You know, the ladies of the streets.'

'Whores.' Prentice found the words for him. 'Or even prostitutes.' He smiled. 'Yes, British soldiers use such women and just as well too. Imagine if they did not... they might go after respectable ladies instead.'

'I've been looking for Major Snodgrass,' Jack said. 'After he brought our women here, he must have joined the garrison. I presume he died at the ghat massacre.'

'I haven't heard his name mentioned,' Elliot said.

Jack shrugged, slightly ashamed of himself for being so callous toward a fellow officer. Although he had never liked Snodgrass, he was one of the 113th and as such a brother-in-arms. 'Let's hope he turns up.'

'He won't be a loss,' Elliot said. 'I never took to him.'

Jack raised his eyebrows. For Elliot, a man of a nearly perennial sunny disposition, to openly say such a thing showed how much this campaign had altered them all.

After the stress and danger of the advance and the horror of the Bibighur, the soldiers – British and Sikh – who had relieved Cawnpore, drank themselves to a frenzy of looting and carnage.

'You two had better keep out of the streets,' Jack said as Mary and Jane sat in the shade within the house he'd requisitioned for the officers of the 113th. 'The men are going crazy out there.'

'How is poor Riley?' Jane asked.

'He's a broken man,' Jack said truthfully.

'He is hurting,' Jane said. 'He is hurting badly. He thinks he could have done something more to help her.'

'What makes you think that?' Jack asked.

'He is a good man,' Jane said. 'Not an angel; he's a bit of a rogue, but he's honest with his wife.'

'We'll be moving on soon,' Jack said. 'We're going to relieve Lucknow next. You two stay here. The mutineers won't be giving much trouble after the drubbings General Havelock has handed them.'

'Who's taking charge here?' Jane asked.

'General Neill,' Jack said. 'He's the man the mutineers fear, so you'll be all right.' He saw the women exchange glances. 'I want no more of your nonsense now, you two!'

'There will be no nonsense,' Jane promised. 'Will there, Mary?'

'Oh, no nonsense at all,' Mary said, and although her face was straight, Jack saw the twinkle of mischief in her deep brown eyes.

'I mean it!' he blustered.

'I know you do,' Jane said. 'Isn't he sweet when he tries to take command?'

Mary smiled without replying, and Jack shook his head. He refused to be irritated by the jibes of a woman. Mary's eyes altered to deep sorrow.

'The well was an awful thing to find.' Jane was looking directly at Jack. 'It will affect you as well as your men.'

'Yes,' Jack said. The images were too fresh in his mind for coherent speech or thought.

'Try not to think of it,' Jane continued.

'My men are angry,' Jack said. 'They want to kill every mutineer, and everybody who might be a mutineer.'

'God knows what General Neill will do,' Mary said. 'He was like a mad dog before. When he gets here and sees this.' She looked away. 'Cawnpore will not be a safe place.'

Jack wondered anew how it must feel to be Eurasian, not quite belonging to either camp. He grunted – he imagined it was a bit like it felt to be the illegitimate son of a general and a kitchen maid.

'My men know you,' he spoke to them both. 'Stay close to the 113th for now. If there is any problem, mention my name if it's an officer, or shout for the 113th if it's anybody else.' He forced a weak grin. 'There you are; you have fifty of the toughest blackguards in the British Army as bodyguards.'

'General Neill far outranks you,' Mary said.

'If Neill or anybody else puts a hand on you,' Jack said. 'I'll blow his blasted head off.' He knew the words sounded very melodramatic; he also knew he meant them. 'That goes for you too, Jane.' He couldn't read the expression in her eyes.

After checking on the safety of Jane and Mary, Jack patrolled the streets for his men, taking the drunk and the stupid and locking them in a chamber to keep them safe. Only at dawn did he slump onto his lonely cot and then the raw images in his mind kept him awake. He stood up again, to find Jane standing in the lee of a waggon, watching him.

'Rest,' Jane said. 'You must rest.'

'No,' Jack said. 'I've got my duty to do.'

There was always his duty to do. His duty kept him sane when life was difficult and vigilant when things were quiet. Now his duty chased away the horrors as he cared for his company. With cholera and sunstroke rife among the British, and Havelock promising to "hang up, in their uniform, all British soldiers that plunder", Jack joined the other officers in rounding up the more wayward of his men.

The 113th gathered in the old stone building Jack had requisitioned as barracks. He harangued them for their ill-discipline and their drunkenness, while all the time he was noting the gaps in the ranks where men had fallen to enemy fire or the equally fatal scourges of fever and cholera.

'The general is gathering boats to get us across the Ganges,' Jack said, 'and then we're off to relieve Lucknow.'

The men nodded. With the usual efficient information service of British soldiers, they probably knew more than he did, and with the habitual reticence of British other-ranks, they hid their knowledge from their officers. Such was the way of the Army.

'You will have heard about the death of Sir Henry Lawrence in Lucknow,' Jack tried to sound unemotional, although the loss of a first-class soldier was a blow to the British position. The men nodded. 'The defenders are still fighting,' he said.

A few cheered, others banged their boots on the ground.

'How are you holding out, Riley?'

'All right, sir, thank you.' Riley's reply was stiff and formal as befitted a private talking to an officer.

'Good man.' Jack looked up as the sentry slammed to attention at his side. 'Yes, Murphy?'

'There's a lady to see you, sir. She says it is important.' Murphy was one of the new men, a Connaught man with a broken nose and the devil in his eyes.

'I've no time for a lady, Murphy; tell her to wait.' Generally, such a message would have set the 113th cat-calling and making obscene remarks, but since the slaughter of the Bibighur, they were quieter and more serious.

'Yes, sir. It's your lady sir.'

'Oh,' Jack wasn't sure if Murphy meant Jane or Mary. 'I don't possess a lady, Murphy. Oh, all right. I'm coming. Lieutenant Prentice will take over here.'

Mary stood outside the door. In a long, pale green dress she must have found in the town, and with her hair in neat ringlets, she could have belonged in any respectable house in Herefordshire.

'I'm a bit busy, Mary,' Jack said impatiently and added, 'are you all right? Has somebody been bothering you?'

'No, nothing like that.' Mary sounded quite excited. 'I might have some good news for you, Jack, and better news for Private Riley.'

'I don't think there can be any good news for Riley,' Jack said. 'He and Charlotte were very close.'

'Somebody found a list in the courtyard of the Bibighar,' Mary said. 'Jane and I copied it out.' She handed it over. 'It's a list of the people killed in the massacre.'

'Who made it?'

'One of the few survivors of the siege, a man named Shepherd,' Mary said. 'Look at the names.'

Jack nodded and scanned the page for Charlotte's name. 'Mrs. Bell; Alpen Bell; Mrs. and Miss Carroll; Mrs. Lupin... Mrs. and Miss Peters.' He looked up. 'I can't see Charlotte Riley's name.'

'It's not there,' Mary said quietly.

'What does that mean?'

'I don't know,' Mary said. 'It may not mean anything.'

Jack rescanned the list, searching for familiar names and finding none. 'Come with me.' He led Mary into the stone chamber where the 113th recovered from their night's exertions.

'Listen to me, men.' Jack held up his hand. 'Mary has found a list of the people recently murdered in Cawnpore.' He dropped his hand; he could have cut the silence with a blunt knife. 'Mary brought it to me in person to tell me that none of the people murdered was from the 113th.'

He saw Riley's head jerk up. 'How about Charlotte, sir?'

'I'll read out the names,' Jack said. 'Listen.'

They did. The men sat in utter silence. He saw Riley shaking, and Logan put a supporting arm around his shoulder. Mary moved closer until O'Neill shook his head, frowning.

Jack felt the lump in his throat. 'You will note there is no mention of *any* of our people.' He lowered the list. 'I know we are all grateful to Mary here.'

Riley was staring, his mouth opening and closing. He took a deep breath to compose himself. 'Sir,' he said, 'does this mean Charlotte is still alive?'

'We don't know quite what it means, Riley,' Jack said. 'All it tells us is that Mrs. Riley was not among the prisoners held by Nana Sahib, and she was not murdered in the massacre.'

'Sir.' Williams spoke out. 'Have you heard anything about Major Snodgrass and the other lads, sir?'

'Not a thing, Williams,' Jack said truthfully. 'The major and the entire convoy of our families have vanished.' He shifted his gaze from Williams to Riley. 'We just don't know where they are. Thanks to Mary, we do know that none of our people was murdered in the Bibighur.'

'So what now, sir?' Riley asked.

'Now we win this war, Riley, defeat the rebels, restore order to India, and in the process, we'll find out where your wife and all our other missing people are.' He saw the stiffening of shoulders and straightening of backs.

Dismissing the men, Jack called Fraser over. Brown faced and grey-haired, Fraser looked out of place in the stiff uniform of the 113th. He came to attention automatically.

'Fraser, you know this country better than anybody else in the army.'

'Probably, sir,' Fraser agreed.

'You know our families were sent off from Gondabad and have not been seen since.' Jack waited for Fraser's nod. 'Do you have any inkling of what may have happened to them?'

'No, sir,' Fraser said. 'I could try and find out if you wish.'

'How?' Jack asked.

'I could tramp the road as a local again,' Fraser said. 'I'm as Indian as I am British Army now.'

'That is amazingly dangerous,' Jack said. 'If the mutineers catch you they'll kill you.'

'And if General Neill catches me, he'll hang me,' Fraser said cheerfully. 'I'll be careful, sir.'

Jack nodded. 'I can't order you to do such a thing,' he said. 'I'll let you think about it for a while.'

'Thank you, sir.' Fraser pulled at the collar of his tunic. 'I'll be glad to get into more sensible clothes.'

'Be careful, Fraser,' Jack said, but Fraser was already changing into the looser clothing of India.

Havelock ordered Mowbray Thompson, another Cawnpore survivor, to create earthworks beside the Ganges while he found some means of crossing the mile-wide river. His offer of an amnesty to any boatman who helped the British attracted a score of locals, and when a steamer chugged up from Allahabad with reinforcements, he had the nucleus of a flotilla. Shortly afterwards General Neill marched in a few hundred more men with vengeance in their hearts and blood on their bayonets.

'Now we'll be moving,' Elliot said. 'Old Holy won't wait much longer.'

Elliot was correct. Leaving Neill and a strong garrison behind, Havelock began the next stage of his march.

'We're going to free Lucknow,' Logan said. 'Cheer up, Riley; Charlotte will be all right. You'll see. She'll turn up when you least expect it and slap you across the head for drinking or something.'

Riley's forced smile lacked any humour.

'Look at the bloody rain!' Thorpe shivered under the constant monsoon deluge. 'It's worse than Worcester in November.'

'That's right Thorpey,' Coleman said. 'Nana Sahib prayed to the great elephant or Kali or somebody to get the rains down.'

'He never did!' Thorpe swore as he stepped into a deep puddle.

'Oh, yes, Thorpey boy. This wetness is all Nana's fault. We beat him so often he turned to religion and ordered the rain.'

Thorpe's face twisted with the effort of thought. 'So if we prayed for it to stop,' he said at last, 'it might work.'

'It might,' Coleman pretended to consider the possibility. 'We'd have to do it the right way of course. It would be no good praying to our god here. We're in India where only Indian gods work.'

'Oh?' Thorpe looked more confused than ever. 'How do we pray to an Indian god?'

Coleman winked at Parker and Williams, who were watching in some amusement. 'The important thing is the sacrifice. You have to find a couple of bottles of rum and give it away as a sacrifice. You can give it to one of their gods or a friend.'

'I would give it to you, Coley.'

'Would you? You're a true friend, Thorpey. I heard that Lieutenant North of the 78th has a few bottles stored away in his baggage—'

'Right lads!' Jack interrupted the conversation before Coleman sent Thorpe on a looting spree that would get him into serious trouble. 'We're moving out soon. Make sure you all have ammunition and caps, fill your water bottles and eat what you can.'

Logan looked at him. 'Fill our water bottles, sir? It's pissing down.'

'So it is, Logan. Well observed.' Jack rode the blow. 'Parker, dump the dog, we've no room for passengers. Riley, the quicker we defeat the mutineers, the quicker we can find Charlotte. Williams...' He spoke to the men individually, making them feel important and part of the whole, checking their morale, ensuring the lazy were fully equipped, bolstering the inexperienced, reining back the over-enthusiastic and preparing them for the ordeal ahead.

'Sir,' Riley asked. 'When are we leaving?'

'Soon, I think,' Jack said. 'Keep your chin up, Riley.'

Used to the armies of the Crimea, Jack thought that Havelock's brigade of about eighteen hundred men plus ten guns was pitifully small to advance across hostile territory and attack a besieging rebel force of unknown strength. But he had faith in Henry Havelock. His forty-nine surviving men of the 113th waited their turn to cross the river as the rain teemed down and the clouded skies pressed upon them.

'Here we go again, then,' Elliot said as they landed on the opposite side of the river, crashed down their boots to prove ownership and began the march toward Lucknow. 'We have General Havelock, the 113th Foot and less than two thousand men against half the mutineers of India, plus God-alone-knows how many badmashes, outlaws, hangers-on, rebel tribesmen and other assorted riff-raff.'

'Put your trust in Havelock,' Jack said, 'and he'll put his in God.'

'Amen,' Elliot said.

Five miles along a road awash with surface water, Havelock halted his force at a village called Mangalwar to wait for his commissariat convoy. On either side of the road, constant rains had transformed the ground into a swamp. Without shelter, the men huddled in miserable groups, sucking on empty pipes and cursing the weather, the officers, the mutineers and unkind fate that had landed them in such a situation.

'The boys aren't happy.' Elliot removed his forage cap, squeezed it to remove the rain water and replaced it on his head.

'They're grumbling,' Jack agreed. 'But if British soldiers ever stop grumbling, I'll really get worried.'

'We've three more men down with dysentery,' Elliot continued.

'As long as it's not cholera they have a chance of survival.' Jack looked back toward the Ganges. Although he didn't admit it, he wondered if Mary and Jane had managed to inveigle a passage onto the commissariat waggons. Part of him longed to see them and part hoped they had remained safe in Cawnpore. Neither liked General Neill, but Jack felt they were safer with him in command than just about any general in the army.

'Sir.' Coleman's salute was so smart that Jack knew it was a prelude to a request. 'There are native houses here, sir, and we're out in the rain.'

Jack understood. 'Be careful when you take them over. There may be mutineers hiding inside.'

'Not for long, sir.' Coleman said grimly.

The 113th had been waiting for Jack's permission and burst inside the houses, so the men were at least out of the worst of the weather.

'There's no pandies here, sir!' Coleman reported happily.

'Let's join the men,' Jack said.

'We're losing men steadily to disease,' Elliot said. 'Not only in the 113th but the other regiments too. We're down to seventeen hundred and seventy- seven men already, and Nana Sahib is at Fatehpur Chaurassi with an army of three thousand and a clutch of artillery.' He patted his hip-flask. 'The pandies are also waiting to contest our crossing of the river Bani.'

'This won't be an easy march to Lucknow.' Jack looked up as water dripped through the roof of their hut.

'If we don't get through,' Elliot said, 'Lucknow will fall, and we all know what that means.'

Jack thought of the horrors within Cawnpore. 'Aye,' he said. 'Don't we just.' He accepted the hip-flask that Elliot passed over. 'Let's hope the garrison in the Residency building can hold out until we get there.'

'At least there are Queen's regiments in the Residency, unlike in Cawnpore,' Elliot took back his flask. 'There are over five hundred of the 32nd, fifty of the 84th as well as a few score artillerymen and a host of officers from the native regiments. There are also about eight hundred sepoys, although only the Lord knows how trustworthy they are.'

'Not a bad garrison,' Jack said. 'Who is in charge now?'

'Brigadier Inglis of the 32nd.' Trust Elliot to know. 'He was born in Nova Scotia and is reputed to be a superb regimental officer. He'll hold firm against whatever the pandies throw at him. Once he hears what happened in Cawnpore, he'll hold out until Judgement Day.' He looked up. 'There is iron in our hearts now.'

'We had enemies in the Crimea,' Jack said, 'but I've never known our men so full of hatred as they are now.'

'God help the pandies if we let slip the leash from our army.' Elliot took another sip from his flask. 'I hope we get our hands on Nana Sahib.'

'I only hope we can get through to Lucknow.' Jack looked outside at the savage rain. With less than two thousand men and surrounded by unknown numbers of a ruthless enemy, only the skill of Havelock and the courage of the ordinary British infantrymen could save them. He glanced back along the road. The baggage train was there, struggling in their wake through this hostile territory of Oude.

In a sudden flash of insight, Jack knew that Mary and Jane had managed to hitch or bribe their way onto it. He didn't like to think of them out there with only a slender escort of British soldiers, yet his duty was to his men. He closed his eyes. Why had these women attached themselves to him? Jane must be in her forties and would be safer and much more comfortable settling in Calcutta or some British-garrisoned town until the present emergency was over and order restored.

And Mary?

Jack shook his head. She was some woman. He struggled with his thoughts, unsure quite how he regarded her. There was no doubt she was attractive. She was also intelligent, thoughtful and capable. He smiled at recent memories and touched the letter in his pocket. Was he only seeking solace after the loss of Helen, or was there more?

'Sir!' O'Neill slammed to attention at his side and threw a salute. 'Some of the lads are short of ammunition sir, and Thorpe's vanished. May I have permission to organise a party to find him before he loses his fool head to the pandies?'

Jack dragged himself back to his duty. 'Thank you, Sergeant. I'll come along. I presume you've asked Coleman where Thorpe is.'

'Yes, sir.'

Jack sighed; the nitty-gritty, hour-by-hour minutiae of an officer's life took up far more of his time than fighting the enemy. 'Come on then, O'Neill.'

On July 29th, with his army ravaged by cholera, Havelock pushed on toward a village and town that shared the name Unao, where the mutineers were in position, as always waiting behind earthworks and artillery.

'March and fight,' Elliot said. 'March and fight.'

'Here we go again.' Jack peered forward. 'These rebels know their stuff, don't they?'

As well as waiting behind the earthworks, the mutineers were in a walled garden beside the village, while they had strengthened and loopholed every house in Unao. Muskets and rifles pointed outward in a hedgehog of death. The mutineers knew they outnumbered the British; they knew the British could not replace their casualties, while a victory could encourage more men to swarm to their standards. In a war of attrition, they held every card.

'Here we go again, Thorpey,' Coleman said quietly. 'Keep your head down, boy.'

'You too, Coley,' Thorpe said. 'I don't want you to get killed.'

'Come on, Holy! Give us the order!' Logan growled. 'Dinnae you fret, Riley. We'll smash they pandies and get Charlotte back.'

There was a narrow road separating the village of Unao from the town, while the monsoon had flooded the ground to the right and swampy ground defended Unao to the left, so the houses were on an island with the road as a causeway. The rains stopped as the British approached, with the return of tropical heat dragging steam from the road and adding a surreal, misty quality to the surroundings.

'We can't outflank this one,' Elliot said.

'We'll go through the front door,' Jack said quietly, wondering how many of his men would be casualties before this day was done. 'Here's Havelock now.'

Looking even more tense than usual, Havelock sat his horse in front of the column. 'Fusiliers, I want you and the 78th to take the walled enclosure. The 64th and the 113th will capture the village.'

'There's no room for manoeuvre,' Jack said. 'No space for feinting or tactics. It will be a straightforward up-and-at-'em attack.' He looked at his men. The veterans were sucking on the stems of their pipes or checking their rifles; they did not appear concerned. The recruits who had more recently joined were blooded now and tried to assume the nonchalance of their comrades. A few talked loudly of the great deeds they would do.

'Just follow orders, support each other and do your duty,' Jack told them. 'You can't go wrong if you do your duty.'

Rain still fell, splashing on the ground, aiding the defenders by increasing the depth of the swamps and flooded fields. Sheltering behind their walls, the mutineers waited until the 78th were moving and then opened fire, catching them on the flank. Some of the Highlanders fell.

'Right, boys!' Jack gave the order and the 64th and 113th stormed forward once again.

'Keep together,' Jack ordered. 'Remember how we fought in the Crimea; support each other. There's nothing the pandies want more than to catch a lone British soldier.'

They advanced at a run, firing by sections as they moved, seeing the muzzle-flare as the mutineers replied from the loopholed houses and the wall around the village. The 64th hit the wall first and pushed over with the 113th a moment behind, yelling, hating the enemy as they remembered the well in Cawnpore. The village lay before them with men firing from windows and doorways, others crowding in alleyways with swords and shields, matchlock muskets and even spears.

'Push on!' Jack fired at a mutineer who leant out from a window. 'Take that house!'

O'Neill led five men, booted in the door, stepped smartly aside as somebody inside fired and barged in. There was an outbreak of firing and Logan emerged with blood on his bayonet.

'It's ours, sir,' he reported laconically.

'That one there.' Jack pointed to a stone built house from where at least four rifles protruded. 'Riley, you and Logan cover us. Thorpe; you and Coleman follow me.' Taking a deep breath, he ran forward, aware of Thorpe on his right and Coleman on his left. In situations such as this, with the enemy in front, there was nobody he would rather have at his side than his Crimea veterans.

The rifles thrust from the loopholes swung and aimed at the advancing British. Lifting his revolver, Jack fired two quick shots, more in the intention of unsettling the defenders rather than with any real hope of hitting anybody. Shouting, he charged forward; he saw the jetting smoke from the muzzle of a defender's firearm, saw a fountain of mud as a bullet hit the outside of a loophole and then he was at the door. It held to his first kick, and he pressed his revolver to the lock and fired, just as Coleman arrived at his side, thrust his rifle through the nearest loophole and squeezed the trigger.

'Try together,' Jack said, and they both threw their weight against the door. It held. 'They must have barricaded it on the inside!'

Momentarily at a loss, he reloaded his revolver with shaking fingers. A mutineer thrust his musket from a window only a yard from Jack's shoulder and fired.

'We could burn them out, sir.' Thorpe was smiling. 'The underside of the thatch is dry.'

'Could you do that, Thorpe?'

'May I, sir?'

'Get a move on!' Jack winced as one of the defenders in a house nearby slanted an ancient matchlock musket to the left and fired. The bullet crashed into the wall an inch from Jack's head. 'Hurry man!'

Ripping open a cartridge and ignoring the bullets slamming into the mud wall around him, Thorpe struck a Lucifer match, applied it to the grease on the cartridge, watched it fondly as the flame grew and threw it carefully onto the roof.

'Spread all over, my little one,' he said softly, stepping back to watch his baby grow.

'Get back you bloody idiot!' Coleman hauled him back to the wall. 'You'll get your fool head blown off!'

'But I like to watch!'

'You'll like my boot going up your arse unless you keep under cover,' Coleman shouted.

The flames spread quicker than Jack had expected so within a few minutes the roof was ablaze. He heard high voices as a man struggled from the nearest window. Coleman shot him through the head. Somebody inside the house screamed, and the door jerked open, with choking smoke gushing out together with a press of bodies. Jack fired into the mass as Thorpe and Coleman were busy with bayonet, boot and rifle-butt. Men fell; there was the stink of scorched flesh and then only bleeding bodies and the heavy panting of Coleman and Thorpe.

'And that's done for you,' Coleman wiped clean his bayonet on the scorched tunic of a mutineer. 'Bloody murdering bastards.'

They moved on. Seeing Thorpe's example, other soldiers had fired the roofs, so the village was ablaze, with bodies – British as well as native – scattered in ones and twos and small groups. One private of the 64th lay amidst a pile of enemy dead, his body slashed and chopped by a score of swords.

'Paddy Cavanagh,' Coleman said casually. 'I met him in Cawnpore. He was a good lad.'

Even with the village on fire the mutineers, joined by warriors from Oudh, resisted with more determination than the British had met since leaving Allahabad. House by house and yard by yard desperate fighting pushed them back. Jack heard the high Gaelic and saw the swirl of colourful tartan as a party of the 78th split in front of a pair of the mutineers' cannon and closed in a melee of stabbing bayonets. Refusing to run, the gunners fought and died around their charges.

'Brave men,' Coleman said. 'I wouldn't care to stand against these Sawnies.'

'We're winning.' Elliot appeared from the right, with O'Neill and Parker at his side.

'Tough fighting, sir.' O'Neill's uniform tunic was ripped, and there was blood on his face, but whether his own or from one of the enemy Jack could not tell.

'Move on!' Riding his horse and gesticulating with his sword, Havelock was never far from the worst of the fighting. 'You've taken the village men; now keep pressing.'

The path between the village and town of Unao was narrow, with flooded fields on both sides and mutineers' muskets firing down the entire length. Havelock spurred his horse, forcing a passage with his men following, exchanging shot for shot with the enemy until they reached the outskirts of the town.

'Here!' Jack threw himself into the shelter of a wall. His men were around him, taking breath, swearing and glad to still be alive.

'We're winning,' Elliot said.

'What next?' Jack snapped open his revolver and reloaded, counting how many cartridges he had in his pouch.

'Sir,' O'Neill was panting. 'Look to the left.'

The mutineers stood in great ranks of men and horses, watching but not advancing. They looked formidable, scarlet uniforms and white cross-belts, shakos and white trousers with irregular horsemen as well as sowars on the flanks.

'There's more in front, sir,' O'Neill said.

Jack counted his men. 'Where's Samuels?'

'Dead, sir,' Riley said. 'A mutineer nearly chopped him in two with a bloody great sword.'

'What happened to the mutineer?'

'Logan happened to him, sir.'

'I see.' The mutineer was dead. Logan was one of the smallest soldiers in the regiment and probably the deadliest in close-quarter fighting. 'Samuels was a good man.'

Like so many British soldiers in so many campaigns, Samuels would be mourned by his colleagues for a few hours and then would lie forgotten in a lonely grave thousands of miles from home. Samuels was the true price of Empire, the blood price of glory, the shilling-a-day private, spurned by the very people he defended and who profited by his sacrifice. Rule Britannia.

'Form line of battle,' Havelock ordered.

Reinforced to six thousand strong, with batteries of artillery, cavalry and great blocks of infantry, the mutineers advanced along the road toward the diminished and heat-exhausted British.

'They don't have to defeat us,' Prentice said. 'All they have to do is fight; kill a few of us, slow us down and retreat. With their numbers, they can't lose. Wounds and disease will whittle us away until we're too few to bother about.'

'The quicker we win and relieve Lucknow the better,' Jack said. 'Thank God General Havelock seems to think the same.'

'They're attacking us this time,' Elliot said. 'Cry Havelock!'

'Havelock!' The 113th echoed him. 'And let loose the dogs of war.'

With the enemy coming straight at them on the only road and with swamp land on either side, Havelock had no choice but to stand square on. He placed four pieces of artillery to command the centre of the road, two more on either flank and had the precious infantry in support.

'Come on, you bastards,' Logan said softly. 'Wee Donnie's waiting for you.'

'They're coming, Logie.' Riley stamped his boots on the ground. 'You won't have to wait for long.'

Jack grunted and nodded; for the first time in weeks Riley sounded something like his old self.

The mutineers marched straight up the road and suddenly halted. Something like a shiver ran through them, with the men in the front ranks pulling back and some of the cavalry edging forward.

'They've seen us,' Elliot said.

'They'd have to be blind not to,' Jack said. 'With our guns pointing straight down their throat.'

'They're forming into battle order,' Elliot said.

'Fire when you're ready,' Havelock ordered, and after an imperceptible pause, the British artillery opened up.

'Fire, lads,' Jack said, and the rifles of the infantry joined the artillery. The noise was deafening, killing all conversation and the result on the disorganised mutineer army was shocking. Iron cannon balls ripped holes in their ranks, knocking down entire files of men. Some of the sepoys darted forward, others pulled back, and the mutineers' artillery pulled right off the road to deploy elsewhere.

The British artillery changed to grape, scything into the mutineers, destroying their cohesion, killing, maiming, dismembering by the score.

'Watch the pandy guns,' Logan jeered, 'they're stuck in the bog!'

It was true; either due to panic or inexperience, the mutineers had plunged their artillery into the boggy ground at the side of the road and now couldn't haul them out. The cannon remained there, useless, as the British guns poured shot after shot into the rebel army.

'They're breaking,' Jack shouted. 'Keep firing!'

With their artillery out of action and British fire unrelenting, the rebels crumbled, turned and fled, leaving hundreds dead and fifteen guns stranded in the marshland.

'That was easier than I expected.' Elliot reached for his hip-flask.

Jack nodded. 'It's another step closer to Lucknow.'

Ignoring the bloodied bodies of the mutineer dead and the men who collapsed with heatstroke and dysentery, the British chased the retreating enemy for mile after mile until Havelock, seeing the exhausted state of his army, ordered a halt.

'Thank God.' Elliot crawled to the shade of a tree and fanned himself with his hat. 'I can't march another yard.'

'Our men are about done,' Jack agreed. He was gasping yet knew he could keep going for a while yet.

Elliot pulled at his flask. 'God, Jack, I wish this was water and not rum.'

'I never thought I'd hear you say that.' Passing over his water-bottle, Jack watched as Elliot took a long drink. 'It makes you long for an English autumn day, doesn't it?'

'I never thought I'd agree to that, either.' Elliot wiped beads of sweat from his forehead. 'Do you think the pandies will stand again between here and Lucknow?'

'God only knows.' Jack shook his head. 'They seem to have an inexhaustible supply of soldiers while we are being whittled away man by man through battle and disease. Unless we get reinforcements, we won't have sufficient force to relieve the residency.' He glanced toward the men. 'Don't tell the men, for God's sake.'

'The general will get us through,' Elliot said. 'Are your ladies with us this time?'

Jack looked back along the road the army had come. 'They will be.' He had a sudden desire to meet them again, to talk to Mary, to know she was there, to know she was safe.

'It's quiet at present, Jack,' Elliot said quietly. 'Go and find her. I'll look after the men if anything happens.'

Jack hesitated between his desire to see Mary and Jane again and his duty and responsibility to his Company. He stood up, shook his head and sank back down. 'My place is here,' he said. 'If the pandies attack or the general orders us forward I have to be with my men.'

'And your women?' Elliot asked gently.

'They're not my women,' Jack said.

Elliot smiled. 'They think they are.'

'Well they're wrong, damn them!' Jack said.

'If you say so.' Elliot crawled deeper into his patch of shade.

'My women.' Jack tried to push the image of Mary from his head and concentrate on his duty. 'They are not my women in any shape or form. I wish they would leave me alone.'

The sun was high now, gradually drying up the land on either side, drifting steam across the British to give an ethereal, near mystical quality to the temporary encampment. Deliberately turning his back on the road to Cawnpore, Jack surveyed his men as they lay supine, gasping in the heat and grubbing for shade.

Thorpe, Coleman and Williams were playing cards; Parker was smiling as he shared the contents of his water-bottle with the dog that Jack had already ordered him to discard and Riley was in earnest conversation with an attentive Logan. Wherever he wandered, the regiment was now his home. After years of striving for promotion and a route away from the 113th and into a more respectable regiment, he was now reconciled with his lot. He lay back, and despite himself, he thought of Mary.

'We're moving again.' Wearily, Elliot pushed himself upright, straightened his tunic and checked the chambers of his revolver. 'Let's see how many more pandies try to stop us.'

They marched on, deeper into rebel-dominated territory, each step bringing them closer to the besieged garrison of Lucknow, with the ground drying under the punishing heat and the mosquitoes feasting on the flesh of perspiring men.

Two hours of marching brought them to the town of Bashiratgunj, where the rebels had decided to make another stand.

'Oh look.' There was no expression in Elliot's voice. 'Pandies. Have they not learned they can't defeat our general? Havelock has them in his pocket every single time.'

'They've taken a strong position,' Jack said.

'They always take a strong position,' Elliot said, 'and Havelock always tosses them out.'

'Aye.' Jack studied the mutineers' lines.

Bashiratgunj was a walled town with a substantial turreted gateway through which the road entered. The walls on each side of the gate were loopholed and battlemented, while the defence was supplemented by earthworks and a wet ditch, rather like a moat, in front. Between the ditch and Havelock's men was a *jhil*, a wide pond. To the rear of the town, out of Jack's vision, a causeway stretched across another deep *jhil* and led to the only exit.

'It's a bit of a bugger.' O'Neill gave his professional opinion.

'What do you think, sir?' Prentice asked. 'Another frontal attack or do we pound the walls with artillery until we destroy them, and then walk in?'

'Not the former, I hope,' Jack said. 'We're losing men like water through a sieve.'

'Sixty-fourth!' Havelock's order ended the debate. 'I want you to march around Bashiratgunj and position yourselves in the rear to cut off the mutineers' retreat. The rest of us are going right for the throat.'

'And may the good Lord have mercy on our souls,' Elliot said and started as the officers and men of the 113th roared out their new battle-cry.

'Cry Havelock!'

'That's my shout,' Elliot complained and joined in. 'Cry Havelock and let loose the dogs!'

As always, the British artillery opened the battle, with the Madras Fusiliers skirmishing in front and the 113th and 78th advancing in a solid line. Five jets of white smoke erupted from the town walls as the enemy artillery responded.

Elliot closed his eyes. 'For what we are about to receive,' he said as the cannon balls smashed into the British lines. Jack saw Lieutenant Henry Havelock, the general's son, go down as his horse was shot. He rose again, grinning like a mischievous school boy and continued the advance. With the Fusiliers as skirmishers, the 113th and 78th ran to the entrenched mutineers.

'Come on, boys!' Jack fired his revolver at the heads bobbing behind the entrenchments. He saw Coleman duck under the swing of a tulwar, saw Thorpe bayonet the swordsman as O'Neill shot a mutineer at close range and May stagger and fall, bleeding from a wound to the neck. Then the mutineers were backing away, the kilted 78th were swarming over the earthworks, and the Fusiliers were hammering at the gate.

'Keep pushing forward!' General Havelock shouted as the mutineers broke and fled into the town. 'Don't allow them to rally!'

There was sense in Havelock's order. Jack could only imagine the horror of a fight among the narrow alleys of Bashiratgunj, where the defenders would know every corner and the British would be in small, isolated pockets.

'Come on, 113th!' Jack followed the Madras Fusiliers into the town, gagging as the stench of packed humanity, untreated sewage, cow-urine and spices smacked him in the face. 'Chase them, lads!' He fired at a huge, bearded rebel wielding a sword, saw a white-trousered mutineer with a matchlock musket, and saw Logan duck down to gut a yelling mutineer.

'Hard going!' Elliot gasped. He had lost his forage cap somewhere.

'Keep pushing!' Jack fired a snap-shot at a mutineer. The man screamed and spat blood.

Suddenly the defenders were running again, leaving a litter of bodies behind them.

Jumping over the man he had just shot, Jack ran on, gasping in the stifling heat, swearing as he slipped on a pile of human entrails, dodging as bullets hummed past him. He tried to shout from a throat closed through heat and dust, tried to encourage his men. He had to keep the momentum; to halt was to allow the enemy time to regroup and the British were at their most vulnerable, scattered inside the town.

'We've beat them again!' Elliot leant against the wall of a house, panting.

'Keep moving,' Jack said. 'Push them right out of town. Don't let them reform.'

House by house and alley by alley the 78th, Madras Fusiliers and 113th Foot shoved forward, shooting, bayoneting, swearing and dying until the mutineers fled out of the rear gate. If they had followed Havelock's plan, the 64th would have been waiting there to destroy the remnants, but they had stopped to exchange fire with the defenders. The mutineers scattered into the countryside, a defeated army that could reform and fight again.

'They're running like hares!' Grabbing a rifle from a private, Elliot fired after the fleeing mutineers. 'Havelock's beat them again.'

'We could have destroyed them if the 64th were on time.' Jack leant against the outside wall of the town. 'Now we'll have to do it all over again.' He looked at his men. Exhausted and blood spattered, they stared at the retreating mutineers even as they sunk to their knees or slumped onto the ground to lie, chests heaving with the effort of drawing in oxygen. Despite this next victory against odds, there was no energy left to celebrate.

'The men are all in,' Jack said. 'One more victory and there won't be enough of us to mount guard, yet alone relieve Lucknow.'

'Here comes Holy Havelock,' Elliot said as the weary infantry stiffened to attention.

'Clear the way for the general!' O'Neill ordered.

'You have done that well already,' Havelock replied, and the men raised a faint cheer.

It was to be their last reason for cheering for some time.

Chapter Twelve

'We're pulling back.' The words ran around Havelock's column. 'We're pulling back to Mangalwar.'

Sick at heart, Jack heard the inevitable comments.

'What? We've got them licked! Why are we retreating?'

'Retreating from the dirty pandies? Bugger that! There's nothing between Lucknow and us but a rabble of scared blacks.'

'Charlotte's up there! We can't leave her!'

'Right lads.' Jack stepped in front of the indignant 113th, knowing every man in every other regiment in the column shared their emotions. 'We've only got eight hundred and fifty fighting men left now, what with battle casualties and disease. There are about ten thousand pandies ahead of us, so the general has ordered a temporary withdrawal and there is no more to be said.'

'Sir… How about the women? What about my wife?' Riley was plainly distraught.

'We'll be back, Riley,' Jack promised. 'You know General Havelock as well as I do. He's not a man to give up.'

Unhappy, the British withdrew back across the land they had won with such courage and suffering. Heads bowed and rifles across shoulders, they marched, hating everything, hoping the enemy would attack so they could take out their frustrations on somebody, anybody.

'We had them licked,' Logan said. 'Dirty pandy bastards. We had them licked.'

'We've still got them licked, Logan,' Jack said. 'This is a withdrawal, not a retreat.'

'Dirty pandy bastards.' Once Logan had a phrase in his head it was hard for him to lose it. 'Dirty murdering pandy bastards.'

They mustered around Mangalwar, with the men glowering in the direction they had just come and the officers discussing their likely next move.

Outside the village, two cannons pointed in the direction of Lucknow.

'What's happening here?' Jack asked as stern-faced Fusiliers marched a pair of rebel prisoners toward the guns. Both men remained erect, with proud faces and no trace of fear.

'The gunners are going to execute them,' Elliot said. 'They've to be blown from the guns.'

Nobody protested; there was no sign of sympathy for the condemned men. Gondabad and Cawnpore had killed any vestige of pity the 113th may have had.

Jack nodded to a pair of trees nearby from which the bodies of two mutineers hung, swaying slightly. 'What's wrong with an old-fashioned hanging?'

Elliot shrugged. 'I'm not sure I want to see this.'

'You've seen much worse,' Jack said.

'Yes, sir, but seeing men killed in battle is different.'

Many of the infantry seemed not to agree as they crowded around to watch. Neither of the mutineers flinched as the Fusiliers pressed the small of their backs against the muzzle of a cannon and tied them in place.

'They're brave men,' Elliot muttered.

'Murdering pandy bastards.' Logan gave his expected opinion.

A stout major ordered, 'Fire', and immediately both cannons gave a muffled bark, and the mutineers disappeared in a welter of blood, flesh and bones. Jack saw a human head lift high in the air to land with a thud on the ground. Parker's dog ran toward it, with Parker in hot pursuit. He pulled the dog away.

'That's another two gone,' Logan said. Riley watched, as expression-less as the mutineers had been a minute earlier.

'Captain Windrush!' Lieutenant Havelock approached, as eager as ever. 'General Havelock requests the pleasure of your company, sir.' He lowered his voice. 'There's a captured native saying he knows you.'

Mangalwar was a typical small Indian town, now crowded with un-happy infantry and the heavy supply waggons, together with palan-quins and dhoolies that carried the wounded and sick back to Cawn-pore for treatment.

'Ah, Captain Windrush.' General Havelock greeted Jack with his in-tense stare. 'Your Private Fraser has returned. He says he has some-thing important to tell you.'

Fraser was wounded. He lay on his side on the ground with blood soaking through the bandages stretched across his chest and his eyes wide open.

'Sorry to see you in this condition, Fraser.' Jack crouched at his side. 'What happened?'

'One of the Fusiliers shot me, sir.' Fraser coughed up blood. 'I was coming into the camp, and he must have thought I was a pandy.' He glanced down at himself. 'I should have changed out of my native clothes first.'

'They'll fix you up in Cawnpore,' Jack said.

'Maybe sir.' Fraser coughed up more blood. 'I may have found your families, sir.'

'Good man.' Jack listened as Fraser's voice dropped. He wiped away the blood. 'Can you tell me more?'

'I heard the natives talking.' Fraser coughed again, and blood drib-bled down his chin. 'They said there is a village near Banda where there are twenty white women and some children hiding.'

Jack thought of Riley. 'I don't know Banda, Fraser; where is it?'

'In the Vindhya Hills, sir, in the forest. I didn't get the name of the actual village.' Fraser's voice faded. 'Near Banda in the hills.'

'Fraser!' Jack bent closer as Fraser's body contorted in a spasm.

'He's a goner, sir,' a Fusilier corporal said. 'I never knew he was one of our spies. I thought he was a pandy.'

'He isn't a spy,' Jack said. 'He's one of my men, a private of the 113th and he's not dead yet.' He stood up, calling for a medical orderly.

It was too late. Fraser died on the damp ground, duty done; he was another forgotten casualty, another casual farthing toward the cost of Empire.

Havelock had been listening. 'Banda is in the centre of a rebellious area,' he said. 'Any British women and children there are in great danger of their lives, and worse.'

Jack nodded. 'Yes, sir.'

'We know what atrocities these savages are capable of,' Havelock said. 'I wish there was some way we could rescue these poor people.'

Jack felt the familiar tingle of mixed excitement and dread. 'There may be, sir. During the Crimean campaign, my men were skilled at operating behind the Russian lines. The 113th countered the Plastun Cossacks.'

'What are you suggesting, Windrush?' Havelock's gaze was even more penetrating than usual.

'I could take some my men and look for these women. If you'll recall, our families were sent away from our cantonment back in May, and they vanished; these women may be ours.'

Havelock pondered for a moment. 'I can't afford to lose any more men, Windrush. I intend gathering reinforcements and advancing to relieve the Residency at Lucknow. Your fifty veterans are too important.'

'I won't take all of them, sir. I could take half a dozen; sufficient as an escort but hardly a diminution of your strength. Lieutenant Elliot is a very experienced officer, and Prentice is also a capable man. They could command my company.' He hesitated. 'The men are a bit down after withdrawing, sir. Imagine the boost to their feelings if we rescue British women from the hands of these monsters.'

'How well do you speak Urdu? Or Pushtu? Or any other Indian language?' Havelock asked. 'Unless you want to spend your days blun-

dering about the countryside, you will have to ask the natives questions, and they won't speak English. No, Windrush.'

'I could translate, sir.' Mary appeared from the shade of a baggage
waggon. 'I know Urdu and Marathi, Bengali and some Gujarati, and I
can make myself understood in Punjabi and Rajasthani.'

For a moment even the collected Havelock looked nonplussed. 'In
the name of heaven, Captain Windrush is proposing marching into a
rebel-held area. It is no place for a woman.'

'It's certainly no place to leave the women of the 113th, sir, with
respect. On the other hand, I know Captain Windrush well. He rescued
me from Gondabad and brought me to safety. I know the dangers, and
my presence will increase his chances of success.' Mary gave a smile
that would have charmed a snake from its hole. 'Perhaps some officers
of the Madras Fusiliers speak the native languages, sir, if you can afford
to lose their services.'

Havelock nearly smiled. 'You are persuasive, madam.' He looked
around the encampment, where tired British infantry searched for
shade while the artillerymen cleaned their guns and men unloaded
the supply waggons.

'All right, Windrush. We are here until my reinforcements arrive,
which hopefully won't be more than a few days. You may take no
more than a dozen men.' He nodded to Mary. 'And this intrepid lady,
whose courage is a beacon for us all to admire.'

'Thank you, sir,' Jack said.

'I trust you will seek the guidance and protection of the Lord in
your endeavours,' Havelock said.

'I always do, sir,' Mary answered at once.

'Then your presence with Captain Windrush will be doubly benefi-
cial,' Havelock looked at her with increased respect, 'for without His
guidance we would all be lost souls in this land as in every other.'

Mary earned Havelock's approval with a firm "Amen" and admon-
ished Jack with a stern look until he added his own quieter contri-
bution.

'Well met.' Havelock looked at Mary with approval. 'Missionary school?'

'Yes, sir,' Mary said.

'Twelve men at most, Windrush, and we won't wait for you. Once you're outside the camp, you're on your own. Look after this young lady as if she was Australian gold.'

'I will, sir,' Jack promised.

Despite the danger and the unfamiliar terrain, it felt good to be outside the stifling rigidity of the column and to command an independent force again.

He had chosen his old Burma hands, Sergeant O'Neill, Coleman and Thorpe, together with Logan who would voice foul-mouthed complaints while fighting to his last drop of blood. There was Riley, the gentleman thief who had married the actress Charlotte at the expense of his family fortune and Williams the miner with hands like shovels and the upper body of Hercules. There was Parker, a new man who never seemed to complain and Kelly, reputedly the best shot in the regiment. Finally, he had Riordan, a Leinsterman with a twisted grin and Armstrong, the deserter with little conversation.

'Is it Charlotte, sir?' Riley asked.

'We don't know,' Jack said. 'We'll find her, Riley if she is there.' He bit off the phrase "if she is alive". Riley would be all too well aware of the possibility of her death.

He saw Mary share a whispered word with Riley and smiled. She was an impressive woman.

They left by night, so any watching mutineers wouldn't see them, and they headed south and east. They followed the minor roads that spread across India like a spider's web, connecting every village and used by travellers, merchants, holy men and hardworking women, farmers, beggars and thieves since time began.

After a couple of hours, Jack called a halt beneath a banyan tree. Each man wore light linen clothes, dyed to a drab colour that the soldiers were beginning to term 'khaki' which was a Persian word for dust-coloured. Each man carried his Enfield rifle with two hundred rounds of ammunition, his bayonet and water bottle, caps and blanket and whatever food he could stuff into his haversack.

'Right, lads.' Jack surveyed the hard, lined faces and bitter eyes. He would trust these men to fight until the end whatever happened and whoever the enemy. 'This won't be a pleasure trip; we don't know if the intelligence is accurate, and if it is, we don't know if these women are from the 113th or are quite a different group. God knows there could be hundreds of British refugees out there, hiding from the pandies, not knowing if we still hold India, maybe believing the mutineers have driven us out.'

'Sir, do you think these women are ours?' Riley asked again.

'I honestly don't know Riley. If they are, then your Charlotte could be among them, keeping their spirits up and looking after them.'

'And nagging at them too, sir, knowing Charlotte.'

There was a small laugh at Riley's words and no need to say more. After a short halt, Jack led the way again, using a map and the stars to guide him through the maze of paths and hoping his men did not fall foul of a larger body of rebels.

'This could be a lovely country,' Jack said when they reached a clearing. They were amidst a range of low-lying hills, with tiny villages perched on the slopes or topping the crests, with stick-thin natives working the fields.

'This *is* a lovely country,' Mary corrected him. 'It is timeless; these people are living the same lives as their great-grandfathers did, and their great-great-grandfathers before them. There is more continuity in these hills than you will ever find back home.'

'Back home?' Jack smiled at the choice of words, and then looked away. 'You are correct. In Wychwood Manor we employ all the latest farming techniques, so we employ fewer farm servants. Each generation of Windrushes makes his mark by introducing some change in buildings or fields or livestock.'

'Not here.' Mary waved a gracious hand. 'These people will neither know nor care who owns this land. It may be the Mughal Emperor or John Company or the Nawab of Oudh. They'll have to pay their taxes, and that is all they'll see of the landowner. Their life revolves around the farming seasons.'

'Exactly like our farmers,' Jack said. 'The weather dictates everything.'

The 113th kept clear of the villages as they moved cautiously to a level plain with areas of cultivated land, patches of scrubby jungle and stands of impressive trees. When the rain began again, Jack realised how difficult his task might be. The smaller paths quickly became quagmires and then bogs as the water levels rose.

'Oh, look. It's raining,' Kelly said.

'So it is.' Parker looked upward. 'It hasn't rained here before.'

'Yes it has, Parky,' Thorpe said. 'Don't you remember? It's rained a lot recently.'

'Nah,' Coleman said. 'You're imagining things, Thorpey. It's been dry as anything.'

'No, honestly.' Thorpe tried to remind Coleman. 'Seriously Coley, we've had lots of rain.'

'Never,' Coleman said. 'You've imagined it. That's why the Queen's so cross with you – you keep imagining things. Never mind Thorpey, Parky and I'll keep you right.'

'We'll need to find higher ground!' Mary had to shout above the hammer of the rain.

'Do you know this area?' Jack asked.

'I used to,' Mary said. 'There is a hill ahead that will take us above the flood.'

Jack consulted his map. 'It's about five miles away, according to this.'

They peered forward into what looked like a waterfall.

'We can make it.' Mary shook rainwater from her hair and smiled. 'It's only rain.'

'There's rather a lot of it though,' Jack said.

'Are you afraid of a little water, Captain Jack?'

'Lead on if you know the way,' Jack said.

'At least the pandies won't attack us in this,' O'Neill shouted. 'Not unless they've got ships.'

'It's like the flood,' Coleman said.

'It's like the flood,' Thorpe repeated and elaborated for those who lacked his knowledge. 'The flood's in the Bible. It rained and rained, and everybody drowned except some fellow who built a big boat and saved all the animals.'

'God, I wish he was here now,' Armstrong said. 'He could build his big boat and save us.'

'It must have been Parker's granddad,' Logan said. 'Parker would build a boat and save all the animals.' He jerked a thumb toward Parker, who was stuffing something furry and living inside his tunic.

Jack led them on, no longer trying to follow the paths, only trudging in the direction he hoped higher ground lay. The water deepened as they progressed, from shin-deep to knee deep and then thigh deep.

'Sir, if this gets any worse we'll lose Logie. He's up to his chest already.' Williams, only a couple of inches taller, indicated Logan who was stretching his head to see above the muddy water.

'Riley, if the rain does get worse, you can hoist Logan on your back.' Jack looked over his shoulder. Mary was the same height as Williams. 'I'll carry you, Mary.'

'There is no need for that,' Mary said. 'I've seen monsoon rains before.'

'Sir, it's getting deeper,' Thorpe said.

'It's only bloody rain,' Armstrong splashed on.

'Keep your rifles and ammunition dry!' Jack cursed as he sunk deep into the soft ground. 'Push on.'

At last, the ground began to rise, and they stepped upward onto a terraced slope.

'This way.' Mary was as animated as Jack had ever seen her. Ignoring the rain, she forged ahead, nearly laughing. 'It's all right; I know what's on the top.'

Turning, Jack encouraged his men onward, counting them to ensure nobody was left behind.

'We can stop here,' Jack called.

'It's better further up the hill,' Mary promised. 'Trust me.'

For a moment Jack remembered the faith the officers of the Native Infantry Regiments had put in their men. They had trusted them and paid the ultimate price; was Mary leading him and his men into a trap? Were there scores of murderous rebels at the top of this hill waiting with muskets and sharp tulwars to massacre them, as they had butchered other unsuspecting British recently?

Jack loosened the revolver in its holster. Mary looked over her shoulder at him. 'It's all right, Jack,' she said. 'Trust me.' There was pain in her eyes. 'Please trust me.'

'I'll come with you,' Jack decided. 'Sergeant O'Neill!'

'Sir!' Only O'Neill would crash to attention and salute even when climbing a muddy hill in the middle of a monsoon.

'I'm going ahead with Mary. You look after the men.' Jack handed over his map and binoculars. 'If I'm not back in two hours, you take charge. Don't go looking for me and beware of mutineers.'

'Yes, sir. Where will you be, sir?'

'Heaven or Hell,' Jack said, 'whichever will have me.' Turning around, he followed Mary, who looked hurt.

'Your men are safe too,' Mary said. 'Do you not trust me?'

'If I did not trust you with my life,' Jack said, 'I would not be here.'

'And your men?'

'Their lives are more valuable to me than my own,' Jack said, truthfully.

Mary flicked rainwater from her hair. 'Beyond the line of trees,' she said. 'Keep up with me.'

She led them along a rain-flooded path that followed the contours of the hill. As Jack approached the trees, he rested his hand on the butt of his revolver, reassured by the solidity of the weapon. He watched her walk in front, hating himself for doubting her even as he admired her swaying walk and the way her dress slithered across her hips. He looked away, remembering Helen and wondering if she had poisoned his belief in all women. *Damn Helen Maxwell.*

The trees formed an irregular line with their tops brushing against the heavy cloud. There was no depth to them and on the far side was a village of stone houses that sat atop the crest of the hill. Low roofs wept rainwater onto narrow streets while bedraggled poultry and animals sheltered behind stone-walled fields.

'Do you like it?' Mary was smiling as she flicked water from her hair. 'What do you think?'

Still wary of a trap, Jack looked around. There was no sign of any men, yet alone the ranks of mutineers he had feared. 'It's a lovely village.'

'It's Bilari; my home,' Mary said. 'This was where I was born.'

'Oh.' Jack released the butt of his revolver and fastened the catch. 'I didn't know that.'

'You're safe now,' Mary said. 'Nobody will bother you, and nobody will inform the mutineers of your presence.'

'I'll bring the men up,' Jack made his decision.

'No need,' Mary said. 'They're right behind you.'

O'Neill stepped out from behind the trees, followed by all the others.

'I ordered you to stay back until I said it was safe,' Jack snapped.

'Did you, sir?' O'Neill sounded astonished. 'I thought you said to follow you and make sure *you* were safe.'

'The sergeant's right, sir,' Thorpe said. 'We was to follow you and make sure you were safe.'

Mary looked away, smiling. 'Your life seems as valuable to your men as theirs does to you.'

'Disobedient blackguards,' Jack grunted.

Mary's laugh rose above the thunder of the rain. 'We'll find somewhere dry for your boys as well.'

'Where does your family live?' Jack looked around with some interest. Bilari looked clean and well organised, with neat houses and walled enclosures.

'Up there.' Mary pointed upwards, where a large house overlooked the rest. 'My uncle is the headman.'

Narendra proved to be a plump, worried-looking man with a plumper and cheerful wife.

'*Jai ram*,' Jack said.

'*Jai ram*,' Narendra replied although he reserved his smile for Mary as Aaryah took her into an encompassing hug and spoke for three minutes non-stop.

'Your men will be comfortable here,' Mary translated Aaryah's words. 'Nobody comes here in the monsoon; it is too much trouble wading through the floods and then climbing the hill.' Aaryah's laughter wrinkled her forehead, nearly obscuring the red mark above her eyes.

'I'll have a couple of sentries on duty just in case,' Jack said.

'The *chowkidars* – the watchmen – will join them,' Mary said at once. 'They know better what to look for.'

When the men were under shelter and Coleman and Thorpe on the first watch, Jack joined Aaryah and Narendra in the airy largest room of their house, with Mary translating what was said.

'We are looking for a party of British women and children,' Jack said. 'They left Gondabad a few weeks ago and have not been seen since.'

Narendra nodded. Mary translated his reply. 'There are British women in Haverpore,' he said at once. 'Everybody knows about them.'

'We don't,' Jack said.

Both Mary and Narendra smiled, with Aaryah listening to the translation and laughing a minute later. She said something that caused Mary to laugh as well.

'What did Aaryah say?' Jack asked.

'Nothing you should know,' Mary said, still smiling.

'Tell me anyway,' Jack insisted.

'It is as well that the British don't know what is going on all around them.' Mary translated and looked at Aaryah, who chuckled and shook her head.

'There was more,' Jack said.

'There was,' Mary agreed.

'Was it about the mutineers and the rebellion?' Jack asked. 'Are these people hiding things from us?'

'India does not all revolve around Britain and the British,' Mary said softly. 'Remember what I said about farmers? The seasons and the weather matter more than anything else.' She smiled again, softly. 'And real life continues.' She tossed back her long hair when Aaryah spoke again. 'Aaryah said that some British officers don't see the obvious even when it's right under their nose.'

Both women exchanged glances and laughed again, leaving Jack feeling slightly uncomfortable. 'I don't understand,' he said, which brought more secretive looks and further laughter.

'You might later,' Mary translated Aaryah's next words.

'These British women,' Jack changed the subject, 'could you take me to them?'

'I could,' Mary said quickly. 'If you can wait until the waters drain away.' Again, she exchanged glances with Aaryah. 'We are on a bit of an island here.'

Only Riley seemed perturbed to learn the flood had trapped them in Bilari. Reassuring him they would leave as soon as it was practicable, Jack set about making friends with the villagers and creating defensive positions in case the mutineers came.

'There is no need for concern,' Mary assured him. 'We can see anybody approaching for miles.' She stood at his side, tall, straight, elegant and more Indian than she had ever appeared before. 'Do you see those hills over there?' She indicated a range of low, wooded heights shrouded in drifting mist or rain; Jack wasn't sure which.

'I do,' Jack said.

'Those are the Vindhya hills,' she said. 'They are only twenty miles away but inaccessible in the floods. We can't get there, and the people there can't leave either.'

Jack noticed Riley watching and listening as Mary pointed to the hills. It must be terrible for him, wondering if Charlotte was there, worrying about her safety every minute of the day and night and not being able to reach her.

'Do you feel she is alive?' Mary asked. She touched Riley's arm.

'Yes,' Riley said at once.

'Then she will be,' Mary said. 'Love is a strange thing. It knows when reason and rationality and logic cannot tell. Trust your feelings.'

Riley did not smile. 'Thank you, Mary.'

'See?' Logan had been sitting on a log, saying nothing as he cleaned his rifle. 'I told you Charlotte was in the pink. Now stop fretting, Riley.'

Jack heard the noise through the croaking of frogs in the dark. He slid his hand to the holster at the side of the bed and grasped the butt of his revolver. He said nothing, lying still as his eyes adjusted to the dark and he listened for the source of the sound. Something was moving in the room, the shape indistinct. He raised the revolver.

'That's far enough! One more step and I'll blow your head off!'

'Jack!' Mary sounded indignant. 'It's me!' There was the flare of a Lucifer and Mary was peering at him behind the flickering flame of a candle.

'What the devil are you doing here?' Jack lowered the revolver.

'Now that is a very foolish question.' Mary kept her voice quiet and swept a hand over her body from neck to knees. 'Move over, please.'

'Oh, dear God.' Jack stared as she dropped her simple dress and stood stark naked at his side. 'Oh, dear God in heaven.'

'Well, Captain Jack,' Mary said softly. 'Are you the British officer tonight, too respectable to even think of a woman who was not of a high caste, or are you Jack Windrush, whose eyes follow me whenever I walk away?'

Jack reached out and stroked the outside of her thigh. 'Come in and find out.'

The rains stopped during the night. Jack heard the quick patter on the roof ease and then cease. He sat up and out of instinct reached for his revolver. Instead, Mary's hand slipped inside his.

'No, Captain Jack. Some things are more urgent even than your duty as an officer of the queen.' She was not smiling. 'You need a woman, Captain Jack; if you think only of your duty, your nerves will stretch and snap.'

Jack let her guide him back down, and for a while, he forgot the weather outside.

Chapter Thirteen

They moved slowly through the receding flood waters with Mary leading them and the men alert for mutineers. Testing each step for the depth of water and mud, hopeful not to meet snakes, the men swatted biting insects, sweltered in the heat and plodded on, swearing.

'Bloody India,' Logan said. 'Somebody told me it never rained in India.'

'They lied,' Parker said.

'What do you think Riley?' When Riley remained stubbornly silent, Logan continued. 'We'll find her, son, dinnae fret.' He swayed closer, so his shoulder nudged Riley's arm. 'We'll find your Charlotte.'

Riley slogged on, thigh deep in water, eyes mobile and jaw set. Watching them both, Jack knew he could never express the pain he felt. These were his men, suffering, and he couldn't help them.

They rested at an isolated village on a ridge of high ground, searched the place for evidence of mutineers and ate what they could from the villagers' meagre stock. 'We'll pay.' Jack passed over a few rupees, hoping that these poor people used such currency. They looked at the coins and salaamed silently.

'There are no mutineers here,' O'Neill reported. 'Only local people and goats. The folk don't understand anything I say to them.'

'Let me try,' Mary said and gave a long speech to the bemused village headman, who shook his head and glanced at Jack in fear.

'They have never seen a white man before,' Mary reported. 'And now a dozen descend on them at one time. They must think we come from the moon. They don't know what a sepoy is, yet alone a mutineer.'

Jack nodded. 'They can think what they like,' he said. 'Have they any news of the white women?'

'Not a word,' Mary said. 'These villagers are poor people, they know nothing.'

Jack grunted. 'You told me that everybody knew about these British women.'

'I was wrong,' Mary admitted frankly.

They left at dusk, wading through the water and asking the same question at other villages in the area, always with the same result until they reached the lower slopes of the Vindhya Hills. Low and wooded, the hills were drier than the plains, but progress was equally slow as they negotiated a seemingly endless series of ridges.

By now Jack's men knew the system. They would move at night and halt during the day, and when they neared a village, Mary and Jack would scout ahead and approach the women. If it seemed safe, Mary would ask about white people, and then they would move on again. The red-turbaned *chowkidar* in the third village in these misty hills grasped an antique sword as he listened. He spoke in a high voice to Mary, pointed behind him and placed himself at the entrance to his village, denying them entry.

'Sound man, that,' Jack approved. 'He's doing his duty and guarding his charges. What did he say?'

'Most of the *chowkidar*'s are steady men,' Mary said. 'You really will have to learn more of the language if you stay here, Captain Jack.'

'Yes, ma'am,' Jack said. 'And if I did, I would be deprived of your company. What did he say?'

Mary gave one of her secretive smiles. 'He said he heard stories of *bhoots* or ghosts deeper in the hills. The ghosts may mean white people, or it may not.' Mary shook her head.

They moved on, still cautious, trusting nobody.

'You hear that, Riley?' Logan nudged him. 'There might be white folks up the hills. Cheer up, man. It could be your missus.'

Riley forced a smile. 'Yes.' He stared forward as if he could penetrate distance and mist. His mouth worked as if he was talking to his wife, or possibly praying.

'Right lads,' Jack said. 'We're marching by day and night now.'

They moved faster, dropped some of their caution and entered villages by daylight, with Mary questioning the headman while the men of the 113th ensured there were no rebels around.

'Riley, you and Logan act as close escort to Mary. Make sure nobody harasses her.' By placing Riley near Mary, Jack had ensured he would be first to hear any news of Charlotte.

The village was small and poor, huddled between two ridges. Jack sent O'Neill and Coleman ahead to scout and waited as insects sought his blood, and a herd of cheetal deer broke cover and vanished before any of the men could react.

'Sir.' Coleman's face was damp with sweat. 'Sergeant O'Neill sends his compliments and could you come at once, sir.' He grinned. 'There are British women, sir!'

'Riley! Come with me. Parker, take over from Riley!'

'You're British?' The voice was thin, with a distinct West Country accent.

'We're the 113th Foot!' Riley shouted. 'Is Charlotte Riley with you?'

'You're British!' The woman emerged from a copse of trees, holding a small child in her arms. 'Oh, thank God!' She was about thirty with her dark blonde hair a tangle on her head, and her clothes ripped past the point of decency. 'Oh, thank God! We've been living with these savages for too long!'

Jack experienced a mixture of sympathy and anger. 'These savages presumably saved your lives,' he said. 'How many of you are there?'

'Seven.' The woman's tears were genuine. 'A mob of our sepoys burned our bungalow and killed my husband, and I grabbed the children and ran.'

'We're searching for women from the 113[th.]' Riley couldn't hold back any further. 'Charlotte Riley? Have you news of my wife? She's about five feet four and...'

The woman shook her head. 'No, no. We're Company infantry, not Queen's.'

'Are there more women here? Have you heard of any other British women and children?' Riley was increasingly anxious.

The woman shook her head. 'There are only us here.'

Riley shook his head. 'There must be more.' He grabbed her shoulders. 'My wife!'

'Come on Riley, son.' Logan put a wiry arm around Riley's shoulders. 'She's not here so she must be somewhere else. We'll find her, don't you fret – we'll find her.'

There were seven civilians, none from the 113th, and although Mary enquired and Jack led patrols around the area, there were no more British survivors in the area.

'They might be somewhere else nearby, sir,' Riley said. 'We can't leave.'

'The local people would know.' Jack watched Logan, concerned that he might take Riley's side. One always had to be careful with the 113th. 'Come on Riley, she's not here.' He turned away. 'We'll find her.'

It was almost a relief to get back to Cawnpore and hand the women into the care of General Neill. Almost a relief, but not quite for the town was less a secure cantonment and more a thinly guarded hospital for the cases of dysentery, fever and cholera.

'Look.' O'Neill leant against the gallows overlooking the courtyard where the women and children of the garrison had been butchered and nodded forward. Two sepoys crawled on hands and knees, surrounded by a group of laughing British soldiers.

'What the devil's happening?' Jack asked.

'It's General Neill's new way of teaching the murdering bastards a lesson,' O'Neill said casually. 'They have to lick up some of the women's blood before we hang them. It spoils their caste you see, and they don't like it one bit. Not one bit, sir.'

'I see.' Jack felt nauseated.

'They raped our women,' O'Neill said, 'and tortured them too, so it serves them right.'

One of the watching infantrymen put his boot on the neck of a naik and pushed his face right down into the blood. 'Lick it, you raping, murdering bastard!' He twisted his boot, grinding the naik's face into the bloody dirt.

Jack felt Mary shiver at his side. 'It's all right,' he whispered. 'They won't touch you. They don't even know you're part native. Why I am as dark as you are and I'm pure English.'

'I did not know they hated the natives so much,' Mary said. 'I thought we were friends in India.'

'So did I,' Jack said. 'The mutineers have broken the faith, I think.'

'The British are doing their best to make sure it stays broken,' Mary said quietly. 'When I see this sort of thing, I feel more Indian than British.'

Jack felt the tension rise between them. 'The mutineers raped and murdered British women and children. Naturally, the men want revenge.'

Mary took a symbolic but significant step further away. 'Hindi men would defile their caste if they raped a Christian woman,' she said quietly. 'The women were murdered but not raped; not unless there were Muslims involved.'

Jack watched as the soldiers continued to torment the sepoys. 'One's as bad as the other,' he said. The cheering rose to new heights when the hangman placed nooses around the mutineers' necks. 'This is a terrible place.' Even as he spoke, he knew India was as much his home as England was.

He walked away and looked in surprise as Mary stepped beside him. 'I thought we had fallen out.'

'Do you want us to fall out?' Her eyes were large and innocent.

Jack remembered Helen's quick temper and sudden mood swings. 'No,' he said. 'Not at all.'

'Then we shan't,' Mary said. 'But I'm not watching these men get hanged for public entertainment.'

'Nor am I,' Jack said and for some reason he didn't understand added, 'thank you.' As they walked side by side, they heard the crowd cheer.

Nodding to Mary, Elliot looked drawn and tired as he gave a half-hearted salute. 'Have you heard the news, sir?'

'Not until you tell me,' Jack responded.

'Havelock has withdrawn all the way to Cawnpore,' Elliot said. 'The attempt to relieve Lucknow has failed. The garrison in the Residency is on its own.'

Chapter Fourteen

With Havelock's return to Cawnpore, India burst into further revolt as a host of minor chieftains and landowners in Oudh were encouraged to rebel. Rather than face a few thousand mutinous sepoys, British India now faced the prospect of rebellion within one of the largest and most important provinces of the country.

'So, you returned safely.' General Havelock looked as lugubrious as ever, if more haggard.

'Yes, sir.' Jack saluted and stood at attention.

'I heard you rescued seven women and children,' Havelock said. 'Good work, Windrush. Now you're back with us you'll wish to resume duty as soon as possible.'

'Yes, sir. My men are keen to relieve Lucknow.'

Havelock gave a stern nod. 'Then they'll be pleased to know that our setback is only temporary. The Lord did not see fit to grant us victory on our first attempt, but we'll try again, and I'll need every experienced fighting man.'

'Yes, sir.'

'You may have heard that Major-General Sir James Outram is taking command here. I fought under him in Persia, and he is a good man.'

'Yes, sir. Will he be leading the force to Lucknow, sir?'

'I will oversee military matters,' Havelock said. 'General Outram will come along in a civilian capacity.'

Jack hid his satisfaction. After Havelock's run of victories over odds, he had no desire for an unknown general to take command.

For the next few weeks the British force gradually built up, while the rains continued, and cholera burned itself out.

'Last time we tried we had about twelve hundred British and a few hundred Sikhs that nobody completely trusted,' Elliot said. 'Now look at us. We have over three thousand men; we know the Sikhs are loyal to a fault, and we have three batteries of artillery and a hundred and sixty cavalry rather than eighteen horsemen.'

'There is some good quality infantry too,' Jack added. 'As well as the regiments we already know there is the 90th Foot; we fought beside them in the Crimea. I don't know the 5th Fusiliers though.'

'I know nothing about them,' Elliot said.

Jack grunted. 'We'll soon find out how good they are.'

In addition to reinforcements, Havelock had been busy gathering boats to cross the rivers Gumti and Sai that barred their road to Lucknow and having artisans make carriages to drag the boats along. In the meantime, engineers constructed a bridge of boats across the Ganges.

'This time we'll get through,' Elliot said. 'This time.'

Jack remembered the well at Cawnpore. 'Oh, God, I hope so.'

On the 18th September Captain Maude took his battery of three guns across the Ganges. The boats swayed under the weight but held and in a hot three-hour duel Maude flattened the mutineers' artillery that attempted to stop him. The sound and smoke reached the 113th as they prepared themselves in Cawnpore.

'It looks like we're going to have to fight all the way to Lucknow,' Elliot said.

Jack saw Mary watching from the banks of the Ganges, her eyes shaded with worry. He waved and mouthed, "Cheer up. Take care."

It was an impulse Jack didn't fully understand. Aware of Mary watching him, he removed Helen's letter from his breast pocket and without reading it, tore it into small fragments and threw it into the air. The pieces of paper fell to the ground like inverted confetti.

'Goodbye, Helen Maxwell.' Jack suspected he had just said farewell to a huge part of his past. It hardly hurt at all.

Mary lifted a hand to wave. Jack didn't know if she appreciated the significance of his action; he was unsure if he understood himself. He did know that Mary's eyes were brown and her gaze intense as she put her fingers to her lips.

On the next day, the 19th September, Havelock again led an army across the Ganges, bound for Lucknow. Jack had augmented his survivors from the previous attempt with men from the garrison and looked over his 113th as they marched over the swaying bridge. Their mood had altered from the grimness of their first attempt to a savage optimism that boded ill for the enemy. He glanced behind him; twenty bullocks hauled each huge carriage bearing the boats for the Gumti and Sai rivers while the battery of three heavy guns could match anything of the enemy. This time they would get through, despite the pelting rain and anything the rebels could throw at them.

'I heard there are eight thousand mutineers at Mangalwar,' Elliot said. 'And they have eighteen pieces of artillery. They still outnumber us nearly three to one.'

'They could have eighty thousand men and a hundred pieces of artillery,' Jack said more than he'd intended. 'We have Havelock.'

'There was a message from the Lucknow Residency as well,' Elliot said. 'They're running short of food, and the pandies are pressing them hard.'

'They'll hold,' Jack said. 'They know we're coming.'

Havelock waited until his whole force was across the Ganges, sent out mounted reconnaissance patrols and at five in the morning of the 21st began the advance.

'Here we come, you pandy bastards,' Logan shouted. 'We're going to get you!' The men of the 113th gave a grim growl and marched on, boots firm on the wet surface of the Grand Trunk Road, faces fixed on the objective. They hadn't far to march before they met the mutineers.

'There they are already.' Elliot pointed ahead. 'They entrench well, the pandies.'

Jack surveyed the rebels' latest defences as he had done so often before in this campaign. They had formed a powerful position on either side of the road. The mutineers had anchored their right on Mangalwar village and in a walled enclosure at the side. Jack could see their heads, matchlocks and swords as they waited for Havelock's inevitable attack.

'They don't give up, do they?' Elliot pointed to the breastworks at the centre and left of the mutineer's line. The muzzles of half a dozen pieces of artillery menaced the British should they choose to advance along the road.

'They're stubborn men, I'll grant you.' After witnessing the massacre at Gondabad and the aftermath of Cawnpore, Jack was reluctant to allow the mutineers any respect, but there was no denying their resilience. After eight straight defeats by Havelock, here they were again, ready to face the general a ninth time.

'They'll be dead men soon,' Elliot said grimly.

The deep boom of the British heavy artillery started this next contest between Havelock and the mutineers.

'Cry Havelock!' Elliot shouted, and the officers and men of the 113th finished their slogan. 'And let loose the dogs of war!'

In this case, the dogs of war were the skirmishers of the 5th Fusiliers who dashed forward in open formation, heads down against the driving rain and boots raising muddy splashes with every step. The veterans of the previous campaigns watched, ready to criticise the performance of this fresh regiment.

'There goes the cavalry!' Elliot said as General Outram led them in a slashing charge on the enemy flank. 'Outram should have had the command you know, but he allowed Havelock to take charge.'

'He knows Havelock has the measure of the mutineers,' Jack said.

With the 5th Fusiliers in front and the cavalry on the flanks, the rebels retreated once more.

'They're running,' Elliot said. 'They just can't stand against Holy Havelock.'

With the 113th having never fired a shot the British advanced. The column passed the dead bodies of scores of mutineers and moved remorselessly forward toward Lucknow. Leaving the artillerymen to deal with the brace of cannon they captured, they pushed the enemy before them as far as Unao where they halted to eat and reform before marching on again.

'Up the old familiar road,' Elliot said.

'For the last time,' Prentice said. 'We won't stop this time! On to Lucknow!'

With any mutineers melting away before them, the British reached Bashiratgunj, scene of three previous victories.

'Will they fight, or will they run?' Elliot removed his forage cap, poured off the collected rain-water and replaced it.

'I hope they fight.' Jack glanced around. 'I'd like one proper battle rather than all these silly little skirmishes. I'd like the mutineers to stand and fight so that we can batter them to pieces. Then we will re-lieve Lucknow and be a huge step closer to putting this mutiny down.'

'There's nobody here,' Elliot said. 'Not even a token force.'

As the rain continued to torment them, they camped on the old battlefield with all its memories.

'Who told me India was always hot and dry?' Thorpe asked.

'Somebody who has never been here.' Coleman gave the stock reply. 'Never mind Thorpey, here come the supply waggons; you can get out of the wet rain into a wet tent instead.'

The rain continued on the 22nd, thundering down on Havelock's column as the British advanced unopposed.

'Where are they?' Thorpe looked around. 'If I was a pandy trying to stop us, I'd be setting ambushes all along this road.'

'If you was a pandy, Thorpey, the rest would throw in their hand and give up,' Coleman said. 'Maybe that's what we should do then; let you join the mutineers. They'd laugh so hard at the thought of you being a soldier they'd be helpless, and we'll win the war and get out of this *bloody rain!*' He faced upward and shouted the last two words, possibly hoping God would take heed and order the deluge to end.

Thorpe looked confused. 'But Coley, I'm British. They'd see I wasn't a native right away!'

'We'll paint you black first,' Parker joined in. 'Then you'd look like a real pandy.'

'No,' Thorpe said. 'I'm not doing it. I'm not joining the pandy army. What would Captain Windrush say?'

'You'd get another medal if you did,' Coleman said. 'And shot if you didn't. I heard the Priest say you was to go away tomorrow to join the pandies.'

'That's right,' Williams agreed. 'I heard him say so.'

'I heard him too,' Whitelam said slowly. 'Old Thorpey's to join the pandies, the Priest said and right quick too; else he'll be hanged at dawn.'

Five paces in front, Jack wondered who the Priest might be. He looked ahead; they were nearing the bridge over the Sai, and intelligence had reported that the mutineers had built earthworks on the further bank. He watched as a troop of cavalry galloped forward to investigate.

'The pandies have left,' they reported. 'And the bridge is intact.'

'Bloody amateurs,' Prentice said. 'They should have blown the bridge.'

'Don't argue,' Elliot said. 'If the Lord offers his hand, we should just accept it.'

Wary of ambush, Havelock's men marched over the high bridge and passed the two empty half-moon batteries on the far side. 'They could have held this bridge for some time,' Jack said. 'Havelock has them panicking now.'

'Maybe they're saving their manpower to defend Lucknow,' Elliot said.

'Maybe they are.' Jack wondered if he may yet see the final decisive battle – Nana Sahib's Waterloo.

They camped on the road, with Havelock firing all his cannon as a signal to the besieged garrison at Lucknow that the relief column was on its way. The gunfire seemed strangely futile in this vast land, achieving nothing except the expenditure of powder and a temporary noise whose echoes soon faded away. Only the murmur of soldiers remained, and the steady patter of the rain.

Elliot produced his silver flask. 'How much longer, Jack?' After the previous attempt to reach Lucknow when the mutineers contested every village and river crossing, this march seemed more like a procession.

'Only God knows, Arthur, and maybe Havelock, if God has let him into the secret.' Jack sighed. 'You're duty officer tonight, Elliot. Wake me if anything happens.' He knew he would hardly sleep but had to appear like a man in total command of his nerves.

India pressed down on them, swallowing the column in its immensity and dwarfing them with its size, scale and history. They marched on, boots tramping, men falling to the heat and disease, intent on relieving the garrison and not caring much about the bigger picture. It was their duty to obey orders and being soldiers, that's what they did.

Elliot glanced at his watch. 'It's quarter to nine in the morning, and already I'm sweating like a pig. At least the rain has stopped.'

'Listen.' Jack touched Elliot's shoulder. 'What can you hear?'

'Three thousand men marching and the tide of history turning in our favour,' Elliot said glibly.

'Nothing,' Jack said. 'For the last days, we've heard the mutineer artillery pounding at the Residency at Lucknow. Now the guns are silent.'

'What does that mean?' Elliot asked. 'Do you think the Residency has fallen? Have the pandies won? Or have they given up and fled before we get to them?'

Jack grunted. 'I don't know, Elliot, but it may mean the mutineers are moving their guns to defend Lucknow against us.'

'They'll need more than artillery to defeat Havelock,' Elliot said confidently. 'He's got their measure and no mistake.'

'We're only sixteen miles to Lucknow, and there's not a mutineer in sight,' Jack said. 'They should be harassing us with their cavalry, placing ambushes wherever they can, hitting the supply column. They're brave men, no doubt, but their leaders are inexperienced.'

'Thank the Lord for small mercies,' Elliot said. 'With their numbers and training, they should wipe us out.'

They marched on, tense, waiting for an attack, suspicious of every noise, every village and every copse of trees. Only their anger at the outrages committed on their womenfolk, their belief in their professional superiority and their faith in Havelock kept their morale high.

'How many pandies are there now, do you think?' Elliot asked. 'Ten thousand, twenty thousand, thirty?'

'We'll soon see,' Jack said. 'Here comes our cavalry.'

The news spread through the column. The mutineers were making a stand at Alambagh, about four miles south of Lucknow.

'Finally,' Jack said. 'Let's hope they don't run this time.'

'Oh, you bloodthirsty thing,' Elliot began, saw the expression on Jack's face and altered what he was going to say. 'The Alambagh is a palace and garden called the Garden of the World,' he said quietly. 'It was the pleasure garden of the rulers of Oudh. What a place for a battle.'

Remembering the Windrush pride in their family estate of Wychwood Manor, Jack surveyed the high walls and angle-turrets of the Alambagh, recognising the wealth and pride of the owner. His family would be envious of the size and scale of this place, which gunfire and the shattered bodies of brave men would soon disfigure.

The mutineers had anchored the left of their line on the Alambagh and manned another two miles of fortified positions in the shelter of a range of small hills. 'They have ten thousand infantry there.' Elliot always knew what was happening. 'Three times our number and they have fifteen hundred of the most skilled cavalry in the world, as well as parks of artillery.'

Jack felt for a cheroot, cursed quietly and nodded. 'So far we've had some pointless skirmishes when the rebels have not stood. Perhaps this time we'll give them a proper towelling.'

'Do you want to kill them, Jack?'

'I want to end this war,' Jack said. 'And the quickest way is to defeat the enemy. Please, God, it's over soon.'

'This is our duty, Jack,' Elliot said. 'We chose it.'

'I know,' Jack said softly.

Once again, Havelock attacked the enemy flank, pounding the mutineers' positions with his heavy artillery as he sent Colonel Hamilton with a brigade around the enemy's right.

'Where are we going?' Thorpe asked as the 113th marched nearly parallel with the mutineers' positions.

'The pandies have put a swamp in front of their flank,' Coleman explained with surprising patience. 'So we either wade through it and get slowed down and drown, or we march round.'

'Oh,' Thorpe said. 'That's smart of them making a swamp.' He ducked as a mutineer cannonball screamed a few feet overhead. 'They're firing at us now.'

'So they are, Thorpey-boy.' Parker said. 'You would almost think we're enemies.'

'We are enemies,' Thorpe said. 'Aren't we?'

'Not at all,' Parker said. 'This is just a field day.'

'You're joking,' Thorpe said. 'Eh, we're enemies, Sergeant?'

O'Neill nodded. 'I'll be your bloody enemy unless you stop talking and get marching, Thorpe. The noise you're making it's a wonder the general can hear himself think.'

'It's they cannon making all the noise, not me,' Thorpe grumbled.

In the centre of the rebel position, the rebel artillery smashed their shots into the marching British.

'They're good shots, them pandy boys.' Williams gave grudging praise.

'Not for much longer.' Riley winced as a roundshot ploughed into the 90th Foot, killing three men. 'Our guns are at them now.'

With a heavy battery in the British centre and lighter guns supporting the flank march on the right, the mutineers were soon under sustained fire. As they marched, the 113th watched the artillery duel between British and rebel gunners with professional interest. One by one the mutineers' guns fell silent, with their crews dead or dying all around.

'Thank God,' Elliot said. 'I don't like marching under fire.'

'If I was the mutineer commander,' Jack looked behind him at the long column of British infantry threading around the swamp, 'I'd send out my cavalry now. What a target – thousands of men out of formation. They could roll us up and end this campaign in half an hour.'

Either the gunners or Havelock must have had the same idea for once the mutineers' artillery was silenced the British guns concentrated on the opposing cavalry.

'Good shooting!' O'Neill enthused as the mutineers' cavalry shredded and fled. '*Shabash* the gunners!'

'Shabash!' Parker said. 'Now there's a good name for my dog. Shabash. Thanks, Sergeant!'

With the enemy cavalry running, the British artillery altered their target to the infantry, pounding the centre and left of the rebel line. Not used to being hammered by heavy guns, the mutineer infantry broke. A stream of running men covered the ground.

'They're beaten,' Elliot said. 'And we didn't have to fire a single shot.'

'They're not all running,' Jack said. 'The Alambagh is holding out.'

Despite losing much of their army, those mutineers who were behind the walls of the Alambagh proved their defiance by opening fire. A cannon ball screamed into the British right, followed by another, with dirty white smoke drifting across the walls.

'They won't hold for long if the Fusiliers have anything to do with it,' Elliot said, 'and the Sawnies are there as well.' He gave a mirthless chuckle. 'Now there's a combination the pandies won't like to meet!'

In a long line of bayonets, the 5th Fusiliers stormed the walls as the 78th smashed through the main gate into the pleasure garden to attack the guns from the rear.

'Shall we join them, sir?' Coleman asked hopefully.

'Stand fast and wait for orders,' Jack snarled. 'This isn't a Burmese donnybrook.'

The 113th could only watch as the Madras Fusiliers followed the 78th into the Alambagh. Attacked front and rear, the rebel survivors left the walls and retreated into the garden with the British chasing.

'That was a smart piece of work.' Elliot snapped shut the lid of his watch. 'Ten minutes flat to clear the Alambagh walls; so much for Nana Sahib's defence of Lucknow. At this rate, we'll be in the Residency before you can say, "Jack Robinson".'

Outside the Alambagh, the British cavalry pursued the fleeing mutineers into the outskirts of Lucknow, where the confusion of buildings slowed them down. Within half an hour General Outram galloped past and spoke urgently to Havelock.

'Aye, aye,' Elliot said. 'Something's happening.'

'Gather round,' the words circulated. 'The general wants to talk to us.'

General Outram sat on his horse, viewing his men with a broad smile on his face and nothing protecting his head from the now-fierce sun. 'Delhi has fallen; spread the good news. We've taken Delhi from the rebels.'

The cheer started slowly and increased to a volume Jack had not heard since the campaign started. Elliot grabbed his hand and shook it enthusiastically. 'We've beaten them here, and we've taken Delhi! Can you believe it? That's where the pandies hoped to rebuild the old Moghul Empire, the nerve centre of the rebellion.'

Jack nodded. 'We'll see,' he said. He thought of the massacre at Gondabad and the horror of the well at Cawnpore. He cared less about Bahadur Shah Zafar and his attempt at becoming Emperor, and much more about Sarvur Khan. Why? Was one murderer worse than another? Was it because Khan had helped massacre a company of the 113th? Or because of the child that Sarvur Khan threw into the burning building?

Jack shook his head. No; it was because of the dream where Sarvur Khan's face tormented him. He knew he would meet the Pathan again and must kill him before something even more terrible happened. He fdidn't understand what, or why; he only knew the two of them were somehow bound together.

'We should relieve the Residency tomorrow,' Elliot said.

'Aye,' Jack said. 'We should. God and the devil willing.'

After chasing the rebels into the suburbs of Lucknow, the British cavalry faced stiff opposition at the Charbagh Bridge and had to withdraw with some casualties.

'It's not finished yet,' Jack said. 'If the mutineers decided to defend the city, street by street, there will be bloody fighting before we reach the Residency.' He took a deep breath. 'This battle, yet alone the war, is not won yet.'

Chapter Fifteen

As the British army waited on the outskirts of Lucknow, the rain had eased off for the first time in days, allowing a window of sunshine and a chance to view the city. With his men secure and already fed, Jack checked the chambers of his revolver, felt for a cheroot and again cursed when he remembered he had none left.

'It's a city of palaces.' Jack stood behind the wall of the Alambagh and traced Lucknow through binoculars he had found abandoned beside the rebel artillery. 'It must have been wonderful before this idiot war started.'

'It was the capital of the state.' Mary was at his side, holding her hat to prevent the slight breeze from tipping it onto the garden below. 'And it is full of palaces, mosques, temples and other public buildings.'

'I've never seen anywhere quite like it,' Jack said, 'except perhaps Valetta in Malta.'

'You'll have to tell me about Valetta some time,' Mary said. 'And all the other places you've visited.'

Some time? That was rather vague, but also exciting.

'See the building there, near the river?' Mary pointed. 'That's the Chuttur Munzil, the old palace. And there,' she pointed further away across the rooftops, 'that's the Kaisarbagh, the new palace.'

Jack nodded. 'Two palaces eh? These princes knew how to take care of themselves while their subjects lived in squalor.'

'I know,' Mary said quietly. 'Unlike back home, where the queen shares her palaces with the poor.'

'Touché,' Jack said, equally quietly. He looked at her sideways. 'Have you been back home?'

'Not yet.' Mary shook her head, so she had to clutch tightly to her hat. 'I want to visit, but I haven't got the tin.' She looked away. 'That's the word, isn't it? The tin – the money?'

'That's one word for it,' Jack said. 'It's a word that schoolboys and young ensigns will say, rather than educated women.'

'I was taught to speak properly in the mission school.' Mary adopted what she evidently considered an educated voice. 'But sometimes I wish I could talk as the British-born do.' She glanced at him and away again.

'You are fine just the way you are,' Jack said. 'More than fine.'

'Thank you.' Her hand touched his arm lightly. 'If I ever visit home.' She paused as he waited. 'Will they like me?'

'Of course, they will like you,' Jack said. 'Why ever would anybody not like you?'

'Because I am half Indian,' Mary said quietly. 'Some people call me half-caste or nigger or black or other things.'

Jack controlled his sudden surge of anger. 'I hope nobody calls you such things when you go home to Britain,' he said.

'I call Britain home, as we all do,' Mary said, 'yet I'm not sure if I think of it as home really.' She sighed. 'I'd like to visit and see all the marvellous things. Buckingham Palace and Hyde Park, Old Father Thames and snow at Christmas, the Queen and horse racing at Epsom, Trafalgar Square and Georgian Bath, the Scott Country and Burn's cottage.'

'I would like to take you to all these places.' Jack realised he meant exactly what he said. He also knew that being seen with an Anglo-Indian woman in Britain would ruin any possibility of social or career advancement. He tried to imagine what his mother, or his brother William and his new wife, Helen Maxwell, would say. *It doesn't matter,* he told himself. *Damn them all.*

'I beg your pardon?' Mary looked quizzical. 'What doesn't matter?'

Jack started. 'Sorry, I was thinking out loud,' he said.

'Oh?' Mary looked sideways at him again. 'You said that Lucknow must have been wonderful before this idiot war started.'

'Did I?'

'Yes, you did,' Mary said. 'I heard you. I thought you soldiers all welcomed wars so you could prove yourselves brave and get promotion and loot.'

'I used to think like that.' Jack remembered his time in Burma when he had volunteered for every crazy mission and led his men on near-suicide attacks for exactly those reasons.

'But not now?' Mary asked.

'Not now.' Jack said no more.

'Why not? What happened to change you?' Mary turned away from the city to face him, her eyes deep and brown and calm as she probed into his soul and waited for an answer.

Jack pondered. How could he tell her of the piles of shrieking wounded at the Redan and Inkerman? How could he tell her of the rows of hanged bodies swaying beside the Great Trunk Road? How could he tell her of the horrors of the march along the Crimean beach with men flailing in the agonies of cholera? 'There is nothing glorious about war,' he said at length. 'It is ugly, sordid and dirty, a failure of politicians, diplomats, kings and emperors to work things out properly.'

'Do your fellow officers think as you do?' Mary asked.

'It is not something we talk about.' Jack thought about Elliot's constant drinking, Kent's seeming desire to avoid anything troublesome and the tense professionalism of Prentice. 'I don't know.' He wondered how much he could trust this strange, complicated woman. 'Gentlemen and officers do not voice their fears or feelings. It's not the done thing.' He waited for her reaction.

'I thought not,' Mary said. 'Yet you told me.'

'I would be obliged if you do not tell anybody else.' Jack knew that even a whisper about this conversation could damage his reputation.

'I will never tell anybody,' she said. 'Please don't tell anybody what I said about being – being what and who I am.'

Only then did Jack realise that she had confided in him as much as he had in her. Their trust was mutual. 'I won't, Mary,' and for some reason he could not understand, he added, 'thank you.'

Mary turned away so suddenly that Jack wondered if he had offended her in some way. 'Over there,' she pointed to the south-east, where two ornate buildings stood within a swathe of green parkland, 'is La Martiniere, where boys from Britain and Europe go to school, and the Dilkusha Palace.'

'Another palace,' Jack said.

'Another palace,' Mary confirmed. 'How many are there in London? Buckingham, St James, Kensington and Windsor.' She continued without waiting for his answer. 'And up-river, where we can't see, is the Machchi Bhawan, the old fort, and a collection of country mansions known as the Musa Bagh.'

'It's a fine city, as I said.' Jack tried to memorise all the names and places although he knew it was pointless. Once he and his men were down on the ground, fighting through the narrow streets and alleys, he would see nothing but blank walls and closed doorways. 'Where is the Residency? Where are our people holding out?' He knew where it was on the map; it was always different on the ground.

'Up there.' Mary pointed to the north-west and gave him a brief, near-nervous smile. 'It's the building with all the holes in it.'

The Residency stood tall on a plateau, not far from the river. To reach it Havelock's men would have to cross the Charbagh Bridge over a canal and then there was a choice. Fight for two miles through a succession of walled palaces or through Lucknow city, where the bulk of the population existed in a maze of narrow streets and flat-topped houses. 'Fighting through to there won't be easy,' he said.

'Do you have to fight all the time?' Mary asked. 'Could you not leave the Army and live in peace?'

Jack considered. If he resigned his commission, what else could he do? Nothing – his skills were all focussed on the military. He had never studied agriculture or business, law or commerce. 'No,' he said, more abruptly than he'd intended.

'Oh.' Mary looked away again. Jack wished he had given a different response. 'When are you attacking?'

'Tomorrow morning,' Jack said.

'Take care,' Mary touched his arm. 'Please take care.'

Jack looked up as the rain began once more. Their little window had ended, and it was time to concentrate on the war again.

Chapter Sixteen

'Are you all set, lads?' The men stood in their ranks, still wearing the travel-worn khaki-stained linen, still holding their Enfield rifles, faces drawn, nutmeg-brown, some shaking with excitement, others striving to appear nonchalant.

'Loosen your bayonets,' Jack ordered. 'Check you each have sixty rounds, caps and a full water bottle.' He watched as they patted and looked through their equipment. 'The pandies will fight this time so watch out for each other; don't go wandering off alone. You'll get lost, and the pandies will gut you like a fish.' The men nodded; by now they were all veterans and they knew what war in India was all about. 'The Residency is still holding out,' Jack told them. 'But we don't know for how much longer. They're short of ammunition and not sure how long the native troops in the garrison will stay loyal.'

Number Two Company, 113th Foot nodded. Some stamped their feet or frowned. 'Here's what we're doing,' Jack said. 'We advance to the Charbagh Bridge, bear right and follow the left bank of the canal to a group of palaces.' The men listened, trying to retain the information on which their lives depended.

'There are bazaars there as well as the palaces. You'll see the Residency then; it's the one where our men are holding out and defending our women.' Jack held Riley's gaze for a moment and looked away. 'We'll have our artillery with us, and we'll move in two brigades. General Outram will lead the first one, including us and the guns, while

General Havelock commands the second.' The men nodded – they knew of Outram as a fighting general. 'Good luck, men. Follow orders, do your duty and support each other.'

'Cry Havelock!' O'Neill took up Elliot's battle cry, and the men all joined in. 'Let loose the dogs of war!' They grinned at each other, knowing that call was unique to the 113th; it had become a regimental tradition.

Shortly after eight the word "advance" came through, and General Outram spurred on his horse toward the Charbagh Bridge.

'Follow the general.' Jack lengthened his stride to lead on his men. On either side of the road, mutineers hid amidst the long rank grass, shooting at the advancing column. More rebels fired from loopholes in the garden walls as well as from the windows on both stories of a substantial house.

'Ambush Alley,' Coleman shouted. 'Keep your heads down, boys!'

A cannon boomed from the right flank, and a nine-pounder ball tore into the second rank of the 113th, ripping the legs off a man. He fell without a sound and stared unbelievingly at the blood that spurted from his stumps.

'Push on!' Jack fired his revolver at the two-storey house, knowing his shots had little chance of taking effect. He ran on, following Outram on his horse, seeing white powder-smoke clouding around the houses and rising from the grass. Fountains of dust and chips of stones revealed where bullets smacked against the road.

Private Riordan staggered as a bullet hit his shoulder. He swore as a second crashed into his knee. He fell, shouting in Gaelic and English. 'Go on boys! Give them hell!'

'Here come the guns,' Elliot yelled. The men cheered when Captain Maude brought up his six pounders, unlimbered and opened rapid fire with grapeshot and canister through the grass before concentrating on the buildings. The rebel fire slackened. The British pushed on.

Losing men, firing back whenever they saw a target, swearing profusely, already hot and sweating, the British advanced. The mutineers' fire increased again, with a battery of artillery on the Lucknow bank opening up as the 113th pounded to the bridge. A twenty-four-pound cannon ball ripped overhead to land somewhere in the column further back. Jack heard somebody scream; there was musketry from houses on the Lucknow bank and a sharp and accurate volley from the high wall of the Charbagh Gardens. More men fell to lie still or roll around the ground, cursing.

'They're ready for us,' Elliot said. 'That's a high rampart.' The seven-foot high earthwork blocked the road from side to side with only a single central gap. Even as Jack watched, the six-cannon battery on the parapet of the earthwork fired again, spraying grapeshot across the bridge.

Knowing an advance would bring heavier casualties than they could afford, the British found cover on the wrong side of the bridge. Out-matched by the rebel artillery, they fired back, with the Enfield bullets kicking up spurts of dust and small chips from the stone walls of the houses and gardens.

'This is the hottest fight so far,' Elliot said as he reloaded his revolver. 'Somebody has taught the pandies how to fight.'

Jack nodded, checked his men, shouted for Thorpe to keep his fool head down and fired in the direction of the twenty-four-pounder. 'Aye; they're fighting now.'

There was a stalemate, British and mutineers exchanging musketry and then there was the jingle of harnesses and the creak of wheels as Maude brought up his faithful battery of artillery.

'He won't get them up that narrow road.' Jack flinched as a bullet whined off the road a few inches in front of his face.

'Yes he will,' Elliot said as Maude set up his brace of cannon. 'He's a brave man.'

They watched as Maude set up his guns, and within a few moments, he opened fire. The mutineers responded at once, with six cannons blasting back.

'This isn't good.' Elliot ducked as a rebel roundshot crashed into a building twenty feet away.

'There goes Outram,' Jack said as the general led the 5th Fusiliers off to the right to storm the walled Charbagh Gardens. 'Once the Fusiliers take the Charbagh they'll be able to fire on the mutineers flank. They may have come late to the war, but they're making up for it now.'

Jack checked the British position. In the centre, Maude's two guns were fighting their unequal battle with the larger and heavier mutineer artillery. Slightly to the left and a few yards forward were twenty-five Madras Fusiliers, firing furiously at the heavily manned houses opposite. To the right of Maude's guns were Jack's 113th, bringing repressing fire onto the Charbagh to give Outram's company a chance. Others of the Madras Fusiliers were lying behind a wall to the rear of Maude's cannon, waiting for the word to advance. General Neill stood calmly beside the wall of the Charbagh, while young Lieutenant Havelock sat astride his horse on the opposite side of the road.

'Keep firing lads, but don't waste ammunition!' Jack remembered the Crimea when his men had sometimes needed to search for bullets.

When any of Maude's men fell, willing volunteers from the 113th or the Madras Fusiliers stepped forward to man the guns. Maude had already taken the place of a fallen gun-layer, with Lieutenant Maitland loading for him. 'Havelock!' Maude shouted over the bark of his battery. 'We're getting murdered here! Do something, for God's sake!'

Lieutenant Havelock kicked in his spurs, riding past Jack to approach Neill. Against the constant hammer of the cannon, Jack couldn't hear what the lieutenant said, but he guessed Havelock was requesting permission to charge. By a strange coincidence, all the guns stopped together as Neill replied, 'I cannot take the responsibility; wait for General Outram.'

'Sir,' Jack ran up, ducking when a mutineer musketeer aimed specifically at him. The ball whined past his head. 'General Neill; I can take my men forward and capture these guns.'

'You will do no such thing, Captain Windrush.' Neill glared at him. 'You will remain where you are until you receive further orders. We will wait for the commander.'

Jack glanced at the high wall separating them from Outram and the 5th Fusiliers. Nobody knew what was happening over there although the crackle of musketry told its own story.

'Captain Windrush' Lieutenant Havelock was grinning, full of fire. 'Are your men ready to fight?'

'We're the 113th!' Jack gave the simple reply.

'Then with your permission, sir, I have an idea.' Lieutenant Havelock said and withdrew to the rear as Jack returned to his men.

'The lieutenant's turned coward,' Thorpe said. 'Look at him; he's running away!'

'Not a chance.' Coleman shook his head. 'Not that young scud. He's his father's son, that one.'

Thorpe frowned. 'Of course, he's his father's son, Coley. You say some right stupid things. It was stupid, wasn't it, Parker?'

Before Parker could reply, Lieutenant Havelock galloped back, reined in his horse in a flurry of hooves and threw Neill an impressive salute. 'You are to carry the bridge, sir!'

'Cheeky young beggar,' Coleman said. 'He's pretending he asked the general for permission. Now watch him go.'

Lieutenant Havelock waved his sword, kicked in his spurs and charged. 'Come on, the Madras Fusiliers!'

Lieutenants Arnold and Tytler of the Madras Fusiliers jumped up from cover and led forward their men. The Fusiliers' boots thundered onto the bridge as the mutineers behind the earthwork rose in a red-coated body while the cannon opened fire with lethal grapeshot.

'It's slaughter,' O'Neill said as the Madras Fusiliers were scythed down. Arnold yelled as grapeshot crashed into both his thighs; he fell, writhing, with Tytler curled beside him, his horse dead and a ball in his groin. Of the twenty-five Madras Fusiliers, twenty-four were down and only a lone private named Jakes upright. Untouched, Lieutenant Havelock still waved his sword. 'Follow me!'

'Come on, lads before the guns reload.' Jack rose and charged forward onto the bridge, knowing his men would follow. If they failed to relieve Lucknow, the rebels would take heart and tens of thousands more might rally to their cause. They could sweep the British out of India in a scarlet storm of bloodshed. Jack had to cross the bridge and push past the pandies. The future of British India, the prosperity of Great Britain and possibly the stability of the world depended on it, for without the British Empire the oceans would lose their policeman and Europe its model of security and resolution.

The 113th followed, yelling, roaring, swearing, firing as they ran, bayonets gleaming in the sun and boots hammering on the bridge. With them were the remainder of the Madras Fusiliers, desperate to avenge their fallen comrades. In front, Lieutenant Havelock and Private Jakes still stood, facing the entire mutineer defence line.

The mixed 113th and Madras Fusiliers crashed across the bridge and threw themselves onto the earthwork. Jack leapt up, grappled for a handhold, felt somebody pushing him from beneath and tumbled over the top. There was a sea of mutineers there, some in white uniforms, some still in scarlet, together with local warriors in all manner of clothing from simple loin-cloths to spiked helmets and chain mail.

Jack shot a white-uniformed mutineer, ducked under the swing of a tulwar, kicked the wielder in the groin and fired at another mutineer who lunged at him with a bayonet. He felt the sting as the spear-point sliced his left arm and then Logan was at his side, yelling his incomprehensible slogans.

'That's for Charlotte, you murdering pandy bastards, that's for Gondabad, and that's for Cawnpore!'

'Cry Havelock!' Elliot shouted, with the cry being taken up along the length of the line. The 113th and Madras Fusiliers spread right and left, bayoneting and shooting, crushing any resistance, killing the artillerymen who had done so much damage and stabbing at their dead bodies again and again.

'Roll up the line!' Jack ordered, dropping cartridges as he reloaded feverishly. 'O'Neill, how many casualties?'

Even during the chaos of combat, O'Neill kept a sharp eye on his men. 'We lost Manson and Evans on the bridge sir, and MacLeod is wounded.'

Jack swore; his company couldn't afford many more losses. 'We'll miss them. Keep the pressure up, push the pandies back before they have time to reorganise.'

'Yes, sir!'

As more British arrived, the mutineers withdrew step by stubborn step. Jack took a deep breath of the humid air. The road to the Residency was won, but only after bitter fighting. He looked back at the litter of dead men and broken bodies on the bridge and its approaches. Was the Empire worth such a price in human suffering? Was anything worth the loss of husbands, sons and brothers? Sliding down, he flexed his left arm where his wound flowed blood. It was only a scratch, but in this climate, it could fester. He would have to take care of it.

As the second brigade marched across the bridge, General Havelock consolidated his success. '78th; advance – hold the road and ensure the mutineers don't interfere with the advance of the heavy artillery. When the rest of the army has passed, act as rear guard.'

Knowing the mutineers were almost certain to attack along this road to delay the passage of the guns, the bearded, kilted men of the 78th looked pleased. 'Aye, sir,' they said and crunched firmly forward as the remainder of Havelock's army followed the pre-arranged plan and turned right to march beside the canal.

'It's bloody hot.' Elliot fanned a hand in front of his face.

Jack nodded, marching with thousands of other men along a narrow lane was not conducive to coolness in India. He looked over his shoulder, hoping the rebels didn't attack while they marched in column.

'Why don't they hit us now?' Elliot echoed Jack's thoughts. 'We're stretched like string, and with the canal behind us, there's nowhere to fall back on.'

'Poor leadership.' Jack repeated what he'd said before. 'We're fighting some of the best soldiers in the world, well trained and brave as lions. If they were better led, we'd be in real trouble.' He motioned to O'Neill. 'Sergeant, take two good men and hurry ahead; see if the mutineers have any nasty surprises prepared for us.'

'Yes, sir,' O'Neill saluted. 'Williams, Parker, you're with me. Come on!' O'Neill hurried ahead, happy to be away from the restrictions of the slow-moving column.

As they neared the Dilkusha Bridge, the British veered north toward the heart of the city and O'Neill returned. 'There's trouble ahead, sir. We've got to cross a bridge over a *nullah* at the Kaisarbagh, and the pandies are waiting for us. The Kaisarbagh is another of these walled gardens, sir.'

'Thank you, Sergeant,' Jack said. 'I'll tell the General.' *Oh God, another blasted bridge!*

'There's no help for it.' Havelock peered over the bridge into the chasm below and then looked upwards, where rebel artillery and musketeers garrisoned a solid-looking building. 'This is the best route. We'll just have to charge them again.' He sighed. 'The Good Lord knows I don't like inflicting casualties on my men. We are still three-quarters of a mile from the Residency, and the rebels seem to be in great force here.'

The bridge was only wide enough for only two men marching abreast, while rebel guns commanded the whole stretch.

'They pick their spots well.' Elliot uncorked his hip-flask and took a long swallow.

Jack nodded. He felt the tension rise within him as he always did before battle. Other officers and many of the men seemed to enjoy the thrill of combat or took it in their stride as part of the soldier's bargain. He was not of that temperament. Every encounter drained him, leaving him shaken, with a head full of images he couldn't lose and nights when nightmares returned him to the monstrosities of war. 'They know their stuff.' How many more battles would there be?

He took a deep breath. It didn't matter how many more. He would face them one by one until this war ended, as he had in the Crimea, or until he was dead or too crippled to be of any use to anybody. That was the soldier's bargain. Once again, the mutineers held the advantage, and the British had only raw courage to pit against accurate artillery. That was the only ace in their pack; that and General Henry Havelock.

As before, the British advanced into a torrent of fire which swept men away and left screaming, limbless wrecks on the ground. Jack rushed forward with his men, saw a musket ball raise chips from the road at his feet and felt a tickle on his scalp as something knocked off his hat. Shaking his head, he shouted something that was intended to be defiant, but which came out as a meaningless gabble.

'Sir?' O'Neill was at his side.

'Charge, damn you!' Jack tried to say. Slipping, he fell against the parapet. For a moment he remained there, staring into dizzying space as bullets and balls cracked and whined all around him, and his men thundered past, and then somebody took hold of his arm.

'Are you all right, sir?' O'Neill looked genuinely concerned. 'Best get you somewhere safe.' There was a sudden roar from the Kaisarbagh, and a charge of grape ripped the length of the bridge, bringing down men in a froth of blood, flesh and splintered bones.

Jack allowed himself to be helped up. 'Thank you, O'Neill.'

'Come on sir, while they're reloading the gun.' Grabbing Jack by the sleeve, O'Neill dragged him off the bridge, just as the cannon fired again, scattering deadly grapeshot.

'The lads can't get past.' Jack tried to shake the dizziness from his head.

'No, sir.' O'Neill was frowning. 'You've been hit, sir.'

'What? Only my arm, a long time ago.' Jack touched his left forearm. The wound was open again.

'No, sir. You're bleeding from your head.' O'Neill put a grimy finger on Jack's temple.

'Am I?' Jack touched the place; his fingers came away wet with blood. 'So I am.' He tried to smile, but the effort made him giddy. 'We'd better push on.'

'We're all alone, sir. The lads couldn't cross.' O'Neill pointed to the far side of the bridge, where the 113th sheltered behind broken houses and isolated rocks.

'We'll have to take the gun without them then,' Jack shouted as the rebels' artillery roared again.

'Yes, sir,' O'Neill replied, and then there sounded a loud cheer and the rattle of musketry on the mutineers' side of the bridge. The firing rose to a crescendo and died away, to erupt again.

'Something's happening, sir!' O'Neill said. 'That was a British cheer.'

A few moments later a kilted corporal strode to the bridge and waved for the Madras Fusiliers and the 113th to cross the bridge. 'Over you come, lads,' he shouted. 'The 78th have done your work for you.'

'How the hell did you get there?' O'Neill bellowed. 'You're meant to be the rearguard.'

'We were fighting off the pandies while you beggars were having your wee stroll beside the canal.' The corporal sounded cheerful despite the bandage across his face. 'We kept them at bay for three hours on the Cawnpore road, threw their guns into the canal and came through the town to help you out.'

'Glad to see you.' Jack pushed himself upright. The ground seemed to be swaying all around him. 'Where are my men?'

'They're coming now,' O'Neill said. 'Houghton is gone though, and Gordon's wounded. Are you all right, sir?'

'We're losing far too many.' Jack pushed O'Neill's supporting hand away, blinking as blood flowed into his left eye. 'Could I borrow your bayonet, O'Neill?'

Removing his tunic, Jack cut off the left sleeve of his shirt, folded it into a rough bandage and tied it around his head. He knew it looked theatrical, but it would serve to keep the blood from his eyes until he could get proper medical attention.

A steady flow of British soldiers was crossing the bridge now, their boots echoing on the stone. They sheltered behind a group of ruinous buildings a few yards from the walls of the Chatr Manzil, the Umbrella Palace and looked forward. Jack counted his men – only forty left standing of the 113th now, and darkness was fast approaching. He didn't relish the idea of a night among this complex of palaces and spacious garden grounds with no defensive lines and thousands of mutineers and other rebels prowling around.

'This place could be paradise.' There was fresh blood soaking through Elliot's tunic and powder burns on his sleeve. 'But this battle's turning it into Satan's playground.' He gestured to the bridge. 'Here are the generals coming along now; I wish Havelock were in sole charge.'

Outram was smiling, apparently pleased at the progress they had made. 'We'll halt here at the Chatr Manzil until the remainder of the rearguard and the heavy guns join us.' He sat erect on his horse amidst the devastated splendour of the Nawab of Oudh's palaces.

'No, sir.' Havelock's decision outweighed Outram's. 'Our duty is to reach the garrison in the Residency; our primary task is to help the poor women and children inside there. God alone knows what suffering this siege has put upon them.'

Jack felt the blood soaking through the makeshift bandage on his head as Outram and Havelock discussed what was best to do. 'We'll be hard hit by an immediate advance,' Havelock admitted, 'but we'll do the thing quickly and get it over with.'

Outram lifted a hand and replied in anger. 'Let us go then, in God's name!'

'He means us, sir,' O'Neill said. 'Are you fit?'

'As fit as you are, damn it!' Jack said.

'We're going through the Khas Bazaar, sir.' O'Neill pointed ahead to a tangle of narrow streets and tall buildings. 'That will be a killing ground for the defenders.'

Jack raised his voice. 'To me, 113th! And stay together, for God's sake.' He swayed, righted himself and looked ahead.

'This will be tough,' Elliot said quietly. 'Dear Father, help me in my time of need.'

Jack glanced at him; Elliot was serious. 'God be with us all,' he said.

With Havelock and a wounded Outram at the head, the British formed column and moved on into the narrow streets and alleyways of the Khas Bazaar. The mutineers waited for them, firing furiously. If men strayed from their units or fell wounded, rebels would drag them away and murder them. Every window held at least one enemy musketeer, while others manned trenches they had hacked across the street.

Some mutineers fired in volleys, others in single shots and the British soldiers were falling for every yard they advanced. As always in battle the noise was constant, the popping of distant musketry and the cracking of rifles close-by, the clatter of lead balls on bayonet and rifle-barrel, the shrieks of the wounded and shouts of defiance and anger of the fighting men, the shouted orders and the wail of the Highland bagpipes.

'This is brutal!' Elliot fired his revolver and ducked behind a wall to reload as a private of the 78th crumpled at his feet, shot through the head. 'This is as bad as Inkerman!'

The dense British column was a perfect target, and although the garrison of the Residency tried to help by firing on the mutineers, man after man crumpled to the ground beneath the rebels' fire.

'Keep together, 113th!' Jack swayed, grabbed a crumbling wall for support and moved on into the labyrinth of the bazaar. His men formed behind him, shooting at anything that could be an enemy, ducking as bullets spattered around them. Musketry rattled so continuously it sounded like a single noise rather than a succession of individual shots as the British fought for every yard of ground.

'Keep going!' Jack shot a bearded man who charged at them with what looked like a scimitar and winced as a musket ball smashed into an arched doorway and sprayed splinters of stone into his face. He saw Riley bayonetting a scarlet-uniformed mutineer as Logan fired at a moving group of three rebels. He saw O'Neill and Coleman combining to deal with a group of screaming men in yellow turbans. He saw a British officer thrust his sword into a rebel's body, only for the man to slide up the blade and hack the officer's head clean off his body.

'Desperate work, eh, Jack?' Elliot fired at the rebel swordsman, shooting him again and again as he lay on the ground.

'Yes. Save your ammunition,' Jack yelled above the sound. 'We might need it later.'

There were more houses, more loopholes with smoke and fire jetting out, more British soldiers falling. Sights and sounds merged into a chaotic succession of horror, of bloodshed and screaming men, of white-clothed rebels firing from dark windows, of Moorish doorways where knifemen waited to spring at stragglers, of British oaths and wild howls of 'Allah Akbar'.

Battered, bloodied and dazed, Havelock's columns emerged from the bazaar to find men of the 78th already waiting.

'Where did you come from?' O'Neill demanded.

'We came the better route.' The same corporal who had spoken to them at the bridge wiped blood from his bayonet. 'You choose the worst places don't you, 113th?'

'We like to do things our way,' O'Neill said.

'Jack!' Elliot hurried up to him. 'Did you hear the news?'

'Not a word.' Jack reloaded; he only had one cartridge left in his revolver although he couldn't remember firing more than three shots.

'General Neill's dead,' Elliot said. 'A pandy shot him in the bazaar.'

'Oh.' Jack had never liked Neill, thinking him a brutal, violent man. 'He was a good soldier.'

'Maybe so,' Elliot said. 'But he was a poor man and a bad Christian.'

Jack could never forget Elliot's religious upbringing. 'I can't argue with that.'

'Listen!' Elliot held up a hand. 'They're cheering in the Residency!' By now, full night pressed down on them, illuminated only by the flashes of gunfire and the reflected orange glow from a fire somewhere to their rear. 'They know we're through!'

The column reformed amidst much cursing and swearing and thrust once more toward the gates of the Residency.

'Come on boys; we're nearly there!' O'Neill shouted encouragement as the 113th formed up, depleted, bloodied but defiant.

There was a group of men at the gates, dim shapes in the dark but wearing turbans and red uniforms. A squad of British soldiers charged them with rifle-butt and bayonet until a gaunt British officer screamed at them from within the Residency. 'They're loyal Sikhs!' he shouted. 'You're killing our men!'

'Oh, dear God in heaven,' Jack said, and pushed his men through the breach. 'Come on, 113th!'

'We've made it.' There were tears in Elliot's eyes as he entered the battered building in which the Lucknow garrison had endured so much and held on for so long. 'We got here.' He sunk to the ground, exhausted.

There were men all around, thin, dirty and tattered, with rifles clutched in hands like claws, and faces drawn and tense.

'Welcome to the Residency,' an officer in an unidentifiable uniform said. 'We've been waiting for you.'

'Roll call, O'Neill,' Jack demanded as the defenders rushed to meet them, hands outstretched in welcome. Their faces, lit by flickering, flaring torches were gaunt, filthy and drawn but also bright with joy.

There was food for the relievers, beef cutlets, mock-turtle soup and champagne for the generals, less for the junior officers and men. Jack looked around the bullet-scarred interior with its rifle pits, trenches and gun batteries from where the garrison had defied all the rebels could throw at them. He had thought the advance was tough, but these people had endured unending hell, with the knowledge that any weakness would mean defeat and slaughter. The lesson of Cawnpore had been well-learned. No surrender, fight to the end, keep the flag flying, save the women.

Men and women emerged from every corner of the Residency, scarred, gaunt-faced, some in ragged uniforms, others with no shoes. Veteran soldiers stared through hollow eyes while women were trying to look composed despite their tears. Even the wounded crawled from the beds in the makeshift hospital to raise a wan welcome.

Jack saw his Highland corporal lay down his rifle and hold out a hairy paw to shake the hand of an elderly lady. The 78th foot, Jack had heard, had lost a third of their strength in the last four days' fighting and here was their reward, a handshake from the women they had fought twelve battles to rescue. In another corner, Coleman and Thorpe were exchanging a bottle of illegally obtained rum for something, and there was Logan, grinning insanely and pushing Riley forward.

'Go on, Riley; she's waiting for you.'

Jack stared and furtively flicked the tears from his eyes as he saw Riley take two slow steps forward to the woman who stood, arms outstretched for him. 'Charlotte.' Riley dropped his rifle and ran forward, enfolding her in his arms.

'You took your time,' Charlotte said. 'I've been waiting and waiting and waiting.'

'I know,' Riley said as Charlotte buried her head in his chest. 'I know.'

Jack turned away. There were other families of the 113th emerging now, some enquiring about their husbands or fathers, others only staring mutely at the loud, blood-stained men who crowded into their Residency. A pair of burly, blood-smeared Highlanders held a huge-eyed baby between them, weeping, while Havelock loudly prayed for the dead and injured.

'Sir?' O'Neill's voice seemed to come from far away. 'Are you all right, sir?'

Jack looked up. O'Neill's face was at the end of a long tunnel, receding into the distance as he sunk away.

Chapter Seventeen

Jack wasn't aware of much over the next days. There were periods of light and periods of darkness. There was a soft voice in the corner and strong arms around him. There was heat, and there was more heat and then a welcome coolness that he didn't wish. He struggled against it, and a familiar voice was speaking. 'Don't be such a baby, Jack Baird Windrush,' and the words were known to him from a very long time ago, and he relaxed and let people do things to him.

There was thunder outside, yet he knew it wasn't thunder, and lightning he knew was not lightning, and then the acrid smell of powder smoke was in his nostrils together with the sickly-sweet reek of blood.

'Jack Baird Windrush.' The words whispered through the night. 'Do your duty, Jack Baird Windrush.' When the words faded, a bearded face leered at him with hate in its eyes.

Jack started up with tight beads of sweat formed on his forehead and streaming in rivulets down his back. Looking into the darkness, he struggled to control his breathing. He had never liked confined spaces. Living in the open air was best for him, and here he was in claustrophobic darkness surrounded by nightmares.

Flies buzzed around his head as he looked up.

'Where the devil am I?'

'You're safe with me, Jack Baird, my lad.' The woman's face was smiling down at him through concerned eyes, and the lines of tiredness were deep in her face.

'Jane?' Jack struggled to sit up, staring. 'Where am I? How did you get here and what the devil—' He looked down at himself. 'What happened?'

'You're in the hospital at Lucknow,' Jane said, 'I came with the baggage and found you wounded.' She touched the rough bandage that swaddled his head. 'You lost a lot of blood, Jack, so only God knows how you managed to get here in the first place.'

'My men?' Jack looked around. There were others in the room, many others, sick and wounded soldiers from every regiment in the relief column as well as from the 32nd Foot who made up the bulk of the original garrison. The air was hot and thick with the stench of unwashed men and human waste.

'Your Lieutenants Elliot and Prentice are looking after them,' Jane said. 'Now you rest. You're not fit yet.'

Jack shook his head, gasping at the pain that even the smallest movement caused him. 'I have rested long enough,' he said. 'I must go to my men. Why have we not left the Residency?'

'Oh, dear,' Jane said. 'That is not a question for a mere woman to answer. You'll have to ask one of the senior officers.'

Jack knew she was mocking him although he wasn't sure why, or how. 'I must get up.' Sliding sideways, he placed one foot on the floor, held on to the head of the bed and stood, only to shudder as waves of dizziness came over him. He closed his eyes and sat down abruptly with Jane at one side and somebody else at the other.

'Mary?' Jack said. 'What in the world?'

'What am I doing here? Caring for you.' Mary looked as tired as Jane. 'Now lie down and rest. You're wounded in the head and arm, and you're not strong enough to do anything.'

Jack became aware of the steady rumble of gunfire. 'Are we still under siege?'

'Yes,' Mary said. 'Lie down. Anyway, you can hardly go out as you are. You'd scare the horses.'

Jack looked down at himself. 'Where are my clothes?' His attempt to cover up made both women smile.

'It's far too late for modesty, Jack Baird. Who do you think has been looking after you these past weeks?' Jane eased him back down.

'These past weeks?' Jack winced as the pain in his head increased with each word he spoke. 'I've been out for weeks?'

'You have,' Jane said quietly.

'Bring me my uniform and my revolver,' Jack said. 'I must get back to duty.'

Mary and Jane glanced at each other. 'You see?' Jane said. 'Just like I said; he's as stubborn as always. All right Jack, if you're sure. We'll help you dress.'

'I've been dressing myself since I was three years old.' Jack ignored Jane's smile. He sat up again. Badly wounded men lay on cots, waiting patiently for death to release them from torment while others muttered in the delirium of fever. 'This is a terrible place,' he said. 'It is not a place for ladies.'

'War is not a place for humans,' Jane said, the words quiet and sincere. 'There is enough suffering in the world without adding more.'

Jack swayed, to find Mary's arms supporting him. 'I'm all right,' he said.

'You're anything but all right,' Mary told him.

'You were always stubborn, even as a baby, Jack Baird.' Jane was smiling, her eyes gentle.

'How the devil…' Jack sat down on the bed. 'How do you know my full name? I never tell anybody.'

'This is neither the time nor the place,' Jane said. 'Wait until you're strong enough.'

'I'm strong enough now, damn it.' Jack threw off Mary's supporting arms. 'I'm not a blasted invalid!'

'You see? Stubborn.' Jane smiled at Mary and sat on the bed at Jack's side. 'As you wish, Jack. I helped name you, you see. Jack Baird was my father.'

Mary's arm tightened around Jack's shoulders. Jack's head felt as if it would explode. 'Why?' he asked at last. 'Why did you name me? Why not my father or my mother?'

'I am your mother, Jack.'

'Oh, dear God.' Jack stared at her. He had known that he was illegitimate and was born in India. 'But you're Eurasian.' He spoke the words without thought and without any intent to insult or offend.

'Is that so bad?' Jane knelt at his side, her face on a level with his.

The other people in this makeshift hospital dissolved into the distance as Jack stared at her. 'I didn't know.' Jack shook his head and ignored the screaming pain the simple act caused. 'How?'

'Now that is a silly question, isn't it?' Jane was smiling through her concern. 'The usual way.'

Jack tried to stand as Mary rubbed his back. 'I have to think,' he said. 'I have to think about this.'

'Take your time, Jack,' Jane said. 'Finding your mother and knowing from where you come is a lot to take in.'

'I don't know what to say.' Jack looked away.

'Go and do your duty,' Jane said, still quietly. 'It is what a Windrush should do. Or a Baird.'

'Yes.' Jack found himself instinctively dressing although a hundred images crowded his mind. He was Eurasian, he was part Indian – he didn't belong in any respectable society. No wonder his step-mother had disowned him. He staggered away, leaving Jane squatting by the bed and Mary with a hurt expression on her face that cut him more deeply than anything Helen had ever said or done. Ignoring the sick and wounded, Jack lurched out of that hellish place of suffering and sickness and into the harsh sunlight of the siege.

'Are you all right, Jack?' Mary had followed; her hand was on his arm.

He drew a deep breath of the dusty, smoke-laden atmosphere and coughed. 'Well enough.' He saw a man with bandages swathing one arm and one leg standing behind a cannon, and an infantryman limping across to his post by the aid of a crutch. 'If these men can fight, then so can I.'

'That is not what I meant.' Her voice was soft.

He knew Mary was watching him, waiting for something. 'So I am Eurasian,' Jack said at last.

'Yes, you are,' Mary said. 'You can't blame your mother for what she is.' A sudden sputter of musketry made her duck.

Jack held her instinctively. 'It's all right; it's over to the left and can't hit us.' His hand fluttered to his top pocket, although he knew it had been empty for many weeks. The half dozen cheroots came as a welcome surprise. 'How did they get there?'

Mary smiled through her weariness. 'Most of your men have visited you, and one pair was very interested in your uniform. I thought they were going to steal it, so I chased them away.'

'Who was it?' Jack already guessed. He sniffed the cheroot, inhaling the rich tobacco scent with great pleasure.

'The small ugly man...'

'Donnie Logan,' Jack said. 'And Riley would be the second.'

'Yes, Riley. He's been terribly anxious about his wife.'

Jack sniffed the cheroot again. Despite his murderous headache and all the mutineers in India, despite the revelation that he was Eurasian, he could face the world again. He had a smoke, he could think about his ancestry later. 'Time to get back to war, Mary.' He kissed her without thinking and limped across the courtyard, ignoring the constant rumble of artillery.

Chapter Eighteen

Blistering sunlight reflected from the interior of the defences as Jack staggered outside. He looked around; eyes narrowed in an attempt to combat the light as much as the pounding of his head. He lit the cheroot and inhaled for the first time in weeks, feeling the smoke relax him.

'Ah, Windrush,' General Havelock greeted him. 'Glad to see you're back on your feet. Your men are in the Chuttur Munzil, beside the Gomti River. That's another of these huge palaces.'

'Yes, sir. May I ask what's been happening?'

'We aren't strong enough to break out,' Havelock said. 'We lost over five hundred men in the final push through the bazaar, and so rather than relieve Lucknow, we are now under siege ourselves.'

Jack nodded – so it had all been in vain. The struggles and the victorious battles, the losses by gunfire and disease, the effort and suffering to relieve the Residency hadn't worked. The siege continued except the defenders had received a reinforcement of a few hundred men. The mutineers had let them in, then banged shut the door.

'What we have done is increased the area we hold.' Havelock was tense. 'As well as the Residency we now occupy most of the buildings to the east including the Farhat Bakhsh and Chuttur Munzil palaces and grounds.'

Jack nodded. 'Yes, sir. That's something.'

'It's not enough,' Havelock said. 'It's a line of gardens, courts and dwelling houses without fortified enceinte, without defences, and closely connected to the buildings of the city.'

'Is there a clear field of fire, sir?' Jack controlled the constant agony of his head. He refused to think of his origin. He must concentrate on military matters and ignore everything else.

'As much for them as for us, Windrush. The rebels have men all around, with musketeers in tall buildings and loopholed walls, plus artillery firing from as close as seventy yards.'

'Yes, sir,' Jack said. 'How about the population of Lucknow? Are any of them loyal to us? Could we start a rebellion among them to rise against the rebels?'

'No.' Havelock shook his head. 'The loyal people are cowed. The rebels rule them by fear.'

'So we're trapped here then, sir?'

Havelock gave a bleak smile. 'Sir Colin Campbell is nearing us with a sizeable force, so our duty is to hold out until he gets here. In the meantime, Windrush, take charge of the 113th.'

'Yes, sir.' Jack hesitated. 'Have you any news of Major Snodgrass and the other men, sir? He was with the women when they left for Cawnpore.'

Havelock shook his head. 'Not a word. The women, God bless them, told me that Major Snodgrass disappeared with their escort en-route. I can only surmise the rebels killed them.'

'Yes, sir.'

Havelock closed his eyes for a moment. 'He will be in the Lord's care, Windrush, as we all are. You will no doubt be anxious to rejoin your men?'

'I am sir.'

'You will find siege warfare different from the campaign so far. This war is about mines and explosives as much as attacks and snipers.' Havelock nodded. 'Your men are listening for mines. Go and do your duty, Windrush.'

'Yes, sir.' Although Jack admired Havelock, he found any conversation with a senior officer a strain and was glad to be dismissed.

Conditions in Lucknow proved to be every bit as grim as they had been on the march from Cawnpore. Men, women and children hung on desperately to their little section of the city while the rebels were constantly ready to snipe them, attack in mass or batter them with cannon. The defenders were thin, most with boils and suppurating sores as well as un-heeded wounds.

Jack winced as he looked around. He had seen the hospital where women who were accustomed to an array of Indian servants and a life of balls and social events tended to men with hideous wounds and dysentery. Now he saw huge-eyed children ignoring the daily deaths, and their parents put on a mask of cheerfulness as shot and shell crashed around them.

'This is no life for a Christian.' Elliot gasped as a cannonball smashed into the wall behind which he sheltered.

'War is no life for a human.' Unconsciously Jack paraphrased Mary's previous words. He had never agreed with her more.

He didn't mention the constant hammering inside his head. Men in bandages and splints stood uncomplaining on guard all around him with Prentice looking efficient as he stalked the walls. 'I was told we are listening for mines.'

'Most of our men are in the cellar,' Elliot said in some disgust. 'Follow me to the pits of the world.'

The cellars were dark and stuffy, lit by small candles that bounced shadows off ancient walls and did little to alleviate the sinister atmosphere. Some of the 113th were busy with pick-axe, shovel and iron bar, widening a four-foot square hole.

'Where's Williams and Logan?' Jack glanced around.

'Down there, sir.' O'Neill jerked a thumb down the hole. 'It goes down deep.' He gave Jack a long look. 'Are you sure you're fit to return to duty?'

'That's none of your damned business.' Jack proved the strain on his nerves before he recollected himself. 'Sorry, O'Neill. Yes, I am fit, thank you. What's been happening here?'

A lifetime in the army had taught O'Neill to shrug off insults and abuse. 'The pandies are trying everything to get in, sir. As well as sniping and full-scale bombardments, they are using mines to place explosives under sections of the wall, so they can blow them up and charge in the breach. Our lads are sinking counter mines and fighting them underground.'

Jack nodded. 'How do we know where the mutineers' mines are?'

O'Neill grinned. 'We use Williams like a pointer dog, sir. He listens for the pandies, and we dig where he directs.'

'Oh, Riley!' Jack saw Riley leaning against a wall, covered in dust. 'Thank you for the cheroots.'

'I don't know what you mean sir,' Riley said.

'Don't you? Well, thank you anyway.' Jack looked down the mine shaft and felt the slow slide of sweat down his back. *Oh, sweet Jesus in heaven, I don't want to go down there.*

'Are you fit to go down sir?' O'Neill asked. 'If you don't feel up to it—'

'I'm going down.' Jack pushed aside his fears. He remembered the explosion outside Sebastopol when he was temporarily buried alive. He had survived that, he could survive this. 'Is there room for more than one man?'

'There's room for two, sir,' O'Neill said. 'Williams and Logan are the best at this. Williams feels totally at home and Logan can nearly stand upright down there.'

'Bring Logan up.' Jack knew he had no choice. An officer should never order a man to do what he would not do himself. He waited until Logan hauled himself out of the mine.

'Hello there, sir,' Logan's grin was genuine. 'Are you going down?'

'Yes, Logan.'

Cursing the constant pain in his head, Jack grabbed hold of the top rung of the ladder and took a deep breath.

'Sir.' Logan handed over the stub of a candle. 'You might need this.'

'Thank you, Logan.' Jack felt for the next rung of the ladder and moved downward with the square of lesser dark above him growing smaller with each step. At the bottom of the shaft, a low tunnel plunged away at an acute angle. Taking a deep breath to control the hammering of his heart, Jack dropped into a crouch and edged down the tunnel, feeling as if the earth was closing in on him.

'Who's there?' Williams peered from behind the small flame of a candle.

'Captain Windrush,' Jack said. 'What's happening? I can't see much digging going on.'

'We've finished the digging at present, sir.' Williams seemed quite at home at the bottom of this constricting tunnel. 'I'm listening for the pandies, sir.'

'Listening?'

'Yes, sir. Sound travels easily through rock and earth. I was talking to some of the Cornish boys of the 32nd; they were tin miners back home, and they've been in Lucknow since the siege began. They said to dig down and listen, and you can hear the pandies hacking away.' Williams spoke in a low tone and tapped his rifle. 'Once I hear where they are, we'll dig across their route and wait.' His grin was anything but pleasant.

'Then what?'

'We kill them, sir,' Williams said.

Jack nodded. The thought of a battle so far underground was appalling. 'You're a brave man, Williams.' He spoke without thinking.

Williams shrugged. 'Thank you, sir.'

'Is there anything you need?' Jack asked.

'Yes, sir, if you don't mind.' Williams tapped his rifle. 'I got one shot with this, sir, and then it's just the bayonet. If I could have a revolver sir, I'd be able to do for more of them.'

'Of course.' Without thinking, Jack unbuckled his pistol and handed it over together with its holster and ammunition.

Williams shook his head. 'I didn't mean yours, sir; you might need it.'

'Better in your hands than mine,' Jack said. 'I can easily get another.' Many officers had died in the siege – he would buy one of their revolvers, and the money would eventually reach their dependents.

Hoping the men would attribute his shaking to his wound rather than to fear, Jack shuffled his way back toward the surface. Gasping and holding his head, he held on to the lower rungs of the ladder before he ascended. The men above were talking, the words distorted until he neared the top of the shaft.

'Treasure,' Riley was saying. 'The Nabob of Lucknow was a rich bugger, richer than Croesus and he was the richest man ever known.'

'I never knew that,' Logan said.

'Well, you wouldn't, would you? Nobody ever told you.' Riley lowered his voice. 'Now this treasure must be somewhere in the city, and I'd wager it's inside the Residency.'

'You mean we've got it?' Logan caught on.

'Why do you think John Company is in this fly-infested country?' Riley said. 'To make money for the merchants, nothing else. That's why we're here, Logie; to make sure the wealthy merchants of the oh-so-very Honourable East India Company get even richer.'

'I thought we were here to protect the Empire,' Logan said.

'And what exactly is the Empire?' Riley asked and answered his own question. 'It's a trading place where merchants and those with shares in the companies make money, and the rest work for them or protect them.'

'Is that right? Can we not have shares then, Riley?'

'You have to be rich to do that,' Riley said.

'How do we get rich?' Logan sounded genuinely interested.

'Steal from somebody else, as the nobs did,' Riley said. 'Or dig up gold in Australia or California.'

'I'd like to dig up gold,' Logan said. 'When I leave the army, I'll go to Australia and get rich.'

'We could get rich here,' Riley said. 'The Nabob's treasure, remember?'

'Riley!' Jack thought it best to interrupt them before Riley returned to his cracksman days and got himself and Logan hanged or transported. 'Bring me up!'

Riley was straight-faced as Jack emerged from the tunnel. 'Here you are, sir, all safe and sound.'

'Thank you, Riley. That's more than you'll be if I see you within a hundred paces of the Nabob's treasure if there is such a thing. Do you understand me?'

'Yes, sir.' Riley came to attention.

'Remember the instructions General Havelock gave about looting? Looters were to be hanged. As far as I am aware, those orders still stand. Think of the noose, Riley, and remember how well I know you and your little ways. If I hear of even one coin going missing, I will personally loop the rope around your neck.' Jack stared at Riley for thirty seconds to drive the message home before he marched away.

Could Riley break into the treasury? More than likely he could. Although Jack knew he would do his duty if required, part of him half-hoped Riley would be successful. God knew that private soldiers had a hard life and it would be good to hear of at least some of them making a success of things. He felt the smile cross his face until he recalled his Eurasian blood and felt the sick slide of despair.

Why me?

It was always worse at night when the images came to haunt him. Now he also had the knowledge that he was part Indian. All the taunts and insults he had heard his men use to address the natives also applied to him. The names circled through his mind – nigger, black, half-breed, half-caste. He could add them to the other names he carried with him – bastard, lower-class, born-on-the-wrong-side-of-the-blanket, unwanted.

He didn't belong anywhere.

But there was also a not-yet-acknowledged pearl. He had discovered his true mother, and she cared for him more than his stepmother ever had. Did her place of birth and race matter? He twisted in mental agony as he wrestled with this new knowledge, so it was a relief when Elliot stood beside him.

'What is it?'

'There's something happening underground, sir.'

It was the news Jack least wished to hear. He reached for his borrowed pistol even as he stood. 'I'm coming.' He glanced upward as he staggered toward the cellars, thinking it ironic that now the better weather had come, he was working underground. This November morning was much more pleasant than summer had been, with the cool season on them and the nights sufficiently chill for a fire. Yet food was in short supply and ammunition shorter for the besieged garrison within Lucknow. Sir Colin Campbell was coming with another relief force, but unless he arrived very soon, things would be unbearable for the besieged garrison.

O'Neill was at the mouth of the shaft with half a dozen men at his back. 'Williams thinks the pandies are up to something big, sir.'

'I'll go down, O'Neill.' Jack checked his revolver and descended the ladder. Once again, waves of panic flowed through him and he stopped to control his breathing. His worst childhood nightmares had included being buried alive, alone in the dark. Now it might just become a reality. To die was part of the soldier's bargain, either in battle or because of disease; to be entombed in the ground was no way for a man to end his life. He took a deep breath. There was no choice – duty dictated he must continue.

'Sir.' Williams seemed not to have moved since Jack's previous visit except the space around him was larger, and Logan was at his side.

'What's happening, Williams?'

'The pandies are on the move, sir, and to judge by the sound, they're in force.'

Logan shifted over, allowing Jack to sit at his side. 'It's good down here, isn't it, sir?'

'You like it, Logan?' Only Logan could enjoy sitting in a dark tunnel scores of feet underground with the possibility of an imminent attack by an unknown number of mutineers.

'Aye, sir. It's nice and quiet and out of the sun.'

'I suppose it is,' Jack said. 'So if you're also nice and quiet we can listen for the pandies.' It was worse in the silence. Jack could hear Logan and Williams breathing as if the earth itself was alive and constricting all around him. The stench of men's bodily aromas filled the air.

'There, sir,' Williams said. 'Can you hear it?'

Jack nodded. There was a definite scraping sound, followed by a steady chunk, chunk of something digging into the earth.

'If you'll permit me sir, it's louder in the dark, somehow.'

Williams blew out the candle, and all Jack's fears returned. He controlled his breathing with an effort and tried to concentrate on listening. Williams was correct; things seemed louder in the dark. The noise of scraping appeared to come from all around, while the repetitive chunking was more immediate, more threatening.

'You, see, sir?' Williams' voice sounded. 'Shall I light the candle again?'

'I'd be obliged, Williams.' Jack hid his relief as the tiny flame bounced light around the tunnel.

'As you heard, sir,' Williams said, pointing to the wall in front of him. 'They've crossed our path here and are working over there.' He indicated his right. 'They're still working, but I'm a bit confused, sir.'

'What is confusing you, Williams?' Jack asked.

'Well sir, the purpose of a mine is to blow a charge of gunpowder under a section of the defender's wall, as you know.' Williams continued before Jack could say anything. 'There is no wall over there, sir. They are passing close to our defences, yet they're not under them.'

'Parallel to them?' Jack asked.

'No, sir, not really.' Williams struggled to disagree with an officer. 'They're moving further away sir, out toward the city if anything.'

'What the devil are they up to?' It seemed as if the mutineers were hacking out a tunnel without any strategic purpose. 'Thank you,

Williams,' Jack said. 'I'll pass this to higher command and see what they say.' He looked back at the dark tunnel to the world above. 'In the meantime, if anything alters, send me a message at once.'

'Yes, sir.'

'When do you get relieved?'

'Oh, we don't, sir.' Logan said. 'We're content down here. No guard duties and no Sergeant O'Neill screaming and yelling at us.' He grinned and leant back against the hacked-out wall. 'This is the easiest posting I've ever had.'

'Even although the mutineers are only a few feet away?' Jack indicated the crumbling dirt of the tunnel, barely a yard away.

Logan's grin widened. 'Won't they be the sorry ones if they break through sir, to find Wills and me waiting for them?' He touched the bayoneted rifle at his side and the tulwar that leant against the wall. 'We'll slaughter them sir, the baby-murdering bastards.'

'Let me know if anything else happens.' Jack couldn't stay there longer. The walls were closing in on him, and his flesh itched and burned with the desire to run. He had to leave.

The room was crowded, with Havelock, looking drawn and sick, sitting at the table beside Outram and a gathering of other officers. As they listened to Jack's report, Outram drummed his fingers on the table.

'As you are aware, gentlemen,' he said, 'the siege is reaching a climax. We are in daily semaphore contact with Sir Colin Campbell's relief column, and we are also engaged in an underground war.' He consulted the paper that lay on the table in front of him. 'We have dug twenty-one shafts and created 3,291 feet of gallery. The rebels have dug twenty mines against us, mainly against the outposts and palaces. They have exploded five; three caused loss of life among us, two did not. We have blown in seven of their mines and driven them out of seven, thanks to the efforts of our miners.' The officers listened as Outram listed the successes and setbacks of the siege. 'And now you tell me of this new mine.'

'Perhaps they have merely lost their way underground, sir?' a captain of the 32nd said.

'That is hardly likely.' Outram unfolded a plan of the defences. 'Now, Windrush, where exactly is your mine?'

Jack stabbed down with more force than he had intended.

'And in which direction was the enemy digging?' Outram placed a small cross where Jack had indicated.

'This way, sir, as far as we could judge.'

'We? Who else was there?' Outram wheezed the words as the dust within the besieged lines worsened his asthma.

'Private Williams, sir. He was a miner in Wales before he joined the army.'

'He would know then.' Outram traced a straight line from the cross out toward the town of Lucknow. 'There we are. If the rebels continue along their present route, they will come to the Shah Najaf Mosque.'

'Indeed, sir?' Jack said.

'Indeed, sir,' Outram confirmed. 'The mosque is some half a mile from our outer walls; far too far for miners to dig.'

The officers nodded, unsure where Outram was taking them.

'However,' Outram said, 'you will note this open space between the mosque and our defences. Sir Colin will have to bring his column across that to reach us.'

'He may choose the same route we did, sir,' somebody said.

'We lost hundreds of men in these narrow lanes.' Havelock's whisper revealed his fragile state of health. 'Sir Colin is a cautious commander. He will have taken note of our casualties and will act accordingly.'

'Exactly, Havelock,' Outram wheezed. 'And Nana Sahib knows that. He will try to stop Sir Colin with every means at his disposal. I suspect he will plant their explosives under the open area and hope to catch Sir Colin's column as it crosses.' Outram looked up, gasping for breath. 'Windrush, I want you to stop the enemy's mine.'

Although Jack shuddered at the prospect of returning underground once more, he gave the only response he could. 'Yes, sir.' He remembered his dream, the combination of stifling dark underground and terrible danger and knew things were coming to a climax.

Chapter Nineteen

They waited in the semi-darkness with flickering candles pooling light onto the rough walls and ceiling. For the fifth time, Jack checked his revolver and the bayonet he carried on his belt. He crouched behind Williams, who had cautiously scraped away the earth toward the mutineer's tunnel. 'How far apart are we?' Jack asked.

'About a spade's length,' Williams whispered. 'I can break through in a minute.'

Jack wondered what was beyond the screen of soil; how many mutineers there were, what they were planning and if they suspected that the British knew about them. He felt the cold sweat soaking through his shirt when he thought of the thousands of tonnes of soil and rock above his head. He didn't want to die down here, so far from the sun and the rain and the wind.

'Ready lads?' He looked at the crouching men with their tense faces, tight lips and bitter-hard eyes. Each man carried his rifle and bayonet and sixty rounds of ammunition. Most also carried a personal weapon for close combat, a weighted blackjack, a captured sword or whatever took their fancy. Three men grumbled under the weight of water-kegs.

He had a dozen veterans with him; good men to fight with and he would choose none better as companions if he were to die.

'Right, Williams; on you go.'

On Jack's last word, Williams lifted a short-hafted pick and attacked the wall with savage energy. 'We have to be quick, sir,' he gasped. 'They'll hear this right away.'

The wall crumbled, soil and rocks falling away under Williams' pick. He grunted, altered the angle of his attack and hauled away a boulder. A small hole appeared.

Without hesitation, Jack thrust the barrel of his revolver through the gap and fired blindly. 'If there are any pandies there, then they'll know we mean business,' he said as Williams lifted his foot and kicked away a larger portion of the wall.

'Come on!' Jack yelled and pushed through the hole, pistol extended in front of him. With no idea what was ahead, he stumbled over the prone body of a bare-chested native carrying a barrel of something, recovered, and looked up.

He was in a larger tunnel, not as dark as the one he'd left, with torches flaring on brackets on the wall and scared looking men backing away. His picket erupted behind him, bayonets ready.

'O'Neill; take five men and form a barrier here. Don't let anybody past. The rest of you, follow me!' Jack turned to the right, where the mine continued into the flame-lit distance.

'The pandies have done a good job.' Williams gave grudging praise as they moved quickly up a broad, sloping tunnel. 'It's better than most pits I've worked in.'

After only a few moments the first shot crashed out behind them, followed by another, echoing terribly in the tunnel. 'O'Neill's in action.' Jack lengthened his stride. 'Come on men.'

Reaching the end of the mine took Jack longer than he had anticipated, and when he did, he stopped in astonishment. He had expected perhaps half a dozen barrels of gunpowder, rather than the fifty or so that were piled up in three explosive tiers.

'If they all went up there would be some bang,' Hutton said. 'Shall we start now, sir?'

Jack nodded. His plan had been to soak the gunpowder, but faced with so many barrels, his supply of water was utterly inadequate. The firing behind them increased, with yells in Irish and English as well as Logan's Glasgow Scots and a cacophony of Urdu.

'Get to the top,' Jack pointed upward. 'Try and spoil as many barrels as you can.' He cursed, wishing he had brought more men and more water. Too late now; he had to work with what he had.

Williams was first up, with Hutton and Armstrong seconds behind. Using his bayonet, Williams stabbed into the uppermost barrel and poured in water. 'That should do it, sir,' he said.

Jack made quick calculations in his head. 'You've each got a three-gallon keg, that's twenty-four pints per man, seventy-two pints in total, and there are fifty barrels of powder. Pour a pint and a half into each barrel.'

'How do we know what a pint and a half are, sir?' Hutton looked at his keg in dismay.

'Estimate,' Jack said. 'Think of a pint of beer.' Drawing his bayonet, he began to prise open the tops or hack through the wood to hasten the procedure. He didn't know how long O'Neill could hold out, or how many mutineers would come against him. Already this operation was taking longer than he'd expected and they had hardly started to dampen the powder.

The gunfire was increasing, each report magnified by the close confinement of the mine and echoing two or three times along the tunnel. 'They're getting closer, sir,' Williams said.

'Hutton; get along to O'Neill and see what's happening. Leave your water.'

Grabbing Hutton's water, Jack frantically opened kegs of gunpowder and poured in water.

'They're coming, sir,' Hutton was back in moments. 'Hundreds of them! The sergeant's wounded and Charlton's dead.'

Jack swore. They had opened and dampened twenty-three barrels of powder, which meant there were twenty-seven remaining and the mutineers were obviously pressing hard. There was a bend in the tunnel about ten yards away; he would try and hold them there. 'Williams – how far are we from the surface?'

The calmest man there, Williams screwed up his face as he looked upward. 'No distance at all, sir. There would be no point blowing this unless we were close.'

'Can you get us up there?'

'Yes, sir,' Williams replied at once.

'Do it then. Leave the powder.'

'Yes, sir.' Williams used his bayonet to hack at the roof of the tunnel as Jack loosened a barrel from the bottom layer and rolled it to the bend. O'Neill leant against the wall and fought one-handed with his rifle and bayonet while Logan and Thorpe slashed and hacked against a press of near naked mutineers. Coleman stood slightly further back, reloading. He knelt and fired.

'Back here, lads!' Jack shouted.

They withdrew slowly, fighting every step as the mutineers pushed at them.

'Sorry, sir. We couldn't hold them.' O'Neill had an ugly wound on his left arm, and blood dripped from his chin.

'No matter! Step aside.' Slicing a strip of linen from his shirt, Jack hacked a hole in the top of his powder –barrel and stuffed in the fabric. Fighting his shaking hands, he scraped a Lucifer and lit the makeshift fuse. The linen smouldered slowly, emitting smoke.

'Let's hope this doesn't bring the whole roof down,' he shouted and shoved the barrel toward the enemy. It rolled ponderously, weaving from side to side along the floor of the mine. At sight of the smoking barrel, most of the mutineers turned and fled, pushing their comrades aside in their panic. One man jumped forward and grabbed hold of the fuse, pulling it out before the sputtering flame reached the contents. Jack swore.

'Shabash!' O'Neill shouted. 'You're a brave man, pandy. Shoot him, Coleman!'

'How are you doing, Williams?' Jack fired three rounds down the tunnel and reloaded hastily before the mutineers could mount another attack. He ducked as a musket ball crashed into the wall behind him.

'There's a layer of rock, sir,' Williams replied. 'It's taking longer than I had thought.'

'Keep trying! Hutton! Give him a hand. Roll me down another barrel.'

The mutineers must have doused the torches, for the mine plunged into sudden darkness; Jack couldn't see what was happening. He fired his revolver again with the muzzle flash bringing sudden intense light. He blinked, unable to see anything at all, closed his eyes and fired two more rounds.

'They're crawling up!' O'Neill's voice sounded weak. 'Logan; Coleman, they're on the ground. Get the bastards.'

Jack opened his eyes as Thorpe managed to re-ignite one of the torches. The floor was a writhing mass of rebels crawling forward with knives in their hands. When the light flared, they jumped up and charged forward, screaming something that Jack couldn't make out. Coleman shot the first one without emotion and then thrust his bayonet through the next. 'There's done for you,' he gasped as Logan sliced sideways at the neck of another and kicked a fourth in the groin with his iron-studded boots.

'Come on then, you pandy bastards!' Logan was yelling obscenities, killing with blade and rifle butt. He staggered as a mutineer slashed at his leg, and then head-butted the man, finishing him with a bayonet thrust to the belly. 'That's for the weans, you murdering bastard.'

Jack fired another round, heard the hammer of his revolver click on an empty chamber and used the barrel like a club to smash the next man on the head. He felt something slice across his ribs, knew he had been cut and kicked upward as hard as he could, grunting in satisfaction at the resulting squeal of pain.

'I'm through, sir!' Williams sounded relieved. 'We've reached the surface!'

'Is the hole wide enough to get through?' Jack stepped back to reload as Logan and Coleman pushed back the next wave of attackers.

'Yes, sir!'

'Pull back, lads,' Jack gasped. The new wound in his side was beginning to hurt as the initial shock wore off. He thrust in the sixth cartridge, closed the revolver and peered down the mine. Shapes were shifting in the shadows. He fired twice and withdrew, limping painfully.

Williams stood at the apex of the powder-kegs, still hacking upwards. 'We've got daylight, sir,' he said.

'Coleman, Logan, help O'Neill to the surface. Thorpe, I need your skills. Where's Hutton?'

'Dead, sir.' Logan was limping, holding his leg. 'Some ugly black bastard done for him with a sword.'

'Right.' There was no time to mourn. There had been too many good men killed in this war. 'Thorpe, you and I are last out.'

'Yes, sir.' Thorpe was at his best when things were desperate. 'What do you want me to do?'

'Blow this lot up,' Jack said. 'We haven't time to wet the powder, so we'll get rid of it before Sir Colin's column arrives.'

Thorpe grinned. 'Oh yes, sir; I'm your man!'

'I'm glad to hear it, Thorpe. I don't want it to explode until we're well clear, and I want it to take the mine down. Can you do that?'

'Of course sir.' Thorpe sounded pained at Jack doubting his professional skill. He looked at the pile of kegs and the tunnel. 'It's a pity you ruined so many of them; I could have blown up half of Lucknow if you'd let me.'

Jack grunted. 'That's precisely why I did not let you, Thorpe. Hurry man; the mutineers will recover and be back anytime.'

'Give me a minute sir,' Thorpe said. 'I have to do this properly.' He tugged at the barrels, checking which ones were soaked and which still contained dry powder.

'Get a move on, Thorpe!' Jack ran to the bend in the tunnel and looked around, jerking back as somebody fired a pistol at him. 'Hurry, man!'

At Jack's shout, the press of rebels increased their speed. He fired twice at the leading man, saw him stagger and temporarily block the passage and then Thorpe was at his side, grinning.

'Right, sir, I've lit two fuses.'

'Jesus, Thorpe! We have to get out first!'

'You said to hurry, sir!' Thorpe sounded indignant. 'So I hurried.'

'Come on, man!' Firing a final shot, Jack followed Thorpe to the head of the mine, where the powder casks provided their only access to the hole in the roof.

Thorpe had laid a spiral trail of gunpowder around the top few yards of the tunnel, with the sputtering flame ending at an open keg at the bottom of the pyramid.

'How long will it take?' Jack asked as he clambered toward the hole. He gasped as the wound in his side opened, and fresh blood seeped out.

'Three minutes sir, and then,' Thorpe waited for Jack beside the hole, 'bang!' He grinned. 'I wish I could see it close.'

'If you do, you'd be blown to bits.' Jack pushed him outside. 'Get up there, Thorpe!' He had one last glance down, where sparks and smoke hissed from the gunpowder fuse, saw the mutineers rush forward and hauled himself outside. Sunlight hit him like a hammer, bright, hard and unfriendly. He stood up, suddenly feeling very exposed. He was about two hundred yards from the Residency, with gunfire booming from both sides and Thorpe hesitating, trying to stare down the hole to watch the coming explosion.

'Thorpey! Sir!' Coleman was standing in the lee of a ruined building about thirty yards away, toward the city. 'Over here!' He gestured violently. 'Hurry!'

Jack heard the crackle of musketry and then saw the mutineers; there were perhaps fifteen of them standing behind a small wall near Coleman. A havildar snapped an order, and their rifles came to the present, and another order had the muzzles pointing directly at him.

'Get down, sir!' Thorpe grabbed Jack's arm and pulled him to the ground an instant before the volley crashed out.

Jack heard the bullets passing overhead and then he was on his feet and running, with Thorpe at his side and their feet kicking up little spurts of dust.

'This way, sir!' Coleman shouted. 'We're over here!'

Jack's men sheltered in the shattered fragments of a house, with Logan and Coleman taking it in turns to load and fire over the wall toward the mutineers. Sergeant O'Neill half lay, half slumped against a broken doorway, with his face drawn and white from loss of blood.

'Sir,' Thorpe said. 'There's nothing happened. My explosion hasn't happened.'

Jack nodded, ducking as something smashed into the wall from behind him. He looked around; there was gunfire from the British defenders in front and much heavier fire from the tangled streets and palaces of Lucknow behind. They were in the middle, a no-man's land where stray shots or falling cannonballs could fall at any second. 'I hope the rebels haven't managed to put the fuse out.'

'I lit two, sir,' Thorpe said. 'That's why I was so long. I lit the one in the middle of the ground so the pandies would think there were only one, and another hidden beside the barrels.'

'Well done, Thorpe.' Jack was surprised Thorpe had thought of a decoy.

A head thrust from the hole they'd made and a rebel miner climbed out and looked around, followed by another.

'Do you want me to shoot them, sir? Or will I shoot the sepoy lads?' Logan swivelled his rifle from side to side in momentary indecision.

'Shoot the sepoys,' Jack decided for him. 'The fuse must have gone out, Thorpe.'

'No, sir.' Thorpe spoke with conviction. 'My fuses won't go out. I know what I'm doing.'

Although they were expecting it, the explosion took both Jack and Thorpe by surprise. Jack felt the shock wave before he heard anything, and then the ground around the mine rose up. It split asunder, sending dirt and rocks and pieces of human bodies in a dirty surge upwards before they fell back in a wide irregular circle. The ground between the explosion and the British positions slid downward to create an immediate and obvious depression. The two rebel miners who'd emerged had vanished.

'Jesus.' Thorpe was staring, open-mouthed. 'That was something worth seeing, sir!'

'Logan, Coleman, Williams!' Jack said sharply. 'Why have you stopped firing?' He pointed at the sepoys. 'They're standing like targets that even a Johnny Raw could hit!'

Shocked by the sudden eruption in the ground, the sepoys were staring at the still-descending debris. Some stood open-mouthed, others had dropped their rifles. Jack heard Logan's evil laugh as he lined up the Havildar and fired, with the bullet taking the man in the chest and knocking him off his feet. Coleman and Williams were a fraction slower and less accurate, with one other sepoy falling.

'Sir!' Thorpe rubbed his ears and shouted. 'Can you hear something?'

'It's only temporary,' Jack yelled. 'Your hearing will come back.'

'No, sir – I mean, can you hear music or something?' Thorpe looked around as a British cannon crashed out, and a ball arced overhead. A mutineer battery returned fire with some interest.

'It's the pipes,' Logan shouted above their temporary deafness after the blast. 'It'll be the 78th inside our lines.'

'It's coming from over there.' Coleman jerked a finger over his shoulder.

Jack ducked as a bullet smacked into the wall beside his head. He eyed the hundreds of yards between their present position and the besieged garrison and knew it would be a killing ground. The besiegers had an unknown number of cannon covering the open area, plus thousands of men with muskets and rifles. As he watched, the mutineers opened fire with a torrent of solid ball and grapeshot that tore up the ground and hammered at the defenders' walls.

Coleman loaded his rifle, aimed and fired. 'There's your leg broken for you, you bastard.'

'We're not going back to the Residency,' Jack decided. 'We're heading for Sir Colin.' For a moment he had a vision of the dour Scotsman who led the Highland Brigade at the Alma and commanded the Thin Red Line at Balaklava. There was nobody in whom he had more confidence, except perhaps Havelock.

Looking over the back wall of the building, Jack worked out their route out of this open wasteland to the shelter of the relieving British column. Without knowing exactly where the rebel positions were, he would have to treat every building as a possible enemy strongpoint and move from cover to cover. He eyed the ground, seeing a surreal landscape of walled palaces and mosques with minarets, ruined buildings and patches of woodland. The whole area was graced by parkland and spoiled by dead bodies, fighting soldiers and the snouts of cannons.

'Follow me, men,' Jack said. 'Keep under cover as much as you can.' He darted to a ruined cottage, whose roof slowly smouldered under the sun.

'This is like walking through a fairytale.' Coleman pointed to a distant palace with tall towers and a beautiful dome. 'You can just see Cinderella living there, can't you?'

'Who's Cinderella?' Fairytales had not been part of Thorpe's childhood.

'She's a sort of princess,' Coleman said. 'Far too good for the likes of you.'

'Stuck-up bitch, her.' Thorpe gave his opinion at once. 'Living out here and thinking she's better than we are. Bloody black bastard, she is.'

'She wasn't black,' Coleman said.

'Then why is she living in India? Stupid bint.' Thorpe grabbed hold of Coleman's arm. 'Over to the right, Coley!'

'Sir!' Coleman hissed. 'Thorpey's seen something.'

'Where?' Jack halted the men. They lay down, searching for dead ground or a bush, rock, anything behind which they could shelter. Armstrong and Williams supported O'Neill between them.

'Over there, sir. In the corner of that broken cottage.' Thorpe didn't point; such sudden movement attracted unwanted attention.

Jack stared through the heat-haze and drifting smoke. 'Whitelam, can you see anything?'

'Yes, sir. Two men, three. They're wearing black shakos and red coats.'

'Mutineers,' Jack decided. There was a clear space in front before the next small copse of tangled trees. 'We'll never make it without being seen.'

'We can take them, sir,' Coleman said.

'We'll have to,' Jack agreed. He lay flat, spying out the land. 'There's a depression from here to that tree.' He nodded toward a lone peepul tree on which a score of birds was sitting. 'When we reach it, we keep down and go around the back of their position.'

'Sir,' Whitelam said softly. 'The birds will make a noise when we reach them. They'll give us away.'

Jack measured the distance from the peepul tree to the occupied cottage. 'There are fifty yards of open ground to cover,' he said. 'We might do it in a rush.'

There were at least three mutineers in the cottage. If each got off one shot, they might kill three of his men. Was there an alternative? Perhaps there was, for men with firm nerves.

'We follow the dead ground to the tree,' he decided. 'Then we stand slowly, so as not to alarm the birds and we walk to the mutineers' positions. God knows we could pass for pandies; we're in rags and are as tanned as they are. We might get close before they realise what we are, and then in with the bayonet.'

It was a simple plan, made in seconds, but it was the best Jack could do.

'How are you doing, Sergeant?'

'Fine, sir, but I'll slow you down.' O'Neill managed a wan smile. 'Best if you just leave me here and get to the British lines.'

Jack frowned. 'You're not thinking about deserting are you, O'Neill?'

'No, sir!' O'Neill said.

'Then stay with us, Sergeant.'

With his heart hammering, Jack led his men through the depression, feeling the sun burning his head and hoping the mutineers weren't watching, waiting for him to get closer. The tree loomed ahead with the birds chattering on the upper branches; he didn't know what kind of birds they were and didn't care.

Jack reached the tree and stood up slowly, breathing heavily. His men followed one by one. He could feel the tension as he stepped toward the mutineers with every yard gained decreasing the distance to cover yet also making him an easier target.

'We could charge them, sir,' Logan said.

'Keep quiet Logan and walk slowly.'

The birds didn't react until the last man arrived at the peepul tree and then they exploded skyward with fluttering wings and loud cries that must have alerted the mutineers. Jack squared his shoulders and put on a swagger as if he had every right to be in the no-man's-land between the British and the rebel lines.

'They've seen us,' Whitelam said softly. 'Their turning our way.'

'Wave,' Jack said and lifted his right hand. 'Confuse them!'

He kept walking, feeling the prickle of tension as the mutineers appeared in gaps of the wall. There were only three, and two pointed their rifles directly at Jack. One of the mutineers shouted something, either a greeting or a challenge and he replied with one word.

'*Shabash!*' and then he remembered his Urdu. '*Jai ram!*' His men followed, shouting 'jai ram' as if their lives depended on it – as perhaps they did, Jack realised.

Judging the distance, he tensed, still waving. 'Right boys,' he muttered. 'Take them!' Jack began the rush, but despite his bleeding leg, Logan was there first, dodging sideways as one of the mutineers fired and lunged in with the bayonet before the man recovered. With the other men of the 113th following, the rebels were overwhelmed, their dead bodies ugly in death, just three more victims of war.

'Keep within the cottage walls.' Jack was breathing heavily. 'In case somebody investigates the shooting.'

Armstrong arrived with O'Neill slung across his back. 'The sergeant's passed out, sir.'

'Look after him, Armstrong.'

'Aye, sir.'

They crouched down, with flies already exploring the dead mutineers. The birds circled for a while and returned to the peepul tree; for them, the incident was over. Jack looked around. Lucknow shimmered under the sun; somewhere artillery fired, and then the shrill notes of a bugle. 'I think we're all right.' He rose cautiously and stepped forward, his heart pounding. Coleman was right behind them, with Logan and Thorpe next. 'That copse there.' Jack pointed ahead. 'Walk quickly rather than run.'

He didn't see from where the shots came; he only saw the spurts of dust they raised and heard the curious double-crash of the original report and the quick echo. 'Move!'

The 113th needed no urging. Dodging and jinking, they scattered and ran to the trees, with bullets thudding into the ground around them. Jack helped Armstrong with O'Neill and joined the others in the copse. 'Anybody hurt?'

'No, sir.' Coleman seemed to have taken up the role of a non-commissioned officer. 'We're all here safe and sound.'

'Did anybody see who was firing?' Jack asked. 'And what's that buzzing sound?'

'I did, sir,' Whitelam said. 'The shots came from over there.' He pointed forward, the direction in which they were heading. 'I think it was our side.'

'Thank you, Whitelam.' Jack moved deeper into the trees and immediately wished he hadn't. Flies rose in uncounted thousands from a layer of corpses. 'Oh, dear God!'

'We can't stay here, sir,' Thorpe swatted vainly at the swarm that now surrounded them. 'They'll eat us alive.'

Jack nodded and spat out a fly in disgust. 'Skirt the bodies and move on. We can't have far to go now.'

'Over there, sir.' Whitelam pointed. 'There's a picket coming out from these buildings.'

'That's the Sikandra Bagh,' Jack said. It was another walled palace, with a secure gateway, corner bastions and loopholes. 'This place could have been created as a soldier's nightmare.'

Carrying Enfield rifles with fixed bayonets, the men wore dun-khaki coloured tunics, dark trousers and white forage hats. A handkerchief shaded the back of their necks. The man who led them wore a red jacket, dark-tartan kilt and strode forward with no attempt at concealment. 'They're ours, right enough,' Jack said. 'Madras Fusiliers led by a Highland major. Ninety-third, I think. Stay put just now.'

Jack emerged when the picket was within a few yards of the copse. 'Well met, Ninety-third!'

Dark lines of weariness marked the face of the major. 'Who the deuce are you, and where did you come from?'

'Captain Jack Windrush of the 113th, sir.'

'113th?' The major frowned. 'I thought you were inside the Residency.'

'Most of us are sir.'

'Oh, I see.' The major gave a small nod of his head. 'Well, your men may have to stay there for some time, Windrush. The mutineers have held us up here at the Sikandra Bagh; the palace over there, in case you didn't know.'

'What happened?'

'We were pushing toward Lucknow when the rebels in the Sikandra Bagh opened up on us.'

The Sikandra Bagh wall was around 150 yards long, with tell-tale spurts of smoke where the mutineers were firing at the relieving, and to Jack still invisible, British column. 'The palace is inside the walls, of course.' The major stood erect as a cannonball ripped overhead. 'We were jammed in a cul-de-sac. These fellows deserve to get hanged for letting any of us out alive. I'm MacRae by the way, of the Ninety-third. Come on, Windrush, and we'll get you back with the column.'

There was the ear-battering crack of artillery as a six-gun battery of the Bengal Horse Artillery opened up.

'That'll be Captain Blunt.' MacRae hadn't flinched at the sound. 'He galloped through the mutineers' fire to get his guns in place.'

Despite the torrent of iron from the Sikandra Bagh walls, sappers were throwing down bankings and making space for a two-gun battery of eighteen-pounders. Within an astonishingly short time, the guns thrust their evil snouts toward the garden walls. Crisp commands heralded the commencement of the bombardment.

'Where could I find Sir Colin?'

'Over there.' MacRae pointed to the massed ranks of the 93rd, which waited, hands grasping their rifles and eyes narrowed. In front, Sir Colin sat astride his horse, talking to their colonel.

'Lie down, Ninety-third, lie down!' Sir Colin spoke in his customary Glasgow burr, so different from the gutter accent of Donnie Logan. 'Every man of you is worth his weight in gold today.'

'Sir!' Jack reported what had happened.

'So you caused that explosion.' Sir Colin was as dour as ever as he scrutinised Jack. 'I remember you from the Crimea. You're a captain now, I see.'

'Yes, sir.'

'Your regiment had a bad time at Gondabad.'

'Yes, sir. We lost the best part of a company and most of the senior officers.'

Sir Colin frowned. 'That was rather careless of you. How did you escape?'

'I had my company away on a route march, sir.'

'You were lucky. Get your wounded man away safe and stay close to me, Windrush.' Sir Colin turned aside as an ensign ran to him with a gasped message. 'Very good.' He raised his voice. 'Ewart!' The colonel of the 93rd came to him, pulling at a fine set of whiskers.

'The eighteen-pounders have made a breach, Ewart. It's time to bring on the tartan,' Campbell said. 'Let my own lads at them.'

'Sir,' Jack stepped forward. 'I have a few men with me. Could I have your permission to join the 93rd?'

Campbell nearly smiled. 'If I recall, you were with the 93rd at the Alma. Don't let your men get in the way, Windrush.'

'We'll be careful, sir.'

The artillery had blown the hole in the south-east angle of the wall, where once a doorway had stood, and the Highlanders were already there. At three-foot square, the breach was smaller than Jack had anticipated, yet the Highlanders did not object. One at a time they pushed through the gap, firing as they entered and fended off the mutineers with their bayonets until the next man arrived and their numbers grew.

'Come on 113th!' Jack led his men in support, joined by Lieutenant McQueen and a squad of Sikhs from the 4th Punjab Infantry. He looked to the main gate, where Subadar Mukarab of the 4th Punjabis was struggling to get in. Mukarab shoved his left arm between the gate and gatepost and held on, despite the defenders' efforts to dislodge him.

'Shabash, Subadar!' Jack yelled and then he was through the gap and inside the garden.

Fighting mutineers filled the place, some still wearing the scarlet jackets, dark trousers and tall shakos of the Company. With Colonel Ewart of the 93rd and McQueen of the 4th Punjabis in the van, the mixed regiments pushed toward the gate and took the defenders in the flank and rear. The pipes began again; with the 93rd's pipe major playing some stirring piece that Jack didn't recognise.

'There we are,' one of the Highlanders said, 'the pipe's playing the *Haughs of Cromdale* for you.'

'It's no' *Cromdale*,'his companion said, 'you're deaf, man. It's *On wi the Tartan*.'

'Is it? I never knew one from the other. Here come the pandies, now.'

'There are thousands of them,' Coleman yelled as the mutineers' volley bowled over some of the attackers. Without time to reload, some defenders threw their bayonetted rifles like lances. A Punjabi fell, speared through the throat. A Highlander looked down in astonishment as a defender lay prone and slashed at his legs with his tulwar until Logan rammed his bayonet into the mutineer's back and twisted.

'And that's done for you, you murdering bastard.'

As the engineers enlarged the original breach more Highlanders and Sikhs rushed through together with men of the 53rd, the Madras Fusiliers and the 90th Foot. Jack saw a Highland lieutenant laying about him with his broadsword, matching the tulwars of the defender's stroke for stroke and cutting a mutineer nearly in half.

'Leave some for us, McBean!' somebody shouted.

'Cawnpore, you bloody murderers,' the 93rd yelled, 'Cawnpore!'

'Havelock!' The 113th responded, 'let loose the dogs!'

The men next to Jack, a red-haired Highlander with a face full of freckles, thrust his bayonet into a sepoy's stomach. 'There's a Cawnpore dinner for you,' he said, shoving the wounded man aside and moving on to the next. Gunpowder blackened the face of the attackers as they shot, stabbed and crushed with musket butt and boots. They fought without expecting or granting mercy, with the high wail of the pipes as a backdrop and the grunts, curses and screams of men rising to the hot sun above. Some Highlanders shouted the Gaelic slogans of the north, the ancient battle-cries that had sounded at Inverlochy and Red Harlaw, while the 113th cursed with the fluency of a lifetime of practice.

Gradually the British and Punjabis forced the mutineers back over the flower beds and past the ornamental trees to the walled enclosure of a two-storied pavilion. 'Keep pushing them!' Jack shouted as McQueen led his Sikhs against the pavilion's two gates. They burst in – Highlanders, Punjabis and the 113th – and the desperate struggle continued, killing, maiming, wounding, swearing, gasping and killing again.

'No quarter!' Somebody shouted.

The Sikhs responded with their famous war cry, *Bole Sohe Nihal, Sat Sri Akal!*'

Knowing that after the massacre of women and children in Cawnpore, the British had suspended their proud civilisation and reverted to their savage past, the mutineers didn't try to surrender. While some tried to hide under the bodies in the courtyard, others climbed onto the roof.

'Shoot these murdering buggers!' Coleman yelled.

With nowhere to run, the rebels jumped off to die in a welter of smashed bones and broken bodies. Only when there were no more rebels to kill did the slaughter end.

Gasping, with his head screaming and the wound across his ribs stiffening, Jack reloaded his revolver and surveyed the shambles of the courtyard and garden. 'I've been in many fights,' he said, 'but never one like that.'

Coleman leant on his rifle. Dyed red with rebel blood, his bayonet was bent and twisted, and his left leg was bleeding from the slash of a tulwar. 'Nor me, sir. It was worse than Inkerman, if not as long-lasting.'

The pile of dead and wounded were as high as Jack's chin, moaning, pulsating, with the men on top still cursing the British and Sikhs who had defeated them. Others lay smouldering across their cooking fires.

'Didn't we get revenge?' A griffin officer shouted, bright-eyed and excited. 'That's the first good revenge I have seen.' He laughed, too high-pitched for sanity, and then his face crumpled, and he began to sob with reaction.

'They were brave men.' With the fury of the battle behind him, Jack had to find a cheroot to stop from trembling.

'Not only men, sir,' Coleman pointed to a woman who lay underneath a fig tree amidst a group of British and Punjabi dead. Dressed in a red coat and rose silk trousers, she clutched a heavy pistol in her hand. A handful of bullets had spilt onto the ground from the ammunition bag at her side.

'She was hiding in the tree and shooting our men, sir,' Coleman said, 'until one of the Highlanders brought her down.'

'I wonder who she was and what her story was,' Jack said. He looked around the courtyard and shivered.

Some of the mutineer dead wore the medals of past campaigns; they were men of famous Company regiments who had fought alongside the British in the Punjab. Jack felt a stab of sympathy, wondering at the twisted politics that had turned friends into enemies and brave men into murderers. Nobody spoke much. There were few shouts of triumph, nothing but a weary acceptance of victory.

'Where next, sir?' Coleman asked.

Jack nodded to the plain between them and the Residency. 'There's that to cross, and then capture the mosque over there.'

'It never ends.' Elliot's voice trembled. 'It never ends.'

The men slumped down, gasping, bleeding, and looking over the field of slaughter. Some swore; others dashed tears of exhaustion from their eyes. 'Bloody pandies,' one youth said, again and again before he began to sob.

Elliot uncorked his silver flask and took a long swallow. 'Is this not just glorious?' He offered the drink to Jack.

Jack shook his head, wordless and reloaded his revolver. He thought of Mary and his mother, shook his head and instead contemplated the next stage in this campaign.

A patch of jungle shrouded the Shah Najaf mosque, while a few poor mud cottages sat under the trees. 'The mosque seems to be last mutineer stronghold.' Intensely weary with killing and suffering, Jack knew he wasn't finished here. He had to face Sarvur Khan at some time. That was his destiny; he couldn't escape it, and the knowledge filled him with sick foreboding. He could not face Jane yet. It was better to immerse himself in his duty.

Oh God, what a mess my life is!

The blood had dried on Jack's wound, so pain accompanied every movement, and his side was stiff. This campaign seemed to be one battle after another and each one tougher than the last. 'After we take the mosque things should be easier.'

He was sick of soldiering, sick of blood and death and suffering, sick of killing strangers and trying not to let strangers kill him. He was tired of wondering what new horrors the next day would bring and of lying awake at night, scared to sleep because then the dreams and memories came. He wanted out. After this war, he would hand in his papers and find some other occupation; he would find something that had nothing to do with destroying human life.

'Easier, sir?' Coleman spoke quietly. 'Is there anything easy in this bloody country?'

Jack shook his head. 'It doesn't seem so,' he said. 'We might get some rest now. I doubt Sir Colin will attack the mosque today.'

'Yes, sir,' Coleman said. He nodded to Logan who arrived with Thorpe and Williams. 'We lost Hutton today, sir, and the sergeant was wounded. There's not many of us left of the originals.'

'The originals?' Jack had never heard Coleman, or any other of his rankers, talk in such a manner.

'The old Burma men, sir, or the lads who stood at Inkerman. There are only you, me, Logie, Thorpey and the sergeant from Burma.' Coleman stuffed black tobacco into the bowl of his pipe. 'I hope O'Neill pulls through, sir.'

'So do I, Coleman,' Jack said truthfully.

'We're like family, eh, sir?' Coleman looked weary. 'Even the sergeant.'

'Hello, sir.' Thorpe leant against the wall of the Sikandra Bagh and slid down until he was sitting on the ground. He watched a dozen insects busy with an unidentified piece of human flesh. 'We're like a family, aren't we?'

Jack glanced at Coleman, who gave a very slight nod.

'Yes, Thorpe, we're like a family,' Jack said.

'I never had a family before, sir,' Thorpe said.

'Never?'

'No, sir. They was burned in a fire, sir, when I was little. I got pulled out, and old Granny Lacey said that if I looked into fires, I would see them, and they would take care of me.' For one moment Thorpe looked lonely, like a small child who had lost everybody who was ever dear to him.

Coleman said nothing. He passed over a bottle of rum from his inside pocket.

Thorpe was staring into space, remembering. 'I never do see them though. I keep trying, keep trying, but Granny Lacey was wrong.'

'Was your grandmother not family, Thorpe?' Jack asked.

'Naw, she was everybody's granny. She was a witch, she helped women give birth and cured horses and stuff like that.' Thorpe put a calloused thumb on the feeding insects and pressed down, crushing them. 'It's good to have a family.' He looked at Coleman. 'You'd be my brother, Coley, and Captain Windrush would be my Da.'

Jack wasn't sure if he should smile or cry. 'I'm glad we feel like a family, Thorpey.' He closed his eyes. He hated the killing yet sometimes, in some rare, illuminating seconds, he could see something noble in the friendship's military life spawned. Men like Thorpe, damaged at an early age, had nothing except the regiment. It gave him structure, friendship and a purpose; he was part of something until he was dead or too old or crippled to be of any use. Then he would be discarded to beg a living on some windy street corner, unwanted and uncared for by the people he gave his life to protect.

'C–Ca–Captain Wi–Win–Windrush?' The ensign was very young, with wide eyes and a stutter.

'I'm Windrush,' Jack said.

'Sir C–Col–Colin's c–c–compliments sir, and cou–could your men join Brigadier Hope's ad–ad–advance on the Shah Na–Najaf m–mo–osque. Sir C–Co–Colin wishes it c–c–leared before nightf–f–fall.'

Jack felt a wave of sick dread wash over him. 'Thank you, ensign. Pray convey my compliments to Sir Colin and assure him we will be there directly.'

Oh, dear God, here we go again. But if I the mutineers kill me, at least my troubles will disappear.

Chapter Twenty

Captain Peel and his Royal Naval gunners had hammered at the defending walls of the Shah Najaf mosque for three hours, firing over the small houses that cowered under the evening heat. Now a mixed battalion of infantry advanced, including the remnants of Jack's 113th. Alongside them were the ubiquitous kilted men of the 93rd, with their bayonets raised and minds full of the slaughter at Cawnpore.

'Oh, God, here we go again.' Elliot drained his hip flask. 'Dear Father, keep us safe in our time of tribulation.'

Jack took a deep breath. 'Come on lads; look out for one another.' He could say no more. He didn't want to be here, yet the alternative of facing the turmoil of his thoughts was worse than fighting the enemy.

'Are you all right, sir?' Thorpe asked.

Jack forced a smile. 'You look after yourself, Thorpe.' He could say no more.

The fading light made the jungle's trees more sinister and the fires lit by the artillery only highlighted the gathering darkness outside. 'I don't like this place,' Thorpe whispered, although his eyes were attracted to the flames as readily as any fluttering moth.

'It doesn't like us either,' Coleman ducked as something shrieked over his head. 'What the hell?'

Glancing behind him, Jack saw a long arrow crash into a Highlander's head, killing him instantly. 'Dear God in heaven; they're using bows and arrows,' he said.

'Jesus; they'll have knights in armour soon,' Coleman said. 'Robin Hood and bloody Ivanhoe.'

'I didn't know you were of a literary mind, Coleman.' Jack tried to hide his fears.

'My Ma used to read to us when I was little.'

'I never knew you had a Ma,' Thorpe said. 'You was lucky, Coley.'

'Quiet. Listen!' Jack said as the thin, insistent sound of a bugle split the night.

'The pandies is coming out to get us,' Thorpe said.

'God help them.' Jack looked to his right and left, where the 93rd Highlanders advanced through the trees toward the loop-holed wall surrounding the mosque.

One of the Highlanders gave a sudden shout, the high Gaelic slogan alien in this hot land, and the 93rd rushed forward, kilts flickering through the undergrowth and bayonets waiting to kill.

'Sir!' Whitelam had better night vision than anybody Jack had ever met. 'The Sawnies have found a breach in the wall.'

Remembering the recent slaughter in the Sikandra Bagh, Jack took a deep breath and ran forward, surrounded by yelling Highlanders and his 113th. Bullets zipped past him, and an arrow plunged into the earth a yard from his feet. Although he was moving fast, his mind focussed on the arrow; he saw it quivering and imagined it in his throat, his chest or his stomach. 'Oh, dear God, protect me!' And then he was in the breach, and Coleman was pushing in front of him, shouting to Thorpe to be careful.

'Come on lads!' Jack threw himself forward and into the unknown beyond. The defending fire stopped. The defenders melted into the dark, and there was an eerie silence as men advanced with no opposition.

'They've run.' Coleman looked around, too experienced to drop his guard. 'It's a trick; remember the dacoits in Burma?'

'Keep alert.' All around Jack, Highlanders and the 113th peered into the gloom as they tested each step, watched the dim roofs and tree tops for marksmen and moved slowly toward the mosque. Flames flickered from the city beyond the walls, highlighting the mosque's tall minaret. Thorpe watched the orange glow, licking his lips.

'You stay with me, Thorpey,' Coleman said. 'We'll look after each other.'

Jack understood the sentiment. When they were fighting, the British soldiers had no time to think. When alone in these very alien buildings with unknown gods and exotic architecture, the more imaginative of them could feel their nerves stretching. Jack remembered one of the few pieces of advice his father had given him: "don't interfere with native gods". It was good advice that John Company seemed to have repudiated, which was a significant factor in the present chaotic situation.

'Keep moving,' Jack said. A stationary figure made a better target for a sniper.

Darkness stared at them from the windows of the mosque.

'Has anybody got a light?' Jack wasn't surprised when Thorpe obliged by scraping a Lucifer and putting the flame to a twist of linen. 'Come on.' He stepped slowly inside with the tiny light a haven amidst the terrible dark.

Despite the damage from artillery and musketry, there was no mistaking the beauty of this place. Jack moved slowly, revolver in hand and boots crunching on what seemed like a covering of coarse sand that got deeper the further into the mosque he ventured. He looked down and felt cold sweat on his back.

'Oh, good God in heaven.' He raised his voice and lifted the glowing linen high. 'Careful now, men. Don't run. Back out slowly and carefully. For God's sake, don't make any sparks with your boots.'

What Jack had believed to be sand was loose gunpowder, inches deep; a single spark could destroy the mosque and every man of the 113th.

'Told you it was a trap.' Coleman was happier that he had been proved correct than afraid he could be blown to pieces any second.

'It was a trap,' Thorpe echoed him. 'You said it was a trap, Coley.'

They withdrew slowly step by step until they left the mosque and then ran to what they hoped was a safe distance. There was no explosion as the British threw themselves down, gasping with shock.

'There must have been about two tons of gunpowder there,' Jack said. 'If it had gone up when our men were there—' There was no need to finish the sentence. 'If it wasn't a trap it was the rebel powder store. I doubt we'll ever know.'

'We'll never know,' Thorpe said solemnly. 'Eh, Coley? We'll never know.'

'You're right, Thorpey, boy.' Coleman gave him a twisted grin. 'You got it right.' He passed across his water-bottle. 'If we died, Thorpey, at least we'd go together, eh? Like brothers should.'

Jack grunted. His head felt as if was ready to explode. 'Well said, Coleman.'

Thorpey took hold of Coleman's hand, and Jack was sure there were tears in his eyes. Coleman shook him off. 'Here, Thorpey, see if you can see any pandies over there.'

He looked around his men. *Please, God, make sure I don't lose more men.* The image of Sarvur Khan entered his head, but the face was weaker, the menace less. 'Come on lads, we're out of here.'

Sir Colin gathered his officers under the clouded dome of the Indian sky. 'Gentlemen,' the gruff Scottish voice was immensely reassuring amidst the backdrop of smoking buildings and shattered palaces. 'We have reached the Residency.'

Jack looked up. After days and weeks, the rumble and hammer of the guns had finally stopped. Guided by Sir Colin, the British had crushed one rebel stronghold after another, pushing to create a corridor between Campbell's small army and the defenders.

Is it finished? Have we won? Oh, dear God, do I have to face myself now?

Sir Colin continued. 'However, you will be aware that we lack the numbers to push out the rebels from Lucknow and hold it.'

Jack felt the agony of defeat. *We must beat them.*

'My plan is to reach the defenders and evacuate,' Sir Colin said.

Jack closed his eyes. An evacuation suggested that the rebels were in too much strength for Sir Colin's army to repulse. This relief of Lucknow would only be a partial success, unlike the recapture of Delhi. The British had not yet won this war. On the other hand, getting the civilians to safety was vital.

Mary and Jane will be safe.

The thought came on a tidal wave of relief. The women's safety was more important than victory. Dear God! From where had that thought come? He was a soldier; it was his duty to fight for Queen, country and regiment. Duty was everything.

Not any longer.

Sir Colin looked up, his dour face as grim as Jack had ever seen. 'Do not think that we are abandoning Lucknow or any part of this province of Oudh to the enemy, gentlemen. We will be back.'

There were solemn nods from battle-weary, worn-down men.

'Windrush; you seem to be expert at moving around the country. I want you to help escort the families to safety.'

'Yes, sir.' *Oh God, not that!* Jack tried to erase his thoughts of Mary and Jane. Despite his sudden desire to have them safe, they reminded him of his Eurasian background. He was not ready to face that, as he had no desire to meet Jane again. It was better to immerse himself in his duty and forget the searing reality of himself.

'The rest of you, continue to defeat the mutineers,' Sir Colin said. 'You may dismiss, gentlemen.'

Evacuating civilians was not the most popular task in any army. There was no chance of glory and civilians were undisciplined, noisy and apt to stray. 'Come on, men,' Jack encouraged his harassed company. 'This is why we have fought across this blasted country!'

The Residency was in an uproar with women, children and men vying to get places on the convoy. There were carriages of all descriptions, native drivers and skeletal-thin draught animals mixed up with British soldiers who displayed their usual mixture of cheerful pragmatism and flexibility as they faced this new challenge.

'Up you get, missus!' Coleman helped an elderly lady to mount a native cart by the simple expedient of taking hold of her arm and pulling hard. 'You sit there and let the driver do the work.' He pressed a granite-hard finger against the native's chest. 'And you – if you even think of joining the pandies, I'll slit your throat from ear to ear; you understand?' The driver salaamed and grinned, probably not understanding a word.

'It's all right, my man,' the lady passenger said. 'I've got this.' She produced a long hatpin. 'If he does not do as I wish I'll stick him. Like this!' She thrust it hard into the driver's backside, so he squealed.

'Good for you, missus! That's the stuff to give them!' Coleman said. 'I wouldn't trust these blackies as far as I could throw them.'

'That's the stuff,' Thorpe echoed, helping the dignified wife of a major into a gharry by shoving her into her seat. 'There you are Missus, and you stick a pin into the driver's arse anytime you like!'

'I'll do no such thing.' The woman stared at Thorpe as if he was something unpleasant on the sole of her shoe. Jack noted she still sported a full array of jewellery, each piece of which would cost more than Thorpe would earn in his lifetime of suffering.

'Well done, Thorpe,' Jack shouted. 'Keep them coming.' He stepped aside as a camel nearly trampled him. 'Who's in charge of this brute? Whoever it is, get the damned thing under control, won't you?'

'I say!' The speaker was about thirty and very blonde, with her wide blue eyes fixed on Jack. 'There are native women on a cart there. Tell them to walk.' The gharry she sat on was piled high with her possessions, while two Indians carried a large leather trunk between them.

Jack frowned. Mary and Jane had squeezed into the back of a tonga, alongside a wounded Eurasian man. For a moment Jack held Mary's gaze as his heart thundered, and then he glanced at Jane. He looked away quickly.

'Why should they walk?' he asked the blonde.

'I have to get my belongings out of here,' she claimed. 'But these blacks are in the cart.'

Ignoring the blonde's wails, Jack approached Jane and Mary. He couldn't meet Jane's eye. 'You two sit tight and don't let anybody say otherwise. If anybody tries to move you, shout for me or any of my men.' He didn't understand his anger, but knew it was genuine.

'How are you, Jack?' Jane looked closely at him. 'You've been in the wars again, I hear.'

Jack touched his ribs. 'Nothing serious,' he said. 'I'll be glad to get away from this place though.' He flinched as Jane took hold of his hand. 'I'll be gladder to get you two away.'

'How are you?' Jane repeated. Her grip tightened as her gaze met his.

'I am well, thank you.' Jack was unsure what to say. 'Try and keep safe.'

'We must talk,' Jane whispered urgently. 'When you have time, please let us talk. I have so much to say to you.'

'Yes.' A wave of unaccountable panic swept over Jack. 'When I have time.' He stepped back. 'I've my duty to do.'

'I know you have,' Jane said sadly. 'Look after yourself, Jack.'

'Jack,' Mary called after him. He turned and lifted a hand in salute as the convoy began to move. He could not talk to her. *Oh, God, what do I do?*

'See those waggons?' Riley spoke in a low tone as he nodded to a separate caravan of carts. A score of Sikh cavalry rode alongside, bearded and professional.

'Aye,' Logan said.

'That's the Nabob's treasure.' Riley's eyes darted from waggon to waggon. 'God only knows what it's worth.'

'Well God is not here, Riley.' Jack was glad to revert to his captain mode. 'But I am. So don't tempt yourself with what you can't have and do your duty as a soldier of the Queen.'

'Yes, sir,' Riley said. 'I was only showing Logan here.'

'Logan does not need to be shown that sort of thing.' Jack raised his voice. 'Come on men!'

In addition to the 113th, the women and children had an escort of a handful of lancers together with men from the Irregular Horse, wild-looking riders with a variety of headgear and weapons. Jack watched them, wondering who had placed such people in charge of civilians.

'Not the escort I would have chosen.' Elliot echoed his thoughts.

'Nor I,' Jack said. 'Keep an eye on them.'

'I will.' Elliot nodded. 'I'll watch your women as well.'

Jack nodded. He didn't deny that Mary and Jane were his women. 'We've got four miles to cover to Sir Colin's army.'

He shouted above the squeal of un-greased axles, the growl of wheels on the hard ground, the clop of hooves and neighs of horses and grunts of oxen. 'Keep them moving! Riley, ignore the nabob's treasure and take care of Charlotte!'

Jack looked up the length of his charge, realised that Mary was watching and half-raised a hand in acknowledgement. While the horsemen trotted around the outside, Jack and his men provided the close escort. As well as guarding the convoy they would tend to the minor mishaps that were bound to occur when a diverse body of vehicles carried civilians along a complicated route.

Running to the front of the convoy, Jack guided the leading horse past the watchful sentries at the Bailey Guard Gate, and then dashed back to ensure the column followed correctly. 'Keep these waggons coming,' he shouted before running to the head of the convoy again.

They passed through the grounds of the Farhat Bakhsh and Chuttur Munzil palaces and on, circling the city to follow the route Sir Colin had thought safest. In places, the engineers had raised canvas screens to hide the convoy from the rebels, while in others, ditches had been dug to provide cover. Jack heard Lieutenant North, in command of the Nabob's treasure, asking who the devil had misplaced a blasted waggon, gave a sympathetic smile and checked his men.

'Williams! You and Whitelam make sure Mrs. Major Mackay is all right! Armstrong! You have better things to do than sweet-talking that blonde woman.' He caught Jane watching him and gave an awkward wave before quickly looking away.

Damn the woman! That's my mother! Competing thoughts crammed into his mind. *What do I do? What do I say?*

The tingle of apprehension came unannounced. 'Be careful men,' he shouted. 'Something's not right.'

'Where, sir?' Coleman was first to reply.

'I don't know, Coleman. I feel it, but I can't see a thing for these damned screens. Where is everybody?'

'Thorpey's over there, sir,' Coleman said. 'Parker is helping some children with their bloody dog, Williams is three waggons back with some loud-mouthed woman, but I don't know where Riley and Logie are.'

'Thank you, Coleman.' Jack hoped O'Neill recovered from his wound quickly. A good sergeant was worth his weight in diamonds. 'Could you—'

The shots punctured Jack's final words, and he moved up to the canvas screen on the right side of the road.

'Tear open this thing, Coleman,' he said, and Coleman jumped to rip a ragged hole with his bayonet.

The escorting Irregular Horse was engaged in a running battle with what looked like their cousins, two sets of wild, bearded men slashing with tulwars and shouting in half the languages of India.

'113th!' Jack shouted at once. 'To me!'

He knew they would be there, bitter-eyed, gaunt of face, with grooves around their mouths, swearing, grumbling and dependable, always doing their best.

'Form a line,' Jack shouted. There was no time for anything fancy, no time for manoeuvres; if these devil's horsemen broke through the Irregulars, they would play merry hell with the unarmed civilians.

'Load! Rod!' The orders came automatically; he saw the Irregulars pushed back by sheer numbers. They fought with sword and pistol, hacking and slashing only two hundred yards from the vulnerable convoy of civilians. Jack thought of Mary and Jane, of Charlotte Riley and those two children with whom Parker had been playing. He shook his head.

The rebels can't get through. They're not killing Mary and Jane.

'Home! Return!' Jack knew his men were there. He didn't have to look. 'Cap!'

'Bloody black pandy bastards.' Logan gave his inevitable comment, muttering under his breath as he struggled to fit the cap. He had never mastered the art of balancing the cap on the ball of his thumb before he placed it on the rifle. For one mad moment, Jack wondered what Logan would say if Jack admitted his part-Indian background. The thought brought a twisted, cynical smile to his mouth.

'At two hundred yards... ready.' Without looking behind him, Jack knew his men were adjusting the range, with Coleman ensuring Thorpe did it properly. Logan was swearing softly, Ryan would be calm-faced and blinking, Parker no doubt thinking about his dog or some other animal he could help.

The Irregulars faltered, and the rebel cavalry burst through, tumbling aside two brave Sikhs who tried to stop them.

'Present!' Jack stepped aside in case Logan or Thorpe fired early. He didn't want to die with a British Enfield bullet in his back.

The rebel horsemen came on at a gallop, brave men yelling loudly.

'Fire!' Jack yelled and saw the jets of smoke from the Enfields. Three of the leading horsemen tumbled with one horse falling end over end and the man immediately behind reining sharply and crashing down to the dusty ground.

'Load! Rod! Home! Return.' Jack gave the orders in a measured sequence, knowing his men were working as hard as they could. The rebel cavalrymen recovered and pushed on, swords waving, warrior faces shouting, horses with gaping mouths and raised hooves.

'Cap.' He heard Logan swearing and Riley's calm voice as he leant over to help.

'Volley at one hundred yards.' Jack waited for the men to adjust their ranges.

'Present!' The rifles slapped down, held by hard, dirty hands and aimed by the unforgiving professional eyes of soldiers who had seen all the horrors that war could bring.

'Fire!' There was another confused horror of injured horses, more men falling off their mounts, more death and then the Irregular Horse charged into the flank of the rebel cavalry, sending them into total confusion.

'They're finished,' Coleman said, just as the scream sounded behind them.

Mary! Jane!

'That's from the convoy,' Riley shouted. 'Charlotte!'

'Riley! Stay with us!' Jack shouted. 'Come on, 113th!' Jack was moving as he spoke, with his men thrusting toward the convoy ahead of him. Impatient, he pushed Williams out of the way and rushed through the gap in the screen.

'Oh, Jesus.' While the 113th and Irregular Horse had been dealing with the rebel cavalry, a score of mutineers had attacked from the other side. Now they were spreading out the length of the column with tulwars and knives.

'Captain Windrush!' Charlotte Riley stood at the side of a cart, pointing urgently down the column. 'They're with your girl!'

Mary and Jane. Oh, God, no!

'Coleman! Go right with ten men. The rest follow me!' Breaking left, Jack ran towards Mary's cart, firing his revolver at any mutineer he saw. These civilians were his responsibility, but it was Mary he thought of, Mary and Jane.

Dear God; that's my mother back there. I've wondered who she is for years and now I may lose her before I've even acknowledged her existence.

Jack suffered a surge of dismay when he saw Sarvur Khan standing on top of Mary's tonga, hacking at the wounded man with his long Khyber knife. Two more mutineers stood beside the cart, both with curved tulwars.

'You!' Jack fired at Sarvur Khan and missed.

'Captain Windrush.' Sarvur Khan sounded calm. 'We meet in strange places.' He was as neat and unruffled as if he was still serving in the officers' mess.

'Come and fight me, rather than murdering children and wounded civilians.' Jack couldn't fire again for fear of hitting the women.

Mary was looking at him, her eyes wide. 'Jack! Be careful!'

'Jack?' Sarvur Khan caught the word. 'This kaffir woman knows you.' His smile was as ugly as anything Jack had ever seen. Sliding forward, he grabbed hold of Mary's hair and pulled her head back, so her throat was exposed. She screamed and scrabbled uselessly with her hands.

'Jack!'

'Watch her die, Jack.'

'No!' Jack ran forward, but Jane was faster. Grabbing hold of Sarvur Khan's knife hand, she pushed it back, catching the Pathan by surprise. He shouted something Jack didn't hear, and, still holding Mary's hair in his left hand, shook off Jane's grip on his right arm. The other two mutineers ran around the tonga toward Jack, tulwars held high.

'Leave these two to us, sir.' Riley was calm as he hefted his bayonetted rifle. 'You get the Pathan.'

Logan didn't say anything as he sidestepped the swing of a tulwar and plunged his bayonet into the mutineer's stomach. 'The 93rd call that a Cawnpore dinner,' he said, twisting the blade and withdrawing to watch the swordsman collapse, writhing, on the ground.

'Good man, Logan.' Leaping onto the tonga, Jack tried to crack his pistol across Sarvur Khan's head. The Pathan jerked aside, so the muzzle only scraped a bloody path down his face. Tempted to squeeze the trigger, Jack knew he couldn't chance it with Mary and Jane so close.

Taking advantage of Jack's momentary hesitation, Sarvur Khan rammed an elbow into his throat and followed through with his entire body weight. Jack fell backwards and for a moment stared right into Sarvur Khan's eyes, seeing the hatred there, and the contempt.

'Eater of pigs!' Sarvur Khan was frothing at the mouth. 'Infidel!'

'Child murdering bastard!' Jack gasped as the Pathan altered his grip on his knife and twisted his wrist, nicking at Jack's already injured arm. Blood spurted scarlet. Weak from his wounds and months of mediocre food and terrible toil, Jack felt Khan force him further back.

He heard Mary gasp, saw Jane shift forward, and with a desperate effort, he managed to bring up his knee into Sarvur Khan's groin. The contact was solid. The Pathan twisted in pain and slashed sideways with his knife, only for Jack to raise his left hand and block the blow.

The force knocked Jack back, so he nearly fell over the side of the tonga. Swearing, he felt the wound across his ribs open and warm blood flow down his side. For a fraction of a second, he had a clear field of fire, raised his pistol and squeezed the trigger. Sarvur Khan didn't flinch as the bullet flicked past his left ear; his foot stabbed out and kicked the revolver out of Jack's hand.

'Jack! Be careful!' Mary screamed, high pitched.

Swearing, Jack reverted to his school-day boxing and jabbed with his left fist, landing a solid punch on Sarvur Khan's nose. There was an immediate spurt of blood. He followed with a right that bounced off the Pathan's shoulder. Sarvur Khan shifted sideways, lifted the knife and slashed at Mary.

'No!' Jane jumped up. The long Khyber knife caught her in the chest, penetrating deeply. Jane sank, mouth open as she stared at the blood that soaked into her dress.

For a single instant, Sarvur Khan was distracted, and Jack pressed the revolver against the Pathan's head. *A bearded face leered at him with hate in its eyes.* Jack squeezed the trigger. The sound was more of a dull thud than the usual high crack. As if in slow motion, Jack saw Sarvur Khan's head dissolve. The back of his skull expanded and then exploded outward, spraying a mess of brains and blood and fragments of bone outward as he fell backwards.

Jack stared at the falling body, remembering all the bloodshed and murders of Gondabad and the battles and horrors since then. Sarvur Khan's body toppled from the cart to lie on the dusty road, seeping blood.

But Sarvur Khan's death didn't matter. Jane, his mother, was hurt. 'Oh, dear God! Jane!'

Jane lay across the width of the cart, blood soaking through her dress and bubbling from her mouth. Mary was holding her close, speaking rapidly.

'Mother.' Jack knelt at her side.

Mary was holding her as her life slipped away. Without thinking, Jack slid his hand under Jane's dress and pushed down on the wound, trying to stop the flow of blood. 'Hold on! We'll save you.'

'No.' When Jane shook her head, blood dribbled from her mouth. 'I'm dying, Jack Baird Windrush.'

'No,' Jack said. 'You're not. I won't let you. I've only just met you again.' He pressed harder as if his hand alone could heal the massive wound made by a Khyber knife.

'You always were a stubborn baby.' Blood spurted with every word Jane said. 'But you can't help me.'

Jack pulled her closer. 'Mother, you can't go yet.'

'It's my time, Jack Baird.' Reaching up, she touched his face. 'Don't be sad. I've waited all my life to hear you say that word.' Despite the blood that covered her teeth, her smile held only love. 'I have seen my son as a man, and I leave him in good hands.'

'Mother,' Jack whispered. He leant closer to her. 'Mother.'

'She's gone, Jack,' Mary said softly.

'No.' Jack shook his head. He knew his men had gathered round. He knew Williams was beside the tonga, stretching out his hand. He knew Coleman was preventing Thorpe from jumping on the cart to help. He knew Charlotte had her arms around Riley and both were staring at him. 'She can't be dead.'

'It's alright Jack,' Mary whispered, 'the angels have come for her, they have taken her to Jesus. She will be all right now, no more pain, sorrow or tears.' She lowered her voice. 'She met her son and heard him call her mother. That was all she wanted.'

'No,' Jack shook his head. 'We didn't get a chance to talk.'

'She's listening now, Captain Jack,' Mary said softly. 'She won't leave you.'

'No,' Jack said, 'but I left her.' For a moment it all made sense; the dream had warned him of the danger from Sarvur Khan. He had known the two of them were intertwined and now he was in the darkness. It was not the physical darkness that he'd feared, but the emotional agony of losing his mother before he had properly acknowledged her existence. Aware that a dozen hard-bitten soldiers were watching, Jack bent down and kissed his mother for the first and last time in his life.

'Sir! There's more rebel cavalry!'

Jack dragged himself back to his duty. There was always one more task to fulfil, one more battle to fight, one more march to make. His was the soldier's lot, and it didn't matter if he was an Englishman, a Scotsman or a Eurasian, he was a soldier of the Queen and an officer of the 113th Foot, and he had his duty to do.

'Come on men.' Jack heard the gruffness in his voice. 'We've got a convoy to get through.' He looked at his mother; he would mourn her later. What had she meant about leaving him in good hands?

He had no time to think about that yet. He would ask Mary; she would know.

Dear reader,

We hope you enjoyed reading *Windrush: Cry Havelock*. Please take a moment to leave a review, even if it's a short one. Your opinion is important to us.

Discover more books by Malcolm Archibald at
https://www.nextchapter.pub/authors/malcolm-archibald

Want to know when one of our books is free or discounted? Join the newsletter at http://eepurl.com/bqqB3H

Best regards,

Malcolm Archibald and the Next Chapter Team

Historical Note

Many of the events depicted in this book took place as described. Although Jack Windrush and the 113th Foot are fictitious, the Indian Mutiny was one of the British Army's most hard-fought campaigns of the nineteenth century. The reasons for the mutiny of the Indian soldiers – the sepoys – are many and varied and include beliefs that the British were violating their religions and decreasing their pay at the same time that the Honourable East India Company was taking over Indian-owned lands.

When many of the sepoys mutinied in 1857, there were 151,000 men in the Bengal Army, of whom only 23,000 were British. Thirteen thousand of the British were in the Punjab, many miles from the scene of disaffection. The remainder were stationed at Calcutta, Meerut and Delhi or scattered in small cantonments across Northern India. In the heartland of the rebellion, between Calcutta and Meerut, there were around 5,500 British troops and around 50,000 Indian or Native troops.

Although most officers of the Native regiments swore their men were loyal, there had been portents of unease for some months. There had been chapattis passed around the villages, although nobody, then or now, really understood the significance of the message, if indeed any message was intended. There had been isolated outbreaks in various regiments of the Bengal Army. There had been rumours of trouble ever since Lord Dalhousie's Doctrine of Lapse had seen native states annexed to British rule, and when the Company sent Hindu regiments overseas, thus damaging their caste, discontent grew.

When the British introduced the new Enfield rifle, trouble came to a head. The paper cartridges had to be torn open with the teeth, and the Indians believed the British had greased them with a mixture of cow fat and pig fat. As cows are holy to Hindus and pigs anathema to Muslims, sepoys of both religions were insulted. Although the authorities saw sense and allowed the sepoys to make their own grease rather than touching the contaminating mixture, the damage had been done. The combination of attacks on their pride, race, money and religion roused the sepoys to mutiny. When some native rulers joined in, the insurrection assumed the aspects of open rebellion, encouraging some revisionist Indian historians to term it the First War of Independence.

Both sides were guilty of terrible atrocities. The mutineers murdered men, women and children in horrible circumstances and the British retaliated by mass hangings and executions in a manner equally barbaric. The initial stages of the war were marked by sieges, with the British besieging Delhi and the mutineers Cawnpore, Lucknow and other smaller stations.

Sir Henry Havelock (1795 – 1857) was born in north-east England and joined the army in 1815. He sailed out to India in 1823 and fought in the First Burmese War, Afghan War, Sikh Wars and Persian War before rising to fame during the Indian Mutiny. He relieved Cawnpore and fought eight victorious battles against the mutineers in his first attempt to relieve Lucknow and another major battle when he and General Outram punched through to the Residency. Once there he was in turn besieged. He lived to see Sir Colin Campbell's relief before he died of dysentery.

Havelock's statue stands in Trafalgar Square, London, inscribed with one of his quotes: 'Soldiers! Your labours, your privations, your sufferings and your valour, will not be forgotten by a grateful country.' However, the soldiers often are forgotten and in 2003 the then mayor of London, Ken Livingstone proposed removing Havelock's statue and replacing it with what he termed a 'more relevant' figure.

Finally, the Eurasians, the product of British fathers and Indian mothers, formed a unique community in India. In 1791 the Directors of the Honourable East India Company banned Eurasians from many military or civil posts on the grounds that they would not command the same respect as purely British men would. However, there were notable exceptions, such as James Metcalfe, with a British father and a Sikh mother, who rose to be aide-de-camp to the Governor-General. There was also James Skinner who raised Skinner's Horse and Robert Warburton who was knighted and became a colonel. In saying that, a manual for Company cadets warned against Eurasian girls with their 'insinuating manners and fascinating beauty' which could help create 'a matrimonial connexion which' the cadet 'might all his life-time regret'.

Time will tell if Jack Windrush either contacts matrimony or regrets his association with Mary Lambert.

Malcolm Archibald

About the Author

Born and raised in Edinburgh, the sternly-romantic capital of Scotland, I grew up with a father and other male relatives imbued with the military, a Jacobite grandmother who collected books and ran her own business and a grandfather from the mystical, legend-crammed island of Arran. With such varied geographical and emotional influences, it was natural that I should write.

Edinburgh's Old Town is crammed with stories and legends, ghosts and murders. I spent a great deal of my childhood when I should have been at school walking the dark roads and exploring the hidden alleyways. In Arran I wandered the shrouded hills where druids, heroes, smugglers and the spirits of ancient warriors abound, mixed with great herds of deer and the rising call of eagles through the mist.

Work followed with many jobs that took me to an intimate knowledge of the Border hill farms as a postman to time in the financial sector, retail, travel and other occupations that are best forgotten. In between I met my wife; I saw her and was captivated immediately, asked her out and was smitten; engaged within five weeks we married the following year and that was the best decision of my life, bar none. Children followed and are now grown.

At 40 I re-entered education, dragging the family to Dundee, where we knew nobody and lacked even a place to stay, but we thrived in that gloriously accepting city. I had a few published books and a number of articles under my belt. Now I learned how to do things the proper way as the University of Dundee took me under their friendly wing for four of the best years I have ever experienced. I emerged with an honours degree in history, returned to the Post in the streets of Dundee, found a job as a historical researcher and then as a college lecturer, and I wrote. Always I wrote.

The words flowed from experience and from reading, from life and from the people I met; the intellectuals and the students, the quiet-eyed farmers with the outlaw names from the Border hills and the hard-handed fishermen from the iron-bound coast of Angus and Fife, the wary scheme-dwelling youths of the peripheries of Edinburgh and the tolerant, very human women of Dundee.

Cathy, my wife, followed me to university and carved herself a Master's degree; she obtained a position in Moray and we moved north, but only with one third of our offspring: the other two had grown up and moved on with their own lives. For a year or so I worked as the researcher in the Dundee Whaling History project while simultaneously studying for my history Masters and commuting home at weekends, which was fun. I wrote 'Sink of Atrocity' and 'The Darkest Walk' at the same time, which was interesting.

When that research job ended I began lecturing in Inverness College, with a host of youngsters and not-so-youngsters from all across the north of Scotland and much further afield. And I wrote; true historical crime, historical crime fiction and a dip into fantasy, with whaling history to keep the research skills alive. Our last child graduated with honours at St Andrews University and left home: I decided to try self-employment as a writer and joined the team at Creativia ... the future lies ahead.

he story continues in:

Windrush: Jayanti's Pawns

To read the first chapter for free, please head to:
https://www.nextchapter.pub/books/windrush-jayantis-pawns

Windrush: Cry Havelock
ISBN: 978-4-86745-643-9

Published by
Next Chapter
1-60-20 Minami-Otsuka
170-0005 Toshima-Ku, Tokyo
+818035793528
7th May 2021